STEEL GODS

The Doberman slid to a halt a few yards from James, who was staring at it. The dog turned swiftly, and sped, sleek and deadly, back towards Vercoe. Vercoe was squeezing the trigger of his gun as the dog launched itself at him. The impact sent him crashing to the ground. He shrieked, tried to club the animal with the .38 he had retrieved from David. The dog ripped the bandage away from his face, revealing an empty eye socket.

Vercoe's shriek turned into a gurgle as the dog sank its fangs into his neck. His blood spurted up over its face. It held on grimly as Vercoe clubbed its head again and again with his pistol.

The gun eventually slid from his grasp. The animal jerked its head up, tearing out his throat. Vercoe's body spasmed, then he lay still.

The dog gazed at Spear, tendrils of flesh hanging from its mouth. It growled, baring its fangs. It was preparing to attack.

Spear stared at the dog. David saw a brief flash of *something* through the air, like electricity. Like a machine that had been switched off, the dog slumped down dead.

D1493904

'The awful shadow of some unseen Power
Floats though unseen among us'

Shelley

STEEL GODS

Scott Grønmark

CORGI BOOKS

To Sara

STEEL GODS

A CORGI BOOK 0 552 13455 4

First publication in Great Britain

PRINTING HISTORY
Corgi edition published 1990

Copyright © Scott Grønmark 1990

This book is set in 10/11pt Plantin by
County Typesetters, Margate, Kent

Corgi Books are published by Transworld Publishers Ltd.,
61–63 Uxbridge Road, Ealing, London W5 5SA, in Australia by
Transworld Publishers (Australia) Pty. Ltd., 15–23 Helles
Avenue, Moorebank, NSW 2170, and in New Zealand by
Transworld Publishers (N.Z.) Ltd., Cnr. Moselle and
Waipareira Avenues, Henderson, Auckland.

Made and printed in Great Britain by
BPCC Hazell Books Ltd
Member of BPCC Ltd
Aylesbury, Bucks, England

PROLOGUE

5 June 1968

The big man sat hunched on the rim of the bath, clutching his belly with both hands, rocking back and forth like a distressed child. As the pain in his stomach blared to a crescendo, he dry-heaved. Acid fizzed in his throat. He caught sight of himself in the mirror over the washbasin. A clown stared back. His permanently florid face had turned purple with the effort of breathing, and his lips were caked with the white calcium solution the doctor had given him to neutralize the acid eating his stomach walls.

A fresh stab of pain made him twist sideways and suck in his breath.

Palmer's guts had been in an uproar since the day Robert Francis Kennedy, the Senator from New York, had announced his intention to run against Lyndon Baines Johnson for the Democratic Party's Presidential nomination. As Kennedy's bodyguard, it was Palmer's job to keep the Senator alive during the campaign, but he knew that if the other side wanted Bobby dead, Bobby would die. They had killed his brother John when he had begun to threaten their interests. Bobby was infinitely more dangerous; he was one of them.

Palmer's stomach cramped viciously. He bent almost double, so that only the swell of his stomach prevented his head touching his knees.

'Sonofabitch!'

He had tried to persuade Bobby that LBJ couldn't be defeated, no matter how unpopular the war in Vietnam had made him. Johnson had promptly withdrawn from the contest – Bobby's doing, of course – and Palmer had headed for the nearest bar to get maudlin drunk on fourteen straight shots of Jim Beam.

He had suffered his first attack of acute gastritis on 4th April when Martin Luther King had been killed in Memphis by James Earl Ray, some redneck asshole supposedly acting on his own initiative. Yeah, sure! Palmer knew who was behind it; Bobby's own kind. Palmer also knew why they'd decided to murder Dr King. The moment LBJ had announced his decision to quit, Bobby had become a serious contender for the Presidency. But to succeed, he needed the Black Vote, all of it. Martin Luther King could deliver that vote. Exit Dr King.

From then on, Palmer's only hope had been that Bobby would fail in the Primaries. Now, eight weeks later in Los Angeles, it had just been announced on television that he had trounced Hubert Humphrey in South Dakota and squeezed past Eugene McCarthy here in California where it really mattered. Senator Robert Kennedy was going to be the next President of the United States. If they let him live; that was something they simply couldn't afford to do.

Bobby had headed downstairs to give a victory speech to his campaign workers in the hotel ballroom protected by two amateur bodyguards and one Ace Agency guard hired for the occasion. Palmer should have been down there, but the announcement of Bobby's victories had sent him rushing to the can with his worst attack of gastritis so far. It felt as if razor blades were lacerating his insides.

A knock at the bathroom door.

'Mr Palmer? Can I go down now?'

'No, kid! You wait for me. I'll be right out.'

The door opened. James Lord, a tall, skinny, blond fifteen-year-old, had often been mistaken for a member of the Kennedy family since joining the entourage eight months back. Munching a caviare canapé, he slouched against the doorframe and stared at Palmer with disconcertingly washed-out green eyes.

'You look real ill, Mr Palmer. Want me to call the doc back?'

Palmer sat up straight, sucked in his breath. 'The pain's easing.'

James shrugged, wandered out again. He had been a gap-toothed six-year-old when Robert Kennedy had met him during JFK's assault on the Presidency in 1960. Bobby had been in charge of the campaign, and James's mother had been one of the campaign organizers in Illinois. James's father, an

6

expatriate Englishman, had been the Marketing Director at the British Tourist Board's Chicago office. After an initial meeting at a campaign rally, Bobby had taken pains to see young James as often as possible. One of Palmer's first jobs after being assigned by the secret service as Bobby's chief bodyguard when he became Attorney General was to accompany him on a visit to the Lords in Chicago. Even to a relative stranger the bond between Kennedy and the child had been obvious; they shared an indefinable quality. The serious, quiet, little boy compelled attention without doing anything obvious to earn it, the same way Kennedy did. Palmer had later learned the exact nature of that similarity when Bobby had asked him to stay on as his bodyguard in a private capacity after John Kennedy's assassination. That was the night Bobby had told him everything. God! that had scared him.

The walkie-talkie on the floor next to Palmer gave a demented squawk; one of the guards informing him that Bobby was wrapping up his speech to the campaign workers in the ballroom and was about to head through to the Colonial Room for a press conference. The guard wanted to know which route they should take. Palmer wanted to warn the guard to avoid passing through the hotel kitchen. He hadn't liked the feel of it when he'd checked it out that afternoon. Too little security – anyone could wander in there. When he tried to give the order, the handset died on him.

'James! Come in here!'

The boy appeared, crunching slush from a Coca-Cola container.

'Help me up. We gotta get down there.'

James hurried over, helped Palmer up off the rim of the bath. The boy knew just how dangerous Bobby's enemies were; they were his enemies as well. His parents' home in Cicero had been firebombed the previous Fall in what the local police had treated as an act of unmotivated arson. Both his parents had died. James had been at a friend's house, but the assassins hadn't known that.

Bobby Kennedy had become James Lord's legal guardian six weeks after the bombing, and Palmer had effectively been bodyguard to both of them since then. Bobby had always insisted that the boy's safety was paramount. 'Whatever

7

happens, they mustn't get James.'

They left the Royal Suite and made their way down in the lift towards the ballroom. As the lift doors opened they heard Bobby's amplified voice: 'On to Chicago! Let's win there!' The rallying cry was answered by a roar from the crowd.

Palmer's lips formed a circle of pain as he and James entered the ballroom just in time to see Bobby disappear into the corridor leading to the kitchen. Palmer bulldozed his way through the crowd of excited campaign workers, James right behind him.

When they had managed to squeeze their way along the packed corridor, Bobby was shaking hands with kitchen workers. His three security guards were close behind, sharp-eyed, alert. Palmer took a deep breath, forced himself not to panic. You saw nothing if you panicked. Cursing the TV lights and camera flashes, he sectioned the crowded room with his eyes, blinking rapidly so that he saw the kitchen as a series of freeze-frames.

It took him ten seconds to spot the potential killer. A slim, dark-skinned, young man crouched on a tray stacker. Blue sweater, white shirt, jeans, clutching what looked like a rolled-up poster. He was smiling as Bobby headed towards him. Next to him on the stacker was a girl wearing a yellow dress with black polka dots. She was smiling as well. It was the smiles that gave them away; malevolent rictus grins.

Palmer reached for his gun and let out a yell as the young man jumped down from the stacker and ripped aside the wrapping paper from the object in his hand. He was holding a pistol. He aimed it at Bobby Kennedy's head, fired.

Palmer had his gun out, but there was no clear field of fire. A volley of shots. Screams. Bobby turned, grasped the Ace Security's guard's clip-on bow tie and ripped it away as he slumped to the ground.

Palmer barged into the crowd towards Bobby, holding his gun pointed at the ceiling. People shrieking, dazzling TV lights, yells, more shots.

Palmer was ten feet from Bobby when he saw the girl in the polka dot dress edging her way round the perimeter of the crowd. Her eyes were fixed on someone behind Palmer. Still grinning, she was using one hand to push through the crowd.

The other was held straight down by her side. Palmer couldn't see what she was holding but he knew it was a gun. People never held anything else in quite the same way they held a gun.

Palmer turned his head, followed her gaze. She was staring at James, but James was in shock, oblivious of her. And then Palmer realized what was meant to happen. They'd planned a double hit; Bobby and James.

Palmer tried to draw a bead on the girl. Too much confusion. He crouched low, snaked between the onlookers. He could see her arm rising. She was still moving forward, bringing the gun up, eyes fixed on James. Someone shrieked as they caught sight of her gun, but in the muddle no one else noticed. She halted, both hands clasping the gun, aimed, began to squeeze the trigger . . .

Palmer lunged at the girl. She caught sight of him at that moment, tried to jerk her head back. The tips of Palmer's stiffened fingers rammed straight into her windpipe. She dropped the gun and sagged to her knees, clutching her throat.

Palmer stood looking down at the girl for a split-second. Should he hold onto her, find out who'd sent her?

He knew from the range at which Bobby had been shot that he wouldn't survive. That meant his job now, his only job, was to protect James Lord. And that meant getting him out of the hotel as fast as possible. There might be another assassin lurking nearby.

He kicked the girl's gun away across the floor, turned and weaved back through the crowd towards James. He grabbed his arm. James resisted.

'I want to stay.'

'Forget it, kid. We're gone!'

He hustled the shocked boy back through the ballroom to reception, and out onto the kerb. A line of cabs was waiting out front. He pushed James into the lead cab, jumped in.

'What's happenin' in there, man?' The driver, a young black wearing shades and a brown leather cap, was leaning back nonchalantly in his seat, sucking a match.

Police sirens wailed in the distance, getting louder.

'Drive,' Palmer said.

The black studied him in the rear-view mirror. 'Hey, man, not till I get an answer.'

Palmer stuck his gun hard into the back of the driver's head. 'There's your fuckin' answer. DRIVE!'

The cab shrieked off, jolting Palmer back into his seat.

'He's dead,' James said, staring ahead, his voice flat, lifeless. 'Isn't he?'

'Yes.'

And Palmer realized for the first time since the shooting that it was true. Bobby Kennedy was dead. Suddenly, Palmer was crying. He hunched forward, half-ashamed of himself, but unable to staunch the flow of tears. He felt James's arm around his shoulders.

'I hate to interrupt,' the driver said. 'But where to?'

James Lord stared out the window of the cab while Cliff Palmer continued to sob.

'Hey, where to?' the driver repeated.

'God knows,' James said.

PART ONE

CHAPTER ONE

8 September 1968

The rain needling his face pricked the running boy back to reality. He glanced up. Low clouds the colour of fresh bruises were scudding across the early evening sky, moving inland over North Cornwall, tumbling towards Bodmin Moor.

The rhythm of David Cauley's thin legs faltered. For thirty minutes his mind had been a perfect blank as his scuffed running shoes ate the narrow, high-hedged road to Padstow. For half an hour he had escaped. But now, as he tried to pick up his stride again his mind was roiling with thoughts and images as ugly and threatening as the clouds lowering above.

He wanted to head straight for home. He wanted to run past St Stephen's School and keep on running till he reached the comforting chaos of London and the sanctuary of his parents' house. He wanted to sleep in his own bed again, all alone in his own room, surrounded by his books, his comics, and his records. He wanted to hear the familiar sounds his parents made as they moved around the house, preparing for bed – his father brushing his teeth fiercely, his mother shooting the bolt on the back door – as he lay in bed with a transistor radio pressed against one ear listening to a pirate radio station. He wanted not to be surrounded by strangers any more. Most of all he wanted never to have to meet Vercoe or Hughes again, because they'd expressed a strong desire to kill him.

Like many boarding schools, St Stephen's was cold, unfriendly and joyless. What made it different was the air of psychotic menace provided by Hughes and Vercoe.

When David reached the outskirts of Padstow he took the left fork in the road and headed for the northern end of town where the school, a glum Victorian gothic mansion, cast a doleful shadow over the houses below.

The thought of Vercoe and Hughes had shot David's rhythm all to hell. He'd never get it back now. He settled for an ungainly trot, barely faster than walking pace. The rain felt good against his hot skin. He tried to concentrate on how good it felt, but Vercoe and Hughes seemed to have taken out a lease on his imagination.

Vercoe was scarier than Hughes, because he had some intelligence, because you knew he actually did the things other kids gave themselves gooseflesh describing. When Vercoe told you he'd raped girls, you believed him. When he said he'd injected himself with heroin, you knew it was true. When he claimed he'd lured an old labrador into one of the empty tourist cottages down by the estuary and skinned it alive, you didn't doubt him.

David slowed to a walk and placed his hands on his hips, steam belching from his mouth.

Two days after the start of term he had been lounging in the window seat of the Junior Common Room, singing along to The Electric Prunes 'I Had Too Much To Dream Last Night' and flicking through a *Paris Match* pictorial on the assassination of Robert Kennedy. The lurid close-up of the Senator lying on the floor open-eyed with blood pooling beneath his wrecked head had chilled him, and he'd slapped the magazine shut.

Ugliness and evil!

Gazing through the window of the Junior Common Room, he had seen Old Max, the labrador, white-muzzled and gentle-eyed, moving slowly up the long driveway towards the school to get his afternoon hand-out of scraps from the cook at the kitchen round the back. David had often wondered who fed the ancient pooch during the holidays. Old Max's back legs were even more arthritic than when David had last seen him three months back. The dog's walk was stiff and precise, as if he was stepping over broken glass.

David saw Vercoe and Hughes heading down the drive towards the old dog. Vercoe's hair was a black, crinkly mop, as close to an Afro as a White could get. His school uniform looked as if it hadn't been washed since last term.

No one else in the school would have got away with it, but Vercoe was the one boy the teachers wouldn't punish. A maths teacher who'd mounted a campaign against him the previous year had died in a lane near the school when his car brakes had failed. A police investigation had established that the brakes had been tampered with. Everyone at the school knew Vercoe had done it, but there was no way of proving it. Since then he'd pretty much done as he pleased, skipping classes, laying in bed till it suited him to get up, going into town whenever he felt like it, disappearing for a few days now and then.

Hughes, Vercoe's creature, was the whitest person David had even seen. Chalk-white skin marred by red blotches of acne, white hair and pink eyes that looked painful and diseased. In contrast to Vercoe, his uniform was spotless, all the creases in place. What made his appearance genuinely bizarre to David was the fact that his small rodent's head was perched on the body of a young giant. At sixteen, Hughes stood six foot three and had the physique of a heavyweight boxer.

As the pair came abreast of the dog, it glanced up at them, blinked, and changed course, attempting to veer off the path. Vercoe's foot was a blur as it lashed out and caught the old dog's back legs. Max let out a howl as he tumbled clumsily. Vercoe and Hughes sniggered, moved on. The dog got to its feet. The hackles on its back rose and it bared yellow teeth. Vercoe and Hughes halted, turned. Vercoe's slightly crossed black eyes looked crazier than ever. Old Max padded heavily towards them. Hughes stood his ground, but Vercoe backed away. There was fear on Vercoe's face. David had never seen that before. The dog shed ten years in the instant it leapt powerfully off the ground straight at Vercoe, aiming for his throat.

Vercoe raised an arm to defend himself. Old Max sank his treeth into it. Vercoe screamed. David smiled. Boy and dog crashed to the ground. Vercoe shrieked as the heavy old mutt continued gnawing on his arm, muzzle wrinkled, lips flared. Hughes shambled over and aimed a massive kick at Max's flank. The dog performed a somersault, landed on its back. Vercoe got up, and, clutching his bleeding arm, walked slowly towards the helpless dog. His crossed eyes were murderous. David felt a shout rise to his throat, but before it arrived he heard someone yell outside.

A tall, slim blond boy was walking down the drive towards Vercoe and Hughes, an American in the year above David, who'd just arrived at the school. David couldn't remember his name. The Yank probably hadn't been warned about Vercoe and Hughes. As David watched, the American raised his arm. Vercoe froze, stared at the new boy.

The LP on the record player in the Junior Common Room came to an end. Silence. A strange atmosphere, a buzz, distant but *there* nonetheless. David pressed his face up against the window. The American was making a big mistake. It was like watching a blind man heading for the edge of a cliff. David's urgent breath misted the window. He rubbed an arm across the glass to clear it. When he could see again, Old Max had righted himself and was hobbling off in the direction of the kitchen, tail between his legs, head down. The American boy was strolling nonchalantly past Hughes and Vercoe. They were following him with their eyes, frowning, puzzled.

The eerie, breathy introduction to Donovan's 'Hurdy Gurdy Man' sounded on the record player, making David jump. The magazine on his lap dropped to the floor splayed open at the photograph of Robert Kennedy he'd wished to avoid.

Ugliness and evil . . .

David picked up the magazine and tossed it on a table. When he looked out the window again, there was no one in sight.

A few days later the story was circulating around the school that Vercoe and Hughes had trapped Old Max and skinned him alive. David believed it, but that hadn't stopped him making the same mistake as Old Max a week later when he'd been awakened in his dormitory in the middle of the night by a fetid, animal smell. Vercoe had been tugging back his bedclothes. David had opened his mouth to cry out, but Vercoe had clamped his hand across it and crawled into bed beside him, mad eyes glittering.

16

David had felt Vercoe's other hand crawling towards his genitals. As Vercoe's fingertips had touched his penis, David had sunk his teeth deep into the hand covering his mouth. Vercoe had yelped and slunk off into the darkness, growling like an animal.

Two days later David had opened his locker to find one of Old Max's twisted, arthritic back legs nestling on top of his books. He'd found the dog's dried, shrivelled testicles in his bed the next night. In the week since then, he'd been awaiting Vercoe's revenge. When the tension got too much for him he sought permission to go running. Without that, he would have gone mad, or run away for good, and he knew that would break his father's heart. St Stephen's was his father's old school, and he cherished an almost mystical belief in its perfection.

David stopped again a quarter of a mile from the school, halfway down Fentonluna Lane. Through the trees to his left he could see the main school building, spiky and threatening in the rainy twilight. To his right were the school playing fields, with a concrete-walled open-air swimming pool in the distance. He bent over to catch his breath and rid himself of the stitch in his side.

Then he heard a voice that made him forget his pain.

'Come on, Old Max. Let's go walkies.'

Fear prickled David's skin like a nettle sting.

Vercoe and Hughes stepped out from behind a tree a few yards in front of him. Vercoe's eyes were crazy slits above his gap-toothed grin. He was holding a hefty hunting knife with a curved blade. Rain was washing what looked like rust off it. Dried blood. David's teeth marks were still visible on Vercoe's hand.

'We won't be interrupted this time,' Vercoe said, conversationally. 'I'm going to enjoy you. Then it'll be Hughes's turn.'

Hughes smiled. His teeth looked green against his luridly white skin.

'He'll enjoy that,' Vercoe went on, 'because he's so ugly he doesn't often get the chance. Then I'm going to give you a personal demonstration of what I did to that fucking dog. I just hope you don't make as much noise.'

A squirt of urine shot down David's leg, shockingly hot. Vercoe had been moving towards him all the time he'd been talking, but David hadn't really noticed. He'd been mesmerized by the evil boy's singsong voice and his berserk eyes. Now he and Vercoe were a couple of feet apart, and Hughes had moved round behind him. David felt one of Hughes's big hands on his shoulders.

He shrieked, dropped his shoulder and ran through the trees to his right, heading across the playing fields.

Three sounds: his pumping heart, shrieking breath, and the pounding splash of boots on the grass right behind him.

And he thought *Dumb. So dumb. If I'd headed for the school someone might have seen me. I'm going to die because I'm so dumb!*

A crash behind him. He glanced back. Hughes had slid in the mud, and was sprawled face down in the grass. Vercoe, lighter, was just managing to keep his footing, and was a few yards behind David. He still had the knife clutched in one hand. Spittle was spraying down his chin.

David slid to a halt, using the edges of his running shoes as brakes, turned, lashed a fist at Vercoe, who shrieked and went skidding across the grass, arms windmilling. The knife bounced out of his hand as he hit the ground.

'Fucker! Stinking fucker!' David yelled, then began running again.

Two options: run around the swimming pool and head for the open fields beyond, or veer back towards the school. But no, neither course would succeed. The older boys might be clumsier than him, but they'd have more stamina. They hadn't just completed a five-mile run. Either way they'd catch him. That left the pool itself. He'd have to get inside, pray that he could find a hiding place. It was a lousy plan, but he couldn't see an alternative.

The six-foot-high wall round the pool was coming up fast. He daren't try the entrance door. Probably locked. He judged his leap, got half way over. The top of the wall caught his stomach. Winded, sucking in air like a drowning man, he looked back. Hughes and Vercoe were up and running again, about fifty yards away, spattered

18

with mud. Vercoe was slashing the air with his knife.

David had to clench his buttocks to stop soiling himself. He hauled himself over the wall, dropped onto the pool's cement surround. He ran around the pool to the changing rooms on the other side. The water was dirty, covered with leaves. David tried the entrance door to the changing rooms. Locked. He could hear his pursuers yelling as they approached the pool. He looked back at the wall. They'd be over it in seconds.

He gritted his teeth, *concentrated*.

One of the changing rooms' frosted-glass windows was banging in the wind a few feet away. He wrenched it open, slipped inside, head-first, pulled it shut behind him, latched it.

Froze in the darkness.

Outside, he heard Hughes and Vercoe clamber over the wall and drop onto the cement. Then silence. Total. More frightening than any noise. He imagined Vercoe out there, sniffing the air like a beast, picking up his scent.

Fear leapt up his gullet, and he had to choke back a yell. What was left in his bladder spurted down his legs. He was going to die, he knew it. An image of Bobby Kennedy floated into his head, lying on the floor of that hotel kitchen, eyes open, blood pooling under his head, everyone yelling.

Evil and ugliness . . .

David squeezed his eyes shut, trying to erase the image.

And then his fear vanished. For an instant, he felt nothing, and then a wave of bleak misery washed through him. It was as acute, as real as a physical pain. It was nothing to do with the thugs outside. It had no cause, as far as he could tell. It was just *there*, a sensation of loss, of grief, unlike anything he had ever experienced. The force of the anguish washing through him caused his whole body to sag. The pain as his knees hit the floor made his eyes pop open.

He heard Hughes and Vercoe moving around the side of the pool towards the changing rooms. And he heard something else, something totally unexpected. Crying. Someone sobbing nearby in the darkness.

David stood and groped his way along the row of cubicles through the gloom towards the source of the sound. The feeling of utter desolation inside him increased with each step.

He stopped at the fifth cubicle along. A boy was hunched on the floor, head between his knees, hands clasped over his head.

'Don't!' David croaked, realizing as he did so that tears were streaming down his own face. 'Don't,' he repeated, lamely, not quite sure what he meant, but aware that, somehow, it was this other boy's misery he was experiencing, not his own at all.

The boy looked up. David recognized him. The new boy, the American. Now, David remembered his name; James Lord. The American stared at him for ten seconds without speaking, and David felt the misery inside himself start to ebb.

'Please,' David said. 'We have to—'

A window broke further down the changing rooms. An object struck the opposite wall, fell to the floor.

'Come out, you little shit!'

David flinched. 'Vercoe and Hughes,' he explained. 'They're after me. Vercoe's got a knife.'

James Lord stood up slowly, sighed. 'I'll get rid of them.'

'No! They'll kill us. I *know* it.'

James Lord wiped a sleeve across his face and made his way along to the changing room door. He unlocked it, stepped outside.

David wanted to follow, to prove he wasn't afraid, but his legs were rooted to the floor. His cheeks burned with shame.

'You again,' David heard Vercoe say, 'Blondy!'

'Me again,' James Lord said, no fear in his voice. 'Why don't you guys just run along.'

David remembered how the American had stopped Vercoe and Hughes killing Old Max. Was he going to pull a similar stunt?

A smack, followed by a 'whoof' as air blasted from someone's lungs.

David ran to the door.

James Lord was lying on the ground, clutching his stomach. Hughes was standing over him. Vercoe caught sight of David, grinned.

He jerked the knife towards David.

'Your turn, Cauley. Come and get it, *shithead*!'

David headed for the nearest wall, but fear had weakened his legs. Vercoe moved swiftly to cut off his escape route. David started backing up towards the diving boards, glanced over at the American. James Lord was sitting up, massaging his stomach. Hughes was towering above him, fists clenched, waiting for him to make a move.

An unexpected sunray speared through the lowering clouds and made the raindrops along Vercoe's knifeblade glint like jewels. The sun disappeared, and the world was plunged back into gloom.

'You should have heard Old Max squeal when I cut his balls off,' Vercoe said, then imitated the dog's agonized yelps. 'Wonder how *you'll* sound, *bastard*!'

David was backed up against the rusted iron ladder leading to the top diving board. He wanted to cry. He wanted to cringe and beg Vercoe for mercy, but even in his terror he realized that would just spur the mad boy on. He could see Vercoe's erect penis straining against his trousers.

Speaking slowly and deliberately, David said, 'They say you've got a dick like a matchstick.'

Before Vercoe could react, David scurried up the ladder. It shook as the knife blade clanged against it, inches below his scrambling feet. He was near the top when the whole apparatus lurched, almost throwing him off. He looked down. Between his feet he saw Vercoe climbing towards him, knife clasped pirate-style between his teeth, hair wild, face smeared with mud. In an act of crazy bravura, which he knew he'd pay for, David crossed his eyes in imitation of Vercoe, before hauling himself up onto the top board. He looked down at James Lord. Hughes was sitting astride him, knees pinning the American's arms to the ground, punching his face. James

Lord was barely putting up a struggle.

Vercoe's head came into view above the top of the board. David swiped at him halfheartedly with his foot, caught the handle of the knife clasped between Vercoe's teeth. The knife clattered to the ground forty feet below. Blood welled from a gash at the corner of Vercoe's mouth, splashed down his chin. He licked the wound with his tongue. His eyes narrowed, became whited-out slits of rage. He dragged himself up onto the board with one surge. David took two steps back along the board, felt it bend under his weight.

Vercoe bounced gently up and down. David had to crouch and hold his arms out from his sides to maintain his balance.

'You're going in for a swim,' Vercoe singsonged, jumping harder on the board, making the whole apparatus judder. 'Then I'm going to fuck you. Then I'm going to kill you.'

David overbalanced and fell on his back. His head was over the end of the board. He could see the dirty water below him. He threshed out with his legs, trying to right himself, strained to get a grip on the board with his hands, but Vercoe's bouncing motion made it impossible. The board bent further at David's end. He looked up, arching his neck. Vercoe was standing at his feet. Blood from the gash in his mouth splattered onto David's legs.

'Dead,' Vercoe said.

He drew back his foot, getting ready to boot David off the board.

'ENOUGH!'

Vercoe blinked. The command had come from below. David looked down. James Lord was still lying on the concrete, but Hughes had got off him and was backing away, his big body suddenly awkward. The American stood up slowly, ignoring Hughes. His face was badly bruised and one eye was rapidly closing as he stared up at Vercoe.

Vercoe returned his stare.

'You're next, blondy!'

Vercoe drew back his foot once more. In the small

section of David Cauley's mind not paralysed by terror he thought *What a stupid way to die*. He should have run away from St Stephen's when he'd had the chance, no matter how much pain it would have caused his father.

As Vercoe's foot arced down towards his side David again heard the command 'Enough!', but this time he seemed to hear it inside his head. It was accompanied by a buzzing sensation, like a mild electric current passing through his body. It was similar to the sensation he'd experienced when James Lord had stopped Hughes and Vercoe attacking Old Max.

Then a miracle happened.

Vercoe's foot went too high, missing David altogether. For an instant Vercoe was standing on one leg, his face registering amazement, then the momentum of his kick overbalanced him and sent him toppling into the pool below.

David heard the kind of smacking sound a diver makes when he does a bellyflop. Water sprayed against the back of his head. With Vercoe's abrupt departure, the diving board vibrated violently and David felt sure he was going to fall off it. He managed to get a grip on both edges and pulled himself upright. When he looked down, Vercoe was thrashing about in the murky water.

Hughes had circled around the back of James, and now made a rush at him, muscular arms outstretched.

David shouted a warning.

James wheeled round on one leg, lashed his foot into Hughes's crutch. The giant albino screamed and fell to the ground, clutching himself.

Vercoe had reached the edge of the pool. He started to haul himself out. Electricity hummed inside David's head again, a pulse of energy . . . and it was as if a hand had been placed on Vercoe's head, and was pushing it back under the leaf-covered water. Vercoe broke the surface again, foliage sprouting from his hair, spluttering. David sensed the electic throb once more, and the invisible hand shoved Vercoe back under.

Hughes, curled up in a foetal position by the side of the pool, clutching his balls, let out a girlish shriek.

A laugh kicked at David's throat. James was standing at the edge of the pool, expressionless. He backed away as Vercoe bobbed up again, coughing and choking. Vercoe thrashed the water with his arms, got back to the side of the pool, hauled himself out. James Lord halted a yard in front of the changing room wall. Vercoe was bent double, wheezing, his frizzy black hair now plastered over his face. He put his hands on his knees, stared at James. A feral snarl came from the back of his throat. He stood up straight, clenching and unclenching his fists. The snarl turned to a growl, became a roar, and he was running straight at the American.

'Get him!' Hughes moaned.

'No!' David shouted.

A split second before impact, James Lord stepped easily aside. Vercoe went charging past, ran smack into the changing room wall. As he crumpled to the ground, unconscious, he left a smear of blood on the whitewashed wall. He rolled over onto his back. His nose was smashed into his face, his lips were torn, and there was a bloody gap where his front teeth had been.

Hughes let out a bleat, crawled to the swimming pool wall, dragged himself over.

David was grinning as he stood up on the board and watched the big boy run away across the playing fields.

James turned, without saying anything, and walked out of the swimming pool. David scrambled down the ladder, ran after him, caught up.

'How did you do that?' David asked. James said nothing. They walked towards the school in silence for five minutes. James was evidently tired, David too excited and confused to know what to say, boogying around his protector in jerky little adrenalin swirls of motion. It was dark now, cold and dark.

Finally, David broke the silence. 'Come on, tell me how you did it! I *felt* it. Like electricity. From *you*! Controlling them! And you did it before, didn't you? That day Vercoe went for Old Max. You stopped him then, didn't you?'

James halted, turned to him. One eye had closed completely. The iris of his other eye was such a subtle shade of pale green it hardly showed at all. There was a grazed bruise on his forehead and his jaw was swollen on one side.

'You mustn't tell anyone,' James said.

'But we *have* to!' David said. 'It was fantastic.'

'No!' James said. 'It wasn't fantastic. It was stupid. I weakened, that's all. I shouldn't have wasted myself on them. Childish.' He shook his head wearily, stared at the ground. 'We don't tell.' He looked up. 'Okay?'

'But we've *got* to!'

'No!'

David wanted to argue, but sensed James was in no mood for it.

'All right.' Disappointed. To himself, he sounded like a whining six-year-old. 'Of course,' he said, trying to be adult.

They walked on in silence again for a while, till they reached the drive leading up to the school. Smoky light drizzled into the darkness from the jagged building's peaked gothic windows. David *had* to have some answers.

'Why were you crying?' he asked.

'For Bobby.'

'Who?'

'Bobby Kennedy. They shot him.' When James added, 'I was there,' his voice cracked.

'Who are "they"?'

James gave a wan smile. 'Oh, boy, what a question! You know way too much already.' He slung an arm around David's shoulder. David shrank a little. He was English; he wasn't used to being touched.

James halted instantly, grabbed one of David's hands, peered at his palm. Frightened, David tried to jerk it away, but James's grip was too strong.

'Can't see!' James muttered. He grabbed David's wrist and dragged him, running, towards the school, halted in a shaft of light coming from the school dining hall. He brought David's palm right up to his unbruised eye.

The American's eagerness vanished suddenly. He let go of David's hand.

'What was that for?' David asked, spooked. It had been a *strange* day.

'When I touched you then, I thought – I thought you were one of us. I really did.' James shook his head, puzzled. 'But you're not.'

'What do you mean? What are you talking about?'

James ignored the question. 'What's your name?'

'Cauley.'

'First name, dummy!'

'David.'

As boys passed them, heading for dinner, James took a deep breath.

'I'm probably making a big mistake, but . . .' He paused. 'What the hell. You seem okay.'

The rain that had been pattering gently for the last hour burst from the sky with a tropical ferocity that made David gasp. James grabbed him by the arm and dragged him away from the dining hall towards the school chapel.

James shouldered open the heavy oak door and pushed David inside. They sat on a pew at the back. Strange-angled beams of light dissected the long, high room. It smelled of dust and cold earth and the sweat of boys. The air was icy. David shivered violently, hugged himself.

'I'm probably going to have to leave here soon,' James began. 'First, there are some things you should know.'

'Leave? When?'

'I don't know. Any time now. I'm just waiting for the signal.'

'But you've only just arrived.'

'They're bound to find out I'm here. When they do, they'll try to kill me.' James's harsh whispers echoed sibillantly off the walls and shivered up to the vaulted ceiling above, where gargoyles mocked them.

'Who are "they"?' David asked again.

'Enemies.'

'I'd gathered that. But why should *anyone* want to kill you?'

'Same reason they killed Martin and Bobby.'

'Martin *who*?' David demanded, his voice querulous with confusion.

'Martin Luther King. There's a war going on most people don't know about. My enemies killed Martin and Bobby. I'm next on their list. They want me bad. They've tried twice already this year.' He smiled grimly. 'Must be getting kinda pissed.'

'Off,' David said. 'Pissed off. "Pissed" means drunk.'

'Dave, I'm talking big stuff here.'

David knew that, and he didn't want to hear it. They were kids, and kids did *not* get involved in assassination plots involving world leaders. Full stop.

'Dave, you know I'm different, right?'

'Yes,' David said. 'You're different.' And maybe, he thought, just a little crazy.

James seemed to sense his doubts. 'I'm not bullshitting you, Dave. You're getting the truth.'

David nodded. 'Go on.'

'I'm different, but I'm not unique. There are others like me. I thought, for a moment, you might be one of us. When I touched you just now I felt something in you, some sort of kinship. I looked at your hand and that proved you're not one us, Dave, but there's *something* in you, some sort of potential.'

David's eyes filled with tears.

'I'm scaring you,' James said.

'Yes.' David's chin puckered. 'I'm frightened.'

'Shh!' James reached out a hand to David's face, laid it against his cheek. David felt a burst of warmth inside him, a healing energy buzzing strong and healthy through his whole being, and he experienced a dizzying sensation of confidence and strength and wholeness. He felt *good*. He felt *right*.

James, smiling, slid his hand round and wiped away David's tears.

'Blow your nose, Dave.'

''Kay.' David scruched up his rain-sodden running vest and wiped his face. The surge of joy was receding.

'Concentrate!' James said. He raised his hand again, held it up in front of David's face. He shifted it so that a shaft of light piercing the darkness just above their heads caught his fingers.

There was something odd about the tips, but at first David couldn't see what it was.

'Look closely, and you'll see my fingertips are straight.' James said. 'See? They run parallel. Yours are all looped and whorled, like most people's. Got that?'

'Yes,' David said. 'What does it mean?'

'Don't ask, just remember. You *ever* see anyone else with prints like these, you let me know. At once.'

'Why?'

'Because it might be important. Will you promise to contact me if you ever meet someone with prints like mine?'

'I will.' He wondered how often he was likley to get a chance to study other people's fingertips. 'How do I find you?'

'Write or wire a guy named Palmer at the following Washington DC post office box number.' He gave the number. 'And remember, that's Washington *DC* not Wash—'

'I know. I'm not an idiot.'

'Says you. Repeat that number.'

David did so.

'Dave, you ever come across anyone else like me, don't mess with them. We're not all good guys. Some of us make Vercoe and Hughes look like boy scouts.'

They heard the chapel door creak open. Weak light illuminated the statues of saints standing in alcoves set in the walls. The room was filled with the sound of rain. David and James ducked their heads.

Someone lurched, snuffling, along the aisle towards the altar. David and James slowly raised their heads.

Vercoe was on his knees at the altar, head bent, crying. In front of him, on a table covered by a white cloth, stood a silver cross.

David glanced at James. There was something hard and vengeful in his expression.

'See you around, Dave,' he whispered, then slipped away.

A roar from the altar. David looked up to see Vercoe powering up off the floor. He grabbed the edge of the table, upended it. Still roaring, he picked up the overturned cross and ran to the nearest alcove, swung the cross at the statue of the saint standing inside it. The statue crashed to the floor, shattered. As Vercoe ran to the next alcove, David caught sight of his mad, smashed face, and shuddered.

David headed for the door, keeping low.

He stood for a while in the rain, listening to the sounds of mindless rage and destruction coming from inside the chapel.

His whole body gave a massive shiver.

Who could be worse than Vercoe?

The police came and took Vercoe away later that evening. Hughes left the school the next day. Two weeks later, over breakfast in the dining hall, David heard a rumour about James. One of the boys from his dormitory claimed he'd slipped away during the night, and hadn't been seen since. David got up right away and went to check the story. James Lord's possessions were gone from the locker beside his bed. In the two weeks since they'd first spoken, they had become friends. At lunchtime, on the day he learned of James's departure, David went to the deserted swimming pool and cried himself dry.

CHAPTER TWO

2 June 1991

The three of them gasped in unison as they stepped out of the coolness of Andy's Kebab House in the hot summer afternoon. Sweat stippled David Cauley's forehead, and he found himself wishing he hadn't ordered a glass of raki after the meal. A man of 37 should know sunshine and spirits don't mix. He made an effort to ignore the queasy feeling in his stomach, determined not to spoil a special day.

His wife and daughter each took one of his arms as they strolled like tourists down Turnham Green Terrace towards Chiswick High Road. For once, passers-by weren't giving him quizzical 'don't I know you from somewhere?' looks. They were too busy studying Anna and Lauris, and that pleased him. He knew they were a good-looking family. Lauris, at 34, was slim and petite, with a round gamine face, short-cut reddish hair and delicate, slightly-freckled fair skin. Her huge, startled-looking hazel eyes made her look at least ten years younger than she was. In contrast, Anna looked older than fourteen. Several inches taller than her mother, her shoulder-length auburn hair framed a longish olive-skinned face. Misty, grey-green eyes gave her a distant, grave air. A friend of the family, a photographer, had suggested that she'd have the looks to become a model in a few years' time. Anna had envinced some interest in the prospect, but Lauris and David had considered it too high-profile a profession. They *had* to keep Anna out of the public eye.

'Can I choose my present now?' Anna asked as they turned into Chiswick High Road.

David grinned. 'That's what today's all about.'

'Have you made up your mind?' Lauris asked.

Anna nodded. 'A holiday in Portugal for the three of us, as soon as possible.'

'But the cottage—' Lauris said.

'We *always* go there,' Anna protested. 'And it's bound to rain all the time. I want to go somewhere where it'll be just like this every day.'

'All right,' Lauris sighed. 'A promise is a promise. But you know what the sun'll do to my skin. I'll come back like a lobster.'

Anna grinned. 'But I'll look great!'

Lauris looked up at David. 'Can we afford it?'

He shrugged. 'No, but we deserve it.' That was true. This was his first day off work from Capital Television News for six months; he was beginning to get stale. Besides, no one seemed to appreciate the effort he was making. He'd been passed over for the last correspondent's job he'd applied for. It still rankled. Lauris had been hard at it as well, putting in ten hour days to fulfil all her silversmithing orders. She'd become so well established in the last few years, a break wouldn't do her career any harm at all. And Anna has spent weeks slaving over her textbooks before taking the entrance exam for the Patterson School. She'd passed with flying colours; hence the celebration lunch and the choice of a present. Hell, yes, they all deserved a treat.

Lauris smiled. 'You go to the travel agent and pick up some brochures. I have to visit the bank. I'd better get some money out while we still have any.'

'We'll meet you outside,' David said. He watched his wife pick her way delicately through the people throwing harsh shadows on the pavement, then took Anna's hand and headed for the SunFun Travel Agency on the other side of the road. They had to sprint to avoid a car. The sudden movement made his left knee twinge. As always, the sensation brought back bad memories.

He blotted them out. This wasn't the day for dark thoughts.

As Anna eyed the brochure rack, David studied her. Her face was a trifle gaunt. The Patterson School exams had been a strain, he knew, and she hadn't been that keen on gaining a place there anyway. She'd made the effort for him, and for Lauris, because she realized it mattered to them.

They were hardly aware of her being different anymore. He guessed the next few years might prove difficult, with boys on the horizon, but altogether there had only been a handful of embarrassing incidents so far. The last one had convinced them to take her away from her school. The headmistress, alerted by shrieks of laughter, had walked into Anna's classroom to discover her teacher, a dumpy little hatchet-faced woman, stripped to her underwear, waltzing with an imaginary partner in front of a class delighted by the impromptu performance. David and Lauris had been called in to see the headmistress, who had said that while she couldn't prove that the teacher's extraordinary behaviour had had anything to do with Anna, she had her suspicions. Anna was a very *unusual* young lady whose influence on her fellow pupils and her

31

teachers was disproportionately strong. In the circumstances it might be best . . .

They'd readily agreed to remove Anna from the school. After the decision had been made, David had lectured Anna sternly regarding her responsibilities. She had sighed and said, 'Daddy, sometimes I just get bored with being good. I only wanted some fun, and that woman's been picking on me all year. But, okay, I'll be wearing a halo from now on.'

They had decided to send her to a school for gifted children where her specialness might not be so evident. Several people had recommended the Patterson School in Kensington. It sounded like a place where special children were helped to appreciate and enjoy their abilities. He hoped Anna would be happy there. Mostly, he hoped her powers would be less noticeable in a group of child prodigies.

He watched as Anna flicked through a brochure, brow furrowed in concentration, weight resting on one hip. Her long, thin legs were dark against her cream shorts.

'Here,' she said, thrusting the brochure at him. 'The Lennox Country Club in Estoril. It's just down the road from Lisbon. One of my friends was taken there last year. Her family loved it.'

He studied the prices, blanched.

'You couldn't make do with just one week, could you, angel?'

She grinned, stood on tip-toe and kissed his cheek. 'Of course.'

Relieved, he got hold of a sales assistant, made the arrangements and wrote out a cheque for the deposit.

Anna took his arm again when they got outside. She gave a little skip of sheer pleasure as they headed for the bank.

There was a small queue of people at the cashpoint outside the National Westminster, but no sign of Lauris. A ten-year-old Ford Cortina was parked clumsily outside, one wheel up on the pavement. The engine was running and the driver's door was open, but there was no one inside. Someone anxious to get cash before the bank shut, David guessed.

He held the door of the bank open for Anna, followed her inside. He shivered as the air-conditioning hit him. Anna halted after two steps, and he collided with her. It was only then that he noticed something was wrong. About ten customers were huddled down the far end of the narrow bank, sitting cross-legged on the floor, hands behind their heads.

A young man stood at the counter, a few feet away from David. He was wearing running shorts, Adidas sneakers and an old 'I Ran the World' T-shirt. His face was covered by a plastic George Bush mask. His left hand was grasping a shotgun, its double-barrel sawn to a length of twelve inches. The gun was digging into Lauris's neck. The fingers of the gunman's right hand were entwined in her hair. Her skin had turned shockingly white. Her teeth were clenched and tiny bleating sounds were issuing from her throat. David could see an artery beating fiercely along her neck.

'With the others!' the gunman ordered. His harsh, strangled voice shook as he gave the command. David hesitated. The gunman dug the gun deeper into Lauris's throat. 'NOW!' the gunman shouted. For the first time, David noticed the bank staff behind the plate glass window that bisected the room cramming bundles of notes into airline bags.

Lauris mouthed the word 'Go!' at him. He turned placed his hands on Anna's shoulders. Her body was taut, like steel.

'Don't resist!' he whispered. 'The quicker he's finished, the better.'

Someone behind the counter would have hit the alarm connected to the local police station by now, and it was only a couple of hundred yards away. The very fact that the robber had chosen this bank meant he was an amateur. If the police turned up, he'd panic, start shooting. And Lauris might die.

David pushed Anna gently towards the back of the bank, where the other customers were sitting. Blood was streaming from the nose of a middle-aged man in a suit. At least someone had put up a fight.

David had to press down on Anna's shoulders to make her sit. He hunkered down beside her.

Lauris's eyes were closed when he looked back at her. Her lips were moving. Praying, he guessed.

An elderly clerk approached the window, carrying two airline bags.

'They're full,' he said.

'Sling 'em over! Don't fuck up, or this slag's a corpse.'

The clerk tossed the bags over the top of the glass divide. They landed two yards from the gunman. His T-shirt was soaked with sweat, and his whole body was shivering with fear and excitement. He let go of Lauris, stepped away from her.

'Thank God!' David breathed out.

'Pick 'em up, you fucking slag!' the gunman growled at Lauris. 'You're coming with me.'

'You *can't*!' David gasped.

'Shut the fuck up!' the gunman shouted, swinging the gun round so that it was pointing at David. 'Anyone tries to follow, the slag dies. Got that?' He trained the gun on Lauris once more. 'MOVE!'

She headed towards the bags with jerky puppet-like movements. As she bent down to pick them up, her eyes met David's. His filled with tears. She looked away.

'We've go to do *something*!' the businessman with the bleeding nose hissed in David's ear.

'No,' said David. 'That's my wife.'

'Oh God!' the man groaned.

Lauris had both airline bags by their straps.

'Get the fuck over here!' the gunman ordered.

Lauris moved stiffly towards him. As she came abreast of him, he pointed the gun at her head.

'The car's right outside, slag. You walk to it, get in. You try and run, your fucking head comes off. Understand?'

Lauris gave a sharp nod.

David heard Anna sob, felt her anguish and anger blare inside him. He heard her getting up. He put out a restraining hand, but too late. Anna was on her feet.

The gunman and Lauris had reached the bank's swing

doors. Keeping the shotgun trained on Lauris, the gunman used his other arm to push one of the doors open. He wedged his foot against it to keep it that way.

'When you're outside, move fast, slag! Remember I'm right behind you!'

'No!' Anna said.

David reached up and grabbed her and tried to jerk her back down as the gunman turned his George Bush face towards them, but Anna shrugged him away.

She began walking down the bank towards the entrance door. The air was suddenly full of an electric buzz, like feedback from an amplifier.

David wanted to shout at her to stop. Yes, sure, she'd done little party tricks now and then, but this was a different kind of game.

The robber aimed the gun at her, sighted along the barrel.

'Okay,' George Bush said. 'You're dead.'

He curled a finger round the trigger, began to squeeze.

Three things happened at once. David leapt up, shouting 'NO!', Lauris screamed and swung both airline bags at the gunman, missing him, and Anna halted, stood stockstill.

David hit Anna flush in the back with both hands as the gun exploded. They landed together in a tangle on the floor. As he looked up, he was aware of the stench of gunpowder in his nostrils. Anna was lying perfectly still, face down on the floor.

'Please, God, no!' David breathed out.

Anna raised her head. David followed the direction of her gaze.

The gunman was taking off his George Bush mask. He looked even younger than David had suspected, twenty-one at most. His mouth was wide open and he was trying to scream. His eyes were bulging impossibly as he stared down at his feet. The shotgun dropped from his hand, clattered on the floor.

David blinked. All that remained of the gunman's left foot was a gory pulp. The blood-splattered top of an Adidas sneaker was lying right in front of David.

Automaticaly, he reached out for it, picked it up. From the weight of it, he realised the gunman's toes were still inside. He threw the object away violently.

Lauris swung the bags at the gunman once more. This time, she connected. He crumpled to the floor, still screaming silently, unable to take his eyes off what remained of his foot.

David helped Anna stand up. Her body was no longer taut. There was a curious expression on her face. Not triumph, exactly, just satisfaction.

At the far end of the bank Lauris, sobbing, sagged down onto her knees.

As David and Anna moved towards her, he heard the businessman behind him say,

'The girl did it. She *made* him shoot himself.'

There was a sinking sensation in David's stomach. This wasn't going to be easy to explain away.

CHAPTER THREE

As David brought his car to a halt fifty yards from the entrance gates of Anna's school, he glanced at the screaming banner headline on the newspaper on the passenger seat beside him.

SUPERGIRL FOILS BANK RAID
TV Man's Daughter Used Supernatural Powers, Witnesses Claim

Terrific, David thought. They'd been so careful for so many years, and now this.

He frowned as he gazed at the gaggle of journalists, photographers and TV camera crews staking out the school. He would have preferred Anna to stay home, but it was the last day of term, and she desperately wanted to say goodbye to her old friends.

His first reaction, after they'd spoken to police and given an exclusive family interview to Capital Television

News, had been to suggest that they flee to their cottage in Wiltshire. It was their secret place, their hideaway, the ownership registered in Lauris's maiden name. They never invited friends there, and kept out of the way of the locals. Even the police would have had a job tracing them.

But, as a journalist himself, he knew the more they hid, the harder the press would chase them. They'd have to bring Anna out of hiding for the gunman's trial, and the more cooperative the family was now, the less hounding they'd have to face then.

The photographers and reporters surged forward. David drove on and parked as near to the gates as he could. He fought his way through the throng and got to Anna just as she reached the gates. She looked less scared than astonished by all the attention. He took hold of her hand as they turned to face popping flashbulbs and a barrage of shouted questions.

'Ladies and gentlemen, please!' No response. 'Fellow hacks!' he shouted. That drew a laugh, and the crowd quietened. 'Okay, here's the deal. Ten minutes of questions and photographs here, now, and then leave us in peace. Either that, or I'm going to let the Inland Revenue in on the secret that reporters ocassionally fiddle their expenses.' Another laugh. Good. He had them on his side. 'First question. Jack Singleton of the *Echo* – it's been years since you had a scoop, Jack. Fire away.'

'Anna, did you make the gunman shoot himself?'

Anna started speaking in a whisper, but gradually her voice gained strength. No, she hadn't used supernatural powers on the gunman. She just got scared and stood up and shouted something at him. She couldn't remember what she'd said, but it made the gunman turn towards her. Her mother had swung the airline bags at him, and his gun had gone off. Her mother was the real heroine. *And* her father, because he'd kept calm. That was all there was to it.

'But the other witnesses say your mother didn't connect with the bags at the first attempt. They say *you* made him do it.'

Anna giggled. 'That's just silly.'

After ten minutes, and after reluctantly agreeing to a shot of himself and Anna cheek-to-cheek, David called a halt to the proceedings.

'And if I find any of you creeping around our house, I won't bother complaining to the Press Council – I'll just kick your backsides.'

Photographers followed them to the car, getting off some extra shots, but the reporters seemed satisfied. Anna blew air out from her cheeks in relief as they drove away.

'Well done, angel,' he said, smiling at her. 'You handled that perfectly.'

'You know what I wish?' she said, staring ahead through the windscreen.

'Tell me.'

'I wish I was ordinary.'

'I know.' He reached across, patted her knee. 'But if you were, your mother might not be alive.'

'I hadn't thought of that.' She smiled at him. 'I suppose I'm just upset about saying goodbye to everyone.'

He had realized there was something different about Anna three days after her birth. He'd been visiting the hospital in Brighton where he'd been a newspaper reporter at the time. He'd been up all night on a 12-hour shift and had been chewing asprin to deaden the screaming pain in his knee. Anna, six weeks premature, had been in a tiny perspex incubator beside Lauris's bed. He'd been leaning over his sleeping daughter, and Lauris had remarked that Anna had her father's chin. 'She doesn't have a chin,' he'd joked, and then Anna had awakened and opened her mouth and let out a wail. At that instant David had experienced a burst of anxiety, a brief flare of unformed, undirected panic. Not his own. His daughter's. He had directly experienced Anna's fear. He had asked Lauris if she'd felt it, and she admitted she had.

'But it's just natural parental empathy,' she'd added.

A few days later, when David had arrived to take his wife and daughter home, the doctor who'd delivered Anna had drawn him aside and asked to see his hands.

'I thought it might be hereditary,' the doctor had said. 'You see, Mr Cauley, your daughter—'

'Her fingerprints are straight. Is that it?'

'Yes, but how did you know?'

'It doesn't matter.'

'I've never seen the phenomenon before. In fact, I've never even heard of it,' the doctor had said, his expression puzzled. 'But it probably doesn't signify anything.'

David had smiled grimly. 'I wouldn't be too sure of that, doctor.'

Later that day, David has posted a card to a Washington DC post office box number.

Now, as he swept his VW Corrado round the Hogarth roundabout he glanced in the rear-view mirror. The red Porsche 959 directly behind him was a handsome, mean-looking car. He'd had the same thought five minutes back when he'd last looked in the mirror.

He squeezed down on the accelerator, abruptly changed lanes. The Porsche glided into place directly behind him. The sun reflecting off the windscreen made it impossible to tell who was driving.

'Dad, what's wrong?' Anna asked.

He realized he'd begun whistling between his teeth, the way he always did when he was nervous.

'I think we're being followed.'

He took the Chiswick turn-off. So did the Porsche.

'Maybe they're reporters,' Anna said, squinting at the side mirror.

'Reporters don't drive cars like that, angel. Neither do the police.'

'Oh!'

'Exactly.' They passed over Chiswick High Road and headed down Turnham Green Terrace, past Andy's. 'I'm going to try to lose it. Hold tight.'

He suddenly swung across The Avenue, heading into Bedford Park's maze of pretty little streets. The Porsche followed. David made a left, a right. The streets were narrow and lined with parked cars on both sides. Accuracy mattered as much as speed. The Porsche was losing ground. A left. Another left. Anna was holding onto the roof strap. A right. He couldn't see the Porsche in his mirror any longer. A left. The Corrado's wheels squealed satisfyingly. One more turn and they'd be back on The Avenue.

He four-wheeled skidded into Bedford Road, shrieked to a halt a few inches from the barrier in the middle of the street. Beyond it, there was a neat five-foot rut running all the way to The Avenue.

He cursed, rammed into reverse, shot backwards.

The Porsche slid into view and halted, blocking his exit.

The doors opened, and two figures he had hoped never to see again stepped out of his past into the sunlight.

At first, he refused to believe his eyes. They couldn't still be together after all these years. It was a nightmare. Had to be.

His heart gave a double beat as he continued to stare through the back window of the car. No, there was no doubting the fact that Vercoe and Hughes were heading towards them.

'Daddy?' Anna's voice was tremulous.

He tried for a smile. He reached out a hand, stroked her cheek.

'Don't worry, angel. I know them. I'm going out to talk to them. You stay in the car. Lock the doors when I get out, and don't open them, *whatever* happens.'

He stepped out of the car, heard the locks click. His mouth went dry, and he licked his lips. He would have given anything for a drink. He realized his hands were shaking, made an effort to control them.

As the pair sauntered towards him, glancing casually up and down the street to make sure no one was watching, David realized that even after twenty-five years they still terrified him.

David leaned against the Corrado, resting an elbow on the roof, trying to appear relaxed. Hughes had grown at least four inches. He must have stood six foot seven. His massively muscled body stretched the fabric of his powder-blue suit. But his face hadn't changed. It still looked as if it belonged on a rat. And his complexion was still that of a vampire. His acne had cleared up, leaving deep pits and ruts behind. His eyes were hidden behind dark glasses.

Vercoe was less recognizable. The impact against the changing room wall the day he had come up against James Lord had left his nose so flat it barely protruded from his face. His eyes were still black, still crossed, and as crazy as ever. His frizzy hair had receded to the crown of his head. The front teeth that had been knocked out at the pool had been replaced. The new ones were unnaturally white against his dirty-looking skin. His face was puffy and flaccid, and criss-crossed with premature wrinkles.

They halted two yards away from David.

Vercoe grinned. 'Long time, Cauley.'

'Not long enough, Vercoe. What do you want?'

'A little slice of your daughter. About £50,000 worth.' The voice was gravelled with alcohol and cigarettes.

Hughes leaned down and peered through the Corrado's windscreen. David looked in to see Anna staring back at the giant in horror.

'You're frightening her, Hughes,' David said. 'Back off.'

The monster looked up at him and grinned, displaying yellow teeth.

'Do what the man says, Hughes,' Vercoe said, not looking at his companion. 'Cauley here's a VIP these days. A big cheese. TV star, no less.'

'And exactly what are you, Vercoe?' David asked.

'We're in the persuasion business.'

Vercoe took a couple of steps towards David, glancing in at Anna as he did so. David's nostrils caught the pungent stench of old sweat. Vercoe's attention to personal hygiene hadn't improved with the passage of time.

'I'm surprized to see you out on the streets, Vercoe,' David said. 'I'd have thought you'd have been locked away years ago.'

Vercoe halted a few inches from him. David had to breath through his mouth.

'I've got friends, Cauley. Powerful friends. I could kill you now, in front of a hundred witnesses, and nothing would happen to me. That's how powerful my friends are.'

'Vercoe, you're boring me. What do you and your ape friend want?'

'I told you. A piece of your daughter.' Vercoe stepped back, stuck his hands in the jacket pockets of his dirty cream-coloured suit. 'We represent a German magazine. The biggest. They want to do a cover item about the bank raid, but only if we can stand up this angle about your kid making the gunman blow his foot off. *If* we can convince them that's true, they'll pay £50,000 for an exclusive. That's a five and four zeroes. Think about it.'

Hughes had moved round the other side of the car and was trying the doors.

'Forget it, Hughes,' David said. 'The doors are locked and the keys are inside.'

Vercoe sighed. 'All we need to do is have a little chat with your daughter. That's all, Cauley. If it works out okay, you'll be fifty grand better off. Where's the harm in that?'

'The answer's no, Vercoe. And if the gorilla touches the car just once more, I'm calling the police.'

Vercoe sniggered. 'You're terrifying us. Isn't he, Hughes?'

Hughes's rodent grin widened. He bunched an enormous fist, smashed it into the front passenger window. It shattered, spraying diamond-shaped fragments of glass around the interior of the car. Anna let out a shriek.

'You bastard!' David shouted.

He lashed out at Vercoe, sent him reeling back, then jumped up onto the bonnet of the car and hurled himself at Hughes. The big man stepped aside easily and David landed painfully on the pavement. Before he could get up, Hughes had him by the throat and was lifting him up off the ground one-handed, and David's feet were dangling six inches from the pavement. Hughes removed his sunglasses and pressed his face close to David's. His eyes were yellow and bloodshot and rheumy. The sight of them close up turned David's stomach.

'Respect!' Hughes growled. 'You show me respect!'

Hughes's grip was so fierce David couldn't breathe.

Out of the corner of his eye, he saw Vercoe reach

through the window Hughes had shattered and feel for the lock on the passenger door. David wanted to shout at Anna to run, but couldn't make a sound. He felt himself starting to pass out.

As his eyes closed, he was vaguely aware of a buzzing sensation coming from far away.

Then, suddenly, he was slipping from Hughes's grasp, crumpling onto the ground. He lay there for a while, too weak to move, just concentrating on getting air into his lungs. Eventually, he propped himself up on one hand, coughing, massaging his throat. His eyes were swimming. He blinked to focus.

Anna had got out of the car, and was standing beside it, staring down the street at Hughes and Vercoe, who were heading for their own car.

As David watched, they got inside their Porsche, and, without a backward glance, drove away.

'Angel?'

Anna didn't respond until the Porsche was out of sight. She moved over to where her father was lying, and helped him up.

'What did you do to them?' he asked.

'I told them I was a perfectly ordinary little girl, of no interest at all to them, and that it was time for them to leave.'

'And it worked?'

'They left, didn't they?'

She looked tired. Dark patches had appeared under her eyes.

'Will it last? Will they still believe that tomorrow?'

She shrugged. 'I don't know, Dad. I've never used the power that way before.' She reached a hand up to her temple. 'I'm not feeling very well.'

'Let's get you home.'

As he wiped glass particles off the front seats, he remembered an order he had been given many years ago. *Always be vigilant for Anna!*

So Vercoe and Hughes had powerful friends. Well, so did he.

CHAPTER FOUR

The pressmen who had been clustered outside the Cauleys' terraced redbrick house in St Alban's Avenue had dispersed by the time David and Anna arrived home. He was grateful his colleagues had stuck by their agreement. Come the trial, though, he knew the deal would be off.

Anna swayed a little as she stepped out of the car. Neighbours' curtains twitched as David helped her to the front door. Lauris opened it for them. The ten milligramme valium tablet the doctor had given her the previous night to help her sleep had left her large hazel eyes glazed.

She put her arms around Anna. 'What's wrong, darling?'

'Tired, Mum. So tired.'

'Up to bed.'

David watched them head upstairs, then moved through to the sitting room, where the curtains were drawn. He poured himself a stiff Cutty Sark. From force of habit, he switched on the TV, checked the news headlines on Ceefax. Mindless laughter from some panel game disturbed his concentration. He killed the sound, sat down on the couch, and gazed up at a print of Max Gertler's 'Merry-Go Round' on the opposite wall. He had never been able to decide whether the stylized riders were laughing or screaming. Today, in the gloom, they were definitely screaming.

Lauris reappeared a few minutes later.

'She's asleep. You look like you've been in a fight.'

'I have.'

'What happened, David?'

She sat down next to him on the couch, took hold of his hand.

He described their confrontation with Vercoe and Hughes. When he'd finished, Lauris got up and opened the curtains to let in some sunlight.

44

'This is getting scary,' she said, staring out the window. 'What did those two *really* want?'

'To find out if Anna was special.'

'Who sent them?' He didn't respond. 'Will they come back?'

'How the hell should I know?' He got up abruptly, went over to the drinks table and poured himself another Scotch, turned. 'I'm sorry. I'm on edge.'

'You'll have to contact him, David.' Lauris sounded resigned. 'He's bound to hear about it anyway.'

He nodded, then walked over to her and took her in his arms.

'It'll be all right,' he whispered. 'James'll know what to do.'

She looked up at him, tears in her eyes. 'I won't let him take her away from us!'

'He won't. He's a friend.' Even to him, the assurance sounded false.

She opened her mouth to say something else, decided against it. 'Make the call,' she said, then let go of him and left the room.

He consulted his filofax, dialled James's number. A ringing tone. As he waited for someone to answer, he remembered back fourteen years to the night James Lord had paid Anna his first and, so far, only visit . . .

David's bladder was screaming with pain when he woke at three in the morning. He slipped out of bed and made his way across the room, on tiptoe, past Anna's cot, avoiding the two floorboards near the door that made a sound like falling timber when you stepped on them.

When he'd relieved himself, he sat down on the toilet lid and yawned. As the newest reporter at London's only all-news radio station he'd drawn the worst shift – the overnight, four on, two off. After six weeks, the stint was taking its toll in disrupted sleep and hunger attacks in the early hours. Like now. He thought about heading for the kitchen, fought the impulse. He stood over six feet tall and had a broad frame, but excess weight didn't sit well on him.

A noise in the house. He held his breath, listened. Nothing.

Probably the lady advertising executive next door performing sexual gymnastics with one of her string of boyfriends. They seemed to change every week. David and Lauris wouldn't have minded, but when it came to lovemaking she was an out-and-out screamer. The first time they'd heard her approach climax they'd thought she was being murdered. Only the rhythm of her headboard banging against the connecting bedroom wall had convinced them otherwise. As for noise, they were getting their own back. Lauris had turned the upstairs front room of the house into a silversmithing workshop. Their neighbour was having to put up with regular hour-long metal-hammering sessions. And when Lauris wasn't beating the hell out of a chunk of metal, the advertising executive had Anna to contend with. After just three months she was developing a fine pair of lungs. A 'For Sale' sign had appeared on the neighbouring house the previous week.

He let out another yawn, decided to get back to bed. His interrupted sleep pattern had introduced him to a new pleasure – lying awake, listening to his wife and daughter's deep, contented breathing gave him an absurd high, made him feel totally at peace.

He tiptoed back to the bedroom, glanced down at Anna's cot. It was empty. His stomach lurched. He peered over at the bed. Lauris hadn't taken Anna in with her.

But if Anna had been awakened during the night, she'd have yelled. Even if a kidnapper had placed a hand over her mouth, he and Lauris would have sensed her panic, as they sensed all her emotions.

A hiccup of baby laughter from downstairs. He realized he'd been holding his breath. He let it out. Somehow, Anna had managed to escape from her cot. He'd buy a new one tomorrow, with padlocks on it, if necessary. He left the room and began to make his way downstairs. He halted at the base of the stairs. All the downstairs doors were locked.

Twelve-week-old babies did not climb out of their cots, make their way down steep flights of stairs and open and close doors whose handles were above their reach.

He heard Anna's laughter again. And an adult voice. He walked along the downstairs hall to the sitting room. He grasped the knob, wrenched it open, hit the light switch.

Anna turned her vague, unfocused gaze towards him, crinkled her forehead.

'Dave, my man!' said James Lord. He was sitting in David's armchair, cradling Anna. One long leg was slung raffishly over the arm of the chair. 'She's got your chin.'

'She doesn't have a chin,' David responded automatically. 'You really scared me.'

'Sorry,' James said. 'I was going to turn up tomorrow, but I couldn't wait to see her.'

'I sent you the telegram three months ago.'

'Tied up.' James looked down at Anna, tickled her chin. She chuckled. 'Old Uncle James was all tied up.'

As David sat down heavily on the sofa, 'glamorous' was the word that sprang to mind. James Lord had acquired glamour in the intervening years. His hair was still blond, his eyes were still a washed-out green colour and he was still slim, but there was an aura about him now that hadn't been there before. Not a glossy movie-star patina: an aura of power.

James looked up as Anna tried to grasp his index finger.

'How'd you get so big, Dave?'

'Why are you still so skinny?' His heart had stopped racing, but there was a shake in his voice.

'I sensed the potential in you, Dave. Didn't know what it meant then. Now it's clear.'

'Explain it to me.'

'What I sensed back then was your potential to father someone . . . special. Someone like me.'

Anna gave up the attempt to get hold of James's finger. Her head lolled back and she was asleep. James smiled at her fondly. 'I just had to see her for myself.'

David took a deep breath. 'That's my daughter, James. I want to know all about her.'

James's expression turned serious. 'I can tell you some of it. Not all. It wouldn't be safe for you. Or Anna.'

'What can you tell me?'

There was a pause before James spoke. His grey-green eyes gazed steadily at David, appraising him. 'Anna's going to be very persuasive. You mustn't be frightened of her, but you mustn't let her get the upper hand either. I know my parents had a hell of a battle trying to control me. You're going to have to learn to set up a mental guard against her, a shield to use when she's really trying to get her own way. Otherwise you'll have a monster on your hands.' He moved her carefully to stop her head flopping back too far. 'Try and teach her not to use her power indiscriminately. It'll frighten people, turn them against her. I spent my early childhood moving from one school to another, because after a while I'd begin to scare the other kids. They sensed I was different from them. Most of all, you must keep her powers secret. There are some people out there who'd try and take her away from you if they found out about her. They'd use her in ways you wouldn't like, ways you—'

'What in God's name is going on?'

David's head snapped around. Lauris was standing in the sitting-room doorway. Her face was puffy with sleep.

'Mrs Cauley, how do you do?' James said pleasantly. 'Nice to meet you, but I really think you should go back to bed.'

David felt the power coming off James. After a pause, Lauris turned and walked back out of the room.

'It's probably best she doesn't know,' James said. 'If she remembers any of this in the morning, tell her it was a dream.'

Anger flared inside David. 'You arrogant bastard! I'll decide what to tell my wife. Okay?' He stood up. 'And give Anna to me!'

James got up, passed her over. 'Don't be angry with me, Dave.'

'Why not? How dare you push my wife around like that in her home. How dare you sneak in here without my permission and steal Anna that way. And stop talking in riddles. "Use her in ways you wouldn't like". What's that supposed to mean?'

James opened his arms wide. 'Dave, my man!'

David felt soothing vibration coming off James. He held Anna tight. 'Don't use any of that mental stuff on me.' He was quivering with anger, an anger he couldn't justify but which had something to do with having his suspicions about Anna confirmed. She was different, like James. A freak. His daughter was a freak!

They studied each other in silence, David glaring, James frowning.

Nearby, a woman yelled: it turned into a choking, gurgling scream.

48

James jumped. 'Was that your wife?'

David shook his head. 'Our next door neighbour getting laid.'

A bellow from the other side of the wall.

'Boy, that guy must be some performer.'

'Judging by her normal reaction, this one's impotent.'

James started to laugh, and, after a pause, David joined in. Suddenly his anger, his sense of violation, eased. The strangeness between them was gone, and for a few seconds it was as if the years had vanished and they were back at school, friends once more. But David knew they weren't, not really. James had changed. There was a hardness to him now that hadn't been there ten tears ago; a hint of something not quite human.

When their laughter subsided James said, 'Dave, I handled this badly. The last thing I wanted to do was upset you.'

They heard the rhythmic thud of a bedhead banging against a connecting wall.

James grinned. 'I can't concentrate with that going on. To be honest, it's making me feel kinda horny. Let's take a walk.'

David paused. 'Okay.'

He went back to the bedroom and placed Anna in her cot. Lauris was in bed, asleep. He dragged on some clothes. He paused at the bedroom door on the way out and breathed in his wife's subtle lilac perfume.

James was waiting for him on the pavement, thin face pointing up at the stars. Steam wraiths twisted up from his mouth into the cold night sky. His slim body was wrapped elegantly in a Burberry coat. A grey cashmere scarf bulked at his throat. The light of a nearby streetlamp glinted off his polished black leather shoes. David felt shabby and clumsy in his jeans and sneakers and a scuffed leather jacket that wouldn't quite zip up over his burgeoning gut.

David pointed, indicating the direction they should take. The long, winding tree-lined street was perfectly still as they fell into step with each other. James looked out of place against the backdrop of small terraced houses; Mayfair would have been a more suitable setting.

'I never apologized for what happened to you after I left St Stephen's,' James said. He gave Dave a sideways glance. 'Left you with a limp. I see.'

'Only now and then.'

'Must have been painful.'

'It was. Still is, sometimes.'

They lapsed into a silence broken only by the scuffle of David's sneakers and the click of James's steel-capped shoe heels. A car started up some way behind them.

As they walked, David studied James. He looked a good ten years older than twenty-four. They reached the end of St Alban's Avenue, headed east along South Parade towards Turnham Green underground station past a row of detached redbrick houses with white wooden balustrades. A brightly lit tube train moved briskly past them high on an embankment a hundred yards away. It was empty, a ghost train.

'What's been happening to you since we last met?' David asked.

'Hid out in various places around Europe for a couple of months. They were close behind me most of the way. They wanted me badly. My luck held, though, and I eventually made it back to the States. Caught up on my education. Went to Harvard Law School. Got married. Got divorced when she realized I wasn't exactly your average lawyer. Now I'm a junior partner in a glitzy practice in Washington. I'm making some headway in politics. Got the remnants of Bobby Kennedy's old machine behind me. I'll be a senator someday, and then . . .' He shrugged.

'President?' David asked, smiling.

'If I want to be.' His tone was serious.

'Simple as that?'

'For an emperor, achievement's easy. It's deciding what you want to achieve that's difficult.'

'Emperor?'

'That's what we call ourselves. Hell, that's what we are!'

'The war you talked about,' David said. 'Is that still going on?'

'It'll go on forever.' James reached in his pocket, pulled out a packet of cigarettes, lit one with a gunmetal lighter. 'As far as I know, it's already lasted thousands of years.'

'You keep talking in riddles, James. I deserve better.'

James halted, tossed his cigarette into the gutter. He placed

50

his hands on David's shoulders. 'If you were a different sort of guy, I'd tell you everything. Maybe. But keeping secrets isn't your style.' James smiled. 'I heard about some of the stories you did on that newspaper in Brighton. You're a good journalist, a real digger, a natural troublemaker. If I told you what was really going down, you wouldn't be able to keep it to yourself.' He removed his hands from David's shoulders. 'Besides, like most of your breed, you drink too much.'

'I'm Anna's father. Doesn't that give me the right to know what's happening? For her sake?'

'It's for her sake I'm not telling you.' James stuck his hands back in his pockets, turned, and walked on. When David had caught up with him, James said, 'Anna needs a normal upbringing with good people who're aware she's different. I might not trust you with most of my secrets, but I trust you to look after her.'

'What if you didn't trust me?'

James shrugged. 'I'd take her away from you.'

David shivered. 'You can't mean that.'

James halted, stared down at the pavement. 'You have no idea how important your little girl might turn out to be.' He looked at David. His green eyes were unsettling in their intensity. 'You have no idea!'

There was a car following them. David realized it had been there since the start of their walk, idling along a hundred yards or so behind, lights off, stopping when they stopped, moving when they did. And he thought James has led them to Anna!

David's voice sounded strangled when he spoke. 'There's a car following us, a Jaguar. I think it's been with us since we left the house.'

He grabbed James's arm, dragged him into a side street. They pressed their backs up against a deep-shadowed wall.

'Got to get back to the house,' David whispered. 'They might try and snatch Anna.'

'Take it easy!' James said.

The car paused at the entrance to the side street. David shrank back against the wall, trying to make himself disappear. The car nosed into the street, pointing at them. David held his breath. The headlights came on, dazzling them. David made to run. James grabbed

51

his arm, holding him in place.

Stay put! *The command was inside his head.*

The car door opened.

'It's good you're afraid, Dave,' *James said.* 'You must always be vigilant for Anna. Anyone shows any interest in her, you let me know.' *He patted David's arm.* 'So long.'

He walked over to the car, got in, slammed the door. The Jaguar swung round sleekly. He recognized the driver. The last time he'd seen him, David had been dangling from a cliff in Cornwall, seconds away from death.

No, he didn't want to think about that now. Too much else on his plate.

The car turned right, heading for Central London. David remained where he was for a few minutes, cold sweat trickling down his flanks.

When he moved, pain shot up his leg. He staggered like a drunk.

He wasn't sure he much liked his old friend any more.

Gritting his teeth, he started to run, ran all the way home.

Lauris was standing in the kitchen, waiting for the kettle to boil, looking vulnerable and frightened.

'Where have you been? There was a man. You were talking to a man—'

'Shh!' *He took her in his arms, squeezed her tight against him.* 'There was no man. No one at all. Just a dream.'

Lauris stepped back from him, still scared. 'It was too real for a dream. You were in the sitting room with a man who was holding Anna, and you were talking about her. Then he . . . did something to me and I was back in bed. And I woke up, and you were gone, and Anna's cot was disturbed, and . . .' *And then the tears came, and David was holding her again.*

'Let's go to bed,' *he said.*

Her face nuzzled in against his chest. Her sobbing gradually lessened, and she allowed him to lead her upstairs.

As they entered the bedroom, they stopped by the cot and gazed down at Anna. David remembered what James had said. You have no idea just how important your little girl might turn out to be. No idea!

Anna opened her eyes and stared up at him intently. There was something terribly knowing about her gaze. His spine froze. She coughed, blinked, closed her eyes.

If James intention had been to scare him into vigilance, he'd done a brilliant job.

'David, you're shaking,' Lauris said.

He turned to her, took a deep breath. 'I have something to tell you. You're not going to like it.'

She wiped her eyes, gave him a determined look. 'Try me.'

When it came down to it, he knew he didn't have the guts to face this on his own.

'It's about Anna,' he said.

'I thought it might be.' She glanced back at the cot. 'She's different, isn't she?'

'James Lord's office. How may I help you?'

'I'd like to speak to him.'

'The Senator is in a meeting right now.'

'Tell him it's David Cauley. He'll want to speak to me. I'll hold.'

He sipped his fresh whisky as he waited. James came on the line after a minute.

'Dave, my man! Do you know you're keeping the President waiting? He's in my office right now.'

The strong, confident voice made him feel better at once. 'We've got trouble, James.'

A slight pause. 'Is Anna all right?'

'For now.'

Another pause. 'Okay, what's been happening?'

David told him. When he'd finished, James said, 'Vercoe and Hughes – I take it they're not working for any magazine.'

'Unlikely. Look, what Anna did to them, will it last? Or will they realize she fooled them?'

'I'm not sure. In the meantime, I'm going to send someone over to keep an eye on you folks. You won't know they're around.'

'Okay, but what about the trial? Anna might have fooled Hughes and Vercoe this time, but it's all going to come up again at the trial. Twenty witnesses are going to say the same thing – Lauris missed the gunman with the bags the first time. They'll say he shot his foot off because Anna—'

'There won't be any trial, Dave.'

'How can you *say* that? You might be a big noise in Washington, but not here.'

James's voice suddenly turned harsh. 'There won't be any trial.'

Silence for a few seconds. 'James?' David said.

'Yes, old buddy?'

'You won't take her away from us, will you?'

'Not if you take care of her, Dave. That's always been the deal.'

As James hung up, David realized his palms were running with sweat.

Two days later, David was back at the reporters' desk in the Capital Newsroom, cruising the wires on the computer, when a colleague opposite him suddenly sat up straight.

'Holy shit, David! Check out the PA story slugged JAIL DEATH.' Whitley Chamberlain, Capital's only black reporter, grinned at him across the desk. 'And never let me hear you say there isn't any justice in the world.'

'Whitley, if this is another of your stupid jokes—'

'Check it out, man! Check it out!'

David found the story, cursored into it.

'A MAN AWAITING TRIAL FOR AN ARMED ROBBERY IN WEST LONDON THREE DAYS AGO HAS DIED IN CUSTODY. 21 YEAR OLD PAUL REYNOLDS, CHARGED WITH THE ATTEMPTED ROBBERY OF THE CHISWICK HIGH ROAD BRANCH OF THE NATIONAL WESTMINSTER BANK, WAS BEING TREATED FOR SHOTGUN WOUNDS AT CHISWICK PRISON INFIRMARY. HE WAS DISCOVERED BY A NURSE EARLY THIS MORNING APPARENTLY STRANGLED TO DEATH WITH A LEATHER BELT. THE AUTHORITIES ARE TREATING THE DEATH AS SUICIDE.'

David read the story twice, then logged off.

'At least your little girl won't have to give evidence at the trial,' Whitley said. They'd been discussing the possibility earlier.

David nodded. 'I know. That's great.'

'Then why do you look as if you just heard your dog got run over?' Whitley's expression turned serious. 'Can you assure me, as a colleague and a close personal friend, that you didn't take out a contract on this guy's life?'

'Hilarious, Whitley,' David said. 'As always.'

Chuckling, Whitley got up and headed for the tea bar.

And David thought, *There won't be any trial!*

'Oh James!' he whispered. 'What's happened to you?'

CHAPTER FIVE

22 April 1992

The RT set fitted to the dashboard of David Cauley's Corrado squawked loudly. Sitting beside him, Anna gave a little jump. David scooped the mike up.

'Yes, base. David Cauley here. What gives?'

'Doorstepper. Ennismore Gardens.' The news organizer, Bill Bride, sounded frazzled already, and the day had barely begun. 'The crew's already on its way. How far away are you?'

'About twenty minutes.' Only then did David remember it was his day off. His response to the call had been a Pavlovian reflex. 'Who are we after?'

'Richard Spear.'

'The Dragon Man? What's the story?'

'Dragon Enterprises has signed a £150 million deal with Libya to provide oil-drilling and refining equipment.'

'With Libya? Are you sure?'

'The story's running on Reuters.'

Spear had a reputation for audacity, but this time, surely, he'd gone too far. A Libyan murder squad had gunned down an exiled political leader in Leicester Square five days back. Two teenage German tourists, a boy and a girl, had been killed during the assault. A Metropolitan policeman, shot as he gave chase to the assassins, was still in intensive care. A Libyan had been arrested in Bayswater and charged with murder. The Libyan President had threatened reprisals against Britain if he wasn't released. Libya wasn't exactly flavour of the month, and the timing of the announcement of Dragon Enterprises' deal couldn't have been more provocative. It was as if Spear wanted to be seen publicly supporting a regime that resorted to terrorism.

'Don't take all day to think about it, Cauley. The editor of the Lunchtime wants a fat minute, so get your backside over to Spear's place pronto.'

'Dear, dear!' Anna said. 'That man needs to learn some manners.'

David hit the 'off' switch, but too late.

'Taking the kiddywinkles to school on the way to work's a sacking offence, as you bloody well know, *Mr* Cauley.'

'Bill, if you'll recall, I'm on my own time this morning. It's my daughter's birthday. I'm bringing her in to show her the newsroom. And she's a young lady, *not* a kiddywinkle.'

'All right,' Bride said curtly.

David mouthed a profanity. He couldn't remember ever hearing Bill Bride apologize for anything. But it was impossible not to sympathize with him. The News Organizer had a hell of a job – deploying twenty reporters and sixty film crew for fourteen hours at a stretch was a killer. If you missed a big story, or decided not to send a crew out on something that later broke big, God help you! Either the job attracted phychopaths, or it turned you into one.

Another voice cut across the circuit. 'You're a pantie-sniffer, Bride.' All conversation on the RT system could be heard by every car within a twenty-seven mile radius of base. There was no way of telling who the speaker was, unless they identified themselves.

'Who said that?' Bride shouted. David could imagine his fat, greasy face reddening.

'And you've got the social graces of a neanderthal.'

The voice was too well disguised for David to recognize it, but he suspected it belonged to a cameraman. Sound and lighting men tended to be conformist; reporters and cameramen shared an anarchic streak.

'If that's you, Jacobs,' Bride shouted, 'you're fired.'

'That's a hurtful suggestion. Bill,' Jacobs said.

'No, Bride,' the mystery voice said. 'This is the voice of your maker, apologizing for shoddy workmanship.'

'SHUT UP!' Bride bellowed.

Anna giggled. 'Pantie-sniffer. Dad, you work with some *strange* people.'

'I know, angel. Believe me, I know.' He smiled at her. 'You want to come along on this, birthday-girl?'

'Try and stop me!'

He caught himself checking the rear-view mirror as they headed through Hammersmith. Force of habit. Silly, now that there didn't seem to be any real need to worry. He'd been aware of someone on their tail for a few weeks after his phone call to James Lord last June. He'd glimpsed the same girl a few times – tall, slim, ash-blonde hair – but he hadn't been certain she'd been sent by James.

He himself had been strongly tempted to track down Vercoe and Hughes, to find out who had ordered them to check out Anna. But he'd controlled his reporter's instincts and let it be. There was always a possibility that such a move might have reawakened interest in his daughter.

Life had returned to normal in time for their trip to Portugal, and things had gone well since then. Lauris had begun receiving write-ups in chic art magazines, and that had allowed her to bump up her prices and turn down pedestrian projects. Anna had started at the Patterson School and seemed to be enjoying it. There had been no awkward incidents. Anna had an explanation for that: 'They're all very weird. Next to them, I'm amazingly normal!' David hadn't been doing so badly himself; there was even talk of a trial as a newsreader.

Yes, life was pretty good.

As they halted at a red light, it started to rain. David groaned. It *always* rained on doorsteppers.

'Music?' Anna asked.

'Be my guest.'

She reached over and switched on the cassette recorder. The first movement of Beethoven's Pastoral Symphony filled the car with a sound so summery he could almost feel the sun on him. He boosted the volume to drown out Bride's conversations with other cars, and because Anna liked her music loud.

As Anna hummed along to the first movement, David tried to recall everything he knew about Richard Spear. It didn't amount to much. Britain's most successful businessman. Publicity-shy, but not to the point of paranoia. Did a lot of business with countries regarded as enemies of the West. Known as 'The Dragon Man'. There'd been a photo-spread about him in a Sunday newspaper colour supplement. He remembered a house full of dragons – dragon-shaped lighters, paintings of serpents, sculptures. Married the daughter of an Earl in the late 'sixties, a wild young aristocrat who'd been mixed up in the sleazy Chelsea-set world of pop stars and 'happenings' and drugs, lots of drugs. As Spear's wife, she had turned into a charity organizer and major art collector. Children? He couldn't remember.

He checked his watch. 8:30. He had to figure out how to deliver a minute plus for the Lunchtime News. A shot of Spear leaving home and getting into his car would take up fifteen seconds. Maybe it'd stretch to twenty. Then some background on Spear's career to date. He'd get the news film library to dig out old footage of Spear, not that there'd be too much of that. Probably more from the late 'sixties than recently, and that would be on two-inch film, so he'd have to get it transferred to half-inch videotape before it could be edited into his piece. Another fifteen seconds. Then a graphics sequence illustrating the extent of Spear's financial empire. Another fifteen seconds. Then fifteen seconds about the Libyan deal – library footage of the country – and a ten second payoff. A piece to camera? Probably not. He'd have to do it before arriving back at the office, and he wouldn't know what to say until he'd been through Spear's file in News Information. And then the whole damn thing would probably be dropped because of lack of space, or the editor would decide to do it in ten seconds over a still photograph of Spear in the middle of a financial wipe sequence.

Ennismore Gardens was buzzing with activity when David and Anna arrived. Spear's house wasn't hard to spot. Outside, a gang of press reporters and two other film crews were drinking coffee out of styrofoam cups and munching bacon rolls. A curtain moved behind a ground-floor window of Spear's white stucco-fronted Victorian home as David slipped into a residents-only parking space twenty yards down the road.

'Can I come, Dad?' Anna asked.

'No, you stay here.' He felt a minor buzz. 'Cut that out or you'll be walking home.'

She folded her hands demurely in her lap. He kissed her nose, flipped his coat collar up and stepped out into the light rain.

He found the Capital camera crew inside their car, parked further along the road. The lighting man and the sound man were playing two-card brag. The cameraman was dozing on the back seat.

'Shouldn't we be set up?' David asked, waking him.

The cameraman shrugged. 'What's the point? Spear never talks. I doorstepped him last year. Waste of time.'

'We'll need general views of the house and shots of him leaving,' David said. 'Let's get moving.'

He was trotting back to his car when he heard his name being called. He looked around. Sammy Moss, a colleague from his radio days, was waving to him from the front seat of a beat-up Audi. David walked over and slipped into the passenger seat. Sammy was fiddling with a portable Üher tape-recorder on his knees. He grinned at David. A diamond sparkled from the centre of one of his eye-teeth.

'Hello, Superstar,' Sammy said. 'Are you sure you don't mind sharing a car with a humble radio hack?'

'Someone has to be rich and famous, Sammy. Might as well be me,' David said as Sammy managed to get his tape wound right. 'Anyway, I heard you were auditioning for us. What happened?'

Sammy shook his head, still grinning. 'My looks are too exotic for the small screen. On the playback I looked like a demented ferret. Your Managing Editor said he'd give me another audition if I shaved and got my teeth fixed. I said I'd do another audition if he shoved his head up his bum.' His smile faded. 'Besides, it wouldn't matter if I looked like Robert Redford. I told your boss I was gay. After that I was about as welcome as a fart in a spacesuit.' He sighed. 'I'm returning to print journalism next month. And *not* to a comic. At least on a newspaper you can look like Quasimodo and sound like Donald Duck and still be a journalist.'

'No, Sammy, you look like Charles Manson and sound like Bugs Bunny.'

'Anyone ever tell you you were funny?'

'Yes.'

'They were wrong.'

Sammy dug a tube of extra-strong mints out of his pocket, popped three in his mouth. David glanced up the road towards his own car. Anna was tracing patterns on the steamed-up inside of the window.

'What do you know about Spear?' David asked.

'As much as anyone outside Dragon Enterprises. I've been studying his business operations for over a year now.'

'How come?'

'I'm writing a book about him. Got two publishers bidding against each other for the rights. I've just shacked up with a young dress designer and he has *very* expensive tastes. Rui Olazabal – lovely name, huh?' David was aware of Sammy checking his face for a reaction. 'Besides, I feel I'm on some sort of mission to expose Spear for what he is.'

'Which is what?'

'The Antichrist. Possibly.'

'Your perchant for understatement is proverbial.'

'Seriously!' Sammy leaned forward, stared up through the windscreen at the front of Spear's tall, narrow house. 'Spear's business dealings are so fucking strange, you wouldn't believe it.'

'Try me.'

Sammy leaned back in his seat, popped another trio of mints.

'First, there's the stuff that makes sense. Consumer durables in Asia. After '68 he set up shop in Hong Kong, Taiwan and Korea and starting cranking out cheap stereos and watches and radios. Made millions. Probably billions. You know, all that stuff with the logo of a dragon curled around the globe on it. He put most of that money into two major areas – the commodities markets and oil. Between 1972 and 1973 commodity prices – stuff like cocoa, rubber and cotton – went up an average 150 per cent. Spear got out when prices reached their peak in the middle of '74. He moved heavily into oil in '72, made another killing when OPEC tripled the price of the stuff in October '73. Some people says he was behind the Arabs' decision to put the squeeze on the West. He moved out of oil in '75, moved back into it three years later just in time for the second big oil crisis, when OPEC doubled the price. After that, he became a major force on the foreign exchange markets – it's rumoured he caused the pound to fall to an all-time low against the dollar in '83 by selling all the sterling he had. When the world economy started moving out of recession, he bought stocks and shares and government bonds in quantities most *countries* couldn't manage. Guess when he decided to sell?

'Amaze me.'

'October, 1987. The very morning of the second great stock market crash. Spear engineered the panic, then moved back into the market when it reached rock-bottom.'

'You've been doing your homework, Sammy.'

'It hasn't been easy. This man covers his tracks, believe me.'

'Everything you've said so far just tells me what everyone already knows. He's a brilliant businessman. There's nothing strange about what he's done.'

Sammy grinned. 'A lot of people, including the FBI, say he's involved in cocaine – production and smuggling – and that's the best profit-making business in the world.'

'Proof?'

'On that score, none. I told you, he pulls the ladder up after him. But Dragon Enterprises maintain an office in Colombia, and no one can figure out why. Spear doesn't have any legitimate business dealings in that part of the world.'

David pursed his lips. Sammy had a habit of letting his theories race ahead of the facts.

'All right, but even if he *is* involved in cocaine, and it's a big "if", that just means he's greedy. He likes to make money, he's superb at it, and he doesn't mind breaking the law. There are plenty like him.'

Sammy beat a rapid tattoo on the controls of his tape-recorder.

'Spear's unique, not *just* because of the way he makes money, or because of the amount he makes, but because of what he does with it.'

Sammy's eyes were glittering with excitement. He was away; David knew the signs. For a reporter, he had a low gullibility threshold. He swallowed each and every new conspiracy theory whole. Queen Victoria's grandson, the Duke of Clarence, was Jack the Ripper. Governments all over the world had conspired to suppress reports of UFO sightings. Elvis Presley was alive and well and living on a desert island.

'Talk has it,' Sammy continued, 'that a hefty slice of the profits from Dragon Enterprises finds it way into the pockets of some pretty unlikely people.'

'Like who?'

'Party bigwigs in the USSR and China, for instance. And Spear's in cahoots with Islamic fundamentalists in Iran, and he's a pal of Libya's President. Has been since they met in London back in '68. Today's deal proves what buddies they are. Who else but Spear could have pulled it off?'

'Oh, come on, Sammy!' David felt disappointed. He'd just been getting interested.

'I have names, I have dates. I know how the money was transferred to these people. I have proof.'

'Show me!'

'Why should I share it with you? What am I – a charity? This is all going in my book. It's going to be the most sensational bestseller of the decade. *The Dragon Man* by Sammy Moss.' He smiled hugely. 'I'm going to be stinking rich.'

'That's not going to be much use in a lunatic asylum. Or in prison, where I suspect Spear's lawyers'll put you. Ever heard of the law of criminal libel?'

Sammy chuckled. 'Oh ye of little faith.'

David's leg was aching. He opened the car door, eased it outside. 'Sammy, when John Kennedy was assassinated, were you one of those who believed Lyndon Johnson was behind it?'

'Certainly.'

'Do you still believe that?'

'Of course not. I was only ten at the time. Besides, I was also one of those people who believed the bizarre rumours about Howard Hughes having long hair and twelve inch fingernails. And I was one of the reporters who broke the story about Sir Anthony Blunt being a soviet agent. And I—'

'Okay, sometimes you're right, sometimes you're wrong. This time—'

'I'm dead right!' Sammy sounded like a religious fanatic.

David smiled. 'I look forward to the book. I enjoy fiction.'

There was a flurry of activity across the street as the door to Spear's house opened. David and Sammy sprang out of the car. David headed for his camera crew. As he did so, he caught sight of Anna in the car. She was gazing eagerly through the window. He was glad her birthday treat had turned out to be more than a dull trip to the office.

Spear emerged from his house. He paused at the top of the steps leading down to the pavement to tug on black leather gloves. David had never seen him in the flesh before. He was dressed in a beautifully tailored dark blue cashmere coat and a dark-grey pinstripe suit. There was a hint of a smile on his intelligent, thin face. He reminded

David of an old film star, but at first he couldn't think who. Then he got it – Laurence Harvey. Spear was handsome in the same louche, sleazy sort of way. There was something decidedly decadent about him. He looked as if sunlight would make him wince.

'Good morning, gentlemen,' Spear said.

'Mr Spear,' David called out. 'Just a few brief questions about the Libyan deal. Isn't the timing clumsy? How do you think the British government will react?'

'I couldn't care less.'

All the reporters started shouting at once. The cameramen and photographers began jostling each other.

A bodyguard stepped up behind Spear, raised an umbrella over his head. The guard was at least six feet seven inches tall. The sight of him made David queasy. It was Hughes.

Spear descended the steps.

'The Libyan deal —' the BBC reporter beside David said. The journalists were all backing off as Spear headed down towards them. There was something in his bearing that commanded respect. He had the same aura of power as James Lord.

David took a deep breath and stepped directly in front of Spear, blocking his path. Spear halted.

'David Cauley, Capital News. If you'd just give us a few minutes, we'll leave you alone.'

'Cauley?' The slight smile disappeared from Spear's face. He glanced back at Hughes, who shrugged in response.

Spear looked back at David. 'Well, well,' he said. For some reason, David's blood iced.

Spear brushed past him. Hughes, following, still holding the umbrella over Spear, jerked his elbow up as he passed David and caught him a sharp blow on the side of the head. David lurched back against the other reporters. Spear was getting into the back of a tungsten grey Rolls Royce Silver Shadow II when Sammy Moss shouted out, 'Mr Spear, why are you supporting a régime that murders its political opponents? Why are you channelling funds into the Soviet Union and China? What the hell are you up to?'

Spear froze in the act of getting into his car. Hughes reached out a giant hand and grabbed Sammy Moss by the scruff of the neck. Spear straightened, turned slowly.

'No!' he said to Hughes, as if addressing a dog, then stared at Sammy Moss. Hughes let go of Sammy's collar.

The newsmen stood perfectly still. No sound, except the patter of rain. For several seconds Spear's malevolent anger blew through them like an evil wind.

'Mistake,' Spear said, quietly, and then he was inside the Rolls and Hughes was closing the door. The spell was broken. The newsmen huddled together in the drizzle as if for protection as the car drove away. Nervous laughter. One of them blew a raspberry.

When the car was out of sight, Sammy turned to David. His sallow skin had turned grey. 'I don't think he likes me.' The remark was meant to sound cocky, but Sammy's voice trembled.

David waited for his cameraman to hand over the videotape of what he'd just shot. As he headed towards the car, he wondered if he'd been too quick to dismiss Sammy Moss's wild stories. Spear's malevolence still clung to him like a fetid stench.

When he opened the car door he could feel Anna's fear skittering around inside like a panicky animal. She was sitting bolt upright, staring ahead, body stiff.

'What's wrong, angel?'

'The big man. The ugly one. He was one of the pair who came looking for me last year.'

'Hughes. Yes.'

'What was he doing here?'

'Working for Spear. A bodyguard, I suppose.'

She bit her lip. 'Was it that man Spear who wanted to find out about me?'

'Could be.'

'Why?'

'I don't know. I really don't.'

'Dad, I'm frightened.'

'Don't be. They don't suspect anything. We'd have

65

heard from them by now if they had.' He smiled. 'Relax, angel.' He leaned over, gave her a quick hug. Instantly, he felt her panic subside.

As he let go of her and started the engine, he saw Sammy Moss still standing outside Spear's house, the other newsmen drifting past him. One of them patted him on the back. Sammy jumped as if he'd been shot.

And David thought, *Mistake!*

CHAPTER SIX

The rain had stopped by the time they reached Capital Television's headquarters on Tottenham Court Road. The sky was starting to brighten. So was Anna's mood: she still possessed a child's ability to wipe unpleasantness from her consciousness and absorb herself entirely in the present. For David, it wasn't so easy.

They drove down to the basement car park, then made their way up in the lift to the tenth floor. David could sense a collective adrenalin rush as they approached the swing doors leading to the open-plan newsroom. A major story had just broken. There was no mistaking the atmosphere. He glanced at Anna. Her eyes were shining with excitement. She could sense it too.

Calvin Scott, the new managing editor of Capital News, was proving a hands-on boss. He had a phone clamped to one ear, a set of cans to the other, and was giving instructions to a reporter standing across the desk while scanning a wire story being held in front of him by a copytaster. David smiled. The newsroom never felt quite right unless it was in a state of mayhem.

At the Intake Desk in the centre of the room, Bill Bride was on his feet, the RT microphone in one fat, sweaty hand, snapping out orders to his crews. With his other hand he was punching out a phone number, while an assistant waved another phone at him, signifying an urgent call.

The newsroom tannoy blared. All activity ceased.

'Newsroom. PA confirm that a bomb exploded at Oxford Circus Underground Station at 10:07 this morning. There are no casualty details yet.'

The blood drained from David's face. Anna gave a gasp of dismay. For several seconds the fifty or so newsroom staff stared up at the tannoy speakers dotted around the room. For those few seconds they were ordinary members of the public, shocked by the news, wanting to know more. But no one was going to tell them any more: they'd have to find out for themselves. Suddenly, the whole room was once again in motion. Anna took her father's hand.

'We'll have to find someone else to show you around. Your Dad's going to be a busy man.'

He led her over to the reporters' desk. Whitley Chamberlain, David's main rival for the newsreader vacancy, had his back partially to them. He was talking fast into a phone cradled in a Popeye the Sailorman shoulder-rest.

'Of course you can't give me any information!' Whitley turned, glanced at David. 'I don't know why government departments *have* press offices, because you bozos never give out any f –' Whitley noticed Anna staring at him. '– any flaming information.' He cut the connection, and gave Anna a little wave. David introduced them.

As Whitley leaned across the desk to shake her hand, he said, 'You don't look anything like your father, Anna. Congratulations.'

Anna giggled.

Francesca, the reporters' secretary, appeared. She was a tall, painfully thin girl in her mid-twenties, who usually sported a variety of bruises courtesy of whichever unsuitable boyfriend she happened to be dating at the time. Today, the left side of her jaw was swollen, as if she'd just been to the dentist.

David asked if she'd mind giving Anna a short guided tour. 'You know – graphics, VTs, the studio, that sort of thing.'

'Why can't I do that?' Whitley complained. 'Afraid I'd want to ask her for a date?'

'Whitley?' David said. 'Flame off!'

He made his way over to the Intake Desk. Bill Bride was trying to juggle two phones and the RT handset at the same time. Sweat was dripping from the end of his nose. Someone in the newsroom had been running a book for several months on how long it would be before Bride keeled over with a coronary. Judging by his present state, David would have bet about ten minutes. He pointed at himself to let Bride know he was back and ready for work, then returned to the reporters' desk, logged into the computer and checked the wires to see if the Oxford Circus bomb story had got on yet. He doubted if there'd be room in the lunchtime bulletin for Spear.

'David! Good of you to come in on a day off.'

Calvin Scott had been lured from a newspaper three months back to take over the news operation. There had been charges that the station's output was becoming too complacently pro-government, and Scott had a reputation for taking an independent line. David hadn't had much contact with him so far, just a pat on the back and a 'Well done!' after a live two-way from a siege in Brighton, when a man who'd barricaded himself in his house with a shotgun had threatened to kill his wife and three children. David had been doing a live piece-to-camera across the street from the house when the man fired the first shot. The police had stormed the building and brought the man and his family out, and the audience at home had seen all of it as it happened, accompanied by David's spare, effective commentary. The specialist media press had tipped the item for all the news broadcasting awards that year.

David's next meeting with Scott had not been so amiable. He had done an item about garages welding together the halves of different cars of the same make wrecked in accidents and passing off the result as one original car. In his piece, he'd named a South London car dealer as one of the culprits. The dealer had issued a writ for libel. David had the proof to hand but Capital News had been unwilling to fight the case. They'd settled out of court. David had gone to Calvin Scott to complain, but had found himself being taken to task for sloppy reporting.

'There's nothing wrong with my reporting,' he'd said. 'But there *is* something wrong with this station's guts.'

Scott's voice had turned quiet and dangerous. 'Don't ever speak to me like that again, Cauley.'

David reckoned the exchange had cost him the chance of becoming a newsreader. Scott would go through the motions of testing him but Whitley would get it for sure.

That had been a month ago. This was the first time Scott had spoken to him since.

'Calvin,' David said, manufacturing a smile. 'What can I do for you?'

'This Spear story,' Scott said, settling a buttock on the desk-top. 'I'd like you to play it up.'

'In what way?'

'Give Spear the credit he deserves. The man's a genius.'

The tannoy speaker blared just beind them. 'Police say at least two people have died following the Oxford Circus bomb blast. They won't comment on rumours that Libyans planted the bomb.'

David jerked a thumb at the loudspeaker. 'Are you going to bother running the Spear item with all this going on? Wouldn't you prefer me doing a live two-way from Oxford Circus?'

'Whitley can do that.'

Whitley stuck out his tongue at David from behind Scott's back.

'I could do a speculative piece on whether the Libyans are behind the bomb,' David suggested.

Scott's Edinburgh accent thickened as his voice grew tight. 'I'd prefer you to do exactly what I tell you, Cauley. And that's a minute and a half on the Libyan deal, marking Spear's previous successes. Let's not kow-tow to the government by mindlessly attacking him. Maybe trade links will prove the key to better relations between our two countries. Mention that.'

'A Libyan citizen just shot down an unarmed British police officer and killed two teenagers in the middle of London. A bomb's just exploded a mile from here, killing at least two people. For all we know, Libya might have given the order for that bomb to be planted. Even if it turned out to be the IRA, we can't rule out Libyan involvement. They've been providing them with funds and explosives for years.' David shrugged. 'I'm going to find it hard to make Spear out to be some kind of hero in the circumstances.'

'Dad?' They both turned. Francesca had returned with Anna, who was holding a cup of orange juice.

Scott frowned. 'Who's that?'

'My daughter. It's her birthday. I brought her in to show her the newsroom.'

Anna sipped her drink, staring at Scott.

'Do the Spear piece, Cauley, and do it *my* way.' The burly man leaned further over David. 'And go carefully. I haven't forgotten that car business.'

As David opened his mouth to reply, the tannoy sounded again.

'Newsroom. The police say at least fifteen people have been injured in the Oxford Circus explosion.'

'*That's* the story,' David said. 'Besides, I don't want to make Spear out to be a saint. I heard some things about him today that were disturbing, to put it mildly. There are rumours he—'

'I don't want your bloody rumours Cauley. This is a professional news organization now. We deal in facts. Something I've noticed you're not altogether happy with.'

Anna's face spasmed with anger. 'Don't talk to my father like that.'

Francesca grabbed Anna's hand, shushed her quiet. The producers at the adjoining desk had stopped work to listen. One of then sniggered.

Scott waved a hand in Anna's direction. 'Get her out of here, Cauley.' He prodded David hard in the chest. 'You'll do this piece, and you'll do it the way I want it, or you're out. There's no room for mavericks here.'

He strode away from the table. Francesca had to tug Anna out of his path.

Anna wheeled round, following Scott with her eyes.

After half a dozen paces, Scott froze in mid-stride.

David held his beath. He was for it now; Scott was going to fire him.

Instead of turning, as David had expected, Scott clutched his stomach and sagged onto his knees, making a high-pitched keening sound.

David's eyes darted towards Anna. Francesca let go of her hand, as if burned. The power was pulsing from Anna in a series of sharp, rapid punches.

Scott keeled over onto his side. His legs were making bicycling movements. He was clawing at his stomach, as if trying to reach inside to rip away the pain.

Several producers ran to help him. David grabbed Anna's arm. He felt her power wham through his own body. He shook her. 'Stop it!' he hissed.

Scott's body gave a jolt. He blinked. 'It's over,' he said, voice weak.

David dragged Anna out of the newsroom, found an empty office, slammed the door shut. He gripped her arms.

'What's got into you? How many times have we told you *never* to do *anything* like that.'

'He – he was being nasty to you.'

'That . . . doesn't . . . matter!' David said, punctuating each word with a vicious shake that made her head flop. Her chin puckered. David let go of her and opened his arms. She stepped inside them. He hugged her, stroked her hair. He could feel her misery inside him.

'Sorry, angel,' he said, keeping his voice quiet, soothing. 'But you mustn't give yourself away like that. The bank robber was different – you didn't have a choice. But what you did just now was stupid. You *know* that. And you must never use your power to hurt anyone that way again.'

He felt her nod into his neck.

He reached in his pocket for a tissue, and wiped her face with it.

'I'm going to order a taxi to take you home. I'll let your mother know you're on your way.'

Reception said the taxi would be there in ten minutes. He rang Lauris.

'I'm sending Anna home by cab.'

'Something's wrong,' Lauris said.

'Nothing. I . . . there's a story I have to do.'

'David, don't lie. What's happened?'

He sighed. 'Anna just gave Calvin Scott the works. It was a pretty spectacular performance.'

Lauris gave an 'Oh!' of dismay.

David smiled at Anna. 'Don't be too angry with her. Scott was giving me a hard time. Let's just say her protective instincts were aroused.'

'Did anyone realize what she was doing?'

'I hope not. I got her away from the scene of the crime fast.'

'I'll be expecting her.'

When David put the phone down, Francesca was standing in the doorway.

'Fran, could you take Anna downstairs and show her where the cabs stop? I've ordered one.'

Francesca kept her eyes on David, as if afraid to look at Anna. 'David, when Calvin had his attack, I felt Anna . . . there was . . .' She shrugged helplessly. 'It was frightening.'

'You're upset, Fran. Naturally. Now please, could you take Anna downstairs?'

Francesca nodded, bit her lip. 'As long as she . . .' Her gaze flickered towards Anna. 'As long as she doesn't touch me.' She turned and walked out of the room.

David guided Anna out of the door. Suddenly, she looked exhausted. 'Go with Francesca.'

'Dad?'

'Yes?'

'Sorry.'

'Sure. By the way, I wouldn't mention anything about seeing Hughes to your mother. It might upset her.' It had certainly upset him.

He kissed her forehead, and she set off down the corridor after Francesca. David sat on the nearest seat and buried his face in his hands.

So far, it had been one hell of a day.

According to Sammy Moss, Richard Spear was a

cocaine-dealing ogre who had the world's economy by the balls and was channelling funds to politicians in China, the USSR, Iran and Libya.

There was a distinct possibility that Richard Spear had sent Hughes and Vercoe to check out Anna, and Spear didn't strike David as being a particularly nice man. The fact that he'd employ a psychopath like Hughes proved that.

Calvin Scott, a man with a reputation for being left-of-centre, had insisted David do a story praising Spear, one of the leading figures of world capitalism. Why? What possible connection could there be between them?

(Mysteries!)

David made a disgusted sound, ran his fingers through his hair.

And his fifteen-year-old daughter had made another human being suffer agonizing pain just because he'd spoken harshly to her father. That wasn't the Anna he knew. Was she changing, the way James Lord had changed? And the *ease* with which she had cut down Calvin Scott had been terrifying. *Just how powerful is she?*

The question frightened him. He stood up, went to the window. It was pouring again. Freezing sheets of rain were billowing against the building. It *all* frightened him, because there was some crazy pattern there, some thread, some link. A link between Spear . . . and Anna

Spear and Anna.

A link . . .

Looking down, he saw a cab pull up in front of the building. Anna appeared a few seconds later, spoke to the driver through the window, got in.

As the cab drove away David murmured, 'Why us?'

Mysteries!

His route back to the newsroom took him past Calvin Scott's office. The door was open. David slowed down as he passed. Scott was standing by his window, looking down at the road below. He was on the phone, talking rapidly. David thought he caught the name 'Anna', but was too far away to be sure.

Scott turned abruptly. When he saw David, his face

flushed. 'Hang on!' he barked into the phone. He strode across the room, slammed the door shut.

David shrugged, turned away.

Mysteries!

CHAPTER SEVEN

10 May 1992

David was lying in the bath, rolling the cooling rim of a tumbler of whisky back and forth across his forehead when he heard the phone ring downstairs.

If it was the office, they could go to hell. He'd only just got back from covering the opening of the trial of the Libyan accused of the Leicester Square killings, and he was bushed.

'For you, David!' Lauris shouted up.

'I'll call them back!'

'It sounds urgent!'

Cursing, David wrapped a towel around himself, padded through to the bedroom and picked up the extension. Anna was playing a rock album in her room next door. He hammered on the wall to get her to turn it down.

'David? Sammy Moss.' There was edge of hysteria to his voice.

'Hi, Sammy. What can I do for you?'

In the two and a half weeks since they'd doorstepped Spear David had considered calling Sammy to pump him for more information about the Dragon Man, but he had been too busy.

'Sammy, are you still there?'

A sigh that could have been a sob.

'Come over here, please,' Sammy said. 'Now.'

He was crying, no doubt about it.

'We're just about to eat.'

'This is *so* important. Please come over, David. I don't know who else to turn to.'

Sammy started crying in earnest.

'Okay. Give me your address.'

Sammy gulped it out and hung up.

David gave Lauris the bad news, and told Anna she could turn her music back up. He dragged on the first clothes that came to hand and set off by car towards Fulham. He parked in front of Sammy's gloomy redbrick mansion block just off the Fulham Road. The interior looked as if it had last been decorated when cars were a novelty. Sammy's flat was on the third floor and the lift was out of order. David was out of breath by the time he'd climbed the stairs.

As he pushed the door to the flat open he saw that the lock was broken. When he stepped inside he noticed an odd, meaty smell, the kind that lingers around a barbecue pit.

The hallway lights were off. He found a light switch. The door in front of him was open. He entered the room. In the wedge of light from the hallway he saw Sammy Moss hunched over on a couch. The smell of burnt meat was strong.

'Sammy?'

Sammy raised his head slowly. His face was streaked with tears and he was clutching a half-empty Vodka bottle. David switched on the sitting room lights. Sammy winced, covered his eyes.

The room had been recently decorated – a striking blend of salmon pink and lime. Not David's taste, but effective. The walls were covered with framed photographs of a young olive-skinned man who David assumed to be Sammy's new lover. David remembered his name. Rui.

There was an object on the carpet in front of Sammy, covered by a dustsheet smeared with pink paint and dark brown stains. The stains looked fresh; they were oozing through from whatever was underneath the sheet. David wasn't sure he wanted to know their source.

Sammy swigged vodka and grinned up at David. His

pirate's smile had turned into the rictus leer of a madman.

'I wanted you to see what the Dragon Man does to his enemies David. I want you to *know* the Dragon Man.'

Sammy grabbed one of the corners of the sheet and flicked it back.

The young man's body looked as if it had been spit-roasted. His skin resembled grilled hamburger. One charred eyelid was closed. The other eye stared up at David.

He turned away, feeling very ill, and quite unreal.

'I was out on a story,' Sammy said. 'He was alive when I found him about an hour ago. I . . . I put a pillow over his face.'

'Yes,' David said, not knowing what he meant, but thinking Sammy had done the right thing.

'Can you imagine how much *pain* he was suffering, David?'

David shook his head, fighting to ignore the repulsive stench in his nostrils.

'*Can you?*' Sammy shrieked.

'No.' On the wall in front of him were more pictures of Rui. It was hard to connect the handsome young man with the horror lying on the carpet. He forced himself to turn around. 'Why?' David asked. 'Why would anyone—'

Sammy laughed. 'Because of my book. Spear didn't want me to publish my book about him. Simple, really.'

'Why Rui? Why not you?'

'Punishment. Revenge.' Sammy's voice was slurred. He took another swig of vodka. 'He wants me to live with this memory.' He was staring fixedly at his lover's corpse.

David went over to the body. Holding his breath, he flicked the sheet back over it. *This thing was alive a few hours ago*, he thought. It hardly seemed possible.

'Did they do it here?'

'The bedroom. The carpet's all charred. Rui must have crawled out here afterwards.' He looked up. 'The pain. Can you *begin* to imagine it?' More vodka.

'I'm sorry to have to ask this,' David said. The facts. He had to root the horror in facts. 'How did they do it? What did they use?'

Sammy's voice was a whisper.

'The Dragon Man breathed on him.'

A wind with a chill flick in its tail was shivering through the trees along St Alban's Avenue when David reached home just before dawn.

He switched the engine off, but didn't get out of the car. He had to think.

He had phoned the police after convincing Sammy not to admit he'd suffocated Rui. The boy would have died anyway. All he had done was spare his lover further suffering. He had also ordered Sammy not to mention Spear's name. The police wouldn't have believed him, and that would have cast doubt on the rest of his story. As it was, they hadn't liked David being there, and Sammy's failure to call them as soon as he had discovered the body had made them suspicious.

'He called me because he needed comforting. To be honest, I think he was in such a state of shock he didn't really know what he was doing.'

The police had figured it all out within a couple of hours. Rui Olazabal had picked up someone in a gay bar, and that someone had turned out to be a psychopath. End of story. According to Sammy, though, Rui didn't visit gay bars. He wasn't promiscuous and he certainly wasn't into any S&M weirdness. As Sammy had phrased it, Rui was a real lady, but that hadn't convinced the police.

Before the police had even arrived, Sammy had told David that he was going to scrap the book about Spear and leave the country as soon as possible. That left David as the only candidate for the role of St George. It was not a part he felt inclined to accept. There was no proof that Spear had had anything to do with the murder. If he had, he certainly wouldn't have been present during the torture. He'd have left that to minions like Hughes or Vercoe. If David made any attempt to pin the blame on Spear, and Spear got wind of it, was there any guarantee Lauris or Anna wouldn't wind up like Rui?

David shuddered as he got out of the car. The wind licked him like a freezing tongue. He stood, looking up at the house where his wife and daughter were sleeping.

Someone else could play St George.

He was going to be very quiet from now on. He was going to be a well-behaved little boy, and just merge into the background. He wasn't going to risk his family being consumed by the Dragon's fiery breath. No, sir!

He headed for the front door. As he searched in his pocket for the key, he glanced up at the sky. The lowering clouds promised a storm. The largest, blackest cloud was slowly changing shape, developing a long tail. As David watched, the cloud roiled and pulsed, until it had assumed the form of a dragon. An enormous, slavering dragon. Staring down at *him*! As he got his key in the front door, the dragon's jaws opened wide. He heard a roaring sound.

David scuttled inside, slammed the door shut behind him. He stood for a long time, his back to the door, eyes shut, body tensed as the thunder vibrated through him.

CHAPTER EIGHT

June 20 1992
'How do I look?'

Anna struck a model pose in the sitting room doorway, one hand behind her head, the other on her hip. The blue dress with white stripes Lauris had bought her that morning made her fifteen-year-old body seem adult and childlike at the same time; it emphasized both the slimness of her hips and legs and the gentle swell of her breasts. David found the effect oddly discomforting; he didn't enjoy being reminded of his daughter's burgeoning sexuality.

'Stunning,' he said, heading over to the drinks table. 'You'll be the prettiest one there.'

'That wouldn't be difficult,' Anna said, letting her body relax and straightening the dress. 'I swear everyone at that school's either a blimp, a skeleton, or a grunk.'

David poured himself a Cutty Sark. 'What's a grunk?'

he asked, spooning ice into his tumbler.

Anna stuck out her teeth and crossed her eyes in demonstration.

'Anna, that's *not* kind,' Lauris said, walking into the room in bra and panties.

'Mother,' Anna said as Lauris stood in the centre of the room, motioning towards the drinks trolley with just-polished nails. 'Bright they may be, but physically, they're non-starters. Unlike your decidedly glamorous daughter.'

She tossed her head, making her hair sway as she flounced out.

Lauris frowned. David chuckled.

'She's only telling the truth, darling,' he said. 'They're a weird-looking crew.'

Lauris shrugged. 'I worry about her becoming smug.'

'She's good-looking, clever and popular. Why shouldn't she be smug? Would you prefer her ugly and *angst*-ridden?'

David handed her a gin and tonic. She accepted it gingerly, fingers splayed, sipped it. 'You're not going in that awful suit, are you?'

'Why not?'

'It makes you look old and fat.'

'I *am* old and fat.'

Lauris's small breasts jiggled inside her bra as she walked out of the room. David experienced a twinge in his groin. He still *loved* the way they did that. He turned to examine himself in the mirror above the fireplace. He'd aged in the last few weeks, mainly due to the weight he'd gained recently. He slapped his gut. It vibrated. He'd have to cut down on booze. His intake had shot up since the night of Rui Olazabal's murder, and his body was starting to bloat.

He sat down, sipped his drink.

Lauris had been nagging him about his alcohol consumption, and about the way he was just tootling along at work, letting the younger reporters snatch the juicy assignments. He'd claimed he was drinking to ease the disappointment of not getting the newscaster's job at Capital, but that wasn't it. Hell, Whitley Chamberlain was better at it than he was. Whitley had presence; he didn't.

Fear was making him drink, and fear had robbed him of his taste for the limelight. It was time to hide in the shadows for a while, where it was cool and safe and nobody noticed you.

He got up, strolled over to the window, and looked out at the familiar street. A harsh wind swirled leaves and litter along the pavement.

He'd been scared from the moment he'd seen Rui Olazabal's grilled corpse. Scared because of the possibility of Spear's involvement, and scared because there was some connection, some *link* between Spear and Anna.

Spear and Anna . . .

He had thought of contacting James Lord to let him know that Spear might have been the one who'd sent Vercoe and Hughes to investigate Anna. But he had decided to keep the suspicion to himself; he didn't want to risk James taking Anna away from them. Last year his old friend had proved he was willing to murder to keep her existence a secret. *There won't be any trial* . . . James would hardly baulk at kidnapping.

He returned to the drinks trolley, poured himself another Scotch. If he drank it quickly, he'd manage to squeeze in one more before they had to leave for the prize-giving ceremony at the Patterson School. He could hear Lauris and Anna in their respective rooms, ransacking drawers, slamming cupboard doors. The sounds made him smile.

His decision not to investigate Rui Olazabal's death hadn't made him feel good about himself, but at least the family was safe. When you came right down to it, that was all that mattered.

'Music!' he heard Lauris call from upstairs. He moved over to the stereo and slotted in a tape of Harry Belafonte calypsoes. They always put her in a good mood when she was getting ready to go out. As the good-time music filled the room he wondered whether he'd been right not to tell Lauris about Hughes working for Spear, and about his suspicions regarding Spear's involvement in Rui's death. But what good would it have done? It would only have worried her.

Anna appeared in the doorway, pointed at the tape deck, placed her hands around her throat and made a gagging sound. David shrugged and Anna disappeared, shaking her head.

Lauris appeared a minute later, carrying a suit on a hanger. She hung it on the doorknob, said 'Wear it!', and headed back upstairs, her neat little bottom swaying as Harry Belafonte began singing about daylight coming and wanting to go home.

David finished his drink, started to undress.

He noticed a faint stain on his shirt cuff, paused. It looked like it could have been caused by anything – coffee, gravy, anything. But he experienced a thrill of horror as he realized what it was. Blood. Rui Olazabal's blood. It was the shirt he'd been wearing the night Sammy had asked him to come over. The sweet, sickening smell of roasted flesh assaulted his nostrils. He swayed slightly, and placed a hand against the nearest wall to steady himself.

'Daddy, are you all right?'

He opened his eyes. Anna was staring at him.

He managed a wan smile. 'Just a bad memory, precious. It's gone now. Gone.'

But it hadn't.

The smell of burned flesh was strong in David's nostrils all the way to the Patterson School.

There were about two hundred parents and children seated in the main hall when the Cauleys arrived. The audience applauded politely as the headmaster and his teaching staff stepped up onto the podium. The assistant headmaster, a young bald man with the insistent, aggressive smile of an insurance salesman, started the ball rolling with a report on recent outstanding achievements by various pupils. A fifteen-year-old girl had won a mathematics scholarship to Cambridge. A fourteen-year-old boy was about to make his debut on the West End stage in a revival of *Lord of the Flies*. There were others, but David's mind soon began to wander. The three Scotches he'd downed before setting off had left him hazy, slightly disoriented. His eyes began to close, and he found himself being nudged awake by Lauris as the headmaster approached the lectern. In contrast to his assistant, the head always looked as if someone had just informed him of a death in the family. When he smiled, it looked somehow brave and sad.

David sat up straight in his chair, made an effort at concentration.

'I have a surprise announcement,' the head began, producing one of his long-suffering smiles. 'As you know, our guest on Prize Day is usally one of our distinguished ex-pupils.' He gave a little cough. 'We have many to choose from. However, our guest today did not attend the Patterson School. Nevertheless, so impressed has he been by our work, by our dedication to excellence, that he contacted me personally and asked if we might break with tradition this one time, and allow an outsider to present the prizes. I have received similar requests in the past – and I have always turned them down.'

As he removed a handkerchief from his pocket, blew his nose and examined the result, the audience buzzed with speculation.

'This time,' the headmaster recommended, 'I simply couldn't bring myself to refuse. Firstly, our guest embodies many of the qualities we admire – among them, immense talent and a fierce will to succeed. Secondly, our guest is himself tonight breaking with one of his own traditions.' The brave smile again. 'He is a man who normally goes to great lengths to guard his privacy. This is his first official public appearance in this country for many, many years. And so I feel honoured to welcome to the Patterson School the country's most successful businessman, the immensely distinguished Richard Spear.'

David's mouth dropped open.

A chorus of surprised 'ohs' greeted Spear's entry through the double doors at the back of the hall. Enthusiastic applause accompanied him all the way to the podium.

Anna grabbed David's arm, gripped it tight.

'Why?' she gasped.

'A coincidence!' he whispered. 'Don't worry!'

'But I have to go up there and meet him.'

'Do what you did to Vercoe and Hughes. He won't even realize you're different.'

'Okay, she said, breathing out. Her grip relaxed slightly.

Lauris leaned forward and stared at Anna. Sitting back, she said to David, 'What's wrong with her?'

'Probably stage fright.'

As Spear shook hands with the headmaster, his face expressionless, David wondered if his presence really was a coincidence.

Spear approached the lectern, and an eerie silence descended on the hall. In that silence, David could detect genuine awe. Spear wasn't just a businessman, he was a legend. The rumours about him were as bizarre as those that had once circulated about Howard Hughes. In Hughes's case, as Sammy Moss had pointed out, the rumours had turned out to be true, but David doubted whether Spear drank a pint of his own urine every day, or that he spent his waking hours being entertained by a constant stream of prostitutes, or that his success in business derived from the practice of Black Magic.

But as he studied the man's thin, arrogant, somehow debauched face, he didn't doubt for a moment that he'd be capable of ordering a minion to grill a human being alive with an oxyacetyline torch.

As Spear studied the audience, there was a suggestion of hunger in the way he held his head slightly forward. His eyes were those of an eagle alert for prey.

David found himself shrinking back into his seat, trying to make himself small, unnoticeable. Anna's hand was still gripping his arm. He patted it. Her skin was ice-cold. He prayed she'd be able to throw Spear off the scent. There was nothing to stop them getting up and leaving right now, but they'd just be drawing attention to themselves.

'When I was a little boy,' Spear began, 'I killed another boy.' A collective gasp from the audience. 'Oh, not intentionally, of course.' Taut spines relaxed. 'We were waiting for a train. We were arguing about something, and the argument turned into a fight. He stumbled and fell onto the track as the train pulled into the station.'

David found himself wondering if it really had been an accident.

'Peter wasn't very bright for his age,' Spear continued. 'But he was terribly interested in how things worked. He might – who knows? – have grown up to be a great scientist. He *might* have discovered a cure for cancer, or a method of food production to feed the millions who die of starvation each year on our planet.' A pause. 'Or he might have been a nobody. It's impossible to tell. What I can say is that I have lived with the guilt of Peter's death all my life. I might, on that awful day so many years ago, have unwittingly deprived the world of a *great man*!' His voice rose on the last words. 'And that's a dreadful possibility, because the world *needs* great men.' He paused. 'Or women.' His face seemed to rest on Anna for a second.

Applause.

David shifted uncomfortably. He glanced at Anna. She had followed his example, hunching her shoulders, trying to disappear. Lauris was sitting forward, listening intently. The Dragon Man had her hooked.

The applause lasted a long time.

'What do I mean by great men?' Spear resumed. 'I mean the men who change our lives, the men who leave their mark on humanity, the men who *matter*!'

As Spear's voice rose in pitch, David experienced a frisson of familiarity. He had heard the voice somewhere before – not at the doorstepper, somewhere else, in an unlikely context. He made a conscious effort not to listen to what Spear was saying, and concentrated instead on his voice. *Where had he heard it before?*

'Strong leadership,' Spear was saying five minutes later. 'There must be followers – and leaders. The boys and girls in this hall tonight are leaders.' He smiled. It didn't look like something that came easily to him. 'It's the job of you parents to make them strong. Help them be *great*!'

The audience applauded enthusiastically. It had been a politician's speech, packed with tricks, a verbal soufflé, puffed with air. But it *had* been an accomplished performance.

The first pupil went up to receive his prize, a fourteen-year-old boy, a physics prodigy who, David guessed, Anna would classify as a 'grunk'. David felt Anna shiver beside him.

'You'll be all right,' David whispered. 'Just do your stuff.'

She nodded, biting her lip. She couldn't seem to take her eyes off the man on the stage.

'Anna Cauley, English and Art,' Spear read out. His tone had altered. There was excitement in it. David realized Spear knew exactly who Anna was.

Anna stood to mild audience applause, but made no move towards the stage. She was staring up at Spear. The applause began to die.

'Go on!' Lauris hissed.

David took hold of Anna's hand. Her palm was sweating. He gave her hand a squeeze. She glanced down at him. He could feel her apprehension fluttering inside him. She had learned over the years to contain her emotions, not to let them spill over so that those around her could feel them, but something about Spear had caught her off-guard.

'You *have* to go up,' David whispered urgently.

Anna let go of his hand and moved along the row. She paused when she reached the aisle, then made her way up towards the podium.

Spear was studying the list of winners, deliberately paying no attention to Anna as she made her way up the five steps to the stage. He finally turned to face her as she walked towards him. The audience had started applauding again, encouraging Anna, mistaking her fear for shyness. Spear was holding the book that was to be Anna's prize in one hand. He extended the other towards her. Anna hesitated, glanced back down at her father. He nodded. She gave Spear her hand.

Spear's whole body stiffened. His mouth opened, but he made no sound. He looked as if he'd been punched in the stomach and was trying to get his breath back.

Lauris gripped David's arm. 'What's happening?'

Anna winced and tried to tug her hand out of Spear's

grasp, but he held her firmly. Her eyes brimmed with tears. Again, she tried to jerk her hand away.

David got half-way out of his seat. *Just make him let go of you!*

The anaemic applause had died. The room was silent. The audience held itself still, not breathing. There was a cough. Another. People shifted in their seats, embarrassed. Spear dropped the book he was holding. As it clattered onto the stage, Anna managed to get her hand free. She turned away from him abruptly, almost tripped in her haste to get down the stairs, ran down the aisle. Spear stooped to retrieve the book he'd dropped, but his eyes remained on Anna.

David and Lauris hurried along the row to meet her. David put his arm around her. Fear was coming off her in rapid waves. David looked back up at Spear, and their eyes locked. Spear's eyes were gleaming with excitement. And something else. Greed? The audience began chattering. Snatches of nervous laughter.

Between them, David and Lauris steered Anna down the aisle. The whole audience was staring at them, but David was only aware of Spear's gaze. As they moved through the exit door, Spear was reading out the name of the next child to receive a prize. His voice was trembling.

Lauris took Anna into the Ladies to calm her down. David waited for them in the middle of the empty entrance hall, chewing his nails, listening to the polite applause from the main hall. A series of little chills rippled along his spine. He felt jittery and panicky, as if someone had crept up on him as he slept and bellowed in his ear.

His leg throbbed with pain. He knew why. As Anna had fought to escape the Dragon Man's grip, David had realized why Spear's voice was familiar. The knowledge had almost made him gag with fear . . .

The fourteen-year-old boy hunkered in the archway at the back of the stage of the open-air theatre and gazed down at the black-headed rock mass thrust like a gnarled leg into the sea below. Beneath a slate-grey sky waves smashed against the Minack rock in fury, trying to ram it back into the granite cliffs behind.

David Cauley zipped up his blue anorak and stuck his freezing hands deep into the pockets.

His first visit to the Minack Theatre had been with James Lord two weeks back, on a cold afternoon when the sun had been so bright it hurt the eyes. James had wanted to see a production of King Lear. When David had asked him why, he had said it was because the play was about power, and he'd smiled and added, 'Power interests me.' After the play, when everyone had left, James had stood in the archway where David was now perched, and shouted:

'Blow, winds, and crack your cheeks! rage! blow!
You cataracts and hurricanoes spout
Till you have drenched our steeples . . .'

And he had laughed crazily, raising his arms high above his head. David, standing directly behind him, watching James silhouetted against the sun, had felt himself alive with the wild thrill his friend was experiencing.

'I've got to come back here and do that when there's a real storm blowing.' James had shouted. 'Wouldn't that be totally far out?'

James had swung round, and had laughed again when he'd seen David's expression. He had jumped down onto the stage and clasped his arms.

'Isn't it great! Aren't people great! A little old lady and a few helpers spent years hacking a theatre out of granite just so's they'd have this as a backdrop.' He made a sweep with his arm to indicate the foaming sea. 'Isn't that fantastic, Dave?'

'I suppose so,' David had said, nervously.

James had let go of him at once, chuckled. 'Sorry, Dave. I forget what an anal-retentive you are. But—'

'What's an anal-retentive?'

'But when you see all the bullshit people do, and you meet pigs like Vercoe and Hughes, you despair. You think, they're all just dumb little animals, and then you see this here, and you think people are all potentially great. It's in you. It's in all of you.'

David had wondered why James kept talking about 'you'. Why not 'us'?

Remembering his friend's excitement, David eased down onto his bottom and let his legs dangle over the edge of the archway. Directly below him were narrow stairs used by the actors to approach the stage. The stairs had no rail, and beyond them was a fifty-foot drop onto rocks. He wondered what it would be like making the ascent on a rough night, shuddered.

He had skipped school that morning and taken a bus all the way across Cornwall to Porthcurno just to be on his own and get some thinking done. It had been thirty-six hours since James had disappeared from St Stephen's. With each passing hour everything he'd told David – about fingerprints, and wars, and assassinations – was beginning to seem more and more like a paranoid fantasy. Somehow, when James had been there, David had allowed himself to be convinced. Now, he wasn't so sure. The one thing he was sure of was that his friend's departure had left a vast, aching gap in his life.

David head a sound, like a shoe scuffing the stone steps. He turned his head. No one there. A disturbing memory of something that had happened earlier that day shimmered at the edge of his consciousness. He made a mental grab for it. It slithered away. He looked back out over the wild sea.

'Please come back!' he whispered.

Feeling himself on the verge of tears, he made to stand.

An arm snaked round his throat and the memory he'd grasped at was there, right up front. A man on the bus, sitting two rows behind him, coat collar hiding his face. There had been something furtive about him. He had been too well dressed to be travelling by bus, and he'd been trying too hard not to pay any attention to David.

David was hauled up into the air. He pumped his elbows furiously, but his attacker's other arm went round his chest, pinioning his arms.

Lips pressed against his ear.

'Where is he?' Barely a whisper.

'Who?' David managed to choke out.

'The American.'

'Which . . . one?'

The grip round his throat tightened.

'LORD! JAMES LORD!' The bellow was deafening. 'Tell me!'

'Don't . . . know. Honest!'

The arm was removed from his throat. A hand grasped his hair and his head was forced down so that he was staring at the rocks below.

'You'll be heading down there if you don't tell me. Your brains are going to be splattered all over those rocks. Understand?'

David did his best to nod. As he did so he could feel his attacker's precise, murderous anger piercing him, like a cold needle. It was the same emotional overspill he had experienced in James's presence, only James's emotions had been large, generous. This man's were hard and mean. So mean.

'Tell me, David!'

'Can't!'

It was as if the fingers grasping his hair had slid through the thin layer of his skull and were gently massaging his brain, trying to squeeze out information. David realized this was what James did to people, this was how he coerced them.

'Can't tell you!' *David shouted as a seagull wheeled, squawking, beneath his dangling feet.*

The fingers slipped away from his brain.

'You don't know,' *the man said, matter-of-factly, and then David was dropping like a stone, feet-first. He crashed into the steep steps twenty feet below, heard a bone crack, bounced off. He twisted in mid air, made a grab for – for anything – got one hand onto one of the steps, gripped with all his strength. He reached up his other hand to the next step and hung there, dangling over the rocks. In his head he heard a clear instruction:*

Let go. Fall. It'll be all right. Just let go . . .

The voice inside his head was soothing. The suggestion sounded terribly sensible. The intensity of his grip relaxed a fraction. His fingers began to slip from the granite steps . . .

Delayed pain from his leg blazed into his consciousness, a white agonizing fire burning out every other thought. He automatically tightened his hold on the steps.

When the pain subsided he heard a shout above him, but with his face pressed hard against the rock from which the steps had been hewn, he could see nothing. His fingers were almost as painful as his legs. As he heard footsteps approach down the stairs he knew his strength would only last another few seconds, and here was his attacker to finish him off anyway. No point in fighting. No point at all.

One hand gave, and he felt the fingers of the other scrape across the granite step as he began to slip down . . .

A big, powerful hand gripped his wrist, and he was hauled upwards. Then he was being carried like a baby, slung over an immense shoulder, back up the steps, and he found himself lying on the stage of the theatre and a florid moon face topped by a snap-brim hat was peering anxiously down at him.

'You hurt?' An American.

'Leg,' David groaned.

The American reached down, laid a hand on it. David sucked in his breath. The pain made his whole body shake.

'Busted,' the American said. 'What did that guy want?'

'Who are you?'

'A friend of James.'

'He wanted to know where James was.'

'What did you say?'

'The truth. I don't know.'

The man nodded, stood up.

'Where's that bastard got to?'

He removed a gun from inside his jacket. David would have liked a closer look. He'd always been fascinated by guns.

'I'll send help as soon as I can,' the man said, scanning the surrounding cliffs. 'Your leg's pretty bad.'

'He was . . . like James,' David said.

The big man looked down at him sharply. 'What do you mean?'

'I felt him inside my head. You know, talking.'

'You sure?'

'Yes.'

'Another one? God almighty!' He shook his head. 'Good luck, kid.' He winced, massaged his stomach. When he next spoke, it was with difficulty. 'I'd better get after that sonofabitch.'

And then he was off, haring with surprising speed up the steep granite seating above the stage. Within two minutes he had disappeared from view over the top of the cliff, and David gave in to unconsciousness . . .

. . . Now, as David stood in the entrance hall of the Patterson School waiting for his family, he realized why Anna hadn't been able to make Spear let go of her hand.

Because Spear was one of *them*! He was like Anna. And James Lord. *An emperor*!

'Hello, Cauley.'

As David turned and found himself staring into Vercoe's black eyes, he knew for certain who had murdered Rui Olazabal. He should have realized the instant he saw the body.

'That little bitch daughter of yours really had us fooled, Cauley. Me and Hughes are going to have to get together with her again some time.' Vercoe's grin widened. 'Should be fun. Daddy!'

'That'll be enough!' Spear's voice.

Fear flared in Vercoe's eyes. He backed away.

As David turned to face the Dragon Man, his whole body was clammy with sweat.

'What do you want?'

Spear stepped closer. David jerked back. Spear halted.

'Take it easy, Cauley. I just want to talk to you about your daughter. Interesting girl. *Different*.'

David's chest constricted. He felt ashamed in this man's presence, appalled by his own cowardice.

'You know Sammy Moss, I believe,' Spear said.

David said nothing. Vercoe sniggered.

'Pity about his . . . *friend*.' Spear enunciated the word precisely.

David's gaze flickered away from Spear. He felt skewered by the Dragon Man's eyes. They read him, understood him, despised his weakness.

'I'd like to help you,' Spear said.

'Why?' David prayed Anna and Lauris wouldn't reappear while Spear was there. 'I don't want any help from you.'

'What you want couldn't interest me less.'

Spear reached out a hand. David tried to step back, to get out of his range, but he collided with Vercoe, who had moved around behind him. Spear's hand clasped David's elbow.

'We're going to be friends, you and I,' Spear said.

'No!' David half-shouted, then flinched as he felt a surge of power ripple through his body . . .

'Better now?' Lauris asked.

Anna studied herself in the mirror above the washhand basin. The bare overhead bulb made her face look haggard.

'Yes. Sort of.'

Lauris placed her hands on her daughter's shoulders. 'Why did that Spear man upset you so much?'

'Don't know.'

Lauris turned her daughter around gently. 'Tell me.'

Anna hung her head. 'He's like me.' She touched her head. 'Here.'

'How do you know?'

A shrug. It was hard to explain; she just *knew*. She had suspected it even before she got up onto the podium, had sensed the mesmerizing power coming off him during his speech. And when Spear had taken her hand there had been an enormous jolt of power, as if their two forces had collided and sent shock waves crashing back through their bodies.

She had quickly given him a mental push to make him release her hand, but he had swatted her feeble effort aside.

'He's powerful,' Anna said. 'But his power . . .' It had felt dark, heavy, threatening. She looked into her mother's worried eyes. 'There's something evil about him. Really evil.'

Lauris shuddered. 'Let's get you home, darling.'

They opened the door to find David standing in the hall, his back to them, watching other parents heading for the exit.

'Daddy?' Anna called out, almost running towards him. She had to tell him about Spear being like her. He'd know what to do, how to protect her.

He swung round as she reached him.

'Hi, angel!' he said, smiling. 'Everything okay?'

Anna blinked. There was something dreadfully wrong

about this. He'd been there in the hall – he'd seen everything. What was he doing *grinning*?

Lauris said, 'Anna has something to tell you about that man Spear.'

'Really?' His grin broadened. 'I was just having a chat with him. He's very interested in Anna.' He reached out, stroked Anna's chin. 'Isn't that nice?'

He began whistling a calypso as they headed for the exit.

'What's got into him?' Lauris muttered.

As Anna followed her parents out of the building it felt as if maggots were squirming inside her stomach.

Wrong! she thought. *So wrong!*

CHAPTER NINE

The running time.

David Cauley didn't need to look at his watch to tell it was 5:30. People in the newsroom always began running exactly half an hour before the start of a bulletin. For most of the afternoon producers would sit at their desks reading wire copy or newspaper cuttings on their story. They'd stroll down to graphics to order a stack, pick up a sandwich and a coffee, study the noticeboards, chew the fat with colleagues about their item, sneak in a few personal calls, or just gossip – who was flavour of the month, who was on the way out, who was sleeping with who.

An hour before transmission the atmosphere turned less casual. Discussions about which clips of VT to use, or what should be the lead story, or how the newsreader's introduction should be written became short and noisy. Requests turned into commands. Discussions became arguments.

Half an hour before the start of the bulletin, there was another change of gear. Computer keyboards clacked madly as scripts were torn apart and reconstructed to accommodate the latest developments in a story. Arguments became ugly rows.

At this stage the newcomers revealed themselves – they started to look scared. The oldtimers just looked strained.

But mainly you could tell there was half an hour to go, because that was when the running started; reporters heading for the dubbing studio to lay down voice tracks; sub-editors scuttling into News Information to check spellings for supers, or facts that, if wrong, could land the station with a hefty libel bill; producers racing to catch a late satellite feed, praying their introductions matched whatever the foreign correspondent was saying in his piece.

David smiled wryly as two producers collided beside the reporters' desk, spraying pieces of paper and recriminations around them.

The running time.

He turned back to his computer terminal. His story didn't amount to much. Like most of the stuff he'd churned out lately it wouldn't make the top half of the bulletin. Overcrowding in Britain's prisons was hardly a ball-grabbing story, and he was damned if he could find a new angle to it. The government had pledged to build more prisons. The opposition had accused them of leaving it too late. That was about it. Library footage, two fifteen-second interview clips (one pro-government, one anti), some new shots taken inside a prison in Oxford earlier in the day in which all the prisoners had their backs to the camera so they couldn't be identified. A minute forty-five max. As far as David was concerned, that was a minute and a half too long.

Usually he'd have had his script written inside twenty minutes, but he'd been at it over an hour and he still couldn't hit on a payoff. 'The government has decided to act at last – but opponents say they're doing too little, too late.' No, he *couldn't* use that one again. 'Todays's announcement by the government will certainly come as a relief to prison officers and prisoners alike.' Nope. The audience wasn't much in favour of molly-coddling jail-birds.

David gripped the bridge of his nose between forefinger and thumb, yawned. His concentration had been ragged for days now, ever since the night of the prize-giving ceremony at Anna's school.

'Haven't you finished yet?'

David looked up. The reporters' secretary, Francesca, had managed to get a producer's job after years of trying. She'd also stopped dating neanderthals whose idea of fun was to bounce her around the room like a squash ball, and had got engaged to a meek little civil servant who treated her like a goddess. Inevitably, she was making his life hell.

'Two minutes,' David said. He tried for a reassuring smile, failed. Francesca bit her lip, loped off towards News Information.

No, David's mind hadn't been right since that night at the Patterson School. Anna hadn't been sleeping well, and Lauris was angry with him about something, but he wasn't sure what. As for himself, it felt as if an enormous problem was lurking like a huge, sinister beast just below the surface of his consciousness, waiting to leap up with a roar when he was least expecting it. But *what* problem? Something to do with Spear? Anna thought so. So did Lauris. Spear was like Anna – they were both telepaths. David knew that. He'd felt the power coming off Spear that evening when he'd been touched by him just after Spear had told him how interested he was in Anna, and how he'd like to help David out.

What was so wrong with that? Did it *matter* if Spear and Anna were alike?

Oh God, he was *so* confused. He'd sleep for hours and wake up feeling as if he hadn't slept at all. He'd read pages of a book and not remember any of it. He'd sit in front of the TV in the evening, drinking too much, and he'd swear there was a voice somewhere, calling to him, and he'd turn the sound down and there'd be nothing but the quiet hum of nearby traffic.

He sighed, turned back to his script. Everything seemed dreamlike these days, as if a piece of gauze had been draped over his mind, turning everything fuzzy, soft-focus.

'Please!' he heard, looked up.

Francesca was clutching her clipboard so fiercely, her knuckles were white. There were tears in her eyes. It had taken her a long time to become a producer; she didn't want to screw up during her first month on the job.

David bashed down the 'too little too late' line, hit the key to print out the script. He stood up and put his arm around Francesca's shoulder.

'Relax. It'll be there.'

She nodded, wiped her eyes.

David's phone rang. Calvin Scott.

'David, come to my office now.'

'I have to lay down a voice track, Calvin.'

'Get someone else to do it. This is important.'

Scott hung up, David cursed. The only other reporter at the desk was a regional journalist down on attachment for a month from Newcastle. The boy had been sitting there all week reading the papers, waiting for a story, any story. David ripped the script off the printer, tossed it at the RJ.

'Voice that,' David said. The RJ buttoned his jacket, began reading it. 'Don't read, just voice. And don't change any of it.'

The RJ looked up. 'The last line's crap.'

'Can you do better?'

'Yes.'

David smiled. 'Okay, do what you want – but do it quickly.' He turned to Francesca. She was on the verge of tears again. 'You know which interview clips to use, Fran. The picture editor's seen all the material – he'll know what to do. You'll be fine.'

He headed off across the newsroom, wondering if he was about to be sacked. His recent performances had been less than inspirational. In the last few months he'd turned into a time-server, an odd-job reporter filling cracks in the bulletins with the minimum of fuss, and that wasn't what Calvin Scott wanted. He preferred bright, dynamic young people with ideas and energy, like the RJ David had just handed his script to. The kid would be changing that script right now, not caring about the lack of time, determined to make his mark.

He halted outside Calvin Scott's office. The problem

96

hiding in his subconscious loomed into view for a split-second. Green eyes blazing at him – an animal of some kind, a vast, scary beast, *glaring* at him. And he thought, *I should contact someone. There's someone I have to tell!* But what was he supposed to tell them?

He took deep breaths, shook his head to clear it. He had to *concentrate*. He could be on the verge of being fired. He'd get another job, but probably not so well paid, and probably not in London. That would mean taking Anna away from her school. They'd have to leave their nice, warm, safe little house.

He stood up straight, sucked in his stomach. He was damned if he was going to allow himself to be scuffed into the gutter like a dog-turd.

He knocked at Scott's door, walked in without waiting to be asked.

Calvin Scott was seated behind his desk. He had a visitor with him. A man, standing with his back to the room, staring out of the window. The visitor turned around slowly.

Richard Spear.

Calvin Scott spoke first. 'Well, David—'

The newsroom tannoy cut across him. 'Newsroom, according to the Soviet news agency, Tass, an attempt has been made to assassinate the Soviet Leader, who is visiting the Ukraine. No details yet.'

Richard Spear was gazing up at the tannoy. 'Dear, dear!' he muttered, and smiled as if at some private joke.

Again, David saw the beast in his subconscious rear into view. As it folded its scaly wings over his soul, he recognized it for what it truly was.

'I thought you'd be *pleased*!'

'I am, David,' Lauris said. She brought the cufflinks she'd been polishing close to her eyes, squinted at them. The two tiny dragons were a perfect mirror image of each other. Fierce little monsters with pointed tongues of flame spiking from their mouths. The man who had ordered them over the phone the previous week would be satisfied. The cheque she'd been sent to cover the commission had been enormous – at least three times what she would normally have charged. She had made a special effort to get the design right, sketching endlessly before getting down to the real work.

'What are they?' David asked, grumpy.

'Cufflinks.'

She held them up for him to see.

'Dragons,' he muttered. His brow furrowed and his eyes went glassy. He clanked his tumbler of whisky down on the workbench.

'Lauris, will you stop farting around with those things and listen to me? I've just been made a correspondent. That means another ten grand a year, a plush office, half a secretary, a better car, status, share options in the company. Can't you even *pretend* to be interested?'

Lauris put the cufflinks down, but continued gazing at them.

'Why, David? That's what I want to know.' She looked up at him. 'We both know your work hasn't been that good recently. And you're not exactly one of Calvin Scott's favourites. Why has he promoted you now?'

'Reliability. Good looks. I don't know.' He scooped up his tumbler, gulped from it.

Lauris stood up, and went to him, reached up and took hold of his jacket by the lapels. 'You know why. You're just not telling me.'

He shrugged her hands off his jacket, turned away.

'When I went to Calvin Scott's office, Richard Spear was there. Don't ask me why, but Spear put pressure on Calvin Scott to give me the new job.'

Lauris studied him in silence for a minute. 'I find that very, very odd.'

'So do I. What can I say? I walked in there, Scott told me about the job, and said I had Spear to thank. Spear shook my hand, said well done, and . . .'

'And what?'

He looked at her out of the corner of his eye. 'Invited us all to lunch this Sunday at his place. It's somewhere in the country.'

Lauris sat back down, shaking her head. 'There's

something very wrong about all this, David.'

'I'm going to get another drink.'

Lauris sat chewing a thumbnail. David was as worried as she was; he wouldn't be drinking as heavily if he weren't. Something had been wrong with him ever since the night of the prize-giving. Something had been wrong with *all* of them. Anna was nervy and sleepless, and David was acting as if he was on amphetamines half the time, tranquilizers the other.

When he reappeared his legs were unsteady. She could tell he'd had a quick belt before refilling his glass. She'd now lost count of his evening's intake – five doubles? Six?

'This invitation – it includes Anna, I suppose,' Lauris said, trying to sound casual.

David made an expansive gesture with his arms, slopping some of his drink onto the workbench. 'He said all of us. I suppose that includes Anna. Certainly. Why not?'

'He's too interested in her, David. The way he reacted to her that night, getting you this job, the invitation . . . it's all because of her, isn't it? Because they're alike. What does he *want*?'

'He's interested in talented children.' He was looking anywhere but at her. 'Anna's talented.'

'No, she's not. She's different. And she's frightened of Spear.' She paused. 'Let's not go.'

'Of course we have to go. He's just got me a promotion. What can I say to him? Thank you and fuck you?'

'Turn the job down. Resign. Get a job somewhere else.'

David's expression turned ugly. He stabbed a finger at her. 'I'm taking that job, and we're going to that lunch. All three of us. Got that?'

'Then at least contact James and tell him about Spear.' She'd been on the verge of suggesting it at least a dozen times in the past few days. 'I know he might take Anna away from us. But maybe that wouldn't be such a bad thing right now.'

'James,' David said. His eyes glazed over. He mouthed the name to himself again, as if trying to remember something.

He turned slowly and wandered out of the room, muttering to himself. Lauris hugged herself, began rocking back and forth in her chair. David had never behaved this way before. There was a war going on somewhere inside him; she and Anna were getting caught in the crossfire.

Anna was in bed half an hour later when Lauris went through to tell her about Richard Spear's lunch invitation. She refused point blank to go. Lauris said she had to, for her father's sake. Anna tried some mental pressure on her mother, a little nudge. Lauris sensed it, resisted it. She sat down on the edge of the bed and took hold of Anna's hands.

'Please, darling. Do it for your father. I think there's something dreadfully wrong with him. He needs our help.' Anna said nothing. 'I need your support, angel. I can't handle this on my own.'

Anna nodded. 'All right.' She turned over quickly.

Lauris kissed the back of her daughter's head. 'Thank you, darling.'

She went through to their bedroom. David had slipped into a boozy doze. She was alarmed by the snuffling noises he was making. When she looked closely, she saw that he was crying in his sleep, the tears squeezing out from behind closed lids. She lay down beside him, held him. Eventually he stopped crying and his breathing became deep and regular.

When she eventually managed to fall asleep, she dreamt about dragons.

'JAMES!'

Lauris awakened with a start. David was sitting bolt upright beside her. He turned to stare at her. 'James,' he repeated, then lay back down and closed his eyes.

Lauris didn't sleep again that night.

CHAPTER TEN

They almost died two miles from Richard Spear's home on the outskirts of Sunningdale when David tried to overtake a slow-moving Escort on a blind corner. The lorry coming the other way missed his car by a fraction of an inch as he braked hard and slewed back behind the crawling Escort.

Anna screamed from the backseat. Lauris shouted at David to stop immediately. They changed places silently while the drivers stuck behind sounded their horns. Lauris drove slowly, not sure that her concentration was much better than her husband's.

The last few days had been nightmarish. David had been undergoing violent, unnerving mood changes. He'd be high one minute, bopping around the house to loud music in a way she'd have found funny another time; the next minute she'd find him slumped in his chair in the sitting room, staring out of the window at nothing in particular, like a stroke victim.

The night before, she had suggested he see a doctor.

'But I'm fine,' he'd said, his voice dreamy, far away.

'David, you're cracking up.'

He had stared at her uncomprehendingly for a while before strolling out of the room, head bent. Half an hour later she'd found him sitting in a deck-chair in the garden, gazing up at the moon, muttering to himself.

Anna had barely spoken for days. Lauris had almost been able to hear her daughter's spine tightening as the lunch with Spear drew nearer. The girl hadn't eaten anything for two days.

Lauris had begged David to take them away for a break to their Wiltshire cottage. 'Let's go there David. Let's go *now!*'

That had elicited a helpless little shrug and an incomprehensible mumble.

As she took the turn-off to Spear's place, she wished she'd put her foot down.

Spear's house was secluded by a dense wall of trees behind a nine-foot-high brick wall. Their first sight of it was through high wrought-iron gates with a dragon motif in the centre. A massive albino opened the gates for them. David grunted when he saw him. Anna sucked in her breath. The albino pointed wordlessly towards the house across a forecourt of cobbled paving. The wide two-storey house was faced with pink-painted stucco, and had a red-tiled roof. The centrepiece consisted of four Tuscan pilasters below a pediment with a circular window set in it like an eye. Immediately above the doorway, also inset into the stucco, was an elaborate heraldic cartouche consisting of three roaring dragons.

Spear was waiting for them by the front door, dressed in country-house tweeds.

Lauris got out of the car first. Spear stepped forward, shook her hand, and welcomed her. She sensed that she didn't interest him in the least. As he shook David's hand Lauris saw that Spear's cufflinks were the ones she had made the previous week.

Spear noticed the direction of her gaze. 'Forgive the subterfuge.'

'Why wasn't I told they were for you?'

'People often try to overcharge when they hear my name.'

'You paid far too much for them anyway.'

'I never pay too much for anything, Mrs Cauley.'

Anna stepped out of the car.

'Welcome, Anna,' Spear said.

She nodded, avoiding his eyes. She was holding her hands behind her back. Spear made no attempt to extend his own hand or to move closer to her. Lauris got the impression he was a little wary of Anna.

He led them inside the house. Dragons everywhere – curtains, wallpaper, even in an inlaid pattern on the marble floor of the main hall.

Spear's wife was waiting for them in a sitting room into which the whole of the Cauley's house would have fitted comfortably. She was a tall, elegant woman in her early forties, whom Lauris recognized as one of the bright young things of swinging sixties London. From a titled family, she seemed to remember. She'd gone out for a while with one of the major rock stars of that decade. There had been some scandal about hard drugs – Lauris remembered a photograph of her lying in some London gutter appearing in a down-market tabloid.

Two teenaged children appeared and were introduced to the Cauleys; Jeremy, a sullen, plain, lumpy boy, and Henrietta, a willowy girl with magnificent black hair and her mother's nervy, equine good looks. Brother and sister instantly retreated, whispering and giggling, to one of the corners of the vast room. Mrs Spear poured drinks from a silver decanter wagon as Lauris sat down on a late-Victorian walnut chaise longue. David asked for a Scotch. Anna refused the offer of a drink. The rest had champagne, a Dom Perignon '64.

'It's a wonderful house,' Lauris ventured, trying to deflect attention from David, who was guzzling his whisky, and Anna, who was sitting perched on the edge of an armchair, hands folded in her lap, staring down at the carpet.

'My wife's choice,' Spear said. 'As are the furnishings and decorations.'

'Are you fond of dragons as well, Mrs Spear?' Lauris asked.

'Only one. My husband.' She smiled. 'I was allowed to do what I liked with the house, but I thought it would be politic to include as many dragons as possible.'

'I don't see St George anywhere,' Lauris said, as David got up and poured himself another Scotch. In the background, Spear's children tittered.

'There is one.' Spear's wife waved a hand in the direction of a gilt bronze marquetry vitrine set against the nearest wall. It was crammed with silver objects.

Lauris got up and went over to it.

The items were so beautiful, they almost brought tears to her eyes; a french perfume-burner, a George IV honeypot, Victorian snuff-boxes, and an early German silver sculpture of a dragon with a helmeted knight clasped in its jaws.

'I thought St George was supposed to have slain the dragon,' Lauris said.

'Not in all versions of the story,' Spear said.

Lauris turned around. 'Then why aren't there any dragons left?'

Spear stood up abruptly. 'Oh, but there are, my dear.' He turned his gaze on Anna, who had not moved. 'Lunch,' he announced.

He led them through a connecting door into a dining room with a long mahogany table set beneath a copy of a Tiepolo ceiling mural.

The meal was an awkward affair. Mrs Spear battled valiantly to find some common conversational ground as they ate quails' eggs, pepper steak and lemon sorbet. She and Lauris discussed art. Then David, who managed to work his way through the best part of two bottles of Chateau Beychevelle '67, tried to explain to Spear's wife how the newsroom worked. Once, he knocked his glass over, and Spear's children giggled. Spear himself ate and said little. He seemed impatient for the meal to end. From time to time, Lauris saw him sneaking glances at Anna, who was sitting quietly staring down at her plate, eating and drinking nothing. Spear spoke to her only once, to ask whether there was something wrong with her appetite. She said nothing, but took a quick, grudging bite of steak and put her fork down again immediately.

Lauris was near screaming point when Spear signalled the end of the meal by standing up.

'I suggest Jeremy and Henrietta entertain Anna while I show the Cauleys around.'

Anna hung back, obviously unwilling to be separated from her parents, but David told her to run along. When the teenagers had left, Mrs Spear claimed correspondence to attend to and disappeared as well.

As Spear led them up the curved staircase Lauris glanced at David. He seemed to be in an alcoholic trance smiling vacantly, barely aware of his surroundings.

Lauris halted half-way up the stairs to study the figure inlaid in the marble floor below.

She shuddered. It was partially human; it had a face

remarkably like Spear's, its mouth belching red flames. Its torso was covered in dragon heads, and dragon wings sprouted from its back. The lower limbs were two vast, coiling serpents.

'It's hideous,' she said.

Spear had halted as well. 'His name is Typhon. In Greek mythology, he was the product of a union between Gaea, the Earth, and Tartarus, the Underworld. He frightened the gods so badly they all fled to Egypt, except for their leader, Zeus. He attacked Typhon with thunderbolts and a sickle made of adamant. Typhon wrapped his coils around him, and severed his sinews. He then imprisoned him in a cave, guarded by a dragon. Two of Zeus's sons managed to free him and restored his sinews. Zeus chased Typhon across Greece to Sicily, where he threw him down into the underworld and imprisoned him by placing Mount Etna over him. They say the volcano's blasts of fire are a result of the thunderbolts Zeus used against the monster. I prefer to think of them as Typhon's fiery breath as he struggles to free himself.'

Lauris looked up at Spear. 'Is he the creature on your company's logo?'

'No, that's Midgard, a Norse dragon, who was thrown into the sea by the god, Thor, where he grew so big he eventually circled the globe.'

'Dragons seem to come to sticky ends.'

'Oh, that wasn't the end of Midgard. He was eventually slain by Thor during Ragnarok – in other words, the Twilight of the Gods.'

'So, once again, the dragon failed.'

Spear's stare chilled her.

'He didn't fail. Thor was overcome by the dragon's breath. Within seconds of slaying Midgard, he dropped down dead.'

Spear turned and carried on up the stairs. Lauris grabbed hold of David's arm, but he hardly seemed to notice. For all the communication between them, they might have been on separate planets. Lauris wished they hadn't let Anna out of their sight. There was a dreadful sense of darkness, of *wrongness* in this house.

Spear opened the first door they came to on the landing, and ushered them inside. It was an oak-panelled study lined with books. In the centre was an oak desk with a red leather top. On it stood a computer and a twelve inch antique terrestrial table globe. In one corner of the room stood a four foot high marble figure of Napoleon in coat and riding boots, as he must have looked on the French army's retreat from Moscow. Above the figure stood busts of Lenin and Mao Tse-tung. The combination struck Lauris as bizarre.

When she glanced at Spear's bookshelves she saw a yard of works on Alexander the Great, next to books on Stalin and Hitler. She was surprised to see a section devoted to Jesus Christ.

'You seem to have an eclectic taste in heroes,' she said, as Spear poured port from a decanter.

'I look upon them more as distant relatives.'

'Hitler?' Lauris said. She glanced at the shelves again. 'Ivan the Terrible? Alexander the Great? What interesting bloodlines you must have.'

Spear handed them glasses of port. 'There's a theory that Alexander the Great was sired by a dragon. Did you know that?'

'That one must have slipped by me.'

David finished his port in one gulp. Spear took his glass, refilled it.

'I think Mr Spear means they're people like him, darling.' David's tone was infuriatingly patronizing, as if he was addressing a six-year-old. 'Powerful men,' he added, oblivious of her irritation.

'Vicious and evil as well, some of them,' Lauris said.

'I grant you that, Mrs Cauley,' Spear said. 'Power isn't always easy to handle.'

'I'm sure six million Jews would agree that Hitler found power hard to handle. And how many Russians died because of Stalin? Fifteen million? Twenty?'

'Oh, let's not argue,' Spear said. 'Sit down, enjoy your port. It's a Taylor's '45.'

David did as he was told. Lauris put her glass down and remained standing as Spear settled behind his desk.

'Why did you get my husband his new job, Mr Spear.'

'Lauris!' David objected, suddenly coming to life.

'What possible motive could you have had?'

Spear shrugged. 'I admire his work.'

'Don't insult my intelligence.'

Spear gazed at her expressionlessly. His eyes were dead, unreflective. 'Very well, Mrs Cauley, I didn't get your husband his new job because of his talent as a reporter. In any case, I detest journalists.' He paused. 'I did it because of your daughter.' His eyes came to life, flickering with a pale green fire.

'Yes,' Lauris said, almost relieved to hear the truth, but dreading it at the same time.

'Anna's a very special girl. As I'm sure you're aware, she has certain gifts.'

Lauris held her breath.

'After I met your daughter I made some enquiries concerning your husband,' Spear went on. David was staring out of the window, apparently unconcerned. 'It seems he was on the verge of losing his job. The Patterson School fees are high. I wish Anna to remain at the school. You couldn't have afforded to keep her there with your husband out of work. I knew you were not the sort of people to accept charity, so I decided to have your husband promoted. Is that clear?'

'Very clear!' Lauris walked over to the desk. 'And now I'd like to make something clear to you. Your interest in Anna is unwelcome. Your meddling in our affairs is unwelcome. If my husband deserves to be fired, that has nothing to do with you. *We* are Anna's parents. *We* look after her as best we can. If we have to take her away from the Patterson School, so be it. It has *nothing* to do with you! Is *that* clear?'

Spear folded his arms. His eyes had gone dead again. 'Your wishes are irrelevant. It's what I want that counts, because that's what's going to happen.'

'You insufferably arrogant bastard!' Lauris turned to David, who was staring at her in dopey bafflement. 'David, we're leaving right now.'

David shrugged. 'If you say so.'

'No,' Spear said. 'If *I* say so.' He stood up and headed around the desk towards Lauris. She backed away.

'David, stop him!' she gasped.

In response, David started to cry. Silent tears trickled down his face. 'Can't . . .' he managed to force out. 'Can't!'

Lauris ran to the door, twisted the knob. A burst of energy crashed through her, shockingly powerful, a tremendous black tidal wave sweeping away her resolve . . .

They'd been sitting in Jeremy's bedroom listening to Heavy Metal music for ten minutes when Henrietta said, 'Your father drinks a lot.'

Anna didn't reply. She continued to flick though the magazine she'd been reading.

'In fact,' said Jeremy, 'I reckon he's an alcoholic.'

Anna slapped the magazine shut, sighed and looked out of the window at the enormous landscaped rear garden. Spear's children were stunningly ordinary. She had thought they might be special, like their father, but she had soon realized they were just silly, rich brats.

'Pathetic, really, drinking like that.' Jeremy said. 'So undignified.'

Suddenly, Anna felt queasy.

'I've no idea why our parents have invited you people round, actually,' the girl said. What was her name? Anna wondered. Henrietta? 'Usually we only have important people to lunch.'

'My father's important,' Anna said, continuing to stare out of the window. The sky seemed darker now. She felt woozy.

Henrietta tossed her head. 'My father says journalists are scum. All of them.'

Anna looked at her. 'Does your father say a lot of stupid things?'

'*Don't* talk to my sister like that,' Jeremy said.

'Oh, drop dead!' Anna said, picking up the magazine again.

'Make me, you silly bitch,' Jeremy said, standing up.

(*Could I?* Anna wondered.)

'You shouldn't anger Jeremy,' Henrietta said. 'He has a

terrible temper. Except with father, of course.'

I bet! Anna thought. There was an air of fear in the house. Did Spear ever really let rip with his family?

She was tempted to teach the two of them a lesson, but decided against it. All she wanted was to escape from this awful place.

'I bet your mother fucks other men,' Jeremy said. 'Men can't get it up when they're drunk.'

'Mind you, she wouldn't attract many men in those dowdy clothes of hers,' Henrietta said.

'Take that back!'

'Piss off!' Jeremy said.

'Ditto!' said Henrietta.

Anna stood up and faced the boy, who was standing with his hands on his hips. He stuck his chin out in provocation. 'Yeah?'

'If you don't take back what you said, your father's going to be very angry with you. And you know what he does to you when he's angry.'

Jeremy and Henrietta exchanged glances.

'If you're so clever, tell us what he does!' Jeremy said.

Anna smiled, tapped her head. 'He uses this, doesn't he?'

Jeremy took a step back.

'How do you know?' Henrietta demanded.

'Because I can do exactly the same.'

'No, you can't!' Jeremy sneered. 'Only father can do those things. He told us that.'

'Yes,' said Henrietta. 'He says there's no one like him in the whole country.'

'Oh yes, there is.'

'Go on, prove it then, you bloody little liar!' Henrietta said. Abruptly, she slapped herself hard across the face.

'Don't mess about, Henrietta,' Jeremy said.

Henrietta was staring at her own hand. There was a livid mark across her cheek. 'I – I didn't mean to do that,' she said.

Jeremy took a step towards Anna, raising his hand. 'You little—'

His open hand suddenly formed itself into a fist with which he clubbed his testicles. He let out a gasp and

109

sagged onto the floor, clutching himself.

Anna looked down at Henrietta. She was staring open-mouthed at her brother. 'Would you like some more proof?'

Henrietta shook her head.

Anna smiled. 'Goodbye, children.'

She left the room and made her way along the landing towards the staircase. She now felt quite sick. She massaged her stomach. She wanted to get out of this house, with its dragons and its creepy atmosphere and the man who stared at her so *greedily*, the man who was like her, but at the same time so unlike her. She wanted to go home, and she wanted her father to be his old self again, not confused and weird the way he had been recently. She wanted never to have to meet Spear again, because he frightened her very badly. He wanted something from her and she had no idea what it was . . .

She halted at the head of the stairs, clutched her stomach. Fog whisps drifted across her consciousness. There were two men below, standing in the middle of the inlaid marble monster in the centre of the entrance hall. Vercoe and Hughes. They looked up suddenly.

Vercoe poked his tongue out at her and waggled it obscenely. She took a step back. A door opened behind her. As she turned the fog in her head became more dense; a thick dark green wall sweeping towards her.

Her parents and Spear stepped out onto the landing, all smiling.

'Hello, Anna,' her father said. There was a stupid grin on his face. He reached out and patted her shoulder clumsily.

'She doesn't look well,' Spear said matter-of-factly.

'Home!' Anna managed to say before the fog enveloped her and she dropped to the floor.

'I'll call a doctor right away,' Spear said. The words sounded muffled.

She felt herself being lifted up off the floor. As she was carried downstairs the fog in her head faded for an instant. She looked up to see Spear's hungry eyes a few inches away from her. She let her head loll back and all she could see was the monster in the hall floor, the monster with Spear's face. Its mouth was open and it was roaring fire.

As she watched, the flames leapt up towards her.

CHAPTER ELEVEN

Consciousness came slowly to Anna, in small surges, like waves sliding their way up a beach, reaching a little further each time. Kaleidoscope impressions of the day's events whirled and flared in her head – Jeremy Spear lying on the floor of his bedroom, holding himself; Vercoe and Hughes leering up at her from the hallway; Spear carrying her down the stairs; flames leaping up at her from the man/dragon's mouth . . .

And the doctor, the tall, stooped man with spectacles that made his eyes enormous. A burst blood vessel in the white of one goggling eye had looked like a gigantic running sore. She remembered smelling his disgusting dead-animal breath as he forced her eyelids wider apart and shone a light into each of her eyes in turn. She recalled shivering as his cold hands moved down over her stomach, and hearing a *snap*! as he pulled on rubber gloves, and the horror she felt when she realized he was *inside* her, probing, scraping . . .

She had wanted to call out to her parents, but had been unable to make any sound at all. Then she had felt a pinprick in one of her arms, and the heavy bank of fog had come rolling in over her once more . . .

Now, Anna opened her eyes.

She was at home in her own bed. Night-time. She tried to turn her head, but her neck muscles wouldn't respond. She had to work hard at getting her mouth open.

'Mother!' she wailed. Her voice sounded like dried leaves crackling in a faint breeze.

'Mother!'

Better.

She remembered Spear insisting she eat some food. It had been drugged, of course. She had to tell her parents about it. And she had to tell them about the examination to which she had been subjected.

She made an enormous effort, managed to lift her head off the pillow.

'MOTHER!'

Exhausted, she slumped back. The fog bank was hovering nearby, waiting for her to give in. She made an effort to hold it where it was, but it began creeping inexorably forwards.

Suddenly, her mother was there, leaning over her, making soothing noises, dabbing cold sweat off Anna's brow with a tissue.

'Spear,' Anna breathed out. 'He poisoned me. It was a trick—'

'There, there!' Lauris said. 'Don't be silly, darling. You have a virus. Dr Sorensen said so.'

Anna was about to tell her what Sorensen had done to her, but then she noticed her mother's eyes; unfocused, cloudy, looking *at* her, but not really seeing her. Instead, they seemed to be staring inwards at some different reality.

Suddenly Anna understood. Spear had been inside her mother's head!

A plastic cup scored with measurement markings was at Anna's lips. Her mother upended it. Anna felt a slimy liquid oozing down her throat, and she could no longer prevent the fog bank from rolling over her . . .

'How is she?' David asked when Lauris re-entered the sitting room.

'Fine.' The word metamorphosed into a yawn as she slumped down beside him on the couch. 'She thinks Mr Spear poisoned her.'

'Poor kid. It was lucky he had that doctor on tap.'

'Yes,' Lauris said. 'Lucky.'

David smiled meaninglessly, turned his vague attention

112

back to the television. The News was starting.

'One of China's leaders, Hua Xianyi, has died at the age of 73, apparently of natural causes. Mr Hua was expected to become China's next Premier. He was widely regarded in the West as the most liberal senior politican in China. In a recent interview, Mr Hua said that democracy was the only way forward for his country – a view that made him unpopular with some colleagues.'

There was a report on the day's events in China, followed by a backgrounder on Mr Hua's career. David felt a sense of disappointment. The sensible little man had seemed China's only hope after the hardliners had brutally crushed the student demonstrations back in '89.

'And now to the United States, where the battle for this year's Presidential election is hotting up . . .'

Not taking his eyes off the screen, David said, 'Spear's not such a bad chap, is he?'

'No,' Lauris said. 'I admit I was wrong.'

David smiled. Then frowned. James Lord was there on the screen, addressing a Democractic Party rally. David tried to concentrate.

' . . . Lord, who despite being only thirty-nine, is hotly tipped as the Democrats' likely presidential candidate next time round. He's spearheading the Democratic Party's campaign in these elections. Today he concentrated on foreign policy.'

There was a close-up of James Lord. 'This country can't afford to make a mistake at the elections. With the Soviet leader still critically ill and with today's terrible news from China, the world could be heading for a new Dark Age. The United States must encourage those two great countries to become more democratic. We can't afford to let them just slip back into their old ways.' James waited for the applause to die down. 'Unless China and Russia become true Democracies, this is going to become a very dangerous world. In that case, this country's going to need a vigorous party with some sort of vision of how the world ought to be. Only we can provide that sort of vision.'

'James,' David said. He shuddered. It felt as if some mammoth bird was hovering overhead, and he was shivering in the dark, freezing shadow of its immense wings.

He wanted to roar with fear.

'Darling?' Lauris said.

A pleading little bleat came from the back of David's throat. Then the menacing beast flew on, and he was left with only a dim memory of fear, and everything was all right again.

He reached for the remote control beside him, switched channels.

He didn't want to see James Lord any more. Too confusing.

CHAPTER TWELVE

'So tell me, what's he like?'

Whitley Chamberlain sipped his wine. The early-evening crowd in Bethell's was noisier than ever, and he had to repeat the question before David heard it.

'What's *who* like?' David asked.

'Spear, of course. Richard Spear. The Dragon Man.'

David poured himself another glass of wine. His item for the Six O'Clock News had been dropped for the Nine, so he'd accepted Whitley's invitation to the local wine bar. He got a kick out of how much Whitley enjoyed his new star status as Capital's latest newsreader. (Whitley preferred to be called a Presenter. 'The others, just read, man. I *present*!').

A girl emerged from the crowd at the bar and asked for Whitley's autograph. He signed the inside cover of her bookmatch, flashed her a big smile, and sat back, sucking in smoke from a Romeo y Julietta cigar, comfortable with the world, having a ball.

'Spear!' he repeated. 'Give me the lowdown.'

'Spear's all right. Not quite what you'd expect, I suppose. Powerful, of course. There's an aura about him –

114

but approachable. You know, he chats away like anyone else.'

David gulped the rest of his wine, poured himself another. He hadn't wanted to go home. Home wasn't really like home these days, what with Anna so ill. It had been four days since the virus had struck her down. And Lauris, well, Lauris was a bit unnatural, somehow. They sat and talked but they weren't getting through to each other. It was as if they were two actors playing David and Lauris Cauley. But, then, everything was strange these days. David heard himself speaking, saying things, believing them, but there was another part of himself saying *No, that's not true. Why are you saying that?* Doublethink.

Odd. Bloody strange. He sometimes wondered if he wasn't going crazy. He was certainly drinking like a madman, but drink was the only thing that seemed to be able to bring the two halves of his warring brain together. When sober, it was like listening to neighbours having a wild argument, but not being able to hear what they were arguing about. When he was drunk, he could ignore the argument.

Weird.

And a sense of danger, of doom, as if he was walking into some kind of trap. Not just himself. All three of them. Anna, especially. Anna was in danger. Sometimes he thought it was from Spear – but Spear was okay. He wanted to help Anna. He wasn't one of the bad guys after all. Lauris agreed with him about that. She'd changed her tune after lunch at Spear's place. 'He's a *nice* man,' she kept saying, as if she was trying to convince herself, as if the words she was speaking sounded strange to her.

'Yoo-hoo!' Whitley Chamberlain was clicking his fingers in front of David's face. 'Ground control to Major Tom. Anyone home?'

David shook his head. 'Sorry, Whitley. I was miles away. What were you saying?'

'I was asking what his place was like.'

'Whose place?'

'Spear's, for God's sake.' Whitley tapped the empty

wine bottle on the table in front of him. 'Maybe you'd better start laying off this stuff, Dave.'

Dave Someone else used to call him Dave. Someone he wanted to contact. *Had* to contact. Because of the danger. The danger to Anna. He shut his eyes, tried to clear his mind, but the mist wouldn't lift.

'Spear's place,' David said. 'Big. Very big. Lots of dragons all over the place. Very impressive. Very . . .' The sentence petered out. 'James!' he whispered. 'Yes. James.' James had been on television the other day, hadn't he?

Whitley sighed. 'Dave, wake up! You're not *that* drunk. What the hell's up with you?' He checked his watch. 'I have to go soon, but before I do, I want you to tell me something interesting about Spear. Anything! Why do you think I invited you for a drink? You know, your company's not that stimulating these days. I mean, I've had better laughs with estate agents.'

'I know,' David said. 'Sorry.' He frowned, like a bad actor trying to look like someone thinking hard. 'Spear. Well, my daughter fell ill at Spear's place, and he called a doctor to examine her. Dr Sorensen. He was there within minutes. I suppose that's what you can do when you've got money. And he took care of Anna, this doctor. He says she's got a bad virus. She's at home, and Sorensen comes to see her every day. Spear's paying for her treatment. Nice of him, don't you think?'

Whitley Chamberlain had paused with his cigar halfway to his mouth at the mention of Sorensen's name.

'What does this doctor look like?'

'Huge eyes. At least, his glasses make them look that way.'

Whitley puffed his cigar alight. 'Sorensen's bad news, David.'

'You know him?'

'Did a story on him last year. Tried to, at least. One of the grubbier Sunday papers got there first. He runs an institute in North London. It specializes in researching artificial insemination techniques for animals.' He squashed his cigar out in an ashtray. 'Before I go

116

slandering the good doctor, let's go back to the office and see what News Information have on him.'

Whitley leafed a ten pound note out of his wallet, tossed it on the table. David staggered slightly as he got up to follow. Whitley took a firm grip on his arm and steered him out of the bar.

News Information came up with three cuttings.

The first, from June 1968, was a report by the Agricultural Correspondent of *The Times* on the opening of the Institute for Genetic Engineering in North London. Dr Sorensen was the head of the Institute, which was to specialize in researching the breeding of livestock for increased milk and meat yields. Richard Spear was among the trustees listed at the end of the article. As far as David knew, Spear had no farming interests, so why had he involved himself with the Institute?

The next clipping, from 1989, reported that Dr Sorensen had recieved an OBE for his services to agriculture in the Queen's New Year's Honours list.

The last item was from a Sunday newspaper, dated the previous year.

TOP SCIENTIST IN HUMAN EMBRYO RESEARCH SHOCK

Dr Edvard Sorensen, 58, the man who got an OBE for his work on breeding bigger and better cows, has turned his attention to human beings! We can reveal that the head of the Institute for Genetic Engineering, whose headquarters are in Hendon, started breeding experiments on fifty women two years ago. The women, all in their twenties with fertility problems, volunteered for the experiments.

'The object of the research was purely to solve the problem of infertility,' Dr Sorensen said last week. 'There was a twenty-five per cent success rate. There was nothing illegal abou⁺ what I did. The Department of Health was informed, and gave the go-ahead.'

But there's been specualtion in the scientific community that the institute might have been tampering with embryos to produce certain types of babies.

One doctor, who wishes to remain anonymous, told us yesterday that Dr Sorensen could well have used patients to

117

try to produce babies of a certain weight, or with a certain eye colour, or even of a certain intelligence.

'Sorensen isn't into fertility,' the doctor said. 'He's into embryo research. He's proved that by tampering with the embryos of cows you can produce calves with pre-defined characteristics. It would surpise me if he's not doing the same thing with his human subjects.'

David crumpled the photocopies of the items into his pocket.

'Well?' Whitley said, ripping the band off a new cigar.

'It doesn't mean he's not a good doctor,' David said.

'A trifle overqualified to be treating your daughter. Virus complaints are hardly his field.'

'Spear wants her to have the best treatment.'

Whitley sucked at the flame of a gold Dunhill lighter. 'It's up to you, but I wouldn't let a man like Sorensen near my children.'

'He's a good doctor. Spear said so.'

'That doesn't sound like a journalist talking. You really trust Spear that much? Anyway, this guy Sorensen lives above the shop in Hendon. What was he doing miles away in Sunningdale? How did Spear know where he was? Why is Sorensen travelling all the way across London just to treat your daughter? What's so special about Anna?' He smiled suddenly, patted David's shoulder. 'Hey, none of my business, right?'

'You're right!' David shouted. 'It *is* none of your fucking business!'

Whitley's spine stiffened. 'Be cool, Dave!' He glanced nervously behind him. The half a dozen other people in the room were staring at them.

'Spear's a good man!' David yelled. 'He wants to help us, that's all.'

No, he doesn't . . .

'He wants to help Anna.' His voice was quieter. 'He's a good man.'

NO HE ISN'T!

Dave sucked in his breath, clutched his temples. That had been *loud*.

'Hey, I have to split.' Whitley gave a tight smile. 'No

offence. Spear's a saint, a real Mother Teresa. Okay?'

And then he was gone.

David grabbed hold of the nearest chair-back, rested his weight on it, stared blearily around the room. He stood up straight, and turned so violently the chair fell on its side.

'Sorry,' he muttered. He stumbled out into the corridor, made his way to the lift, and rode it down to the basement car park.

Why in God's name is a geneticist looking after Anna? Why does she need to be so heavily drugged? WHY ISN'T SHE IN HOSPITAL?

He walked quickly from the lift to his car.

No, Spear knows what he's doing. He called Sorensen because Sorensen's the best, a real star, a . . .

He halted by his Corrado, leaned on it. His head felt as if it was about to explode. He rested his forehead on the roof of the car.

Sorensen didn't have a bag with him. He took Anna into another room at Spear's house to examine her, but we saw him arrive – and HE DIDN'T HAVE A BAG!

But he'd had the bag with him when he'd left. The bag was already at the house *waiting for him*!

'Oh God!' David whispered.

No, Spear's okay, he wants to help. He's a good—

David raised his head a few inches, slammed his forehead down against the roof of the car.

Spear's a good man.

This time David slammed his head so hard against the car-roof it made a dent.

(A good man . . .)

'Fuck off!' he shouted. Another slam. His head was aching, but the other voice in his head, the one that kept telling him that Spear was a good man, was growing fainter.

'FUCK OFF, SPEAR!'

He drew blood with the next whack. He felt it trickle down over his eyebrows.

A good—

'GET OUT OF MY FUCKING HEAD!'

When the echo of his roar died away, he realized he was

standing with his fists clenched above his head, as if expecting an attack from above.

Silence. Just his own harsh breathing.

He got into the car, examined his face in the mirror. An ugly bruise was rising fast around a two-inch gash in his forehead. He started the engine, reversed out of the garage at speed.

As he headed away from Tottenham Court Road he realized that his head was clear for the first time in weeks. His anger had blasted away the effects of alcohol as well as Spear's insidious whisperings.

By the time he was speeding up the ramp onto the Westway section of the M40 he knew he was being followed. A red Porsche 959. He slowed and shifted across two lanes. The Porsche did likewise. He let it catch up, altered the angle of his rear-view mirror.

Vercoe's crossed eyes were staring at him from the car behind.

CHAPTER THIRTEEN

When David reached home, he waited long enough to see Vercoe pull up some fifty yards down the road before getting out of the Corrado and simulating a drunken lurch to his front door. He made a play of finding it difficult to get the key in the lock, stepped inside. As he did so, he experienced a peculiar sense of relief. The years of fearful waiting were over. The worst had happened. *Let battle commence*.

'Lauris?'

She wasn't in the sitting room or the kitchen, though the lights were on. He headed upstairs. The door to Anna's room was open. Lauris was pouring some of the clear liquid that Dr Sorensen had left with them into a spoon. Anna was unconscious, lips slightly parted. Lauris put the bottle down and raised Anna's head. Anna groaned and her eyelids trembled. Sorensen gave her an injection each day to keep her quiet. Lauris and David had been given strict instructions to give her a tablespoonful of the liquid every night 'to make sure she sleeps comfortably'. Sleep? The poor child was drugged to the eyeballs. She'd lost several pounds in weight already. Her cheeks were gaunt and there were dark patches like bruises under her eyes. She looked like she was dying.

Lauris moved the spoon towards Anna's lips

'Don't!' David said. The spoon jerked in Lauris's hand and the liquid splashed over the pillow.

'Oh, David! Look what you've made me *do*!' She turned round and reached for the bottle. David strode across the room, grabbed the bottle and hurled it against the nearest wall, smashing it.

Lauris stared at him, open-mouthed. 'What are you doing?'

He leaned over Anna, wiped cold sweat off her brow. 'Trying to save Anna's life.'

'I don't think we should ignore Dr Sorensen's instructions.'

David looked at her. 'There's nothing wrong with Anna. She doesn't have any virus. Spear must have given her drugged food at that lunch. Sorensen was waiting to step in and pump her full of tranquilizers.'

Lauris's eyes were unfocused. 'But Mr Spear, he's—'

'Yes, I know. A good man.' He walked over to her, took hold of her by the shoulders. 'Listen to me, darling. I don't know exactly what Spear's up to, but I know we're in danger.' Lauris was twisting her head from side to side, refusing to meet his gaze. He shook her, hard. 'Listen! Spear has placed some kind of a mental block on both of us. He's made us believe he means us no harm. When you stepped into his study last Sunday, you were scared of him, and rightly. By the time you stepped out, you thought he was a great guy. Just think back, and ask yourself why. What made you change your opinion of him?'

'No!' Lauris slipped from his grasp, backed away across the room. 'No, David. You're wrong. He's a good man.

He just wants to help. Anna's ill. He wants her to get better. He—'

Anna let out a moan.

'If anything happens to her, David—'

'Look, ask yourself this. Why would anyone with a virus need to be kept unconscious? Why?'

'Dr Sorensen's a good doctor, David. It's not up to us to question what he thinks is best for Anna.'

David let out a long breath. He held out his hand to the bed. 'Look at her, Lauris. That's our daughter. She's suffering because Sorensen is *making* her suffer.'

'No, David, I think you're wrong, and I'm going to give her her medicine. If you try and stop me—'

He moved across the room towards her. She tried to back out of the door, but he was too quick for her. He slapped her hard across the face. She gasped, raised a hand to her cheek.

'Lauris, we don't have time for this. Snap out of it. I did it, so can you.'

'You've gone mad,' she said, her voice breathy. 'Raving mad.'

He grabbed her and manhandled her over the bed and forced her head down so that her face was inches from Anna's.

'Look at her, for God's sake! Look what Sorensen's done to her. Does it look like she's getting better?' He twisted her round, shouted in her face. 'Fight him! Fight Spear! There's another voice inside you. *Your* voice. Listen to it!'

Then Anna spoke. A thin scratchy sound from impossibly far away. 'Help me!' Her eyelids fluttered open for a few seconds. 'Help me, please.' Then she was gone from them again.

Lauris's face crumpled. Tears welled in her eyes. 'Oh, David, what's happening?'

He took her in his arms, gently this time. 'I'm going to tell you everything I know. I should have done it a long time ago.'

Lauris twitched the curtain back. A leaden, overcast

dawn. Vercoe's Porsche was still there. She could just make out a figure apparently asleep in the driving seat. There was another Porsche parked directly behind it. Hughes was leaning against it, pumping a metal hand-exerciser. That made sense; Vercoe followed David, while Hughes covered the house. She let the curtain fall back into place.

David was sitting on Anna's bed, dipping a sponge into a bowl of cold water and wiping it over her forehead. Anna had awakened several times during the night, but each time she had slipped away again after a few seconds.

Lauris's mind was swirling with David's stories about James Lord and Sammy Moss and the Dragon Man, but she knew she had to make an effort to understand. It had taken David several hours to convince her that Spear meant them harm. When she thought of Spear she still felt a warm glow of admiration and trust – the Dragon Man's mind games had worked better on her than on David.

Lauris sat down on the other side of the bed, took a deep breath.

'You should have told me about Hughes working for Spear – and that you thought Spear ordered Sammy's lover killed. I'd have been on my guard against him.'

He rubbed a hand over his bleary eyes. 'I know that now.'

'There are a few things I don't understand.'

He gave a weary grin. 'Only a few?'

'How did Spear get mixed up with Vercoe and Hughes? It can't just be a coincidence.'

'I don't think it was. I reckon Spear met up with them back in '68 when he was trying to find out what had happened to James Lord. Maybe he heard about them when he was digging around for information at the school, figured their abrupt departure might have had something to do with James. They probably told him about the incident at the swimming pool and obviously mentioned the fact I was there. It's likely that's how Spear got onto my trail. After that?' He shrugged. 'Spear must have hired them. They've probably been with him ever since.'

He dipped the sponge he was holding into the basin on

his lap, gently stroked Anna's cheeks with it.

'What was Spear doing at the Patterson School?'

'I've no doubt he was there to meet Anna, make sure she really was an emperor.'

'But how did he find out about her in the first place? You said she fooled Vercoe and Hughes.'

'I've no idea.'

Lauris took the sponge from him, began to wipe Anna's forehead.

'What will Spear do next?' she asked.

'Who knows? Take her away from us, I suppose.'

Anna moaned, shifted her head a little.

'What do they want from her, David?'

He shrugged. 'I don't know. Right now the important thing is to figure out how to get her away from them.'

'What can we possibly do?'

'I'll have to ask James, but I can't phone him from here. It's probably bugged. I'll have to leave for the office in a few hours at the normal time. We mustn't let Spear know we suspect anything. I'll contact James and get some instructions. Meanwhile we've got to pray that Anna recovers before that bastard Sorensen arrives here with her next shot.'

'Can't we just make a run for it?'

'No, Vercoe and Hughes are still out front. I don't want those psychos after us.'

'But if you're at the office, how do I stop Sorensen injecting Anna?'

'Anna has to stop him.'

At that moment Anna's eyes blinked open. This time, they stayed open.

CHAPTER FOURTEEN

Before leaving for work, David phoned the secretary he shared with the Court Correspondent and gave her the day off. When he got to Capital Television, he went through

124

to the interconnecting office, which he knew would be empty. The Court Correspondent had taken off earlier that week for what he'd described as a 'holiday stroke nervous breakdown'. David reckoned his own phone might be bugged. Wiping the tiredness from his eyes, he phoned Capital's Washington Correspondent at home to find out if he knew James Lord's whereabouts.

'Why do you want him?' the Correspondent asked.

'Personal.'

'Don't piss him off by phoning at this time. It's three in the morning. You've already managed to screw up my sleep.'

'Do you know where he is?'

Reluctantly the correspondent gave him the name of a hotel in Houston. 'It's where politicians usually stay.'

The slamming of the phone almost punctured David's eardrum. He got the number of the hotel from International Directory Enquiries and dialled it. The desk clerk was reluctant to put him through, but he eventually got a frazzled-sounding aide.

'No way am I going to wake James up for some limey journalist, okay? We're in the middle of a frigging election campaign here, managing about three hours sleep a night. Phone back later. Goodnight!'

David went to the canteen on the floor below, loaded up on coffee and bought a pack of cigarettes. He hadn't smoked in fifteen years, but he had to keep his nerves at bay. The first puff made his head waltz, the second made him feel sleepy. He began to untense after the third.

A lightning flash whited out the room for several seconds. He was reaching for the phone again when he heard the phone in his own office ring. He guessed it was the editor of the One O'clock News looking for a report from him. He was already composing an excuse as he went through to answer the call.

'Good morning, David.'

His palms turned clammy. It was Spear.

'Hello, Mr Spear. How are you?' He was pleased he'd had the cigarette. It was helping keep the fear out of his voice. He dragged deeply on it.

'I'm phoning about Anna. Dr Sorensen tells me she's not getting any better. If she hasn't improved by tomorrow, he thinks it might be wise to admit her to his clinic. The facilities are excellent.'

'No!' David said sharply, too sharply. 'We feel better having her at home.'

A slight pause. 'I'm sure you do, but we have to do what's best for Anna.'

'Yes, of course.' He *mustn't* make Spear suspicious. He made his voice dreamy. 'We'll do whatever you and Dr Sorensen think is best.'

'Good, that's better, David.' Another pause. 'Is anything wrong?'

David screwed his eyes shut against another lightning flash. 'Nothing's wrong, Mr Spear. I'm just worried about Anna.'

'Of course. We all are.'

Spear put the phone down. David lit a new cigarette with the butt of the old one. His mouth was dry with panic. He gulped down one of the coffees, reached for the phone again.

The door opened. Calvin Scott walked in.

'How's our new star correspondent?'

'Fine. Just checking out a story.'

'Interesting?'

'It should make quite a splash.'

'Great!' Calvin Scott sat on the edge of David's desk, making it creak alarmingly. 'But you'll have to put it on the back-burner for the time being. There's a NATO summit meeting starting in Venice tomorrow. I'd like you to cover it.' He smiled. 'Bit of a treat, eh?'

'That's kind of you,' David said. 'But my daughter's ill and I don't want to leave her.'

Calvin Scott's smile froze. 'You've evidently mistaken an order for a request. You're going.'

'Send someone else.'

'There is no one else.' Scott stood abruptly, glaring at him.

David said nothing. Scott strode to the door, slammed it on the way out. As David moved back to the Court

126

Correspondent's office he wondered why Scott had been so insistent. He could name several other reporters who were available and would have covered the summit just as competently as himself.

A call to the radio station where Sammy Moss had worked before Rui Olazabal's death revealed that he'd set up shop as a stringer in Hong Kong. Directory enquiries told him there were three subscribers there listed as S Moss. David tried each of them in turn. The first two turned out to be strangers. The third didn't answer.

He felt his eyelids droop and realized he needed sleep. There was nothing more he could do for the moment. He just made it back to his own office couch before passing out.

A lightning shaft awakened him four hours later. There was a note pinned to his shirt. 'Tough at the top, I see!' It was signed 'Whitley.'

He yawned, stretched and made his way back to the Court Correspondent's desk. There was still one cup of cold coffee left. He drank it, lit a cigarette. A thunder rumble shook the building.

He phoned Houston again. James Lord had left two hours back. The aide whose sleep David had disturbed had evidently not bothered to pass on his message. He phoned the Washington Bureau of an American network which had financial ties with Capital and provided them with news pictures on a reciprocal basis.

The news editor told him James Lord was due to address a rally in Austin in about an hour's time. The network was covering it, and, yes, they'd get their reporter down there to pass a message to James Lord.

'"Anna's in danger". That's the message.' He gave the man his phone number.

'Sounds intriguing.' The news editor said. 'Do I sense a story here somewhere?'

'Oh not really. The world's at the mercy of a bunch of power-crazed telepaths, and one of them's trying to murder my daughter, as far as I can tell. He pushed me off the top of a cliff once, years back. And James Lord, well, he's another of these telepaths, but he's a good guy—'

He heard a groan down the line. He knew the sound well – the newsroom got an average of fifty fruitcake calls a day.

'No, don't worry, I'm not out to lunch. It's just been a bit of a hard week.' That struck him as funny as well, and he had to choke back a laugh. 'You've got my name. Check me out with Capital here or our Washington Correspondent. Whatever you do, get that message to James Lord.'

'Okay.' The man sounded doubtful.

'Please,' David added.

'Okay.' That sounded better.

He dialled Sammy Moss's number again. Sammy's voice was slurred and gravelled with sleep, as if he had been drinking heavily, or doing drugs.

'Sammy, it's David Cauley.'

Silence.

'Don't say you've forgotten me.'

'It's four in the fucking morning, Cauley. What's this about?'

'The Dragon Man,' David said.

Another silence.

'I want to talk about the Dragon Man, Sammy.'

'I don't.'

'Those things you told me about him. Do you have proof?'

A long sigh down the line. 'Are you seriously going after him?'

'No choice. He's after me. I have to protect myself.'

'The only protection's invisibility. The man's poison. He ruined my life. You go after him, he'll destroy you. Get out of his line of fire.'

'It's too late for that.'

'Then you're finished.'

The line went dead.

Anna was asleep when Lauris made her regular half-hourly check at two in the afternoon. She decided not to

128

awaken her. Anna would need all her strength to deal with Sorensen.

She went back downstairs to the kitchen at the back of the house. She switched on the kettle and sat at the breakfast bar, waiting for it to boil. The kitchen was a mess. There was a pile of unironed clothes in a wicker basket in front of the washing machine, a stack of dishes in the sink, and a regiment of unwashed cups and glasses on the drainer. Old shopping lists were attached to the fridge with ladybird magnets. It all seemed so domestic, so bloody *normal*.

The kettle boiled, clicked itself off. She got wearily off her seat, spooned Red Mountain coffee into a red and yellow ceramic mug, poured in water. Through the kitchen window she saw the sky lowering overhead. The storm had been rumbling most of the day, and the atmosphere was still heavy. It felt as if a weight was pressing down on her head.

She sipped the coffee.

Spear's a good man. He just wants to . . .

'No!' She shook her head. Spear's voice was like a worm twisting around inside her brain. She felt disgusted. Somehow it was worse than physical violation.

The front doorbell blared. Lauris shrieked, dropped her mug. It shattered on the floor. Coffee sprayed over the clothes in the basket in front of the fridge.

She skited the fragments of the cup aside with an angry swipe of her foot. She headed down the corridor and forced a wan smile onto her face before opening the door.

'Dr Sorensen, welcome.'

Anna opened her eyes when she heard voices in the corridor outside her bedroom. She shut them just as the bedroom door opened.

She was aware of a shadow falling across her. Fingers at her wrist.

'Yes, she's not doing so well, Mrs Cauley.'

'Is she in any danger?'

'Probably not.' A sandpaper voice, slightly accented. A curling, wheezing cough, bringing up phlegm. This afternoon, Sorensen's halitosis had a metallic quality.

'You're not sounding so well yourself, doctor,' Lauris said.

He ignored the comment.

'If she hasn't improved by tomorrow, we'll have to admit her to my clinic. Just to be safe.'

Anna heard her mother move closer to the bed. 'We'd prefer that she stayed here.'

'Mr Spear has phoned your husband about the matter, I believe.' Sorensen sounded irritated. 'Mr Spear feels Anna would be better off in my clinic.'

'In that case, of course, it would be fine,' Lauris said. 'Whatever Mr Spear wants.'

Anna wondered how the doctor had managed to miss the heavy sarcasm in her mother's voice. Anna risked opening her eyes a fraction. Sorensen was bending over his doctor's bag, withdrawing a hypodermic syringe. Lauris was standing behind, glaring at him.

Sorensen closed his bag and turned with the disposable syringe in his hand, the needle pointing up at the ceiling. He moved towards Anna, his monstrous, goggling eyes fixed on her.

He bent over her, placed the needle against her arm. Anna wanted to give him a massive blast, make him experience real pain, let him know what helplessness and humiliation were like. But she'd only done that to someone once in her life, and it had left her drained for days. She wasn't sure she had enough strength for that. Besides, the whole point was not to give the game away.

Her mother coughed loudly, evidently afraid that Anna was not awake. Anna felt the needle press against her skin. She opened her eyes wide. Sorensen gave a surprised grunt. His eyes widened grotesquely. Anna gathered her power, shot a bolt at him.

Her mother gasped.

Abruptly, Sorensen turned and placed the hypodermic, still full, back in his bag.

'That should keep her quiet, Mrs Cauley. Don't forget to give her the booster tonight.'

'Of course, doctor,' Lauris said.

He left the room and Lauris followed. Anna felt exhausted. She heard the front door shut. A minute later she felt her mother's lips against her brow. 'Well done, darling.'

Relieved, she allowed herself to drift into a doze.

David glared at the phone, snapped his briefcase shut. It hadn't occurred to him there'd be any problem contacting James Lord, but it was 4:30 and he hadn't heard back.

'Dammit!' he muttered, heading for the door.

The phone blared behind him. He dropped his case, ran to it.

'Cauley here!'

'Dave, it's James. I only just got your message. What sort of danger is Anna in?'

David explained briefly.

'Why didn't you tell me about Spear earlier? I warned you to be on your guard.'

'Why the hell didn't you tell me Spear was the guy who tried to kill me that day at the Minack? Besides, I was afraid you'd have taken Anna away from us.'

'Damn right I would! What in God's name possessed you to take Anna to his house?'

'Spear put some kind of a mental block on me and Lauris. Had us both believing he was a wonderful fellow.'

'Hang on!' David heard James asking someone to keep the noise down. 'Tell me about this Dr Sorensen.'

'A geneticist rumoured to be involved in human embryo research. According to Anna, he gave her an internal examination last week.'

A pause. 'That's very bad news.'

David gripped the phone tighter. 'James, tell me what's happening. What are they planning to do to Anna? We're so damned frightened . . .' He had to swallow to stop himself from crying.

'Easy, Dave. Easy! The reason they want Anna so bad is that she's female. They're not planning to kill her, that I can assure you. Far from it. As for you and Lauris, I think you really could be in danger. You don't matter to them.

Now just calm yourself and tell me what the position is at your house.'

David cleared his throat. 'Lauris is there with Anna. Anna's still very weak. The place is being watched by Hughes. Vercoe's job is to tail me. As far as I know, he's outside this building right now.'

'Can you get Lauris and Anna out of the house without being seen?'

'Difficult. Maybe impossible.'

'You'll have to manage it, Dave. You've *got* to get Anna away from there, take her some place they won't be able to find her. That's the number one priority. You'll have to do it tonight, before Spear realizes he's no longer got control of you. As soon as he realizes that, he'll kidnap Anna.'

'I'll do my best.'

'I'll fly over there. I'd better take care of this myself. Hang on.'

James was off the line for a couple of minutes. 'I'll be arriving at Heathrow tomorrow in my own plane around 08:20 your time. I want you at the airport to meet me. I'll be arriving at Terminal 3. *Don't* bring Anna with you. Just get her safe. Understood?'

'Yes.' David slammed the receiver down, grinned.

Fighting back. It felt good.

The storm that had been rumbling and flashing over the city all day had spent itself by the time David brought the Corrado to a halt in the street parallel to St Alban's Avenue. The evening was grey and cold.

Giving Vercoe the slip had proved simple; he had arranged for a reporter of a height and build roughly similar to his own to drive his Corrado out of the Capital underground car park and take the scenic route around the West End. David had waited five minutes before booking out another of the news pool Corrados and driving away. There had been no sign of Vercoe on the journey home.

He lit a cigarette and tried to figure out which of the houses on the west side of Rusthall Avenue backed onto his own. He knew it belonged to the Sharmas, an Indian couple who owned a newsagents shop around the corner in

Southfields Road. The only way to get Anna out of the house undetected would be through one of the houses backing onto theirs. If they used the Sharmas' house as an escape route they'd only have to negotiate the fence that separated their two gardens.

He just hoped the Sharmas were at their shop, taking care of business. He checked his watch. 7:30. The corner shop would be open for another half an hour at least.

He got out of the car, checked the road to make sure no one was watching and approached what he guessed to be the Sharmas' front door. He rang the bell. No response. He hunkered down and peered under a flower pot by the front door, searching for a spare key. Nothing there but a few bugs. He lifted the rubber mat in front of the door. Again, nothing. He removed the white plastic casing from the external gas meter. Bull's-eye. The key was hidden inside a matchbox.

He opened the door, stepped quickly inside and closed it behind him. He held his breath, listened. Silence. He trotted quickly through the house. Garish ornaments, sweet, spicy smells, everything neat and clean. The french windows at the back of the house were locked, and this time he couldn't find a key. He stood back and kicked at the lock. It gave instantly, and the door swung open. He ran across the Sharmas' back garden, clambered over the fence into his own. He crouched down in the flower bed and studied the back of his house. There was nothing obviously amiss. The kitchen was dark, but above it a light glowed dimly from Anna's bedroom.

He opened the back door and made his way through the kitchen. A radio was on somewhere in the house. He was half way down the corridor leading to the sitting room when he realized the man's voice he could hear wasn't coming from any radio.

He froze. The voice was Richard Spear's.

CHAPTER FIFTEEN

Instinctively, David took a step back. He bumped into something large and solid. The something moved. Before he could turn, a hand was clamped over his mouth. An arm gripped him round the waist and he was lifted clean off the floor. It had to be Hughes.

He was carried, struggling, along the corridor. The sitting-room door was booted open and Hughes toted him inside.

Lauris was sitting on the couch by the window, Spear beside her. She looked up at David with a vaguely puzzled expression. Hughes lowered him so that his feet touched the foor. Instantly, David gave a sharp backward kick. His heel crashed satisfyingly into Hughes's shin. Hughes yelled, let go of him. Spear began to rise off the couch. David lunged towards him, fists balled. Their eyes met for a split-second. David suddenly found himself on his knees. He tried to stand, but his legs wouldn't obey. He stuttered forward on his knees, hands reaching for Spear, but a terrible wave of exhaustion washed through him, and he let his hands drop. He had never been so tired, so utterly, completely spent, and he thought it would be nice to lie down on the floor and just sleep and sleep, and then he felt huge hands grab him under his arms and he was being hauled across the room and his eyes just wouldn't stay open . . .

And then he was sitting in his chair, near the couch, and his body was shaking and he was wondering why it was shaking, because he felt rather good, quiet and dreamy, as if on the edge of sleep, and he had to concentrate on what Mr Spear was saying. Something about having Anna's best interests at heart, and maybe it would be best if Anna went to stay with Dr Sorensen for a while, because she really was dreadfully ill, and it was their duty to make sure she got well again.

Lauris nodded, smiling, and David heard someone say 'yes', and realized it was his own voice.

But, Spear went on, Anna might be a little apprehensive about leaving the house – they knew how badly children sometimes reacted at having to leave their parents – so it might be best all round if Lauris were to take her a cup of tea or whatever she normally drank. Spear would put something in it, a mild relaxant to keep Anna calm and help her see that going away for a short while might not be such a bad idea.

'You're right,' David heard himself say, and Lauris was nodding again and David nodded as well.

'So you'll give her something to drink, Mrs Cauley,' said Spear.

'Certainly,' Lauris said, nodding away like a mechanical toy.

'Good,' David said. 'That's good.' But there was another voice screaming at him from far away, shrieking *No! No! No!* It was annoying, distracting, expecially when it was so hard concentrating on what Mr Spear had to say. He dimly realized the voice was coming from inside his own skull, so he shook his head to get rid of it, and after that everything was dandy. Just . . . dandy.

'I'll go and make a cup of . . .' Lauris said, her voice slurred. She frowned. 'Cup of . . .'

'Tea,' Spear supplied. 'That won't be necessary. Hughes can do that. You can take it upstairs to Anna and make sure she drinks it.'

Hughes. Yes, David remembered Hughes being there, but he wasn't in the room now.

'Hughes!' Spear called out as he reached into his pocket and brought out a tiny white packet folded like a homeopathic prescription.

Not right! David thought.

'Hughes!' Spear repeated, his voice sharp. 'In here!'

A panel of the sitting-room door blasted open as Hughes's head burst through it. He gazed at them, blood cascading from a deep gash above his left eyebrow. A broken tooth dropped from his mouth onto the carpet. His head disappeared from view. They heard a shout of fear, instantly followed by a tremendous crash as the whole of the door shot across the room. Hughes rolled to a halt in the middle of the floor. He gazed up at where the door had been, whimpered.

Suddenly, reality rushed at David. It was like a torrent of cleansing water smashing through him.

Anna appeared in the empty doorway. She looked at her father, then her mother.

Spear stood up. He opened his arms in a welcoming gesture, took a step towards Anna.

She turned her eyes on him. They filled with hatred. She raised her arm and pointed at Spear.

'You!' she shouted, her voice strangely deep, adult. 'Get out!'

Spear's body shuddered. He sucked in air. His skin turned a sickly grey colour.

'Anna!' he breathed out.

Anna opened her mouth wide. A roaring sound. The word 'Out!' endlessly extended. As her body began to shake, the room started to vibrate with her power. The very walls of the house quaked with it. David's brain felt as if it was expanding, straining against his skull, trying to burst through the bone.

Spear clutched his head. Veins stood out on his neck and temples like twisted cord. He made a keening, whining sound like a wounded animal. He stared at Anna as long as he could, then dropped his eyes. He shouted something – 'witch' or 'bitch' – then stumbled out of the room, hands still clamped to his skull, as if trying to stop it exploding. They heard him lurch down the corridor to the front door.

Hughes, still cowering on the sitting-room floor, took after his master, scampering out of the room on all fours, a whipped hell-hound.

Anna sagged onto her knees and covered her face with her hands. David went to her, knelt beside her, clutched her to him. She was limp, like a rag-doll, spent, crying weakly against his chest. And then Lauris had her arms around them and they were all kneeling in the centre of the room, forming a protective circle against the horror determined to destroy them.

The anonymous BMW Spear used when driving himself was parked behind Hughes's Porsche. He slid into the driver's seat and sat, hunched forward, forehead against the steering wheel, eyes shut tight, sobbing with pain and humiliation.

The girl was stronger than him. Her power was immense, terrifying. She had almost ripped his mind apart with one sustained blinding shaft of pure energy.

Compared to him, she was in another league. The knowledge hurt almost as badly as the crippling ache in his head.

He made an effort to pull himself together.

The girl was stronger than him, but he was smarter, surely.

He knew how exhausted he felt after using his powers for anything more demanding than the parlour games he had been playing with David and Lauris Cauley. Anna would be wiped out now for hours, maybe even days. If he was going to take her, he would have to do it *now*! He knew he could never again risk confronting her on equal terms. She'd destroy him.

He heard a tap on the car window, looked up. Hughes was staring in at him with the pathetic look of a child who has just seen its father humiliated.

Spear waved him away. Hughes disappeared back to his own car.

Spear wiped his eyes, looked over at the Cauleys' house. It was fortunate Sorensen had noticed the full syringe in his bag upon returning to the Institute. If he hadn't, the Cauleys might have had a chance to spirit Anna away. And the fact that one of the technicians responsible for pre-flight checks on James Lord's private jet had got himself into trouble with acquaintances of Spear's over gambling debts in Vegas the previous summer had finally proved useful. He knew all about James Lord's plan to fly to Heathrow the next day.

What would Cauley do now? he wondered. He couldn't risk staying in there. He'd know Spear would come for Anna, and he'd realize that in her condition there was little she could do to resist him. Cauley would decide to flee, get

137

Anna away. But how? Not out the front. That would be suicidal. He'd never make it to the . . .

. . . car! Spear cursed. The Corrado was nowhere in sight. Of *course*! Cauley had entered the house from the *back*!

He started the BMW, pulled up alongside Hughes's Porsche. Hughes wound the window down, holding a handkerchief to his bleeding forehead.

'Stay here,' Spear said. 'I'll drive round the back in case they try to get out that way.'

'Yeah, yeah,' Hughes said.

Spear's lips twisted. 'If you ever use that tone with me again, Hughes, I'll kill you.'

Hughes's spine stiffened as Spear's black BMW shot off down the road.

Anna had lost consciousness a few minutes after her battle with Spear. She was still unconscious as David carried her through the open french windows into the Sharmas' house. Lauris was right behind them, dragging a hastily-packed suitcase.

'Hello?' David called out. No response. Relieved, he headed across the sitting room. He took special care not to bump Anna's head as they moved into the dark corridor leading to the front door.

'It's okay,' he called to Lauris. 'They're not home yet.'

The corridor was so narrow, he had to move sideways down it.

He was ten feet from the front door when it swung open.

The young Indian couple stared in disbelief.

'Good evening,' David said.

'Good evening,' Mr Sharma replied. Mrs Sharma just nodded.

Lauris squeezed past David, still dragging the suitcase, and said, 'Excuse us.'

The Sharmas stepped aside as the Cauleys left the house.

David didn't look back until they were all in the Corrado. When he did so, the Sharmas were peering at them through their sitting room window.

David gave a little apologetic wave. Mr Sharma waved back.

David checked his rear-view mirror as he took off from the kerb, relieved that no one appeared to be following them.

He didn't think anything about the black BMW directly in front.

CHAPTER SIXTEEN

David swung off the M4 into the Swindon junction service area just after 8:30. They were only twenty minutes from the cottage, but the petrol gauge had been flashing warnings at him for a quarter of an hour and he didn't want to risk being stranded on a country road.

He pulled up at a petrol pump, turned in his seat. Anna's face was grey and gaunt. When Lauris had checked her pulse after they'd been travelling for half an hour it had been weak, but David hadn't wanted to stop to find a doctor. He'd figured the quicker he put some miles between his family and Spear the better.

Now, Lauris was asleep as well, Anna's head cradled in her lap.

David got out of the car, closed the door quietly. As he filled the tank, he glanced at the slip road leading into the service area, checking for a red Porsche.

He slotted the petrol pump nozzle back into its holder, walked across the forecourt. The night was cold, and he shivered.

Inside, he scooped cellophane-wrapped sandwiches off a shelf, grabbed some soft drinks out of the fridge and joined a line of three people at the cash desk.

He glimpsed a bottle of Scotch behind the cashier's desk. It whispered 'Drink me!' to him. He looked away quickly. There was some whisky at the cottage. He'd treat himself to a couple of belts while they waited for the doctor to arrive to examine Anna. It would help him sleep, and he'd have to be up early to get to the airport in time to catch James Lord.

The girl at the cash desk weighed about fifteen stone and had fingers like sausages. She kept adding up wrong. The man in front of David eventually said 'For God's sake!' and stalked off. As David took his place he glanced out at the forecourt. Lauris had woken up and was peering anxiously out the back window of the car.

David rapped his knuckles on the shop's picture window, earning a glare from the lard mountain at the cash desk. Lauris saw him, smiled in relief. David smiled back, showed her the food he was buying. She gave him a thumbs-up.

A black BMW pulled up behind the Corrado, then a coach swept into the garage and hid both cars from view.

Drunk soccer fans poured off the coach, shouting, shoving each other, kicking empty beer cans ahead of them.

Lauris looked down at Anna, stroked her head. The poor child looked half-dead.

Back at the house, Lauris had told David Anna was not well enough to be moved.

'She's going to be a lot sicker if she stays here,' he'd said.

He had been right, of course. Spear wouldn't have let them stay in the house indefinitely without attempting another assault, and Anna was in no state to repel him.

Anna's tongue lapped dryly in her mouth. Lauris wished David would hurry up with the soft drinks. Anna was seriously dehydrated. Her eyes were moving rapidly behind her eyelids. She bleated as her brow furrowed. Bad dreams, Lauris thought. No wonder.

'Angel,' she whispered, her eyes filling with tears. 'Poor angel.'

A young thug lurched against the car, shaking it, then peered through the window. He made an obscene gesture. Lauris looked away. The thug staggered off, turned, and hurled a half-empty beer can at the car in one easy motion.

It bounced off the windscreen, leaving a trail of froth across the glass.

Lauris sighed, and lowered Anna's head gently onto the seat. She snatched a cloth out the back and stepped out of the car.

She winced as she stretched to get all the beer off the glass; she'd ricked her back clambering over the fence into the Sharmas' garden. There was still a smear over the driver's section of the windscreen. She spat on the cloth, rubbed the mark vigorously. When it was gone, she tossed the sopping cloth into a nearby bin and got back into the car, next to Anna. She tried to pull the door shut. It wouldn't budge. She tried again, looked up.

Hughes was grinning down at her. As she opened her mouth to scream he wrenched the door open all the way and clamped a giant hand over her face. The back door on the other side opened. Spear reached in and tipped a packet of white powder into Anna's open mouth. He placed one hand on top of her head, the other under her chin.

Lauris squirmed, tried to kick at Spear. Hughes lifted her easily out of the car. The last thing she saw was Anna awakening, eyes widening in terror as she fought not to swallow what was in her mouth.

Lauris bit deep into Hughes's hand. She felt her head being jerked savagely to one side. Something inside her gave a reverberating crunch. For an instant, she was aware that she could no longer see or hear anything. There was a flare of pain, and then all feeling left her body.

One of the hooligans barged into David as he was trying to shoulder open the door of the shop. The jolt made him drop everything he was carrying. Cursing, he bent down and picked up the sandwiches and cans again as the lout's friends jeered at him.

He made his way around the football coach, froze when he saw the car.

They've gone to freshen up . . .

But why leave both back doors wide open?

He threw cans and sandwiches aside, started to run.

Froze again when he saw one of Lauris's shoes lying

next to the car. Its heel was broken off.

Needlepoints of fear raced over his body.

CHAPTER SEVENTEEN

The red Porsche 959 was doing a steady 90 miles an hour in the fast lane when David caught sight of it ten miles from the Hungerford turn-off.

He'd been doing 110 all the way from the service area. Now, he slowed and shifted over into the middle lane forty yards behind the Porsche.

He had sat in the car back at the petrol station for several minutes, sweating with panic, his guts roiling, trying to fight back tears, think rationally. He could have contacted the police, but if Spear was with Lauris and Anna it wouldn't have done any good. Ater a minute of talking to Spear the police would be apologizing for bothering him. No, his first priority was to find out who was driving the Porsche. If it was Hughes or Vercoe, he'd contact the police. If it was Spear, he'd try and tail him to his destination.

He slewed back into the fast lane, hit the accelerator, gradually gaining on the Porsche till he was right on its bumper. No good. He still couldn't see inside.

He shifted back into the middle lane after allowing some young people in an open-top sports car to shoot past. He started to sneak up on the Porsche, hovered in its blind spot for a minute, then eased the Corrado forward.

Lauris's head was lolling against the side window. Her eyes were open, but they didn't seem to be seeing anything. He still couldn't see the driver. He gave the accelerator a squirt, eased forward. And saw Hughes.

David eased back on the accelerator, slid behind the Porsche in the fast lane. He fought the sensation of sick panic in his stomach. *Where was Anna?* On the back seat? Where else could she be? Now that he knew Spear wasn't in the car, he could contact the police on his cellphone. He prayed Hughes wouldn't pull any crazy stunts when they tried to pick him up, but that was a risk he'd have to take.

The Porsche's indicator blinked, and it glided into the middle lane. David wondered if Hughes had spotted him. There was an exit ahead. Hughes kept on signalling, left the motorway.

David swore. He had to slew across three lanes to make the exit, weaving between cars. Lights flashed at him, horns blared.

He dipped his headlights, allowed the Porsche to pull ahead. They were on an unlit two-lane country road. There was no oncoming traffic and no cars ahead of the Porsche. David was desperate for a roadsign. He couldn't call the police until he knew where he was.

They'd gone about three miles when he saw a sign. *Ashmolden 5m.*. That would provide the police with a good enough fix. He reached for the car phone.

It rang. Puzzled, he picked it up. 'Yes?'

'Hello, David.'

Hearing Spear's voice almost caused him to lose control of the wheel. The Corrado wobbled dangerously. He had to drop the phone to grab the wheel with both hands. When the car was steady, he picked up the phone again.

'Close one, David,' Spear said.

'Let me have them back. Please. I'll agree to *anything*. You'll never be bothered by us again, I promise.'

'It's unfortunate things can't be that way, David. But they can't.' A pause. 'Goodbye.'

The Porsche was slowing down in front of him. David squeezed the brake pedal. A tremendous blow made him drop the phone and wrenched his other hand from the wheel. The Corrado went into a skid. He span the steering wheel against the direction of the skid, got the car under control again. He glanced at the rear-view mirror. A car right behind him, a BMW with its lights off, inches away. Spear had followed him off the motorway, but he'd been too intent on the car in front to notice.

The BMW spurted forward again, catching the Corrado's rear on the left. The Corrado went into a 360 degree spin. When it came out of it, it was hurtling towards the

Porsche. David span the wheel again to avoid the car in front, then the Corrado was smashing through a wooden fence and bumping crazily between trees and he was ramming down on the brake pedal . . .

He felt the impact as the bonnet of the Corrado concertinaed against a tree. He shot forward. His head smacked into the windscreen, shattering it. The last thing he was conscious of was the sound of breaking glass . . .

The *whoomph!* of petrol catching fire awakened him. The stink of it was pungent in his nostrils. The pain in his head and chest was excruciating. He opened his eyes. He was in the driving seat of the Corrado. The windscreen was smashed and the steering wheel column had crumpled. Blood was seeping from his chest. Another *whoomph!* and a dazzle of light from behind.

Someone beside him; Lauris, head to one side, staring at him, her neck at a strange angle, her eyes open but dead, quite dead.

Heat blazing against the back of his head. Hair burning, crackling. He launched himself forward. The seatbelt tugged him back. He scrambled at the catch. As he did so, his hand brushed the ice-cold skin of Lauris's arm. He found the catch, released it. He lunged forward again, got half-way through the windscreen. Strength gone. His legs were burning. He made another lunge, tumbled onto the ground. He lay, wheezing, staring up at the branches of a tree directly above him. They were garish in the light from the burning car. His chest ached. Sparks spat over him, burning his face. He rolled over onto his knees. The explosion was seconds away. He could *feel* it, gathering right behind him. He surged up off the ground, lurched forward, staggering, and then the explosion came and he was lifted clean off the ground and he was flying through the darkness, shrieking . . .

CHAPTER EIGHTEEN

Plunging headlong, screaming, pain scything his body . . .

David half-swallowed a shout as he awoke from the nightmare. A Heathrow Airport security guard was staring at him from the other side of the Terminal 3 Arrivals Hall. David managed an apologetic smile. The guard turned and walked away.

Lauris is dead, Lauris is dead, Lauris . . .

He shook his head fiercely. Anna might be alive. *That's* what he had to concentrate on. He had to hold himself together long enough to tell James Lord what had happened. James would figure out how to get Anna back. Meanwhile he had to take all his pain and grief and exhaustion and scunch them up into a tight little ball and bury them deep inside himself. He had to keep going. *Had* to!

He stood up, swayed, made his way over to a newsstand, bought a paper. He skimmed the headlines, couldn't take them in. He glanced up at the arrivals' board clock. 8:10. James wasn't due to land for another ten minutes. It would take him at least half an hour to clear customs.

David's left leg almost gave way. He returned to his seat, flopped down on it.

His chest was badly bruised, but the wound had proved superficial. He had cleaned it up when he'd reached the motorway service area two hours after the explosion. He'd washed his face and hands vigorously and combed his hair. After that, he had looked no worse than someone who'd spent a rough night on the tiles. He had to wait an hour and a half at the service area before a lorry driver heading for London had agreed to give him a lift. David had fed him a cock-and-bull story about being drunk and getting into a fight at a party and his girlfriend losing her temper with him and stranding him on the way home.

The lorry driver had dropped him off at the Heathrow airport intersection. He'd bought a shirt and a pair of trousers at a twenty-four-hour shop. Apart from his singed hair, some bruises, and a cut on his face, he didn't look so bad. Inside, it felt as if someone had tied his guts in a tight knot. But he'd made it through the night, and soon James would be there to take over, Spear would be facing an adversary capable of defeating him, Anna would be back with him, and . . .

and Lauris is dead, Lauris is dead, Lauris . . .

The sob almost ripped his bruised chest apart. The guard was back, staring at him.

David got up, headed upstairs to the coffee shop, ordered a cup and found an empty table. He gulped the coffee down, and tried not to think about anything.

'Finished?'

He looked up. A bored-looking young black in a green uniform with a blaring transistor radio jammed in his top pocket was pointing at his cup.

'Yes, sure,' David said.

The record on the radio came to an end. DJ prattle followed. ' . . . funky *soul* sensation. I'll be back right after the news with a solid *soul* classic, Otis Redding and *I've Been Loving You Too Long*.' The waiter moved on, the voice on the radio grew fainter, but David kept himself tuned to it, pleased to have something to concentrate on.

'There's been an attempt on the life of James Lord, one of the leading figures in this year's American Presidential Election . . .'

Static on the radio. David wheeled round. The waiter was fiddling with the radio, trying to find another station.

David shouted 'No!' ran over and ripped the radio out of the waiter's pocket.

'Hey, man, what the fuck—'

'Shut up!' David growled, twisting the dial. He found the station again, rammed the radio against his ear.

' . . . last night, after a rally in Texas. Mr Lord's condition is said to be critical. Doctors are now operating to remove a bullet lodged near his heart. A security guard, Cliff Palmer, died after being shot at point blank range attempting to protect Mr Lord. Another guard was wounded in the attack, but his condition is described as satisfactory . . .'

David let the transistor drop from his hand onto the floor.

Spear knew, he thought. *Spear knew James Lord was coming here to save Anna. Spear arranged the shooting because of Anna.*

'Excuse me, sir.'

David blinked. The security guard had followed him up to the restaurant. The black waiter was standing behind him, scowling.

'He's going to kill us all,' David said. He felt his legs give way and he was lying on the floor. The linoleum felt cool against his cheek. Someone was trying to raise his head but he didn't want to remain awake any longer . . .

PART TWO

CHAPTER NINETEEN

The worst moment of all came when the police told him that Anna's body had been found in the wreckage of the car along with that of her mother. What remained of her was too charred for identification purposes, but her dental records left no room for doubt; it was Anna.

For many nights David sat and drank and contemplated revenge. Sometimes, he thought about killing himself. At first, he had to spend a lot of time with the police. He told them he had been taking Anna and Lauris away for a weekend break. They were driving around, looking for a country hotel. They had been forced off the road by an oncoming car. The Corrado had crashed, caught fire. He couldn't remember anything after that. He couldn't explain how he had got to Heathrow or what he was doing there. A doctor had examined him and diagnosed partial amnesia resulting from concussion and shock.

Initially, the detectives investigating the case had been aggressive. David's colleagues at work claimed he'd been behaving strangely for the past few weeks, and that his drinking had recently got out of hand. Had he been drunk the night of the accident? Had he run away from the scene so the police couldn't breathalyse him? Or had he deliberately murdered his wife and daughter and tried to make it look like an accident? Had he panicked afterwards and gone to Heathrow intending to flee the country?

Those two detectives had quickly been removed from the case. Their replacements had been friendlier, positively sympathetic.

Even in his befuddled state, David guessed that Spear had interfered to get the police to stop probing. He must have found out that David hadn't named him or Hughes, and had persuaded someone to throttle back on the investigation.

The inquest was brief, the verdict accidental death. That night David had moved out of his house, away from everything that reminded him of his family, into a service apartment near the office; bare, functional, featureless.

He watched the news every night in case there was any change in James Lord's condition. He microwaved Lean Cuisines when he remembered to eat. He began to drink his whisky neat, occasionally straight from the neck of the bottle. He listened to tapes of Robert Johnson and Hank Williams; their misery and pain seemed to make his own emotions easier to bear.

Calvin Scott attended Lauris and Anna's funeral at a crematorium near the river in Chiswick. Whitley Chamberlain turned up, together with Francesca. Some relatives and friends were there, but David barely noticed them.

Halfway through the ceremony, while a clergyman he had never met intoned platitudes about Anna and Lauris, David's red, tear-puffed eyes wandered over the wreaths resting against the coffins.

Richard Spear's name was on one of them.

David stepped forward from the front pew, shrugging off Calvin Scott's restraining hand. He picked up the wreath and tore it to shreds. The vicar ploughed on gamely. The members of the congregation, paralyzed by shock and embarrassment, stared at their own feet. When the wreath had been utterly destroyed, David fell to his knees and cried, his hands bleeding where wire and thorns had ripped them.

After the coffins had slid out of sight into the unseen flames beyond, Calvin Scott led David out of the church to a nearby section of the riverbank overlooking Eyot Island.

'What can I do for you, David?'

He waited a minute before replying.

'I have to get back to work, Calvin. Right away.'

'Be at the office tomorrow.'

For the next three months he worked harder than he ever had in his life, seven days a week, twelve, sometimes fourteen hours a day, volunteering for any and every story, trying to white out his mind so that he wouldn't have to think about his murdered family or Spear or anything.

When he got back to his apartment each night he poured himself one large Scotch which he could never finish before exhaustion overtook him. At first the nightmares which had poisoned his sleep since the murders continued to wake him every night, but after a few weeks of his new régime they grew less frequent. He would wake up at seven, catch the news on Radio 4, shower, walk the ten minutes to work and if there wasn't an assignment waiting for him, he'd demand one. If that didn't work, he'd cruise the wires till he found a story to sell to one of the editors. His new manic persona led people to avoid him; that was fine. He didn't want to talk to anyone about anything but work.

Whitley Chamberlain took him aside one night just as he was about to head for his apartment, and suggested he ease off, take a break.

'You're looking dreadful, man. You're going to fall apart if you keep this up.'

'Thanks, Whitley, but I'm fine. Really.'

'By the way, that Sorensen business. Did you ever get to the bottom of that?'

'It doesn't matter now.'

'I know, but—'

'See you around, Whitley.'

Two months after his return to work, there was a gathering of European Community ministers at No. 10 Downing Street. According to the press handout, the meeting was to discuss measures against the rising tide of drugs flooding the Continent. But in David Cauley's report, which had gone out at the start of the Nine O'Clock News, he had argued that the ministers would be spending most of their time discussing the future of the Soviet Union. The Soviet leader was still in intensive care ten weeks after the attempt on his life. There were three candidates for his job waiting in the wings. Two of them could be relied on to continue his policies of openness and democratization, but one, Piotr Marenkev, the leader of the Moscow Communist Party, recently appointed to the Politburo, was urging a return to hard-line Stalinism.

While David's original piece was going out the Ministers' meeting broke up, and a press statement was issued. Various new anti-drug measures had been agreed. In addition, the Ministers had sent a joint message of sympathy to the Soviet government, urging them to carry on their leader's work during his absence. The implication was plain – Europe didn't want Marenkev as the next leader. David's guess was that the Soviet people might feel the same way. There had already been spontaneous anti-Marenkev demonstrations in Red Square. The editor of the Nine had decided to return to Downing Street for a live two-way, with David answering questions put to him by the presenter, Whitley Chamberlain. David rehearsed a few phrases while the Outside Broadcast unit set up cameras and lights.

The lights came on two minutes before he was due on air. David screwed his earpiece in deep so he could listen to talkback from the studio gallery at Capital. He heard the assistant editor say he hoped David wasn't drunk, and was pleased to hear the editor defending him.

'Cauley hasn't touched a drop in weeks. Right now he's the best damned reporter we've got.'

David listened to the countdown, drew in his breath and tried to bulk out his shoulders. He'd lost a lot of weight recently and his suits tended to hang awkwardly. He stared into the camera, adjusted his tie, checked his flies, coughed, listened to Whitley introduce the item.

'Those Downing Street talks have just broken up. We're going over to our correspondent there, David Cauley, to hear what's happening . . . David, any positive results?'

'Yes, Whitley, it seems clear from a joint statement issued after the meeting that, as we expected, the ministers spent most of the time discussing events in the Soviet Union. They've urged the Soviet government not to abandon their leader's policies during his illness, and it's obvious . . .

They're dead. Anna and Lauris. Dead, dead, dead.

Whitley broke the silence. 'David, did the statement make any direct reference to Piotr Marenkev? You said in your piece earlier that the general feeling in Europe was he'd plunge the world back into a Cold War if he took over.'

. . . dead, gone. Alone. All alone. Dead . . .

'David . . .'

Suddenly, David was crying, just staring at the camera, not knowing where he was, tears rolling down his cheeks, unaware that his notes had slipped from his hand.

CHAPTER TWENTY

6 January 1993

'How are you feeling, David?'

'I feel better. Much better.'

It was true. There was a dreadful ache inside him that he guessed would always be there, and there were still occasional nightmares and unexpected tears, but his mental condition had improved markedly during his ten-week stay at Dr Elizabeth Iremonger's psychiatric clinic on the edge of Epping Forest.

Dr Iremonger smiled, and her fat hamsterlike face creased with dimples. Her smile was infectious and David returned it. She was brisk and down-to-earth and cheerful. As far as he was concerned, she had saved his sanity.

'Do you think you're well enough to leave us? Be honest, David.'

He gazed out the window at the Clinic's tree-lined grounds. It was peaceful here, soothing, and a part of him didn't want to leave at all. But he had to.

He looked back at the doctor. 'It's time I was on my way.'

She slapped his file shut, beamed. 'No more of this nonsense about Richard Spear then.' It was more of an order than a question.

'I've got that under control.'

He had been so helpless after his on-screen breakdown that he'd blurted out everything to the doctor. He had told her all about Spear and about how Lauris and Anna had really died. She hadn't believed him, of course. 'A paranoid fantasy created by your subconscious mind. You need someone to blame for your wife and daughter's deaths, because you can't accept them as cruel accidents.' Yes, it sounded right. He guessed if he'd been in Dr Iremonger's shoes he might have reached the same conclusion. At one stage, even he had developed doubts regarding Spear's involvement. He had begun to sound like those sad people who wrote letters in green ink to newsrooms the world over claiming that the CIA were bouncing poisonous rays at them off overhead satellites. But no sooner had his doubts emerged than he himself had received a letter that confirmed Spear as the monster he knew him to be.

Now, as he sat across the desk from the doctor, he touched the breast pocket of his jacket. He heard the airmail paper crackle inside: it was a reassuring sound.

'So, it's back to work right away?' the doctor asked, opening a desk drawer and dropping David's file inside.

'Do Capital actually want me back? What happened must have really embarrassed them.'

'No one blames you. You've seen all those sympathetic articles in the papers. Capital have received over a thousand letters from viewers wishing you well and wanting to see you back on the screen. Capital *want* you back. I had a talk with Calvin Scott about it just yesterday.'

'That's nice,' he said. 'But I might feel a bit like a freakshow exhibit if I returned immediately. I'd like to take a holiday first, just a couple of weeks.'

She pursed her lips. 'Is that really wise, David? Won't it lead to a lot of brooding?'

'You've taught me a lot, doctor. I've learned to accept that Lauris and Anna are dead and that there's nothing I can do about it. I've learned to be thankful for all the good years we had together.'

'Will you return to your house?'

'Not at once. In a month or so, maybe. I'll know when I'm ready for it. Right now, I'm not.'

She opened her mouth to say something, changed her mind.

'That's fine, David. You go on holiday, contact me as soon as you get back. I'll tell Capital you'll be ready to return to work in two weeks' time.'

She stood up, and David followed suit. She walked round the desk and they shook hands.

'Thank you, doctor. You've been wonderful.'

'So have you. When I first saw you six weeks ago, I never suspected you'd come this far this quickly.' She walked him to the door, opened it. 'Where are you thinking of holidaying?'

'I haven't decided yet,' he lied.

'Send me a postcard.'

'Will do.' He wouldn't. She'd guess what he was up to; he'd told her all about Sammy Moss. He bent down, kissed her cheek, then walked quickly along the corridor to reception. He collected his suitcase at the desk and walked into an overcast winter morning.

A newspool Corrado was waiting for him out front, keys in the ignition, courtesy of Capital. He appreciated the gesture, but would have preferred another make of car. He slipped behind the wheel, turned the key in the ignition. For a split second, out the corner of his eye, he saw Lauris in the seat beside him, neck twisted, staring at him. He blinked; the image vanished.

Dr Iremonger had helped him to face his tragedy; she had taught him to grieve properly. But it was the letter in his pocket that had given him a reason for living.

He had to become St George. He had to destroy the Dragon.

All he needed was the right weapon.

He mashed his foot down on the accelerator. The car shrieked away from the clinic, tyres spurting gravel.

CHAPTER TWENTY-ONE

The colours were all wrong. The sea was yellow; the dense wall of exotic, unfamiliar trees forming a backdrop to the beach was a dark, jungly green; most disconcerting of all, the sand was as black as night.

David extracted a packet of cigarettes from his safari jacket, lit one. He slid sunglasses over his eyes to blank out the weird colours. Now, Cheoc Van Beach looked like most any other beach, except for the sampans gliding across the South China Sea between the southernmost tip of the colony of Macao and the Chinese mainland half a mile away.

Anna would have loved it.

He made his way down to the water, threading his way between European businessmen and their wives, all glistening with suntan oil. He removed his blue canvas espadrilles and let the muddy water lap over his sore feet. The seventeen-hour flight to Hong Kong had left him jetlagged; the change from an English winter to an oriental city with an atmosphere like a sauna had added to his exhaustion. One ragged night's sleep in The Peninsula Hotel on Kowloon's Golden Mile hadn't helped much.

A series of cryptic calls from Sammy Moss followed by a note pushed under his door in the middle of the night had led to him taking the fifty-minute hydrofoil trip to the island of Macao that morning. He'd lunched off baked seacod and cheese at a Portuguese restaurant in town, then hired a Mini-moke and driven to Coloane, one of the three islands that formed the colony. Sammy Moss was an hour late, and David was starting to get nervous. Had Spear got wind of their meeting? Was Sammy still alive? If he was, was he really working for Spear? Was this all some plot to get rid of David?

He shook his head, managed a tired grin. If Spear had wanted to kill him, he could have arranged it more easily back in London.

Two chubby little American boys ran screaming into the water right in front of him.

He took the note he had received from Sammy out of his pocket, read it again. 'Cheoc Van Beach, 100 yds east of the Pousade de Coloane, 5pm today.' He folded the note, put it away. There was the Pousade, a Portuguese hotel with a beachfront restaurant and bar, a short way along the shore, its suntrap patio littered with boiled holidaymakers sipping beer and munching tapas. He was in the right place, so where the hell was . . .

Maybe Sammy didn't write the note!

No sooner did the thought enter his head than he heard Sammy say, 'Hello, David.'

Sammy looked years older than when they'd last met the previous summer. His body had ballooned in the interim; he'd gained at least thirty pounds, maybe more. His new gut was straining against his loud beach shirt, and David couldn't help staring at it.

'At least one of us has lost weight,' Sammy said, not smiling. His eyes had once glittered with excitement and suspicion; there was something dead about them now. 'Food comforts me,' he added defensively.

'You're late. I was worried,' David said.

'I've been watching from the trees for an hour. I don't want anyone getting hold of this.' He tapped a bulging package clamped under one arm. 'Let's get a drink.' He reached into a pocket, brought out a tube of mints, tossed three in his mouth.

They headed up to the hotel in silence, found a table on the patio. Sammy ordered a bottle of Portuguese white wine, and three p...tes of tapas.

'Why did we have to meet here?' David asked.

'I have a lover on the island. These days I have to take it where I can find it. There aren't too many gay Chinese.' He looked around the patio. 'He's a nice young man. I help him out.'

The wine and food arrived. David decided to allow himself a glass. It was delicious. Sammy went at the chunks of spicy sausage as if he hadn't eaten in a week.

'What made you change your mind about helping me?'

David said when he'd finished his glass of wine. He fought back the temptation to pour himself another.

'I heard about your wife and daughter.' Sammy wiped his greasy hands on a paper napkin, sat back in his chair, belched. 'It wasn't an accident, was it?'

David shook his head.

'Why aren't you dead?' Sammy asked.

'Luck, I suppose.'

'Yeah, luck. Same sort I had.' He paused, scanned the patio once more. 'I think about Rui every day. Poor bastard.' He looked at David. 'He was the one, you know. The one who would have made me happy.' He leaned forward, pulled the last plate of tapas onto his stomach and started shovelling the food into his mouth.

'Why aren't *you* dead?' David asked.

Sammy slid the empty plate back on the table, wiped his beard. 'I've kept my head down. I've spent the past few months tiptoeing around in the shadow of the Beast, trying to keep downwind. I *hope* he's forgotten about me.' Trembling blobs of viscous sweat were rolling down his puffy face. He jerked his head round suddenly, looked behind him.

'There's no one watching us,' David said. Sammy's behaviour was making him jumpy.

'You wouldn't be able to tell,' Sammy said dismissively.

David reached forward and tapped the package on the table.

'Will this help me nail Spear?'

'If you can get someone to use the material. It'd have to be radio or TV. Publishing anything takes too long – Spear'd get wind of it. TV News would be a good bet. No one knows what's on the running order till the last minute. All you need is for one editor to agree to it. There'll be you, the programme editor and a picture editor involved – no one else need know.'

'What do I put in the piece?'

Sammy clicked his fingers at a waiter, ordered another bottle of Bucelas and more tapas. The patio was beginning to thin out as people strolled into the hotel to prepare for dinner.

160

Sammy raised a hand and pointed across at China, where the sun was setting.

'There's a powerful Communist Party cadre over there, called Hung Xiang, a member of the Standing Committee of their Politburo. He's one of the top contenders for Hua Xianyi's old job, but he isn't exactly in Hua's mould. He's a throwback to the days of Chairman Mao. Whenever Mao felt power slipping away he'd instigate some lunatic revolutionary crusade. The Great Leap Forward in the early sixties almost destroyed the country's agriculture and industry. The Cultural Revolution in '68 wiped out the intelligensia, destroyed education. Hung Xiang's planning another Cultural Revolution, only he wants it on an even bigger scale than the original. He believes Western capitalist influences must be purged from the system, and the only way to achieve that is through mob rule and mass murder. He thinks the student demonstrations in '89 justified his stance. It'll be Pol Pot and Cambodia all over again, only the total population of Cambodia was eight million. The population of China's over a thousand million. Next to this boy, Mao was a moderate.'

'What's that got to do with Spear?'

'The Dragon Man's been channelling funds to Hung for years, funds that have allowed him to stockpile weapons, set up a private army, and buy influence inside the armed forces and the rest of the central government. Spear's money has virtually guaranteed Hung getting into power.'

'Why would Spear do that? Does he expect business favours from Hung after he takes over?'

'There isn't going to *be* any business in China when Hung gets control. He doesn't believe in it. And if he's in charge when the People's Republic of China takes over Hong Kong and Macao in '97, God help all of us!'

'Do you have real proof that Spear's given Hung money?'

'It's all in the dossier. Cheques and bank statements showing where the money came from – mostly Spear's businesses in Hong Kong and Korea – and where it went to, namely Hung personally, or contacts of his.'

They were the only customers left on the patio. The sun was sinking fast. Sammy scooped up what was left on the tapas plate. 'It's all in there. Use it, David, but keep my name out of it. My life isn't that great, but it's the only one I've got.' Sammy stood up, wheezing. 'Remember when you used to think I was paranoid?' He gave a quick smile. 'Welcome to the club.' He turned, walked a few yards, halted. 'Nail that bastard, David. For all our sakes. I meant what I said in my letter – he is, without doubt, the most dangerous sonofabitch in the world.'

As Sammy Moss descended the steps leading to the beach, the sun disappeared behind China. The world was suddenly cold, and David shivered.

It took him an hour just to skim the dossier. Fat bugs thwacked against his face as he sat in a pool of light coming from the window of the hotel restaurant. Once, he looked up to see a face silhouetted above the rim of the patio. It disappeared instantly; he wasn't sure if he'd really seen it.

When he'd got to the end of the dossier, he felt sick with excitement and dread. The sheer *scale* of Spear's operations defied comprehension. How in God's name was he going to get anyone to believe it all, to believe *any* of it?

When he stood up, he found that his limbs were shaking. His left leg was aching. It hadn't done that in a while. He suddenly felt scared and alone out there in the darkness. It felt as if someone was watching him, as if the very eyes of the Dragon Man were on him. Clutching the dossier against his chest, he headed into the hotel, found the bar. He had renounced hard liquor, but right now he needed a stiff drink. It felt as if an iron hand was squeezing his heart. He ordered a large bargaço, gulped the white spirit down in one. The petrolly liquid blasted his stomach, sent waves of warmth back up through his body.

He looked around the bar to make sure he wasn't being observed, then left the hotel and headed across the patio.

He was half-way down the steps leading to the illuminated beachside carpark when he noticed three Chinese boys goofing around inside his Mini-moke. They were about eleven or twelve and raggedly dressed. One of them was sitting in the driver's seat fiddling with the ignition key.

David yelled, 'Hey, cut that out!'

162

The children saw him, giggled. The engine came on.

David opened his mouth to shout again. His cry was swallowed by an explosion that ripped the car apart. When he came to, he was lying at the bottom of the steps. He shook his head, blinked. The car wasn't there any more. He put out a hand to push himself up, touched something warm. He looked down. A tiny, slim, delicate hand. A child's hand. David gagged.

Shouts above him, faces at the hotel's windows, people running across the patio.

He scuffed the severed hand aside, began searching frantically for the dossier. It was lodged in a thorny bush alongside the steps. He grabbed it, grazing his hands in the process. People were running down the steps. He let them pass, then began to skirt the perimeter of the car park. Debris from the Moke had been scattered hundreds of yards. There was a crater where it had stood. Smoke and flames swirled in the cauldron-like hole. Other cars had been damaged in the blast. One of them was on fire and the owner was leaping around it, screaming for a fire extinguisher.

David headed for the trees behind the beach. He couldn't afford to get mixed up with the police. They'd hold him here in Macao, and he'd be a sitting duck for Spear. He had to get the dossier back to England. Nothing else mattered.

The vegetation was dense. He had to move slowly, feeling in front of him with one hand. An animal brushed against his legs – something low and heavy with metal-hard scales – and he yelled. Razor sharp leaves sliced into his upper arm. A giant moth fluttered against his face. He lashed at it, cursing, almost dropped the dossier.

Ten minutes passed, twenty. He began to wonder if he was ever going out of there. His nostrils were full of the lush, corrupt stench of rotting vegetation. He stopped to vomit up the bargaço he'd had at the bar. He tried not to think about the child's hand he had touched. The dossier was all that mattered, the *only* thing, because with it he could destroy the monster, cleanse the world . . .

Suddenly he was on a two-lane tarmac road. It had to be

the main road leading back to Macao. He had no idea which direction to take. He paused, tried to get his breath back. Something moved inside his shirt. He pulled it up. An enormous furry spider was clamped to his chest. It's body was at least three inches across. David froze. The spider raised one of its front legs, delicately explored David's chest hair, set it down and scuttled swiftly up towards his chin, all its legs rippling.

David shrieked, beat it off. The spider landed on its back. Its legs waved madly and it managed to right itself. Instantly, it raced towards him. As it touched his foot, David jumped back. He raised the package above his head, smashed it down on the still-moving spider, hammering it flat. Without much caring where he was headed, he set off down the road, skin crawling.

He had gone about a hundred yards when he saw the car, half hidden by bushes at the side of the road. The engine was still running, but the lights were off. The nearside door was open. He approached it warily, wishing he had some kind of torch.

Sammy Moss was lying across the front seat on his back. His mouth was wide open in a silent scream and his eyes were staring in horror up through the windscreen. Below his bloated stomach there was a gory black mess. Blood was still oozing down his legs. His genitals had been ripped away.

David placed the dossier on the roof of the car, closed his eyes, reached in and grabbed Sammy Moss's shirt-front. He heaved the corpse out of the car. Sammy's hot blood soaked his trousers. He lugged the corpse round the side of the car and rolled it into the foliage beside the road.

Don't think don't think don't think . . .

He retrieved the dossier and slid behind the wheel of the car. He pulled the door closed and reversed out onto the deserted road.

Don't think don't . . .

He switched on the lights and drove away.

Two police cars passed him at speed, blaring their horns to make him shift over. If they were on their way to the

164

Pousade, it meant he was heading in the wrong direction. He did a U-turn.

He reached down and felt the package next to him. It was sticky with the innards of the spider he'd killed.

Sammy and he had both lived in the shadow of the Beast for too long. For Sammy, it was too late. For David, it was time to step out into the light.

CHAPTER TWENTY-TWO

David's finger hovered over the front doorbell for two minutes before he could bring himself to push it. While he waited for a response he took deep breaths and tried to calm himself. He had to appear as rational and self-possessed as possible. He rang the bell again. A light went on two floors above him.

He checked the road. The suburban street was silent. The mock-Tudor houses lining it were all dark. The cars and the bare trees were covered in frost, and David's breath formed twisted steam phantoms.

As far as he could tell, he had not been followed since leaving Macao, but as Sammy had pointed out, how would he know? Spear's people would have found out by now that the attempt to kill him had failed. They'd know he'd flown back to London, but he hoped they hadn't managed to trace him to the anonymous seedy hotel off Bedford Square he'd checked into under the name 'David St George'.

He heard a chain being slid back, turned. The door opened. Calvin Scott peered at him through red rimmed eyes.

'By Christ, this had better be good, Cauley!'

'It is.'

'Who is it?' a woman's voice called down.

'Don't worry dear, it's someone from the office. I'll be up in a wee while.' Scott ushered David inside with an irritated gesture, then led him into an immaculate sitting room furnished in a cloyingly twee style. A glass-fronted cabinet housed holiday mementoes, including a straw pony with a sombrero on its head.

'No, it's not my taste either,' Scott said, noting the object of David's attention. 'Sit down there. What time is it anyway?'

'Just after three.'

'Oh God!' Scott ran a hand through his mussed hair and retied the cord on his dressing gown. 'A drink?'

David shook his head.

'Well I'm bloody having one.' He went to a drinks cabinet and poured brandy from a decanter. He sat down opposite David. 'Speak!'

David cleared his throat. 'I'm about to hand you the biggest news scoop you've ever had. Correction. That *anyone* ever had.' He paused, lit a cigarette. 'Now, not everyone would agree, of course, but I reckon life improved for a lot of people in the eighties.'

'I'm already not believing this conversation, Cauley.'

'Bear with me, Calvin.' He paused. 'I might have that drink after all.'

'Get it yourself.'

David went over to the trolley, poured himself a brandy. This was going even more badly than he had anticipated. He could have done as Sammy had suggested and try to slip the item about Spear on the air without Calvin Scott knowing in advance. But there was a strong chance Scott would simply deny the validity of the story afterwards, citing David's mental condition as a reason for dissociating Capital from his allegations. Getting the managing editor on his side now would add immeasurable weight to the case against the Dragon Man later on. Scott had revealed himself as an admirer of Spear, but he was too good a news man to pass up the opportunity to break as red hot a story as this.

David sipped his brandy, took it back to his chair.

'The Soviet Union started to loosen up, things seemed to get better in China for a while, the Middle East got rid of Ayatollah Khomeini, and the Americans went some way towards clipping Gaddafi's wings when they bombed

Libya back in '86. The Iran-Iraq war ended. The Russians got out of Afghanistan.'

'Thank you for the history lesson.'

'Despite setbacks, things are generally still improving. There are fewer nuclear and chemical weapons than there used to be. The States has stopped fooling around in Central America. India got a ruler more interested in getting the people fed than striking political poses. Israel and the PLO are heading towards an agreement. Africa's still an unholy mess, but the new South African government's trying to reach an accommodation with the ANC on power-sharing. There's hardly a dictator left in South America. What it all boils down to is that fewer people live under tyrants than they did ten, fifteen years ago. There aren't as many fanatics around as there used to be, and, as a result, I'd guess, there's less misery.'

Calvin Scott swallowed the rest of his brandy, banged the goblet down on the coffee table in front of him.

'All right,' he snapped. 'I've had enough of your Mickey Mouse analysis of world affairs.'

David stubbed out his cigarette. He wasn't going to be deflected. 'The fanatics are on the way back. That's obvious. In the Soviet Union Marenkev's beginning to look like the next leader. The old order there hasn't liked the recent changes. They want things to be like they were. In China, the man most likely to wind up on top is Hung Xiang – a real maniac, by the sound of it. In Iran the position of the Head of State is being threatened by an out-and-out Khomeini-ite, Ayatollah Hossein Kashami, who doubles up as the Minister of Justice and Minister of the Islamic Revolutionary Guards Corps. He's about as fundamentalist as you can get, the kind who thinks you should have your finger chopped off for picking your nose. He wants to give more power to the Revolutionary Guards, which'll mean more terrorism and kidnapping, and, eventually, have the Islamic nations band together to declare a Holy War against the United States. Not good news. And there's—'

'Get to the bloody point!'

David nodded. 'All right. The point is that the fanatics,

the hard-liners who're going to bring misery to millions of people, and death to millions more, are all being funded by one man.'

'Richard Spear,' said Calvin Scott.

A brief silence broken by a clock chiming in the hallway.

Calvin Scott got up and poured himself another drink. When he turned towards David, there was a sad smile on his face.

'"David cannot face the fact that his wife and daughter perished accidentally. *Someone* must be responsible. For David, that someone is Richard Spear, whom his imagination has transformed into the Devil Incarnate."' Scott walked back to his chair, perched on the arm. 'That's a direct quote from Dr Iremonger's report on you. I'm disappointed in her. She said you were cured. Quite obviously, you aren't.'

David reached into his jacket and took out the letter he'd received at Dr Iremonger's clinic. He handed it to Scott.

'That's a letter from Sammy Moss. You remember? He's the journalist whose boyfriend was murdered, the one who was writing a book about Spear.'

'I remember him.' Scott opened up the letter.

'You'll notice a phrase in there. "The most dangerous man in the world". If I'm suffering paranoid delusions about Spear, then I'm not the only one.'

Scott refolded the letter, handed it back without comment.'

'I've just returned from Hong Kong, where Sammy Moss gave me irrefutable proof of Spear's involvement with these fanatics.'

'Why isn't Moss with you?'

'Sammy's dead. He was murdered the day before yesterday, after talking to me. Someone acting on behalf of Richard Spear tore away Sammy's private parts. I found his body just after a bomb destroyed the car I was about to drive off in. The explosion killed three little Chinese boys. I doubt that'll worry Spear too much. After all, he killed my wife and my daughter. He's not an oversentimental man.'

'Why should Spear want you dead?'

'He knows I'm after him. Sammy died because the information he gave me was dynamite. Used right, it'll destroy Spear.'

Scott got up, went to the window, twitched back the curtain.

'Cold night,' he said. 'Dr Iremonger said you believed Spear had mysterious telepathic powers. You were convinced your daughter had them as well. Do you still believe that?'

'I don't want to get into that, Calvin. It's irrelevant to Spear's political activities. All I'll say in support of that theory is that you wound up giving me a correspondent's job despite the fact that you had little respect for my work.'

'Just prior to your breakdown, your work was excellent.'

'But before you appointed me as a correspondent, I was lousy. We both know that. Spear *made* you give me the job.'

'Okay, let's leave that aside.' Scott let go of the curtain, turned, frowning. 'Where's this proof Moss is supposed to have given you?'

David reached in his briefcase, extracted a large brown envelope bound with sellotape, and placed it on the table. 'It's all in here, Calvin.'

Scott stared at the package. 'Is that the only copy?'

'No.' David leaned forward, opened the package and removed its contents. 'There's about 350 pages here. It'll take you a while to get through.'

Scott walked around the table, his eyes on the dossier, keeping his distance from it. 'And if I believe what I read?'

David clicked his briefcase shut, stood up. 'We'll do an item on the news tonight, consisting of a five minute VT package and a live ten minute studio spot. That should give me enough time to tell at least some of the story. I'll stick to what's in the dossier – I won't mention my family or Sammy Moss. I've already written a draft script. It's there with the dossier.'

Scott was staring at him. David met his gaze. 'Will you read it?'

Scott sucked air in through his nostrils, eventually nodded.

'Call me when you've made a decision,' David said. 'I'm at the Belvedere Hotel. It's listed in the phone book. Ask for Room 83.' He walked to the door, opened it. 'If you decide not to run the item it goes to the opposition. Understood?'

'Understood.' Scott's voice was quiet.

'If you contact Richard Spear, you'll be signing my death warrant, Calvin. It's up to you.'

David closed the front door of the house on the way out, leaned back against it. He had no idea whether he'd been convincing, but at least he'd started the ball rolling.

Now, at last, he could get some sleep.

Calvin Scott stood in the centre of the sitting room for a full ten minutes, staring at the document on the table.

'Calvin?' he heard his wife call down.

His face spasmed with irritation. 'Go to sleep!'

He walked to the phone, lifted the receiver, paused.

'Damn!' he muttered. He tapped out a number with savage stabs of his index finger.

'This is Calvin Scott . . . I know it's late. Later than you think.'

CHAPTER TWENTY-THREE

When David awakened he was lying in bed on his side, facing a wall covered with dirty flock paper. Traffic sounds from outside. Drizzly grey light.

And the realization that his wife and daughter were dead. It came every morning, a few seconds after waking up.

He lay very still and closed his eyes, tried to plunge back into sleep, but it was no use. He had dreamt about them during the night. For once it had been a happy dream, no horror. More of an extended memory than a dream; the memory of a day at their cottage in Wiltshire, a day in August when the sun had shone, and warm breezes had stirred the trees fringing their garden. He and Lauris had made gentle love in the afternoon after lunching on lobster and chablis at a local restaurant. Lying in bed, they'd heard laughter from the garden and gone outside to find Anna, five-years-old, in ecstasy, surrounded by wild geese.

'David,' Lauris had gasped. 'Geese can attack children!'

'She seems to have them under control.'

Anna was whirling round and round, laughing, the sun flashing like gold in her auburn hair. Reassured, Lauris had put her arm around David's waist and squeezed him and he'd looked down to see tears of sheer pleasure in her eyes. He'd kissed her, and then gone whooping in amongst the cackling geese to scoop Anna up in his arms, feeling her happiness exploding inside him . . .

It had proved harder to bear than the dreams of death and horror, for now he had to face afresh the fact that they were dead, and that there would be no more golden days.

He tried to blot the thought from his mind. Today was the day for revenge. Today was the day he would slay the dragon.

He yawned, turned over.

And saw Richard Spear sitting on a chair in the far corner of the dingy hotel room. He was reading the original copy of Sammy Moss's dossier by the dim light coming through the window.

Spear lifted his eyes from the document.

'Entertaining,' he said.

'Accurate?' David asked, finding it hard to speak. The moisture was suddenly gone from his mouth.

'Remarkably.' Spear placed the document on a small coffee table beside his chair. 'Sammy Moss always was a gifted journalist.' Spear reached behind him, slid the curtains further open. 'Of course, no one will believe a word of it, let alone use it.'

David sat up, swung his legs out the side of the bed.

171

'You'll be finished by this evening, Spear. If I were you, I'd start running now.'

'You're not the Marshal and this isn't Tombstone.' He reached up a hand to smooth his immaculate hair. 'If you think my dear old friend Calvin Scott is going to blow the whistle on me, you're mistaken. Very close, Calvin and I. Have been for a long time. He phoned me just after you left that depressing bourgeois home of his. He's very worried about you, David. He thinks you're destroying yourself with this lunatic crusade against me. He wants to save you from yourself.'

A hoover started up in the corridor outside. A couple in the next room began to argue. French by the sound of it. David thought about shouting to attract attention, decided against it. Spear would convince anyone who came to investigate that everything was just fine.

'I don't need Calvin Scott. Capital isn't the only TV company. I've sent copies of that document to every radio and television station and newspaper in London.'

'No you haven't. They'd have tried to contact me by now for a reaction. Besides, no one would use that material without checking you out. The last time you had any publicity was when you cracked up on national television. Why should anyone believe a word you said?' Spear stood up. 'There are only two dossiers in existence. Calvin Scott has one. The other's here with us, and *it* won't be going anywhere.'

'How can you be so sure?'

'Because you're going to die.'

Outside, the hoovering stopped. A door slammed in the next room. Silence.

'Calvin Scott will know you did it. He'll come after you.'

'Calvin does what I tell him to. He believes in me. Calvin's a committed hardline Marxist. Has been all his life. He's convinced I share his ideals. I've assured him my goal is to achieve a world government based on the principles of Marxism–Leninism.' He paused to let that information sink in. 'Besides, how do you imagine I found out about Anna? Calvin phoned me right after she almost

172

killed him in the newsroom. He knew I'd spent years looking for someone like her.' Spear shrugged. 'David, it's time to die.'

Yes, David thought. *Maybe it is.*

'Anna. Lauris. Why did you kill them? At least tell me that.'

Spear shook his head. 'Even Calvin Scott doesn't know the reason for that. Only myself and Sorensen.' He wiped one hand along the top of the small drinks fridge. There was a bottle of Scotch on top. It hadn't been there when David had gone to sleep. Spear examined the dirt on his hand, slapped it off. 'Let's just say they had to die for the good of the cause.'

David jumped up from the bed, grabbed hold of the bedside table, hoisted it one handed above his head. He ran, naked, towards Spear, intent on smashing his brains out . . .

He halted suddenly, puzzled to find himself in the middle of a hotel room holding a table. He let it drop, lowered his arms.

'Listen to me, Cauley,' Spear said. 'You've lost your wife and child. Calvin Scott isn't likely to give you back your job now, not after last night's performance. You're mentally ill. That's obvious from all your wild delusions concerning me – I'm supposed to have killed your family, I'm supposed to be taking over the world, God knows what else. It's all very sad.'

David was only vaguely aware of Spear's words. His whole being was enveloped by a black, freezing fog of grief and hopelessness. All at once, everything seemed meaningless. He experienced a deep desire not to exist.

'No one would blame you, Cauley.' Spear's voice was a distant murmur. 'No one would blame you for killing yourself.'

Then Spear was handing him something. He took it, barely able to summon the energy to grip the object. He looked down at it. The bottle of whisky.

'The bathroom,' Spear said.

David walked across the hotel bedroom on leaden legs, entered the bathroom.

Spear was behind him. 'The cabinet,' he said.

David pulled the cabinet door open. Bottles of pills; tranquilizers, narcotics, painkillers.'

'They'll do the job, Cauley. They'll release you.'

David placed the whisky bottle in the washbasin, opened one of the pill bottles and tipped the contents into his mouth. He stood for a while, head back, mouth full of pills, not knowing what to do next.

'The whisky,' he heard. 'Drink some.'

David picked up the bottle, twisted the cap. It seemed to take forever to get it off. He poured whisky into his mouth, swallowed.

No! No! No!

Another voice, so far away, so far . . . He looked around to see where it was coming from, but there was no one there except Spear, standing by the bathroom door.

'It's for the best,' Spear said.

Spear had to help him get the cap off the second pill bottle. He tipped the contents into David's palm. David drank more whisky to wash the pills down. All the while the bleakness was growing inside him. The voice screaming at him in the distance grew fainter. More pills, more whisky. Unable to stand any longer, he sagged onto his knees and slumped gratefully against the base of the bath. He lay there, legs splayed, staring up at the ceiling, wanting everything to be over.

Suddenly, the fog dispersed. He realized what he'd done.

Spear was staring dispassionately down at him.

'Yes, that's right, Cauley. You're dying.' The singsong, soothing quality had left his voice. 'It shouldn't take more than half an hour. You'll be unconscious long before that. Count yourself lucky you're not Rui Olazabal. He took hours to die.'

The room was spinning now. It was like being at sea in a rough storm. His stomach lurched.

He tried to move, to get up, imagined himself rising to his feet, but when he managed to focus his eyes for a few seconds, he found that he was lying on his front, staring at the floor, a strand of drool hanging from the corner of his mouth.

All over . . .

But still there was Spear's voice.

'. . . daughter, David. Before you go, I must tell you something amusing about Anna . . . may surprise you . . .'

Oblivion.

Then he was awake, and the world was lurching beneath him.

God I feel so godawful. Can't feel this bad. Not possible. Nobody can feel this bad and be . . .

Alive. Yes, he was alive. Sort of.

Someone was puking, making a spectacular racket. Could that be him? More retching. Yes, it was him all right.

He opened his eyes. Lavatory bowl. That made sense. He closed them, didn't want to look. Someone punched his stomach. He opened his eyes again, saw slim hands gripped over his belly. Someone holding him from behind. A woman. He could detect scent in amongst the whisky stench. The delicate-looking hands punched inwards just below his ribcage and he was vomiting again.

'Hey!' he managed to slur out.

'More!' a voice said. The accent sounded American.

'No!' he tried to say, but she punched inwards at his stomach once more and he was gagging. Nothing came up.

'No more!' he said, quite clearly.

'Okay,' he heard, and then he was drifting back into unconsciousness, feeling bad, but so *pleased* to be alive.

Hospital. He recognized the smell at once.

A small, clean private room. Grey light was squeezing between the slats of a Venetian blind. He was lying on top of the bedclothes, dressed in a white gown tied at the back. There was a white plastic name tag on his wrist and a butterfly feed taped to the crook of his elbow. The tube in his arm was attached to an IV unit standing by the side of his bed.

He did not feel good. Blinding headache, nausea, and

ribs that felt as if they'd been used as a punch-bag.

He remembered Spear being in his hotel room, and swallowing whisky and pills and waking up to find someone holding him over the lavatory, making him throw up. Then there had been a stretcher and an ambulance and nurses and a tube being forced down his throat and his stomach roiling.

His throat felt as if it had been sandpapered.

He moved gingerly into a sitting position. There was a plastic bell-push affair dangling from the wall beside the bed. He pressed it.

After a minute, a young nurse with a pretty oval face entered the room. A stray lock of blonde hair hung down over her forehead. Without saying anything, she took his pulse, checked the pupils of his eyes, and lifted the strip of tape to make sure the butterfly feed was still in place.

'How did I get here?' David asked.

'Ambulance,' she said, making notes on a chart hanging from the end of the bed.

'Who called the ambulance?' His voice was a rasping whisper.

'If you want conversation, I'll fetch the doctor.'

She returned after two minutes in the company of a tired-looking young man with thinning sandy hair. He went straight to the foot of the bed and unclipped David's chart.

'You seem to be over the worst of it. We'll keep you in for a day or two. You'll be on liquids till tomorrow morning. A psychiatrist will be along to see you later. No doubt you'll also be receiving a visit from a representative of some well-meaning Christian organization.' The doctor clipped the chart back in place, looked at David for the first time. His eyes were hard, angry. 'Luckily I don't have to worry about your mind or your soul. My job's to get you out of here as soon as possible.' He withdrew a pen from his breast pocket. The nurse was staring glumly at David.

'Why are you treating me this way?' David asked.

'We have five year-old children dying of leukaemia in this hospital, Mr Cauley. Two young men on the critical list, stabbed because they walked down the wrong street last night. Old women beaten to a pulp in their own homes for the sake of five pounds. As far as I'm concerned, people like you are a waste of time.'

'Thanks,' David said. 'You're obviously a deeply sympathetic person.'

'The quicker you give me some details about yourself, the quicker I'll be able to get back to helping genuinely sick people.'

'I'll co-operate if you'll agree to return my clothes.'

'You're not allowed to leave here till the police have interviewed you.'

'I thought you were anxious to get rid of me.' David decided to stop needling the doctor. Spear would know he was still alive and which hospital he'd been taken to; undoubtedly he'd be planning another attempt on his life. 'Look,' David went on, 'I didn't say anything about leaving. I just want my wallet. I'm worried about some things in it. My cheque book, some credit cards.'

The doctor studied him for a few moments.

'Nurse, are the patient's things here?'

'They must be,' David said. 'Or you wouldn't know my name. I was booked in under an alias at the hotel.'

The doctor and nurse exchanged glances.

'I can hardly dress up in my wallet, can I?' David said.

'All right,' the doctor said. 'Now, let's get this over with.'

The questions took a few minutes. The doctor and the nurse left. The nurse reappeared a short while later and handed him his wallet.

She stood by the bed for a few moments, staring down at her feet.

'Do you want something?' David asked.

'I . . . I didn't realize who you were. When you were answering the doctor's questions I remembered the story about your family dying. I saw you on TV the night you . . . Well, you know what I mean. I'm sorry.'

She turned and quickly left the room.

He checked the contents of the wallet. All there. Now all he needed were some clothes. He got up off the bed, and, wincing, holding his aching ribs, tried to make it over to the window. He'd forgotten about the IV unit attached to his arm, and had to lunge to stop the apparatus crashing to the floor. He felt so dizzy he had to sit down on the edge of the bed for several minutes.

He took a gulp of water to ease his raw throat, unplugged the IV tube from the butterfly feed in his arm, and just made it over to the window.

He was on the fourth floor of a Victorian hospital. He recognized Praed Street below him. They'd brought him to St Mary's, Paddington. He was in one of the rooms in the Isolation Unit, where they kept infectious disease cases and anyone requiring police supervision – IRA informers, criminal supergrasses, ministers of the realm, people like that. David wondered what he was doing in one of the private rooms. Had Spear somehow fixed it?

Below, the road was jammed with cars and the grey sky was darkening into twilight. It was about five o'clock. He'd been in the hospital for approximately eight hours, plenty of time for Spear to arrange a transfer from a public ward.

A red Porsche slewed to a halt by the kerb beneath him. The driver got out and approached the hospital's side entrance.

Vercoe.

CHAPTER TWENTY-FOUR

David hobbled towards the door, but was too woozy to make it all the way. He had to grab hold of the end rail of his bed for support. His mind was perfectly clear, but his legs were like jelly and his ribs were screaming with pain. He considered summoning the doctor, decided there wasn't enough time for that. He scanned the room. His only hope would be to surprise Vercoe, attack first. The one object he might have the strength to lift was a portable aluminium bedpan near the door. He staggered over to it, picked it up. It was light, maybe too light to do any real damage.

He took up a position behind the door, waited, praying his legs would stand the strain.

Thirty seconds later, the door started to open. A pause. David felt his knees giving way. The door opened further. A metallic clanking sound. He saw an instrument trolley edge its way around the door. Vercoe was masquerading as a hospital worker.

David raised the bedpan as high as he could. A head appeared. He swung the bedpan. It made a dull thunk as it crashed against the intruder's skull.

His victim let out a groan and sprawled onto the floor. It wasn't Vercoe. It was David's nurse.

He just had time to grunt in surprise before the door opened again. Vercoe stepped into the room. He drew a short-barrelled Colt .38 Detective Special from a speed holster under his right arm.

He closed the door behind him, glanced at the nurse on the floor, grinned.

'Whoops!' he said.

He flipped his gun up in the air, caught it by the barrel.

'Time for your medicine, Mr Cauley.'

David was still holding the dented bedpan. He tried to lift it again as Vercoe moved towards him, but didn't have enough strength left. Vercoe raised his gun, preparing to club David with the butt.

David flipped up the bedpan at the last second, catching Vercoe's testicles.

Vercoe sucked in his breath and fell to his knees. David crashed the bedpan down over his head. Vercoe's body gave a twitch, and he was unconscious.

David tottered backwards, sat on the bed, let the bedpan slip from his hand.

Summoning what little strength he had left, he got off the bed and laboriously dragged Vercoe's clothes off and put them on. The stained cream suit fitted badly and there was a four-inch gap between the top of his socks and the bottoms of his trousers. The shoes caused the most trouble. He had to bend his toes almost double to get them on. He slipped Vercoe's Colt .38 into his pocket along with his car keys, and went to the door. He opened it a couple of inches, checked the corridor. His doctor was standing outside the next room along, talking to a nurse. David shut the door, leaned against it.

A wave of lethargy washed over him. Tired, so tired. If he ever got out of this hospital he'd sleep for a—

A hand grabbed his ankle, twisted it. David choked back a yell.

Vercoe was conscious, but only just. His eyes were flickering up under his eyelids. David removed the gun from his pocket. Vercoe saw it, opened his mouth to cry out. David smashed the butt down against his head. Vercoe's naked body tremored, and he was out again.

The nurse was also beginning to stir.

He put the gun back in his pocket, eased the door open once more. The doctor was still in the corridor, but he had his back to David now.

He stepped out of the room, headed down the corridor away from the doctor. He went through swing doors and came to a service lift. He pressed the button to summon it.

There was a cry of 'Doctor!' behind him. The nurse had come to.

The lift seemed to have got stuck on the first floor. David knew he didn't have the strength to get down the stairs under his own steam. He'd have to ditch the shoes for a start.

A yell, close by. He ignored it. The lifted started moving again.

2 . . . 3 . . .

'Hey, Cauley!'

David looked around.

The doctor was running towards him down the corridor, about to hit the swing doors. As he swept through them the lift door opened. David stepped inside. The doctor grabbed the edge of the door as it began to slide shut. He let go when he realized David had a gun aimed at him.

The doctor backed off. Keeping his eyes on the doctor,

David pressed the ground floor button. The door began to slide shut. David winked at the doctor just before he disappeared from view.

The Porsche was still sitting out front. David shouted with relief as he eased into the driver's seat and kicked off Vercoe's shoes. The car started first time. As he eased it away from the kerb, he wondered if he had hit Vercoe hard enough to kill him.

He found himself hoping he had.

CHAPTER TWENTY-FIVE

David pushed himself out of his sleeping bag, yawned and stretched. His ribs were still sore, and his feet ached, but eleven hours of exhausted sleep had helped work the drugs out of his system.

He felt almost good.

A weak winter sun was watering light out of a cold dawn sky. Nearby, someone was whistling. He shoved his sleeping bag and belongings further under the bush he had used for a shelter. There was an airline hold-all beside him. He removed a bulging supermarket carrier bag from it, extracted a can of tuna fish and gouged his way inside with a tin opener. He scooped the contents into his mouth with his fingers, then ate a packet of peanuts, followed by a tin of pineapple rings and a bottle of Appletize. After he'd wiped his greasy hands on the grass, he lit a cigarette, sucking the smoke in deep. The whistler – a gardener, he guessed – was heading away from him.

His luck had held the previous evening. He had driven back to his house in Chiswick, reckoning that, no matter how fast the police put out an APB on him, he'd still be able to get in, grab whatever he needed, and get out before they even thought of searching for him there.

It had been hard going inside the house again, crammed as it was with poignant memories, but he'd had little choice. He had deliberately kept his mind busy with the task at hand. He had found the sleeping bag in the attic: he'd bought it fifteen years back, for reasons now obscure to him, and it had never been used. He'd found the hold-all up there as well, and this he had stuffed with clothes and food. He had put on two shirts, old jeans, thick woollen socks, heavy duty walking boots, a chunky fisherman's sweater, a longshoreman's woollen hat, and a padded anorak. He had raided the larder, shovelling tins into a plastic bag, along with a tin opener, soft drinks, a packet of stale cigarettes they'd kept for guests, and a box of matches.

He'd left Vercoe's Porsche parked in front of the house and driven Lauris's beat-up old VW Beetle down to Grove Park, near the river. He had parked outside the grounds of Chiswick House. The original mansion had been demolished a long time ago, leaving behind an eighteenth-century Palladian villa.

The grounds were a bewilderingly complex mixture of serpentine canals, woods, and geometrically-arranged bush-lined avenues. It was wild enough to hide out in, and easy to sneak in and out of. He knew the lay-out pretty well; he and Lauris had often taken Anna for picnics there on Sunday afternoons. He had taken a chance on it not being too well-guarded. It was run by a heritage society too short of cash to afford night-guards.

He flicked his cigarette over the bush and stood up warily. No one in sight. He stamped his feet to get his circulation going. The sun was growing stronger; it was almost warm against his face. He glanced at his wrist before remembering that his watch was with his other possessions back at the hospital. He had seen a watch of Lauris's lying on her dressing table the previous evening, but he hadn't been able to bring himself to take it.

He guessed it was about 7:30. Time to get moving.

Life had become simple. Now that he no longer had a copy of Sammy Moss's document, there was only one way to stop Spear; by killing him.

He reached inside his anorak, withdrew Vercoe's revolver. It smelt of oil. Above the cross-hatched hand-grip, just below the trigger, stood the company trademark, an oddly whimsical prancing horse.

He grinned. St George had found his steed.

TV REPORTER IN HOSPITAL ESCAPE DRAMA

Television News reporter, David Cauley, 38, escaped from a central London hospital yesterday before police could question him about an alleged suicide bid.

Cauley was rushed to St Mary's Hospital, Paddington, after being found unconscious in a room at the Belvedere Hotel, Bloomsbury. He had booked in late the previous evening using the name 'David St George'.

Hotel receptionist Cathy Hunt, 23, said Cauley was in a nervous state when he booked in at 10 PM. 'He wanted to know where he could find a photocopier. He seemed very agitated.'

Cauley left the hotel a short while after booking in, carrying a bulky brown package. He returned to the hotel at 5 in the morning. An ambulance was called to the hotel three and a half hours later. The caller, who used the phone in Cauley's room, did not identify herself. The hotel receptionist remembers a slim woman in her mid-twenties entering and leaving the hotel shortly before the ambulance arrived.

Ambulancemen found Cauley naked on the floor of his bathroom, surrounded by a half-finished bottle of whisky and several empty bottles of pills. He was rushed to St Mary's, where his stomach was pumped. He regained consciousness just before 5 PM. A few minutes later he ASSAULTED a nurse and ATTACKED a male visitor, rendering both unconscious. He then stripped the visitor, put on his clothes and fled the hospital, brandishing a gun. The visitor, who has not been named, is being kept in for observation with a suspected skull fracture.

David Cauley, whose wife and daughter died tragically in a car accident earlier this year, AMAZED TV viewers by having a nervous breakdown on screen during a live broadcast from Downing Street four months ago. He has recently been undergoing psychiatric treatment.

The Managing Editor of Capital Television News,

Calvin Scott, 49, called yesterday's incident 'a terrible tragedy'. He said Cauley, one of the most talented reporters on television, had never got over the death of his wife and daughter. 'Wherever he is, I plead with him to give himself up. His job at Capital is still open. We all want to see him well again.'

Police say anyone sighting Cauley should report it immediately. He is armed, and could be dangerous.

As David folded the paper, he wondered who the girl was who'd saved his life. Where had she come from?

He tossed the paper onto the Volkswagen's backseat. He unwrapped a Mars Bar and bit off a chunk. The papers he'd read had made no mention of Lauris's VW. The police probably hadn't even realized he'd taken it. As for the possibility of being recognized, it didn't worry him. He hadn't shaved for four days, he was wearing his hair brushed down over his forehead and his rough clothes weren't what people associated with TV newsmen. He wondered what sort of story Vercoe had given the police. They'd no doubt been interested to know exactly how David had managed to get hold of a gun.

His main worry now was that Hughes would eventually realize that David was tailing him. He'd been following Spear's Rolls-Royce around town for three days. It was only a matter of time before Hughes or Spear spotted him. So far, their routine had proved the same each day – they'd leave Spear's Ennismore Gardens home around nine, drive to Dragon Enterprises HQ in the City, and head back just after seven.

David lit a cigarette, shivered. It had been raining almost constantly for the past two nights and his clothes were damp. He couldn't afford to get ill now. It was Thursday morning. He'd got a pretty accurate idea of Spear's routine. He just had to decide when and where to kill him.

He couldn't afford to wait much longer. Even if Hughes didn't spot him, someone might find his gear in the grounds of Chiswick House. The whistling gardener had passed within a few feet of him that morning.

The door of Spear's house opened. David sank down low in the driver's seat. Hughes emerged first, glanced up and down the road as usual. His eyes seemed to linger for an extra second on David's car. David stiffened. Hughes's head turned in the other direction.

Spear, who was wearing a Russian fur hat, looked slightly nervous when he appeared. David smiled. Spear knew David was out there somewhere, and that he had a gun, and he wasn't enjoying the knowledge.

Spear and Hughes halted on the pavement. Hughes said something. Spear spat angry words back. Hughes flinched visibly and hurried to open the back door of the Rolls-Royce. Spear dipped inside.

David smiled. The Dragon Man was distinctly uneasy.

The Rolls pulled slickly away from the curb. David stubbed out his cigarette, jammed the last of the Mars Bar into his mouth, and started the VW. He kept well back, letting a couple of other cars get in front of him.

When he pulled out of Ennismore Gardens onto Kensington Gore the Rolls wasn't in sight. He checked his rear view mirror, saw it. Hughes had decided to take a different route. A device to flush out a tail? He wondered if he should abandon pursuit. Curiosity got the better of him.

He did a U-turn. A taxi driver screamed abuse at him. The Rolls turned up Kensington Church Street, heading North. David hoped Spear wasn't planning a trip out of London. The VW wouldn't be able to keep up with the Rolls on a motorway. Sixty-five was its top limit.

After twenty minutes the Rolls came to a stop in a quiet road in Hendon. David was forced to drive past it and park in the next street on the left. He got out of the car, and peered round a hedge at the end of the road just in time to see Hughes open the back door. Spear stepped out, glanced about him and walked across the road towards a redbrick Victorian mansion that looked as if it might have been a school at some stage. There was an ugly windowless concrete annexe tacked onto one side of the building. As Spear approached the gate, a uniformed guard emerged and opened it for him. Spear walked up to the main door.

It was opened by a tall, stooped, grey-haired man.

Dr Sorensen.

There was no handshake. The two men went inside.

Hughes was leaning against the Rolls, arms folded. He turned his head, and David jerked back behind the hedge. Waited. When he next looked, Hughes had got back into the car.

There was a bronze sign by the gate. David had to screw his eyes up to read it. *INSTITUTE FOR GENETIC RESEARCH*.

He was about to head back to the VW when the sensation hit him: a mixture of misery, fear, and confusion. And a terrible sense of loneliness. The sensations were distant, faint, but real, so real they made him halt in mid-stride, and he realized he was crying.

He wiped his face angrily, walked briskly to the car. Seeing Sorensen had reminded him of Anna's suffering, that was all.

When he slid in behind the wheel of the VW, his mind was made up. Spear would die tomorrow.

CHAPTER TWENTY-SIX

David eased his legs out from behind the empty dustbins. He had to clamp his teeth together to halt a shivering fit. His hands were jammed under his armpits. The rain swirling down the alley burned against his face. The chill had taken a fierce hold on him overnight; he was a sick man.

He had intended to strike that morning, but the refuse men had arrived a few minutes before Spear's departure. He had been forced to act the part of a derelict, shouting abuse, staggering off, hoping he'd be out of sight before Spear emerged from his house. He had half-expected to find the police waiting for him in the alley beside Spear's house upon returning that evening, but it had been deserted.

It was Friday evening, and he knew he had to get it over with now. He prayed Spear hadn't headed for his mansion in Sunningdale straight from the office. David wouldn't be able to make it through the weekend; another night sleeping out in the rain would land him in hospital.

A sound behind him. He wheeled around. The alley ended in a solid brick wall. Something moving back there in the darkness. He reached for his gun.

A black plastic dustbin bag danced towards him out of the gloom. He relaxed, checked the cheap digital watch he'd picked up the previous day. 7:05. Spear was due home in five minutes.

David got to his feet. His limbs were freezing. Another trembling attack shook him. This time he didn't resist it. He leaned back against the side wall of Spear's house with the rain lashing his face for a full minute before he felt strong enough to make his way to the end of the alley.

He checked the street. There was a parking space just big enough for a Rolls right in front of the house.

He mentally rehearsed his plan of attack.

Hughes always got out of the car first and checked the road before opening the nearside back door. He'd check the road again before telling Spear it was all right to get out. Spear would step out of the car and move aside as Hughes shut the door. As Hughes did so, Spear would reach in his pocket for his front-door key, then hand Hughes his briefcase.

That was the moment to strike, the instant the case was being handed over. Neither Spear nor Hughes would be watching the road. In that split second David would have to leap out of the alley, aim the .38 and shoot. The distance was only five yards, but he'd never shot a gun before in his life. It would have been better to shoot Spear at point-blank range, but that wasn't going to be possible. Spear would only need a second to grab hold of David's mind and freeze him to the spot. The bullet would have to be travelling towards Spear before the Dragon Man realized what was happening.

David had decided to ignore Hughes and concentrate on pumping as many bullets into Spear as he could manage.

Hughes would kill him in turn, but he was prepared for that. This was a kamikaze mission.

The only thing he regretted about the plan was that he would never know why Lauris and Anna had been murdered, but any attempt to solve the mystery could jeopardize his main objective.

The Rolls nosed into the street. Hughes was visible behind the windscreen, but it was impossible to tell whether Spear was in the back.

David drew the gun from his pocket. He had checked the chamber. Six bullets. The .38 felt familiar to his hand. He had handled it a lot in the past few days, getting used to its weight and balance, making sure he could grasp it comfortably with two hands.

The Rolls slowed as it approached Spear's house. A Mini Metro shot past it on the inside and slipped into the empty space. Hughes had the Rolls stopped and was out and running towards the Metro before it had come to a halt.

He leant menacingly over the bonnet, rapped his knuckles against the driver's window.

The driver, a teenage girl, peered up at him, evidently unnerved by the giant's freakish appearance.

'Move this piece of *shit* or I'll roll right over you, bitch!'

The Metro stalled as the girl attempted to drive off.

'Hurry it up, *bitch*!' Hughes yelled.

For a moment David considered running behind Hughes's back to the Rolls and shooting Spear through the window. But the Dragon Man might see him coming. Besides, he couldn't be sure that Spear was actually inside.

Hughes swaggered back to the Rolls as the Metro shot off down the road. He slipped behind the wheel, eased into the space. When he emerged from the car again, he barely bothered checking the road.

David gripped Vercoe's gun with both hands. It felt right; heavy and solid and efficient.

Hughes approached the back door of the Rolls. David tensed. Hughes walked past the door, round the back of the car, and opened the boot.

'Shit!' David hissed.

Hughes removed a suitcase from the boot, which he slammed shut, and carried the case up to the front door of the house.

David's shoulders slumped in disappointment. Spear wasn't in the car. He'd probably driven down to Surrey for the weekend in his BMW. How the hell was David supposed to get at him there? By the time Spear returned to London on Sunday night, David wouldn't be in a fit state to shake a fist at him, let alone shoot straight.

He jammed the gun back in the pocket of his anorak. Hughes returned down the steps of the house and approached the Rolls once more. He went straight to the back door, opened it. David drew the gun again. It suddenly felt huge and clumsy, almost too heavy to lift. His throat was dry. He had to stifle a cough.

Spear stepped out onto the pavement.

A chill shiver wracked David's body. He rammed his jaws together to control it, biting so hard he felt a tooth chip.

Hughes shut the back door. Spear held out his briefcase. Hughes reached for it.

Die, you bastard! David thought.

He raised the gun and stepped out from the shadow of the alley.

There was a sensation like a block of concrete landing on his neck, and then the world pitched and turned upside down, and then there was nothing, just nothing at all.

CHAPTER TWENTY-SEVEN

No traffic sounds, no voices, just a smattering of birdsong and the wind sussurating in the trees. The room was dark, but there was light behind the curtains near the foot of the bed.

The pain in the back of his neck made David gasp when he tried to sit up. He reached his hand round and gingerly probed a lump the size of an imbedded tennis ball.

His ribs were aching and so was his leg, but at least his fever seemed to have passed.

He sat up – this time the pain was just about bearable – and tried to figure out where he was.

Spear's mansion?

For a moment his stomach felt as if it was dropping through space.

As his eyes adjusted to the gloom he realized he had guessed wrong. The room was too small and ramshackle to be part of Spear's country home. This was on a different scale; more like a small room in a cottage. He glanced up at the black rafters tracing an erratic course across the ceiling above him. It all seemed so terribly *familiar*.

His leg almost buckled as he got out of bed. After a minute he managed to hobble over to the window and pull back the curtain.

A pallid sun bleaching morning mist. A half-acre garden fringed with trees, and, beyond them, fields.

Their garden.

He was at the cottage.

He turned and looked back at the room, now awash with pale light. Pencil drawings. Water-colours. Pin-ups. Anna's bedroom.

Dreaming, he thought. *Must be.*

Someone whistling softly in the kitchen directly below him.

He was naked except for his underpants, and there was no sign of his clothes. He went to the bedroom door and stepped out onto the landing.

The whistling changed to humming. He made his way to the top of the stairs past a wall lined with framed photographs of himself and Lauris and Anna. A colour snap of Anna smiling, astride a pony. An arty black-and-white blow-up of Lauris, apprehensive at an exhibition of her work at Camberwell Art School. David himself, shaking hands with the Prime Minister, who had been visiting the Capital newsroom.

He ducked his head, and made his way down the narrow stairs. The cottage smelt damp. The heating had been turned on recently, and the wooden building was creaking.

David halted in the kitchen doorway.

The girl had one of the lids of the Aga open and was frying bacon in a pan. Thick steel-grey hair hung far down her back. The colour of it made her look older than David guessed her to be. Twenty-two, twenty-three at most. She was tall and broad shouldered. Slim hips, neat buttocks, long legs. She was wearing an oxblood rollneck sweater tucked into tight black cord jeans and hippyish black leather pixie boots, turned over at the top.

'What did you hit me with?' David asked.

'The edge of my hand.'

She didn't flinch, didn't look around. It was as if she'd known he was there all along.

'What else do you do with it? Chop wood?'

She looked at him over her shoulder, smiled, still chasing bacon around the pan. Nice face. Wide jaw, a big mouth with lots of perfect white teeth, eyes that turned up, smiling, at the corners. Her accent had told him she was American, but he would have been able to tell that from her face and her expression alone; confident, outgoing, direct. It was the face of someone who'd bounce back from disaster. Just looking at her made him feel better.

'There's a robe in the living room,' she said. 'Come back and I'll give you brunch.'

There was a log fire blazing in the sitting room. A white cotton robe lay on the couch. He shrugged it on, returned to the kitchen.

There was a plate of crisp bacon and fried eggs on the stripped pine kitchen table. He sat down and ate the meal with big slabs of hot buttered toast.

The girl brought steaming mugs of coffee over to the table when he had finished and produced his cigarettes from her pocket. He lit one, leaned back in his chair. The pain at the back of his head was receding.

The girl was watching him over the rim of her coffee cup.

'I should be angry with you,' he said.

'For saving your life?'

'For saving Spear's. He'd be dead by now if it weren't for you.'

The girl put her cup down. 'The way you were holding that gun, you'd probably have done more harm to yourself than to Spear. You've never used a gun, right?'

He ignored the question. 'I've seen you somewhere before.'

'James sent me over to keep a watch on Anna after your old school pals came looking for her.'

'Your hair's different.'

'It was dyed.' She ran a hand through her leonine mane. 'This is real.'

'How did you know about this place? We've always kept it secret.'

'When I was tailing you last year you came down here for a weekend.'

He nodded. 'Okay.' He sipped his coffee. 'What's your name?'

'Beth Palmer.'

'Palmer? Isn't that the name of the man who got shot when they tried to kill James Lord?'

'He was my father.' A shadow passed over her face.

'He saved my life once.'

She nodded. 'Cornwall, '68. The first time Spear tried to kill you.'

'You seem to know a lot.'

'Everything, just about.'

'Was your father an emperor?'

She smiled. 'Dad? No. He was Bobby Kennedy's protector. After Bobby died, he became James Lord's. That's my job now.'

'You?' It sounded patronizing. He realized he'd annoyed her.

'Dad trained me for it all my life. I've known about the emperors since I was eight-years-old. Took up karate when I was nine. Learned how to shoot the same year.'

'Heavyweight boxing and brain surgery the year after that?'

'Tee-hee!'

192

'Sorry.'

'Look, I know what I'm doing. Okay? I'm not some cute-assed bimbo playing at spies. I'm a professional.'

David reached up to touch the back of his head. 'I realize that.'

Her expression softened. 'Still painful?'

'Only when I breathe.' He swallowed the last of his coffee, lit another cigarette. The heat from the Aga was easing his pains. He was amazed to find himself thinking about making love to Beth, and that made him uncomfortable. The last time he'd sat talking over coffee in this kitchen, he'd been with Lauris.

'What brought you to England this time?' David asked.

She got up, poured more coffee for them, brought it back to the table. 'I want to find out why the enemy tried to kill James Lord.' Her voice grew quieter. 'And why Dad died.'

Her shoulders had slumped. She squared them, sat up straight. David noticed her breasts jutting out from her sweater, forced himself to concentrate on her face.

'I began tailing Spear a couple of weeks ago. One morning I followed him to that crappy hotel you were staying at. I didn't realize you were there. I saw Spear go in and come out again forty-five minutes later. I had to find out what he'd been doing in there. When I got to your room you were just about dead, pulse about half normal rate, choking on your own vomit. I helped you as much as I could, phoned an ambulance, and split. I guessed you'd be okay. I got on with tailing Spear. Then, dammit, *you* showed up again. For a while we had us a regular convoy – Spear's car, yours, and mine. Remind me to give you some tips on how to tail a car. You're really lousy.'

'I wasn't spotted.'

'That gorilla-chauffeur of Spear's must have a single-figure IQ.'

'You're probably flattering him.'

'Anyway, I figured you were fixing to do something whacky, so I hung around to stop you.'

'Do you want Spear to live?'

'He's the reason my father's dead. My father was a

good, *good* man. I very much want Spear to die. As badly as you do. Only *you* were going to make a hash of it. Besides, we can't kill him till next week.'

'Why not?'

She arched her back and ran the fingers of both hands through her hair. The motion made David's loins ache. He hadn't thought about sex for months, had imagined his libido to be dead.

'According to our intelligence sources,' she said, 'there's a big meeting due at Spear's place in the country next Wednesday night, eight o'clock. There's people coming in from all over the world to be there. We have to know what that meeting's about and who shows up. It might explain why my father died.'

'And my wife and daughter.'

'Yes,' she said. 'I'm sorry.'

'After the meeting, will you kill Spear?'

'Yes.'

'How?'

'Explosives. Semtex. I'm going to wire the mansion before the meeting, see who turns up, eavesdrop on the proceedings, and then blow the whole bunch of them to hell.'

She looked and sounded like a young girl excited at the prospect of throwing a big party.

'What about Spear's family?'

She shrugged. 'They'll probably stay in London that night. If they don't, too bad.'

'Sentimental, aren't you?'

She stood up, went to the window. She stared out at the garden for a while before speaking. 'When I was sixteen and my father told me what the point of all those years of training had been – all the exercise and the unarmed combat and the shooting, and all the other spycraft stuff – I wasn't too thrilled, to be honest. I mean, it was fun up till then, but I didn't want it to get serious and important. I wanted to go to college, study, get a neat job in New York, meet a handsome, rich, kind man and settle down to raise clever, good-looking, spiffy children and live in a mansion apartment on Park Avenue and have a big house

194

in the Hamptons.' As she turned and leaned against the window, the morning sun turned her hair to silver fire. 'But Dad explained that wasn't the way it was going to be. At first, I told him I wasn't sacrificing my life for some noble cause. But then he explained exactly what the cause was, what I'd be fighting against, and after a while I began to see it wasn't something I could just turn my back on. Dad told me I'd have to make myself hard, tough, tougher than him, because I'd be asked to do things that would go against my nature. That included murder. At some stage, he said, I might have to kill innocent people. Could I do that? I thought about it for a long time. I realized if I was going to dedicate myself to fighting Spear and his kind, I'd have to be willing to go all the way. So, if Spear's family are in that house on Wednesday, I'll be sorry about it.' She shrugged. 'But if I have to kill them to get Spear, I'll do it.'

David found himself wondering whether Beth had had anything to do with the supposed suicide of the bank robber the previous year.

'Would James approve of your plans?'

'He does approve.' She smiled. 'He came out of the coma two months back. We decided to keep it quiet in case Spear and his crew came after him again. Our side isn't exactly calling the shots right now. Spear's one hell of an operator, and James admits he was concentrating too hard on the election to provide effective opposition.'

David stood up, walked over to her. 'Why did Lauris and Anna die?'

She looked him straight in the eye. 'I don't know. It doesn't make sense. Especially Anna's death. Not even James can figure out why Anna was murdered.'

'Who are the emperors, Beth? Exactly who are they?'

She shook her head. He moved closer to her.

'If James is one of them, why aren't he and Spear working together?'

She squirmed out from under him, backed into the centre of the room. 'There's no reason for you to know any more than you do. It would be better if you didn't.'

'My wife and daughter are dead. That gives me the right to know.'

'Please, David. I'm under enough pressure already. Don't make it harder for me.'

He paused. 'Okay. Just one more question. How can I help?'

She walked over to him, took his hands in hers. 'To be honest, you'd just get in the way.'

He looked down at her hands. They were surprisingly slim and soft. It was hard to believe she'd used them to knock him unconscious.

'Do you know the lay-out of Spear's place?' he asked.

'No,' she admitted. 'I'll have to play it by ear.'

He smiled. 'I've been inside. I had lunch there. Spear gave us a guided tour.'

'Oh, wow!'

His smile turned to a grin. 'But if you're *sure* you don't want me along—'

'Cut that out!' She went up on her toes and kissed him lightly, quickly on the lips. Her breath was warm and sweet. 'David?'

'Yes?' His heart was tremoring.

'Draw me a floor-plan.'

He laughed.

'What's so funny?'

'You, you incurable romantic.' He let go of her. 'You'll find paper and pencils in the sitting-room bureau.'

She paused at the door on the way out.

'Your wife,' she said. 'I was looking at the photographs. She was very pretty.'

'Yes,' he said. 'She was.'

'I . . .' Beth said, halted, dropped her gaze. 'I'm sorry we met this way. But I'm not sorry we met.'

Then she was gone and he could hear her riffling through the drawers of the desk next door.

He sat down at the kitchen table and awaited her return.

Yesterday, he had not cared about dying. Now, he wasn't so sure.

CHAPTER TWENTY-EIGHT

Spear poured himself another glass of port and, leaning back in his Federal dining chair at the head of the twenty-foot-long mahogany conference table, gazed up at the painting on the wall opposite.

On one of her regular visits to Sotheby's, his wife had come across a fourteenth-century woodcut of a demon with a serpent in one hand and a bag of gold in the other, riding a dog-faced dragon. A Cambridge medievalist had identified the figure as Astaroth, the grand treasurer of hell. His wife had commissioned one of her friends to paint a picture based on the woodcut. As with the marble mosaic of Typhon in the main hall, she had asked the artist to give the demon her husband's face.

Spear sipped his port. They had been married for over twenty years, yet she could still think up ways to keep him amused. There was little warmth in their relationship, but his power – and his money – excited her. All he asked in return was that she didn't bore him.

The Grand Treasurer of Hell. He allowed himself a smile.

Jeremy and Henrietta were arguing somewhere close by. His smile froze. They knew better than to make noise in the house when he was in residence.

His wife had disappointed him in only one respect: she had been unable to bear him an emperor child. His peers had assured him that his children would be ordinary, but he had somehow imagined he would prove the exception to the rule. He hadn't. After Henrietta's birth he had taken his disappointment out on his wife. She had disappeared for three months. Vercoe had eventually found her, covered in sores and scabs, in a sleazy Earl's Court basement flat littered with rusty needles. Sorensen had supervised her recovery. They had not slept together since. He knew she occasionally took drugs, and that she had formed some sort of perverted sexual liaison with Hughes and Vercoe, but he had agreed to turn a blind eye as long as she was discreet.

Henrietta began shrieking at Jeremy just outside the door of the conference room.

Spear rose from his chair, intending to punish them. He heard the word 'father'. The noise stopped. He decided to ignore the transgression. His family would be setting off for London within the hour, and would not return until after The Meeting. He dismissed them from his thoughts and concentrated on the gathering that would finally establish him as the undisputed leader of the group. It was a position for which he had fought hard in the past few years. Two emperors from his own side had had to be disposed of because of their opposition to him. There had been at least three plots against his own life during the last five years, mainly emanating from Moscow. But that was all in the past; the time was now ripe for him to assume his proper role as leader. There had been discontent amongst the group for almost a decade which had seen them retreating on all fronts. But things had recently begun to turn their way, thanks to Spear's careful planning. Hung Xiang and Marenkev were poised for power, and James Lord was in a coma.

It was *their* turn to take charge. The other side had enjoyed ten years of power, but they lacked the will to *keep* control.

On Wednesday, Spear would be able to tell his colleagues that the world was theirs *forever!*

He shut his eyes and rehearsed what he was going to say to them. At first they'd be cynical, determined to be unimpressed. They'd glance at each other in a way that would suggest Spear had finally gone insane, the fate of so many of their predecessors. They'd be angry at the risk he had asked them to take in attending. They'd be wondering whether they could capitalize on his apparent weakness to seize the reins of power for themselves. He would wait for one of them to question his authority. Then, when he judged the moment to be right, he would play his trump card.

And that would be that. He would be their King, the Emperor of Emperors.

He opened his eyes and grinned.

Their god!

The grin slowly died. There were problems. A rumour had reached him that James Lord had emerged from his coma and had gone into hiding somewhere in the States. Bad news. He was the only emperor Spear genuinely feared.

He turned, stared out of the nearest window. A crescent moon. Somewhere out there was David Cauley, a man still alive despite three attempts on his life. If James Lord was the only emperor who frightened Spear, Cauley was the only human being. He was neither physically strong, nor particularly intelligent. Yet Cauley was alive, and he shouldn't have been, and that made Spear nervous. It was as if some force was protecting him, a force seemingly beyond Spear's control.

He gazed at the moon, forced the doubts from his mind. Soon, neither James Lord nor David Cauley would matter a damn. Soon, he would be beyond challenge.

He grinned. *Soon!*

At first, David thought it was an animal. But when the night wind quietened for a moment and the sound continued, he realized it was Beth crying somewhere below him.

He got up and pulled on his dressing gown. He opened the bedroom door and listened, recognizing the sound of raw, aching grief.

He made his way softly down the stairs, halted outside the sitting room. Beth's misery made him feel ashamed. He'd been so wrapped up in his own grief he hadn't really given much thought to her. She had lost her father. From the way she had spoken about him, David should have realized how close they had been.

He opened the sitting-room door.

She was lying in a foetal position on the couch, hands over her face. Moonlight washing through the window glinted off the tears trickling between her fingers.

He went to the couch, knelt beside it. Beth must have sensed his presence, but didn't move.

'Beth,' he said, his voice husky. 'Beth, please don't.'

Then her wet face was pressed against his chest, and she was hugging him, sobbing.

He placed his arms around her. Her robe had fallen open and his hand brushed against one of her breasts. The nipple was hot and hard. He felt himself becoming erect.

He groaned.

She looked up at him.

'Yes,' she said. Her voice was a croak.

'What do you mean?'

'Make love to me.'

'No, I . . . not here.'

'*Please!*' she whispered urgently. 'Oh please! I need you.'

'No!' he said. 'Not like this.' But even to himself, his words sounded unconvincing. He wanted her just as badly. No. She was right. *Needed* her.

He tried to get up, but she held him, and then her lips were against his and she was reaching inside his robe to take him in her hand.

He shuddered at her touch. He opened his mouth and moved his hand so that her erect nipple was burning his palm.

'Yes,' he moaned.

There were three mirrors on the wall of the ranch-house sitting room. James Lord watched himself in all three as he made his way from the picture window that looked out onto a snow-covered Colorado valley over to the kitchen hatch.

He didn't much like what he saw. He had hoped to be walking normally by now. He had managed to pick up some speed in the past two months, but it was obvious to anyone watching that there was something wrong with the left-hand side of his body. The leg was slightly stiff, the arm rigid and unmoving, and his torso had a crook to it.

It wasn't the walk of a future President. John Kennedy had been plagued with appalling back pain all the time he'd been in office, but in public he had appeared the epitome of vigorous good health. Roosevelt had been stuck in a wheelchair, but his big, robust upper body and strong voice had offset any impression that he was crippled. With James, it would be different. When he moved there was no getting away from the fact that he just looked plumb *wrong*. He hadn't been able to risk getting in the best medical help while he was in hiding. Now he was beginning to wonder if it was too late to correct the partial paralysis afflicting the left-hand side of his body.

He wandered back across the room, flopped down on a chair next to the main window, and stared out at the snow. He'd loved the view when he'd first arrived eight weeks before, shortly after emerging from the coma. Now he was sure he'd never be able to hear the word 'panoramic' again without feeling queasy.

Outside, a guard strolled by, cradling a shotgun. James waved at him. The guard acknowledged the gesture before continuing on his rounds.

James tried to reach out his paralysed arm to a can of beer perched on a stack of *Time* and *Newsweek* beside his chair. Nothing happened. He strained his whole body. The fucking arm just *lay* there. He willed it to move. Nothing. Felt tears coming on, fought them back. He could command other people to do exactly what he wanted them to do, but he couldn't move his frigging arm one lousy inch.

He twisted his whole body, picked up the beer with his right hand, took a pull on it.

He'd have been able to cope if Cliff Palmer had still been alive. He hadn't realized what a tremendous source of strength the big man had been until he'd lost him.

He felt another maudlin attack coming on. He struggled up out of his seat, overtipping the stack of magazines. He walked to the window, slid it open and stepped out onto the porch.

Freezing silence. He felt as desolate as the landscape. Everything had gone wrong. *Everything!* And it was his fault.

Anna Cauley was dead. The girl who could have changed the world was dead. He should have kidnapped her that night fifteen years ago when he had sneaked into David's house and seen her for the first time. Sentimentality had got the better of him. If Dave Cauley had been a stranger he might have considered it, but he hadn't been able to bring himself to make his old friend suffer that way. No, he couldn't have lived with the guilt, but he should have done *something*. He should have arranged for a permanent watch to be kept on Anna. That way, he would have known about Spear's interest in her sooner.

Now, it was too damn late.

Again, he wondered why Spear had had her killed. It made no kind of sense. Spear had obviously seen the same possibilities that James had seen. Why else involve the geneticist Sorensen? Had Anna's death been an accident? He doubted it. Spear wouldn't make such a grotesque mistake; he was an emperor.

He dismissed the mystery from his mind, began cataloguing his other blunders. He had been so obsessed with the forthcoming elections, with making his mark now so that he'd be able to run for President in '96, he hadn't responded to what was happening elsewhere, hadn't divined the pattern of events – China, the Soviet Union, the Middle East. God, why hadn't he *done* something?

The wind howled, spat a snow flurry over him. The right hand side of his body was freezing. The left hand side was as neutral as wood.

He re-entered the chalet, slid the window shut.

A computer terminal was flashing in the far corner of the room. He walked over to it.

By his own negligence he'd been forced into a position where his only possible response to the opposition was murder. And he was shovelling the responsibility for the monstrous deed onto the shoulders of a twenty-two-year-old girl whose early life had already been sacrificed in his cause. Maybe he should go himself, confront Spear directly. Like a gunslinger. He smiled crookedly at the thought. He hadn't the strength for that. Before the assassination attempt he might have considered it, but a lot of his strength had leaked away. He wasn't sure he would win against Spear in his present condition, and it wasn't a battle he could afford to lose.

Or maybe he was just a coward.

He could see his own reflection in the computer screen. 'Dumb bastard!'

His voice was blurred, as if he had a wad of cotton wool stuck in his mouth, but at least the paralysis in his face, like that in his leg, was only partial.

(Why did Spear kill her? Why?)

Should he call the operation off? Should he tell Beth to pull out, forget it? It would help salve his conscience, but it would leave Richard Spear alive. And Spear was planning something, something big, and that meant trouble on a cosmic scale.

He closed his eyes and concentrated. There was a well of light deep inside himself, a source of strength, calmness, *certainty*. He let himself fall down, down, down, plunged into the light, felt it sparkle and tingle through his whole being. Then he was rising, rising fast, fast and sleek, like an eagle, strong and sure . . .

His eyes opened.

He reached his right hand out to the computer keyboard. He had to know what was going to happen at the Wednesday meeting. *Had* to. And he had to make sure that Richard Spear died.

No more foul-ups!

His expression was grim as he began tapping the keys.

The tiny beep awakened Beth. She felt warm and languorous. She lay in the darkness, on the couch, staring at David's face. Despite the beard growth and the dark patches under his eyes, he looked impossibly young in repose. There was something childlike about him. In a way, he seemed younger that her, but then she hadn't experienced much of a youth.

She reached out, traced a finger over his lips. She had awakened once to hear him mumbling his wife's name, and she had not felt good about that. She had seduced him, here, where he and his family had enjoyed such good times.

David frowned in his sleep, and she withdrew her hand from his face.

She tried to console herself with the thought that David was still a reflectively young man. Lauris had been dead for six months. Was he supposed to remain celibate for life? And did it matter *where* they made love? They had needed each other. Besides, she found him attractive. Last year, when she had been shadowing Anna, David had struck her as a puffy, unhealthy-looking man hurtling towards middle age. Now he was pared down, lean, and it suited him.

The beep sounded again. She slipped off the couch, made her way to the corner of the room where the small lap-top computer was plugged in. The word 'Message' was flashing in the top right-hand corner of the screen. She pressed the button marked 'Send message'.

Situation report, it read.

She typed in her own message. *AOK. D. knows layout of lair.*

Don't take him!

He insists.

No!

You try and stop him!

A pause.

You don't have to go through with this.

She smiled before tapping in her answer. *Yes I do. I'm sleepy. Stop beeping!*

Beep you! she read. She chuckled and made her way back to the couch and lay down beside David.

Dawn light was trickling in through the window and the birds had started singing. It was a good sound.

CHAPTER TWENTY-NINE

A cold, crisp night. Clear, far too clear.

Beth and David ran across the narrow road behind Spear's estate, and crouched in the shadows of a brick wall beyond which lay the rose garden.

They were dressed in black. Beth had insisted they smear their faces with moistened earth, commando-style. The action had made David feel vaguely silly, like a child play-acting.

Beth checked her watch. 'Three, on the dot,' she whispered. 'We've got fifteen minutes to get in and out.' She placed a hand on his arm. 'David, could you not make that whistling noise through your nose? It's kinda deafening.'

'Sorry.' How could she stay so bloody calm? She'd been keeping the house under sporadic surveillance for the past few days. In order to get in and plant the explosives in what Spear had described as the 'conference room' on the ground floor, they'd have to get past at least three Dobermanns who patrolled the grounds at night. If the dogs didn't get them, there was always a chance that Hughes or Vercoe would. David hated to think what Vercoe would do to him if they ever met up again.

'David, wouldn't it be better if you stayed here till I returned?'

He wanted to shout 'Yes!', but instead said 'No' in a way he hoped sounded convincing.

'You're not coming into the house, you know that,' she said.

'Okay.'

'And if anything happens to me, you must try and get away. Your job then is just to find out what happens here on Wednesday. You know how to use the surveillance equipment. Take photographs of whoever turns up, record what they say, and report back to James.'

His hands were beginning to freeze. 'Let's get on with it.'

She leaned forward in the darkness and kissed his cheek, taking him by surprise. She scrambled over the brick wall. It took him twice as long to clear it. He made a racket as he landed clumsily in the middle of a rose bush on the other side.

'Quiet!' Beth hissed.

He extricated himself from the thorns, tearing his trousers and sweater.

Good start, he thought. *You're obviously a natural.*

Beth was already weaving her way between the patterned flower beds. David followed, crouching low. His ribs had improved in the past few days, but his leg was still sore.

He slid to a halt beside her at the small iron gate leading out of the rose garden. The mansion, a hundred yards away across a wide, formal garden, was in darkness, except for a light coming from a second-floor window. Spear's study, David calculated. He imagined the Dragon Man hunched over his desk, plotting. Better he was up there than taking the air. Much better. He felt thankful that the emperors' psychic abilities didn't work both ways, or Spear would have been able to sense their presence.

Beth was rummaging in the bag strapped across her stomach. She withdrew hunks of meat, tossed them into the garden.

David started to say something. She shushed him quiet.

'Your hair,' he whispered. 'The moon.' Her silver hair was a sparkling cascade.

She reached inside the bag again, dragged out a woollen longshoreman's hat. They heard padding sounds nearby. Beth squeaked as she hurried to get the hat over her head. David reached out, tucked in stray strands of hair.

Then the dogs arrived. Two of them. Slim strong beasts, oily black coats. They were beautiful as they glided towards the lumps of meat. As they gulped the beefsteak down, they sounded ugly.

'Good boys!' Beth whispered. One of the animals' heads shot up. Strands of raw meat hung from its mouth, and its muzzle was covered with blood. It cocked its head to one side. Its mad killer's eyes seemed to be staring straight at David. He felt his bowels shrivel. The dog took a tentative step towards the rose garden. Another.

And then sneezed. It was a big, wheezy sneeze, the kind a fat man produces. Another sneeze. The dog barked, angry. Then its companion sneezed as well, a howling screamer. David imagined dog-snot zooming across the lawn. Then both dogs were barking and sneezing and snuffling, rubbing their muzzles on the ground, going round in circles, mad with rage and confusion.

David glanced at Beth. She was smiling. 'You were right,' she whispered. 'English mustard powder. Wow!'

The cacophony increased, and suddenly David was crying with suppressed laughter.

'Shut up!' Beth hissed.

He clamped a hand over his mouth and keeled over onto his side.

Through his tears, he saw a figure at the window of Spear's study. The Dragon Man himself. His laughter died.

Footsteps.

'Shut up, you stupid fucking animal!'

Vercoe's voice. David held his breath. The ground shook. Big, heavy steps.

'What the fuck's up with them?' Hughes said. He kicked one of the dogs. It slunk away, still sneezing.

'They've been eating something. Looks like meat,' Vercoe said. 'Did you let them in the kitchen?'

'Of course not!'

Vercoe bent down, picked up a chunk of meat. 'Steak. I wonder who gave it to them?'

'How the fuck should I know?'

'It's your job to know, apeman!'

Vercoe stepped up to the rose garden gate, scowling. From where he was crouched, David saw that his head was heavily bandaged. Vercoe's crossed eyes were darting about. It would be a miracle if he didn't spot them. David saw Beth reach into her bag, half remove a gun. He pulled the .38 from his own pocket.

'Watch out!' Hughes said. 'The Boss is looking.'

'Let's get these fucking animals shut up. I couldn't stand another mindfuck from Spear right now. I haven't recovered from the last one yet.'

'You shouldn't have let Cauley get away.'

'What about you, you bastard? Who let him escape from the car? He'd have been dead if you hadn't fucked up.'

Hughes reached down, grabbed the collar of the nearest dog just as it let out another enormous sneeze. He whacked it across the head.

Vercoe turned away from the rose garden, loped off in pursuit of the other dog, hooked his fingers inside its collar. They led the animals away across the lawn, and around the side of the house.

Spear was still silhouetted against the window. He disappeared from view after a minute.

David let out his breath. 'The third dog,' he said. 'You said there were always three.'

Beth shrugged. 'Maybe it's sick. We'll have to take a chance on that. Let's get in now while they're busy with the dogs.' Perspiration was running down her face, streaking the dirt on her cheeks.

David noticed that the light had gone out in Spear's study.

'Let's wait!' he said. 'Spear might still be watching.'

'No! We go right now. If you're scared, stay here!'

She opened the gate. It squeaked. She slipped through it. David followed. They bellycrawled across the lawn. By the time they'd reached the back of the house David's elbows and knees had been scraped raw, and he could barely catch his breath. Beth placed a hand over his mouth and grimaced at him.

He nodded after half a minute to signal that he could breath without making too much noise. She took her hand away.

'What if there's an alarm system?' he asked.

'I've thought of that. I've seen Hughes and Vercoe move in and out of the house at night without switching anything on or off.'

'But what if it's set now?'

'We're in trouble.' She took a strip of celluloid out of her bag and inserted it between the sash windows. David heard the latch slip open.

She slid the bottom half of the window up a foot, then it got stuck. She couldn't shift it further. She squeezed through the gap, head first.

David let his body sag against the outside wall of the house. Whatever happened now, he'd justified his insistence on accompanying Beth. If he hadn't reminded her to cover up her hair, Vercoe and Hughes would certainly have spotted her. He looked up at the moon. Tomorrow, Spear would die. The realization made him feel good.

He heard footsteps on the gravel path that led around the house.

He scuttled along the base of the house to a bush set against the wall five yards away. He squeezed his body in underneath it, trying his best not to make any noise. He lay perfectly still as the footsteps got nearer. They sounded incredibly loud.

He hoped to God Beth could hear them too, and that she'd stay inside until whoever it was had passed. He slid his hand into the pocket containing Vercoe's gun.

A foot crunched gravel inches from his ear. Silence. He looked up. Through the tangle of the bush he could see a figure standing directly above him, facing the bush, looking down at it. He could have reached out and grabbed the person's leg. The man turned his head one way, then the other.

The moonlight glinted in Spear's eyes.

In his own ears, David's heartbeat sounded like an earthpounder.

Spear looked down at the bush again. David tensed, waiting for him to say something.

He heard the sound of a zip being pulled. There was a fierce spray of liquid, dripping down onto him through the bush. Had it started to rain? He turned his face away, in case Spear saw his eyes.

Why didn't the bastard speak? He *had* to have seen him. Why else would he be standing there for so long?

Then David realized, with pristine clarity, exactly what was happening. Spear was taking a leak. He hadn't seen David at all. He'd been looking around to make sure no one saw him having a piss. David could feel Spear's urine hot against his back.

Crazy laughter bubbled up from deep inside his stomach. This was *too* bizarre. He rammed one hand into his mouth, bit hard into it. Not enough to quench the hysteria. He bit again, harder, felt the bones in his hand mash together, tasted blood.

The rain stopped. He heard Spear close his zip. Then the Dragon Man was walking away from him.

David shifted his body.

Spear was strolling nonchalantly along the path, hands in his pockets. David was about to let out a sigh of relief when Spear halted by the window through which Beth had entered the house.

David eased the gun out of his pocket, drew a bead on Spear. It was strictly against orders, but he wasn't going to let Beth die. His hands began to shake. He thought of Lauris and Anna and the blazing car, and his hands steadied. He wouldn't miss. He'd get Spear in the stomach, leap out, and shoot him in the head.

Spear reached out and grabbed the bottom of the window. David began to squeeze the trigger.

Spear slammed the window shut. Shaking his head, he resumed his stroll.

When he was out of sight, David eased his body out from under the bush and headed for the window. As he began to slide it open again, he felt someone doing the same from the other side, stepping back.

Beth's face appeared.

'All done,' she said.

He helped her out onto the path.

'Who shut the window?'

'Spear.'

'Oh God!'

'Exactly. A close call.'

'You're all wet,' she said. 'And your hand's bleeding.'

'I'll explain later. Let's get out of here. *Please!*'

'Okay, down on your belly.'

'Bugger that!'

He took off before she could argue. He ran as fast as he could, but Beth still managed to reach the rose garden first. He followed her in, shutting the gate behind him.

He felt safer at once. No one could see them from the house now. He let out his breath and turned, feeling triumphant. They'd done it. They'd really done it.

Beth was waiting for him, smiling. She ripped the hat off her head, stuffed it in her bag.

'Some team, huh?' she said. Her eyes were shining with excitement. Her hair was a wild sweaty tangle. He wanted to make love to her right there. He opened his arms, stepped towards her.

He caught sight of the Doberman out the corner of his eye, a black shadow speeding like a missile through the night. It was on him in an instant, teeth sinking into his throat, and he was falling backwards, staring into its berserk eyes, his body vibrating with its growl.

'Close your eyes!' Beth hissed. He did so. The mustard powder was like sand pattering against his face. The dog gave a mighty sneeze, let go of him. David just had time to see Beth putting the box of Coleman's mustard powder back into her bag before he himself let out a howling sneeze. She grabbed him, dragged him up off the ground, and pushed him towards the wall. He was blinded by sneezes, eyes streaming, helpless. She got beneath him, rammed her shoulder up against his buttocks, and he was tumbling across the road on the other side of the wall. Beth took hold of his arm and dragged him along in her wake.

When they were back in the car and Beth was looking in her bag for the keys, he reached over and patted her hand.

'Beth,' he said, his voice thick with mucus.

'Yes?' she said, aggressively.

'Thanks for a real fun evening.'

CHAPTER THIRTY

10 February 1993
The first raindrop hit the tip of David's cigarette, extinguishing it. He tossed it aside and flipped up the hood of his anorak.

'Getting anything?' he asked.

'Wet,' said Beth.

They were stationed in the woods across the road from

the entrance to Spear's mansion. From their vantage point, ten yards from the road, they could see the main door through the wrought iron entrance gates. Beth was busy positioning a directional microphone to pick up anything being said in the conference room immediately to the right of the main door.

'Can you hear anybody?' David asked, lighting another cigarette, hiding the flame of the match so it couldn't be seen from the house.

'Just background atmosphere. There's no one in the conference room yet. When the talking starts, I'll be able to adjust the mike.'

'Are you sure you'll be able to pick up conversations with that thing?'

'Positive. The room's got nice big windows. That's just what we need.'

Beth sat back on her haunches, evidently pleased with her work. 'I *hated* this part of my training, the technical stuff. Dad used to shout to get me to concentrate.'

The bark of the tree David was sitting against was digging into his back. He shifted slightly, and massaged his torn elbows through the material of his anorak. Beth had dabbed disinfectant on his wounds when they'd got back to the cottage just before dawn. The stinging pain had made him yell. Afterwards he'd made love to her, gingerly. Their foray into Spear's house had left adrenalin coursing through her system, and she'd ridden him to a wild climax. Her abandonment had frightened and excited him.

As he'd lain beside her afterwards, too exhausted to sleep, he had wondered if what he felt for her was more than the product of circumstances. Could he be falling in love again? When he had finally fallen asleep, he had dreamt that a noise awakened him and that he'd gone to the window and Lauris had been standing at the far end of the garden, head bent. He had called her name and she had looked up. Smiling sadly, she had turned languidly away from him to disappear through the trees, while he shouted her name and hammered at the window.

Now, Beth came over and sat beside him against the

oak. She removed the cigarette from his lips, took a puff, and put it back. She reached in the bag strapped to her stomach, took out a rectangular metal object about the size of a cigarette packet, studded with two buttons.

'The detonator,' she said. 'If anything happens to me, press the buttons simultaneously. Don't feel any compunction about using it.'

She placed the detonator back in the bag. He said nothing. She took out two pairs of binoculars, and handed one pair to him. He pinged the cigarette he was smoking into the woods behind him, trained the binoculars on the house. The rain made it difficult to see, but after a few minutes a figure appeared at the gates – Vercoe, dressed in waterproofs. Beside him was a Doberman on a leash. David guessed Hughes would be patrolling the rear of the house.

The dog barked. Vercoe tugged its choke chain to kill the sound. The front door of the house opened, and, for an instant, Spear was silhouetted against the bright light of the hallway. The door closed.

Vercoe opened the gates. The dog was straining at its leash, eyes bugging in the direction of David and Beth. Vercoe began walking across the road towards their hiding place.

'Oh God!' David moaned.

'Shut up!' Beth commanded. 'Don't move.'

Vercoe and the dog had reached their side of the road. David and Beth sat perfectly still, not breathing. Vercoe, squinting against the rain, peered into the woods.

David heard a rustle, shifted his eyes to see Beth reaching into her bag.

Car headlights speared the woods. David and Beth ducked as the lights swept the tree immediately above them. They looked up in time to see Vercoe leading the dog back across the road. He stopped in front of the car, a blue Mercedes, blocking its path, then moved round the side and peered in the window. The dog leapt up, scratching the car with its paws.

Vercoe waved the car on and it rolled slowly towards the house.

The driver, an enormous thick-set man with hair cut short, like a soldier, got out, looked around, and opened one of the rear doors. The passenger got out of the car just as the front door of the house opened to reveal Spear. The passenger, a small round man in a dark suit, ran through the rain to the door. He and Spear shook hands, exchanged a brief, formal hug. Just before the door closed, David caught a glimpse of the visitor's face. A camera clicked beside him.

He lowered his binoculars slowly, mouth open.

'It can't be,' he said, too loudly. The Doberman at the gates pricked its ears.

'It is,' Beth said, wiping rain off the telephoto lens of an infrared camera. 'The photograph will prove it.'

'Impossible.' But the man had appeared in news reports too often recently for there to be any real doubt.

It had been Piotr Marenkev, the head of the Moscow Communist Party.

'Okay,' he said, 'it's Marenkev, but how the hell did he get into the country without anyone seeing him?'

'Marenkev's an emperor. He goes were he wants. Some mental pressure, and who'd remember seeing him?'

Before he had a chance to say anything else, another visitor arrived. This time they got a good look, almost ten seconds in profile as Spear greeted him. Again, there could be no question about the visitor's identity. The birthmark on his chin was unmistakable. It was the man who had been quoted as saying that ten million deaths would not be too high a price to pay to keep the revolution pure in China – Hung Xiang.

Beth managed three quick snaps before the door closed.

'Were you expecting this?' David asked.

'No. We knew the meeting was supposed to be important, but we had no idea the head honchos were going to show.'

She moved over to the directional microphone. She put on headphones and made minute adjustments to the mike's position. When she was satisfied, she switched on a tape recorder encased in a canvas bag.

When another car appeared she returned to David's side.

'Small talk,' she whispered. 'My guess is they won't get down to business till everyone's arrived.'

The new arrival was Ayatollah Hossein Kashami. Black-robed, bearded, bespectacled, he looked a mild, respectable figure compared to his driver, a combat-jacketed Iranian revolutionary guard.

Kashami did not allow Spear to touch him, merely acknowledged him with an unsmiling nod.

A minute later, another arrival. A black-haired sallow man with a trim moustache, wearing a white suit and a camel hair coat draped over his shoulders like a 1950s Italian film director. He slung a friendly arm around Spear's shoulder and grinned at him before they stepped inside the house.

'Who was that?' David asked.

'Emilio Juarez, the Cocaine King. He controls the economy of three South American countries. About half the coke snorted in the States is imported by good old Emilio. He's South America's biggest exporter. Of *any-thing*! His pet American politician could be standing for the Presidency in '96. If James Lord doesn't win that election, Emilio will effectively be running the United States.' She blew air out from her cheeks. 'As far as I know, there haven't been as many emperors as this at one meeting in twenty years. Whatever they're planning, it'll be an earth-shaker.' She looked straight at David. Her eyes were hard. 'Would you really object to me wiping out this crew?'

'Maybe not. But it's not as simple as you make it sound.'

She made her way back to the tape recorder. She listened on the headphones for a few minutes before returning to his side.

'They've started arguing. They're all demanding to know why the hell Spear's placed them in danger by dragging them all this way. He's enjoying himself, giving nothing away. Kashami just called him a name I'm sure doesn't appear in the Koran. And Emilio doesn't sound like he's smiling any more.'

The rain had grown fiercer. Freezing streaks whipped across their faces.

'What's Spear waiting for?' David asked. He was dying for a cigarette, but he couldn't risk lighting one while Vercoe was still on patrol at the gates.

'Spear told them there's one more guest due.'

'Any ideas?'

'None. But the way he announced it, it sounded like it was going to be a real big surprise.'

'It's probably the Devil himself. He'd feel at home.'

'In some ways I think those people in there *are* the Devil.'

David shivered, wiped rain off his face. He became aware of a strange poisonous vibration in the air, a dark, murderous pulse, emanating from the mansion. It scared him; it was like listening to the very heartbeat of evil.

He thought he understood what Beth meant. The men in there tempted the world; they offered escape from reality through drugs and warped religion and violence. Especially violence. They created the circumstances in which people could behave like beasts. And that was the work of the Devil.

'Can you feel it?' Beth asked.

He nodded.

As the atmosphere from the mansion polluted the air around them, they sat in silence, awaiting the last arrival. David peered through his binoculars again. Even Vercoe looked scared. Perhaps it was dawning on him what a minor league monster he really was; a playground bully hanging out with demons. The Doberman's tail was curled between its legs. It kept glancing back at the house, shivering.

As David lowered the binoculars, he wondered if Spear's initial intention had been to make Anna one of them, part of the darkness. Maybe, just maybe, she was better off dead.

Car headlights streamed through the rain.

'This is it,' Beth whispered. 'The big surprise.'

They both then raised their binoculars.

As soon as Vercoe heard the car, he opened the gates. Spear's Roll Royce swept past him, on up to the house. Spear had the door open before the car had halted. Hughes

216

got out of the driver's seat and opened the back door. The first figure to emerge was Dr Sorensen, wearing a raincoat with the collar up. He reached back into the car to help out another passenger.

When David saw who it was, his mouth formed a silent 'No!'

CHAPTER THIRTY-ONE

It was hard to tell whether or not she was dreaming. During her incarceration dream and reality had become easy to distinguish. When she was awake, voices sounded too loud or too soft, objects within her cell appeared incredibly close or miles distant. Any movement took effort, a massive effort. And she was always in the same place.

The cage.

In her dreams she could hear and see normally. She had her power back. And she was always somewhere outside, escaping from the doctor and Spear, feeling wind and rain on her face, running, running towards her parents. They were calling to her, encouraging her, as if she was taking part in a race. But no matter how fast she ran she could get no closer to them, and when she called out to them to come towards her, to help her, her voice was a silent scream, with no force behind it . . .

But now, as Sorensen helped her out of the car, handling her as if she was a precious, fragile object, she couldn't tell whether she was back in the cage, imagining it all, or if this was really happening. If it was a dream, she would start running as soon as she got out of the car. If it was reality, that would prove impossible.

Sorensen placed a blanket over her head as he pulled her off the seat into a standing position. She could feel wind against her face. The sound of the rain was astonishingly loud. She blinked up at the house she was being led towards, vaguely recognized it; she had been here before.

Her back ached. Her belly felt enormous, heavy. She placed a hand on top of the bulging mound her stomach had become. Her mind swirled with white mist. She could grasp thoughts and ideas clearly for an instant, but then the fog would billow around them, hiding them from her. Now, she grasped the fact that the house before her was Spear's mansion.

And then the realization disappeared, shrouded in mist.

She sensed the atmosphere coming from inside the building, the doomy, black feeling of destruction and desolation, of hatred and violence . . .

She moved on rubbery legs, Sorensen's hands supporting her. He was talking to her, but she couldn't make out what he was saying.

The front door of the house opened as they approached it. A man stood there, waiting for them. A man she knew. A man she feared.

Spear.

Dream, she thought. *Just a dream!*

That meant she could run away, escape.

She tugged herself out of the doctor's grip, shucked off the blanket, and began running hell-for-leather along the driveway, towards the main gates, away from the house . . .

Blinked.

She was still in Sorensen's grasp, the blanket over her head, and she was still moving towards Spear.

So this was real.

Spear's eyes widened greedily as she approached.

She turned as they reached the door, looked back into the night, and flung out a silent cry for help . . .

. . . and David heard it. It tore a sob from his chest. He rose up from the base of the tree he'd been leaning against and took a step towards the road . . .

Found himself sprawled on the ground, Beth on top of him, her hand over his mouth.

'No!' she whispered. 'Vercoe's still at the gate.'

She took her hand away from his mouth, got off him.

He turned over and sat up. He was crying. Part joy, part anger, part fear.

'She's alive,' he said, knowing it sounded stupid, just wanting to test out the phrase to see if it sounded convincing. He looked at Beth, who had moved over to the microphone. He turned the statement into a question.

She nodded briefly.

'She's pregnant,' he said. 'Did you see that?'

Beth put on headphones, signalled for him to do the same. He crawled over to her on all fours, took the spare set.

The police evidence at the inquest had been fixed. That stuff about finding Anna's charred remains in the boot of the car had been phoney. Spear must have paid the police a visit. Or maybe he'd just had them bribed.

Beth prodded his arm, recalling him to the present. He put the headphones on.

She's alive!

'. . . angry and upset, naturally.' Spear's voice was faint, but clear. 'You've been put to a lot of trouble. For some of you, the trip has been dangerous.'

Someone else spoke, but David couldn't make out what they were saying.

'. . . just listen to what I have to say,' Spear went on. 'You'll see that I was right to bring you here. The only way you'd believe what I have to tell you is to see it for yourself.' A pause. A scraping sound. A match flaring into life? Someone puffing at a cigar? 'The eighties were a bad time for us, let's admit it. But we've begun to fight back. The next decade will undoubtedly belong to us. In the natural course of events, we might expect the other side to regroup, grow strong again, make some inroads into our success. That's the way it's always been, back and forth, throughout history.' Another pause. When Spear spoke again, David could hear the pleasure in his voice. 'No more! There will be no more power-sharing, no more compromise. We will no longer have our schemes and dreams destroyed by *them*.'

Another interruption. 'Wait!' Spear commanded. 'Tell

219

me, what has been our greatest weakness – a weakness shared by the other side?'

'Numbers,' David heard someone say. A deep, thickly accented voice. Maybe the Russian, Marenkev.

'Exactly,' Spear said. 'Numbers. We know what we want to do, and we know how to achieve it, but there simply aren't enough of us to carry our plans through. *That's* what's going to change.'

Murmuring.

'. . . fucking get on with it!' David heard. Vaguely American.

'No doubt, Senor Jaurez, it was impatience that caused you to lose two major drugs shipments to Florida last month. Fortunately, I'm not impatient. I plan ahead, and you're all going to be damned grateful for that.' Spear moved out of range. David could hear muttered conversations between the assembled guests, angry, bitter words. He heard a door open and slam shut. All conversation halted for ten seconds. The silence was followed by an excited buzz.

'Let me introduce you to our other guests,' Spear said. His voice had grown louder. 'This is Dr Sorensen, an expert in genetics. He has been looking after this young lady.'

David heard the room gasp.

'Pick her up, Sorensen,' Spear said. 'Excuse me, gentlemen, the girl is heavily sedated, but she's all right.'

David heard the phrase 'child sex'.

'No,' Spear said, trying to sound amused. 'We're not all depraved here in the West, Marenkev. This is Anna Cauley, an English girl, fifteen and a half years old. As some of you might have sensed, she is one of us.'

David glanced at Beth. Her eyes were wide with fear. There was an outburst of chatter in the room. Spear's voice rose above it.

'Anna was inseminated on the seventh of July last year. She will give birth in just over six weeks' time, at the start of April. The child she produces will be my daughter. More significantly, and the reason I've asked you all to travel thousands of miles to be here, that child will be an emperor.'

Even with the headphones on, David could hear Beth gasp beside him.

A stunned silence in the room. Then everyone talking at once, yelling. The evil throb emanating from the mansion intensified. David could feel it quake through his body.

It was a full minute before Spear could make himself heard above the racket. David could barely concentrate on what he was saying. Anna was pregnant with Spear's child. *Spear's*! Had he actually . . . ? David shuddered.

'I see you've successfully grasped the implications of our experiment,' Spear said. 'From the day the child is born, *we* will be in control. Forever!'

Excitement blasted from the mansion like rolls of thunder.

David ripped off his headphones.

'What does that mean?'

Beth squeezed the headphones tight against her ears. David reached out, plucked them from her head. The movement dislodged the directional microphone.

'Beth, what does it mean?'

'It means we're through!' she whispered. 'All of us. Finished.' She reached in the bag strapped to her stomach, removed the detonator. 'Or we would be, if it wasn't for this.'

The fingers of her other hand reached towards the buttons.

'You can't!' David said.

She glared at him again. 'Why not?'

'Anna's in there. She'll die.'

Confusion entered her eyes for a moment, disappeared. 'I have to! No choice!'

'My daughter's in there, damn you!' David growled.

She turned away from him to face the mansion, placed her fingers on the two buttons.

David unlooped the binoculars from around his neck and brought them crashing down against Beth's head. In the same instant she stabbed down on the buttons with her fingers, but only made contact with one. David tensed.

221

Nothing happened. The detonator slipped from Beth's hand and she keeled over onto her side.

The Doberman at the gates began to howl. David could see it squeezing its muzzle between the iron bars, fangs bared. Vercoe peered into the darkness beyond the gates, opened them. David hurriedly unstrapped the bag from Beth's stomach. He stuffed her equipment inside and slung it over his shoulder. Vercoe had reached the edge of the wood. He started a slow sweep of the trees with a flashlight. The beam juddered as the dog bucked at the end of its leash.

David grabbed Beth under the arms and dragged her deeper into the wood. The beam of the light slithered over the spot where she had been lying a split second before.

Then he was on his feet, carrying her in his arms, running wildly through the night.

CHAPTER THIRTY-TWO

David checked his watch. 11:30. He recommenced chewing his fingernails, winced. In the hour he'd spent prowling around the sitting room of the cottage, waiting for Beth to regain consciousness, he'd bitten every nail to the quick. He poured himself another Scotch. He'd had three already, but the alcohol wasn't having any effect.

He went to the phone for the fifth time since he'd arrived back, picked it up, held the receiver to his ear, slammed it back onto its cradle after a few seconds. Who could he call? Who would believe him? 'World conspiracy? Uh-huh! Telepaths? Sure. Straight fingerprints? Of *course*, David, of course!'

It was the hope that was so hard to cope with. Anna was alive, and there was a chance of getting her back. Anything he did now could jeopardize that possibility. He *mustn't* make the wrong choice.

He went back to his chair, sat down, resumed worrying his raw nails.

He couldn't even count on Beth helping him decide what to do. She'd been on the verge of murdering his daughter. His pregnant daughter.

It was Anna being pregnant that had made Beth reach for the the detonator. Why? What was so significant about her carrying Spear's baby (*Damn him!*). There were other emperors. What would be so different about this one?

He stood abruptly, went over to the couch, shook Beth awake.

Her eyelids flickered. She groaned, looked around. She let her head drop back and stared up at David expressionlessly for a few seconds. Her eyes caught fire suddenly and she was pummelling him with her fists. He grabbed her wrists. It took all his strength to control her.

'You stupid *bastard*!' she shouted. 'You *really* screwed up!'

'You were about to kill my daughter,' he said quietly.

Some of the anger drained from her eyes, but they were no friendlier. 'It was the right thing to do.'

'You can't mean that.'

'It was *right*!'

'Nothing could make that right.'

She looked away. 'I have to contact James to let him know we failed.'

Still holding her wrists, David brought his face close to her's. 'WE DON'T DO ANYTHING TILL YOU TELL ME WHAT'S GOING ON! I WANT TO KNOW EVERYTHING. NOW, DAMN YOU!'

The room seemed eerily still after he had stopped shouting. Beth was shaking. He let go of her.

She rubbed each of her wrists in turn. In his rage, David had almost broken them.

'I must know,' David said, his voice now hoarse.

'Yes,' Beth said. 'First, a drink. Please.'

He got up, poured her a whisky, returned to the couch.

'The emperors,' he said. 'Tell me everything.'

She sat up, sipped her drink. He sat down next to her.

Beth cleared her throat. 'Right. Emperors are freaks, basically. Just as nature sometimes produces children with

223

two heads, or siamese twins, it occasionally comes up with an emperor. They've got parallel fingerprints and slightly different brain structures from ordinary human beings. The differences are so minor a brilliant nuerosurgeon wouldn't notice them unless he was looking for them. Emperors have no other physical characteristics in common. Mentally, they tend to be domineering, intelligent, arrogant. People are attracted to them by their aura of power, by their charisma.'

'Their mental powers?'

'You've seen your daughter in action. They're telepaths, but only in one direction. They can't read your thoughts but they can make you do what they want you to do. They can place a thought in your head and make you believe it's yours. It's an intimate power – it works best one to one. It sort of works with a crowd – they can hold people's attention – but emperors can't make a whole roomful of people believe something they know to be false. One to one, they can make you believe anything.'

She took another sip of her Scotch, leaned back and fingered the wound on her scalp.

'Is their power finite? Do they run out of juice? I remember the day Anna forced Spear out of our house, the effort seemed to exhaust her.'

'They're like athletes – their energy shouldn't be frittered away. They have to have time to recoup afterwards. James says if he really has to use his power, it leaves him feeling like he's just run a marathon.'

'What motivates them? What do they want?'

'Power, control over others. They often become politicians, because that's where the power lies. Or businessmen, like Spear, because money's power as well. They don't have appetites for things like drugs or sex or money for its own sake. Physical pleasure is low on their agenda.'

'Okay, so power turns them on. But what do they do with it when they've got it?'

'Depends which side they're on. They see themselves as a separate race from human beings, a race whose destiny is to control us. For some of them, I think power's just an end in itself.'

'Numbers?'

'Impossible to say. Right now, we know of seven in the enemy camp, including Spear. There are five in James Lord's, including him. But there could be dozens more scattered around the world, unaware of their potential, keeping their heads down because they're guilty about being different, scared they'll be punished if they're found out. Emperors don't realize exactly what they are until they meet others of their own kind. That's a pretty haphazard process. James might never have known unless he'd met Bobby Kennedy. Spear must have had a similar experience – we know he met Gadaffi at an Embassy reception back in London in '68, before the coup that put Gadaffi in power. Maybe that's when he found out about himself.' She looked at him. 'Anna might have been safe today if you hadn't met James Lord.'

David nodded. He felt calmer inside, but he was still angry.

'Why are the emperors divided into two camps?'

'They're like ordinary people. Some emperors are good, some bad. James amuses himself by making out lists of historical figures he reckons were emperors. Hitler was one. He thinks Jesus Christ was another. It's difficult to imagine two more different figures. James believes Christ is the most powerful emperor the world has ever known. Of course, that doesn't mean he wasn't the Son of God.'

'But Christ didn't convince everyone. They crucified him.'

'James thinks they crucified him because they knew he was an emperor. People understood these things better before the age of science.'

'If Christ was an emperor, why didn't he stop the crucifixion?'

'Maybe he didn't want to. Would his teachings have had as big an impact if he hadn't died on the cross?'

'I suppose not.' David snapped his fingers. 'Spear thinks Christ was an emperor as well. There's a row of books about him in his study. Along with works on Stalin and Hitler and Napoleon.'

'James reckons Jack the Ripper was another. Sex

murders are all to do with power. If the Ripper was an emperor, it would account for his ability to get out of tight spots and it might explain why nobody remembered seeing him.'

'So is it nature or nurture?' David asked.

'Could you run that by me again?'

David shrugged. 'Are emperors born good or evil or does their upbringing and environment make them the way they are?'

'We don't know if that's the case with human beings, let alone emperors.'

'True.' He paused. 'What I mean is, do you think Spear could turn Anna into someone like himself?'

'It's happened to others in the past. Mao Tse-tung started off wanting a better life for the Chinese people. He wanted to wipe out starvation and end exploitation by Chiang Kai-shek's warlords. After ten years in power Mao collectivized agriculture. Millions died of starvation. He built up a massive secret police force that used murder and torture. In 1966 he engineered the Cultural Revolution, and we now know how much evil that produced. Mao turned bad.'

David thought of the change he had discerned in James Lord over the years. *There won't be any trial!* Had power corrupted *him*!

'How come one group doesn't get the upper hand and wipe out the other?'

'The Balance,' she said. 'James is always talking about it. Nature just seems to have a way of evening things out. When the bad guys have been on top for a while, the good guys find more emperors, and vice-versa. James reckons the Second World War could have been the first time one side went for a clean sweep, but Stalin and Hitler fell out and that's what saved us. Since then the initiative's regularly passed from one side to the other, though James's side had been doing pretty well until a few months back. As Spear pointed out, a lot of good things happened in the eighties.' She paused, gave a hopeless little shake of the head. 'But all those advances aren't going to count for anything if Spear gets his way.'

'When Spear told the other emperors Anna's baby was going to be one of them, that terrified you. Why?'

She held out her empty glass. 'Another?'

He got up, poured out some more Scotch.

When she'd taken a gulp of her fresh drink, she said, 'I hope what I'm going to tell you will help you forgive me for trying to kill Anna.'

'Let's hear it.' He did not feel particularly forgiving.

'The real reason neither side has been able to gain a permanent advantage, the thing that keeps the world in a sort of moral twilight, is that emperors can't reproduce. When they mate with ordinary human beings, their children are always normal. Otherwise, they'd have taken over the world centuries ago. Total control. Mankind would have had as much chance of survival as Neanderthal man.'

'Man would have fought back.'

'Other species didn't do so well against man, did they? There's a growing concensus that Evolution hasn't all been gradual. Species, *some* species, at least, have evolved by gigantic leaps. For instance, giraffes started out as short-necked creatures. Fossil evidence proves that. Now, all giraffes have long necks. Go to any zoo. So, the old theory went, giraffe necks gradually got longer as they stretched to reach food higher up in the trees. That process is supposed to have taken hundreds of thousands of years. Gradually, short-necked giraffes disappeared from the scene, because they couldn't stretch high enough to get at the food.'

'I don't see the relevance of any of this, but what's wrong with the theory of gradual change? And what does it have to do with emperors?' He lit a cigarette, puffed at it impatiently.

'Nowhere in the world has anyone ever found any fossil remains of a giraffe with a medium-length neck. Plenty of short-necked giraffes. No medium. Now do you see?'

'No.'

'The new theory is that the first long-necked giraffe was a freak – an emperor, if you like. The freak giraffe could get at the food more easily. He survived. He mated with an ordinary giraffe. Maybe some of their offspring had short necks, some long. The long-necked ones survived, mated with each other. The changeover didn't take hundreds of thousands of years. One minute there were short-necked giraffes, the next, maybe only a century or two later, there were none. That's why there are no fossil remains of medium-necked giraffes. They never existed.'

David mashed out his cigarette. 'You're saying that if emperors could reproduce, we'd suffer the same fate as short-necked giraffes. We'd die out.'

'Or they'd turn us into slaves. Neither prospect's particularly appealing.'

'But surely they'd have done that already if they'd wanted to. All they need do is mate with another emperor.'

'Anna's the *only* female emperor known to either side. As far as anyone knows, she's unique.'

David stared at Beth for a long time. Eventually, as understanding dawned, he said, 'Good God!'

'Exactly.'

'But there must be other female emperors.'

'Maybe. Boadicea and Joan of Arc were probably emperors, or empresses. Catherine the Great of Russia, Queen Elizabeth the First here in England. Who knows? It's unlikely that Anna's the only one there's been throughout the whole of history. But she's the only one in modern times who's come into contact with another emperor.'

David stood up. 'So Spear made her pregnant. Anna's going to have a daughter. That daughter's going to be an emperor. He'll have more daughters by her. Sorensen can fix it so they'll be female. As soon as Anna's children reach puberty, they'll be made pregnant by other emperors. And so on and so on, until—'

'Until life get's tough for us short-necked giraffes. And for James Lord and his people. They'll wind up as a guerrilla group fighting a rearguard action against Spear's progeny.'

David wheeled round. 'The Balance,' he said. 'Gone forever.'

'Moral darkness,' Beth said.

David shut his eyes. He could see a black, evil, poisonous mist oozing over the face of the Earth, and from the depths of that mist he could hear screams of agony and despair . . .

'And there's nothing we can do about it,' Beth said, her voice dead.

David opened his eyes. 'Yes there is.'

She looked up at him. 'What?'

'Get Anna back.'

'Oh, sure. Now, why didn't I think of that?' She shook her head. 'We don't even know where she is.'

He grinned. 'Yes we do.'

CHAPTER THIRTY-THREE

The Doberman sounded big as a horse as it splashed across the sodden back garden. Its low growl was loud in the quiet of the night.

Spear wheeled round, biting the cigar clenched between his teeth. Brandy slopped over the rim of the goblet in his hand.

The Doberman was heading straight for him. It was an ideal guard dog; it would automatically attack anyone it had not been trained to obey, and Spear had deliberately chosen not to have the dogs trained to respond to him. He enjoyed mastering them afresh each time they went for him. It kept him alert.

He waited till the animal was just on the verge of leaping before gathering his power and aiming a mental bolt at it. It was too late for the dog not to leap, but now it had to obey the mental command not to harm Spear. It twisted in mid-air, squealing, missed him by inches. It hit the ground clumsily, on its side, went tumbling over and over. It slithered to a halt, picked itself up gingerly, stared at him. It growled, and began heading towards him again.

He gave the dog another bolt. It twisted its body and

bit through its testicles, howled.

Vercoe came running round the side of the house, halted when he saw the mutilated dog.

As Vercoe dragged the whimpering animal away, Spear sipped his brandy and puffed at his cigar. Plumes of smoke wafted up into the night sky.

He had won.

The other emperors had accepted him as their unquestioned leader. Even Marenkev. Their tributes had been embarrassingly fulsome, but he had enjoyed them. It had taken him years to become their master. By the time he was ready to relinquish that position, the new generation of emperors would be in place. He was going to start a dynasty that would never be overthrown.

His descendants would control the world as easily as he had the Doberman.

He pulled back his arm and hurled the brandy goblet in the direction of the rose garden. He lost sight of it, and stood still, waiting. Eventually, he heard it shatter. The sound of destruction made him smile. Soon, the world would echo with it.

James Lord sat on his porch high up in the Colorado mountains, waiting for dawn. He wanted desperately to see the distant clouds blush with the morning sun.

He had sat for hours staring at the computer monitor after receiving the news about Anna. The last message had been particularly chilling: *To the Devil, a daughter*. As he had sat there, flesh crawling, stomach churning with a fear more devastating than any he had ever experienced, he had not known what message to send back. The world was to be ruled by Calibans; he had delivered it into the hands of brutes. The earth would become one vast prison camp, an enormous torture chamber.

Brutal images flickered against his mind's eye. The Nazi death camps, twisted limbs piled like gnarled sticks, the stench of burned flesh; lines of emaciated, exhausted zombies trudging across the endless bleak, freezing wastes of the Gulag Archipelago; the streets of Phnom Penh, Khmer Rouge soldiers skewering babies with bayonets, the sick being hurled from hospital windows to certain death . . .

The reply he had eventually tapped into the computer had been:

Do you know where Anna is?

Yes.

There had been tears in his eyes when he'd tapped in the next message: *Save her, if possible. If not* – (here, his hand had started to shake) – *terminate.*

Beth's reply had been a long time coming. *Understood.*

Afterwards he had poured himself a drink and lain down on the couch, but there had been no chance of sleep. The order he had given had made him feel dirty, as if the odour of old puke clung to him. But he had once been sentimental; he had allowed the infant Anna to stay with her parents. That softness had brought the world to the brink of total horror. He must not be soft again. If Anna Cauley gave birth to an emperor under the control of Richard Spear, the next century would belong to psychopaths.

Giving up his attempt at sleep, he had wrapped himself in protective clothing and gone out onto the balcony to await the light, craving it, suddenly frightened of the dark. Frightened because he might have signed the death warrant of an innocent child. And frightened of something else. After an hour spent sipping neat vodka and staring down at the eerie glow of the snow-dusted valley below the house, he admitted to himself that he was terrified in case he no longer possessed the power. He had not truly tested himself since the attempt on his life; he had been scared to, in case it wasn't there.

Just after he had stepped out onto the balcony, one of the guards had appeared and asked him if he was all right. He had nodded and sent him on his way. Now, the guard was back, looking up at James, asking if he hadn't better go inside.

'It's mighty cold out here, Mr Lord.'

The sky above the distant mountains had begun to lighten.

James shrugged the blanket from his shoulders, rose.

He had to test himself, had to *know*. He stood crookedly, leaning to one side, as if a strong wind was blowing against him.

He stared down at the guard, then shut his eyes, concentrated.

Now!

He opened his eyes, felt the power leave his body. The guard stood stockstill for a moment. James's stomach twisted with anxiety. The guard wheeled round, lifting his rifle as he did so, loosed off two quick shots into the dawn sky. They echoed amongst the mountains for a long time. The guard lowered his rifle. As he turned back towards James, his expression was puzzled.

'I'm sorry, Mr Lord. I swear I heard something behind me. No, felt it, more like. When I turned, it was *there*! Something.' He shook his head. 'Sorry.'

'Don't be sorry,' James said, smiling. 'You're alert, that's good.'

There were violet streaks in the sky. Light was returning to the earth.

The guard was still standing there, looking confused.

'I'll be leaving here sometime today,' James said. 'We'll use the plane. Tell them to get it ready for a long haul.'

'How long, Mr Lord?'

'England.'

Just as he turned and headed inside, the first rays of the rising sun caught his back. It felt warm and good.

CHAPTER THIRTY-FOUR

Light from a streetlamp above Beth's Mitsubishi Galant GTi glinted off the barrel of her pistol as she checked the magazine.

David hadn't really studied it before.

'Swiss gun, isn't it?'

She slid the magazine back into the butt.

'Nine millimetre SIG. One of the finest pistols in the world.' She gave him a sideways glance as she slipped the gun into a shoulder holster under her short black leather jacket. 'I thought you'd never fired a gun in your life.'

'I haven't, but they fascinated me when I was a kid. My father found all my gun magazines one day. You'd have thought he'd caught me reading hard porn. He made me throw them away.'

Beth stared down the leafy suburban street. 'Strange. Your father wouldn't even let you read gun magazines. Mine took me to a shooting gallery twice a week.' She paused. 'This was his gun. It was still in its holster when they killed him. He must have been slowing down.' She cleared her throat, sat up straight. 'If any shooting needs to be done, leave it to me. I don't want you blowing my head off.' She glanced at her watch. 'Five to five. Time to get moving.'

'Beth, you've been keeping something back. What is it?'

'Don't start that again.'

She had been acting furtively since receiving her last message from James Lord. She had barely spoken a word to David in the past twenty-four hours. The cottage had been thick with her tension. It wasn't fear, exactly: something else was troubling her, something to do with James's message.

'What did James tell you to do?'

She said nothing, kept staring straight ahead.

'You point that gun anywhere near Anna,' he said, 'I'll be forced to kill you.' No response. 'That's what James's message was about, wasn't it?'

'I . . .' She lowered her eyes. 'If things go wrong and we can't get her out, I'm supposed to shoot her.'

'If we can't take her with us, we leave her. Understood?'

'I have to obey James's orders.'

He reached for her chin, forced her head up. 'James isn't here. I am. And I have a gun. Remember that.' He let go of her chin. 'That man used to be my friend. Now . . .' He shrugged. 'Let's go.'

They got out of the car. A chill wind was gusting leaves down the pre-dawn street. They made their way to the end of the road and halted. The Institute for Genetic Engineering was in total darkness, and there was no sign of any guard at the gate. David closed his eyes for a moment, trying to pick up any vibrations that might indicate Anna was inside. The sense of confusion and hopelessness he had experienced when trailing Spear to the Institute had been Anna's, but he hadn't realized that then. Now, he felt it again. It was much fainter this time – a tiny tremor of despair.

'She's in there,' he said.

'You can't know that.'

'Yes, I can.'

Beth stepped out from the shadow of the bush at the end of the street. A car came careering down the road, doing about sixty, almost out of control. In its headlights, David saw a guard behind the gates of the Institute. He tugged Beth back into the shadow of the bush. The car slewed past them, skidded round the next corner.

'I saw a guard in there, just behind the gate.'

Beth pressed back the edge of the bush. 'How are you at acting drunk?'

'I've had some practice.'

'Okay. I'll go first. When I reach the wall beside the gate, you head down the road. Act drunk, but don't make enough noise to wake the neighbourhood. When you're level with the gate, do something to attract the guard's attention. Fall down or something.'

'And this is spycraft?'

'It'll work. That's what counts.'

She checked the gate once more to make sure the guard wasn't watching, ran lightly across the road, and, crouching, padded along the pavement. When she was beside the gate she straightened, pulled her gun out of its holster, and pressed her back against the redbrick wall that ran along the front of the institute. She motioned at David with her gun.

He tottered out from behind the bush, went highstepping up the road, lifting his knees, leaning back. He manufactured a belch that echoed down the street, and began a lugubrious rendition of *What the World Needs Now*

234

is Love Sweet Love. He glanced at Beth. She was holding her nose as a comment on his performance.

When he was level with the gate he deliberately dropped some coins from his anorak pocket.

'Shit!' he slurred. He bent down, straight-legged, made it look as if he was trying to pick up the coins, cursing all the while. Out of the corner of his eye, he saw the guard approaching the gate. A big beefy black man in uniform.

David stood up straight. 'I say, old boy, you couldn't lend us a hand, could you? Dropped all my money. Can't get home.'

The guard sucked on a hollow tooth for a few seconds, then said, 'Fuck off!'

'Well, that's not very pleasant.' David belched. 'Is it?'

The guard shrugged, began to blend back into the shadows.

Beth made frantic signals at David.

'Hey!' David called out. 'You look like a fucking gorilla in a cage. When's feeding time?'

The black stuck his head between two of the gate's iron bars, eyes blazing. 'Man, I told you to fuck—'

Beth slammed the butt of her gun against the guard's forehead. He sagged against the gate and slid onto the ground. She had the gate open by the time David reached it. He lugged the guard into the shadows.

Beth ran swiftly up to the front door. There was a coloured-glass porthole window beside it. She smashed it with her gunbutt, reached in to unlatch it, and slithered inside. She opened the door for David a few seconds later.

They headed down the nearest corridor in the direction of the windowless annexe at the side of the house. Another uniformed guard was running towards them, holding a gun. Vercoe was right behind him, trying to get his own gun out.

Beth loosed off a shot without slowing down. There was a flash of light, and the guard fell forwards, blood pouring from his mouth. Vercoe turned, began to run away.

'Halt or you're dead!' David shouted. Beth fired a warning shot that almost deafened him.

Vercoe froze.

Beth ran past him to a metal door at the end of the corridor. There was a number-lock device attached to the wall beside it.

David grabbed Vercoe's collar, dug the barrel of the Colt hard into his neck.

'Open it!' he shouted.

'Don't know how!' Vercoe yelled.

David jabbed the gun fiercely against Vercoe's skull.

'Open it!'

Vercoe reached out a shaking hand, punched in a combination. The door began to slide back. Vaporous light poured into the corridor from the room beyond.

David slammed Vercoe up against the wall next to the sliding door. 'I'd like to kill you, but I'm going to leave you to Spear.'

He brought the gun down in a short, vicious arc. As Vercoe slithered unconscious onto the floor, David followed Beth into the annexe.

Muted striplighting. A laboratory; books, a workbench, an examination table. One corner of the room had been turned into a wiremesh cage, containing a bed and a bank of electronic equipment – an ECG, an electroencephalogram, a CAT-scanner. Several monitors were stacked one on top of the other. A constant stream of numbers flickered across the bottom screen. Above it, another screen displayed a multi-coloured depiction of a fully-formed foetus, a blue patch pulsing in the middle of its chest.

Anna was on the bed, naked, eyes closed, a mass of wires attached to her body. There were needle tracks on her scrawny arms. Electrodes had been taped to her shaved skull.

Beth rattled the door of the cage. David motioned her to step aside, crashed the door open with his foot. A sob escaped his throat as he approached the bed. He halted.

'Keep going!' Beth shouted, moving past him. She began ripping away the wires and electrodes taped to Anna's body. David removed the IV feed from Anna's arm, then turned and lashed at the bank of monitoring equipment with his foot, sent it crashing to the floor.

236

Sparks, warning beeps, curls of smoke.

He turned, lifted Anna up off the bed. She seemed to weigh nothing at all. With Beth leading the way, he ran down the corridor back towards the front door. When they reached it, a shot rang out. A fist-sized hole appeared in one of the door panels. Sorensen was at the top of the stairs, a gun in his hand. Beth loosed off a shot at him. He dropped to the floor, out of sight.

Beth covered David as he ran from the building. The guard he'd left by the side of the gate lurched at him out of the darkness, fists balled. David skidded to a halt. Suddenly, Beth was there, chopping the guard's windpipe with the side of her hand. He made an ugly wheezing sound as he reeled back into the shadows, clutching his throat.

David kicked the gates open, and they ran across the street. Beth overtook him and had the back door open when he reached the car. He lay Anna along the backseat, squeezed in beside her. Beth got in the front, revved the engine. The tyres gave a pained squeal as the car bulleted away from the kerb.

CHAPTER THIRTY-FIVE

'We've got to get her to a hospital,' David said as they headed up off the Marylebone Road onto the M40 motorway.

He was stroking Anna's chalk-white face. She was still unconscious, and her breathing was ragged.

'We can't chance it,' Beth said, taking the car up to eighty in the fast lane. 'How do we explain how she got in this state? The hospital would be onto the cops in a flash.'

'She needs a doctor, Beth.'

'We'll talk about it when we reach the cottage.'

'Now! She's sick.'

'Later. I have to ask James what to do.'

'*Fuck* James!'

'I have,' she said.

He jerked his head up.

'You should have told me.'

'It's none of your business!' she shouted over her shoulder.

Stunned, he shifted his gaze back to Anna. She looked near to death. 'She needs treatment.'

'She'll get it, but not right now. I just have—'

The police siren cut off the rest of her sentence. The patrol car's headlights lit up the inside of the Mitsubishi as it roared up behind them.

'Take the next turn-off!' David ordered.

Beth slewed across three lanes, just in time to make the slip-road.

'Kill the lights!' he shouted.

She switched them off.

'Second exit off this roundabout . . . Good . . . Left-hand fork.'

They were racing down Wood Lane towards Shepherd's Bush. The police car was fifty yards behind as they shot past BBC Television Centre.

'I can't outrun them,' Beth yelled.

'You *have* to!'

They were about to enter Shepherd's Bush Green, a four-lane one way system coiling around a small park. David hooked an arm around the passenger-seat headrest, keeping Anna pinned to the backseat with his other hand.

'Straight ahead!' he ordered.

'It's one way.'

'Just do it!'

A taxi was heading straight towards them. Beth crashed her hand on the horn. The taxi tried to get out of their way, but Beth caught the side of it. The Mitsubishi fishtailed as it glanced off the cab, and they were heading the wrong way around the park. David glanced out the back window. The taxi had broadsided to a halt, blocking the sliproad that would have allowed the police to follow them the wrong way around the Green. The police car was forced to take the standard route. The cars were parallel now, on either side of the park, heading for the same intersection.

'Stop!' David yelled.

Beth rammed down on the brakes. David lost his hold on the headrest. Anna rolled off the backseat onto the floor, groaned. They skidded to a halt. The police car was still moving.

'Across the Green,' David shouted.

'There's no road!'

'Through the railings!'

Beth twisted the wheel, headed for the park railings, hit them at an angle. They sagged. The car stalled. She restarted it, backed across the road, narrowly missing an electric milk float. The back of the Mitsubishi crashed into the window of a betting shop, shattering it. Beth smashed her foot down on the accelerator, shot forward.

The police car had halted at the intersection. Lights were going on in windows all around the Green. This time the Mitsubishi hit the railings front on, flattening them. They were hurtling across the Green, down a cement path, back towards the entrance to Wood Lane. The taxi was gone, and their way out of the Green was clear. The police car had reached the breach in the railings and was following them across the park. A lamp-post loomed up at them out of the darkness. Beth span the wheel, but too late. The Mitsubishi clipped the post, but managed to keep on going. The post fell across the cement pathway behind them. They rammed the railings on the other side of the Green. The car juddered violently, but they were back out on the road. As they skidded into Wood Lane David saw the patrol car hit the fallen lamp-post and do a cartwheel.

The police siren was dying as Beth speeded back up towards the motorway.

David let out a whoop, then he heard a faint, confused voice.

'Daddy?'

He reached down, lifted Anna up off the floor of the car.

She looked up at him for a moment. 'Daddy,' she

239

repeated, then her eyes crossed and her head sagged against his chest.

Anna was still unconscious an hour later when they arrived at the cottage. David carried her upstairs and laid her on the bed in her old room. He switched on the bedside light. The sight of her gaunt, grey face brought tears to his eyes. Her body was filthy. Her sunken cheeks and shaved head made her look like a victim of the Nazi death camps.

'They didn't even bathe her,' he said. 'How could they treat her this way?'

'I'll get her cleaned up,' Beth said, sounding brisk. 'Look for something we can wrap round her.'

When Beth left the room, David saw Anna's veined belly ripple. The baby was moving around inside her. Spear's baby. He shuddered, went to Anna's cupboard, took out a kimono-style cotton robe.

Beth reappeared with a tin basin full of hot, soapy water, a sponge, and a bath-towel. She washed Anna meticulously, and towelled her down afterwards. David produced the robe and held Anna while Beth struggled to get it on her.

'Can we call a doctor now?' he asked when they'd finished.

'Not yet,' Beth said. 'I'll look after her while you get some sleep.'

'You sleep. I couldn't.'

'Okay. I've just got to send James a message, tell him she's safe.' She halted at the door on the way out. 'David, tonight, I couldn't have killed her. I know that now.'

He wanted to believe her. He nodded, not looking at her. She left the room.

He sat down on the edge of the bed, and stared at Anna, trying to grasp the fact that she was here, really here. It didn't seem possible.

Beth came back a few minutes later. 'James isn't logged in.'

'What does that mean?'

'I'm not sure.' She shook her head. 'I'll worry about it when I wake up.' She yawned. 'See you later.'

Anna's eyes flickered open a few seconds later. She stared at her father for a long time through half-shut lids, her face expressionless. Then her eyes shifted about the room.

'Where?' she asked.

'The cottage,' David said.

'The cottage,' she repeated and looked back at him. 'How?'

'It doesn't matter.' He placed his hand over hers. It was painfully thin.

'Mummy?' she asked.

'She's not here.'

'Dead.' It was a statement.

'Yes.'

Her eyes filled with tears. 'I knew.'

David leaned forward, kissed her cheek.

'I couldn't fight the doctor,' she said. 'He kept injecting me, and I couldn't use my power on him. He kept me so . . . so foggy. Couldn't fight.' Her eyes became unfocused. Her other hand slithered up over her belly. 'I'm going to have a baby. I don't know how. A baby. I remember a ride in a car and then I was in a room with a lot of men. They were like me. And Spear was there, and he said it was his baby.' Her eyes closed. 'His.'

And she was unconscious again.

David experienced a strong temptation to clasp her swollen belly and *crush* inwards with both hands to destroy the thing inside her.

Ugliness and evil.

He stood up and quickly left the room.

CHAPTER THIRTY-SIX

Spear's lips were pursed as he emerged from the cage after a cursory inspection. When Hughes had awakened him at the mansion to inform him that Anna Cauley had been kidnapped he had gone, literally, crazy. He vaguely remembered running, screaming, through the house, destroying everything that came to hand – paintings, mirrors, windows. God alone knew what the damage amounted to. Hughes had fled the house to hide in the grounds until Spear's initial burst of rage had passed.

Now, as Spear halted in front of Sorensen and Vercoe, the rage was still there, throbbing inside him, but he was the master of it.

Vercoe was sitting on an examination table, shoulders slumped, staring at the floor. Stitches protruded like barbed wire from a livid gash in his skull. Sorensen was standing beside him. The doctor returned Spear's gaze defiantly. His shoulders were squared, as if he was bracing himself for a possible blast.

'All right, Sorensen, it wasn't your fault. You did your best.' Spear paused. 'Tell me, will the baby be in danger now that you're no longer treating the girl?'

'Yes,' Sorensen said. 'Anything could happen.'

'Then we better find her quickly. Might the girl herself die?'

'Probably not. Again, it's hard to tell. The antenatal preparations have been seriously disrupted.'

'Go upstairs and pack some clothes, doctor. I want you with me when we find the girl.'

Evidently relieved, Sorensen left the room. Hughes appeared a few moments later.

'The guards?' Spear asked.

'Both dead. They won't be found.'

'That's good.'

Spear turned to Vercoe. 'Look at me,' he said quietly.

Vercoe lifted his head slowly. His crossed eyes were glassy and bloodshot.

'You let Cauley get away when you went to the hospital to kill him. From the fact that Cauley knew where to find his daughter, I deduce that he witnessed her arrival at the mansion the other night. You were on guard duty.' Spear's anger was like a beast stirring within him. 'This morning you allowed Cauley to stroll in here and kidnap his daughter. She was your responsibility.'

Hughes shuffled backwards, heading for the door.

'Stay!' Spear ordered. Hughes halted. 'Vercoe, you seem to have been having trouble with your eyes. They're obviously not working very well. Things escape them.'

Liquid dribbled onto the concrete floor of the annex as Vercoe's bladder voided.

'The uselessness of your eyes offends me, Vercoe.'

Vercoe threw up an arm, as if warding off a blow. There was a warm feeling in the pit of Spear's stomach, an anticipatory tingle as he gathered his mental energy.

Now, he would find a proper release for his anger. He reached a finger of energy into the dark, bubbling cesspit of Vercoe's mind.

Vercoe reached a hand up to his own face, formed a circle with his fingers, and tore out his right eye.

'Why hasn't James responded?' David asked, sinking down onto the sitting-room couch. Anna had woken up a few minutes before, and had stayed conscious long enough for him to feed her some soup. She was sleeping again now.

Beth swung her chair away from the computer in the corner of the room, and shrugged. 'I don't know. Maybe there's a fault in the system somewhere. I can't even tell if he's received the message.'

'We have to decide whether to call in a doctor.'

Beth stood up, stretched her arms. 'Anna's okay, isn't she? There's no need to panic.'

'Now I've got her back, I don't want to risk losing her again just because we didn't hear from James.'

Logs shifted in the fireplace. Above it, a carriage clock chimed the half hour: 7:30.

Beth walked over to the couch and sat down beside David. 'It upset you, hearing about James and me. Why?'

'I was disappointed in him, taking advantage of you.'

'How do you know it wasn't the other way round?'

'Was it?'

She looked away, into the fire. 'It seemed right at the time. Dad was sick and I was deputizing for him. James was taking care of some business in Germany – he had a meeting with another emperor. We were staying at the

243

Four Seasons in Hamburg. One evening he took me for a ride on the lake, and we had dinner. Afterwards, we had drinks in his room. I was telling him how I felt I hadn't really had a childhood, and he said he felt pretty much the same. He told me what a strain it was being an emperor, how he could never really relax, and how he wished he could lead a normal life. Ideally, he would have liked to remain a Washington lawyer, and meet a nice girl and settle down, but he knew that was out of the question. He'd tried it once, and the marriage had failed. His wife had gradually realized there was something strange about him, and it had freaked her out. Besides, he said he had this power compulsion to cope with, this worm twisting around in his stomach.' She smiled, remembering. 'And then we were making love. I don't really know how it happened. It just did. I don't think he used his power on me. I'd always wondered what it would be like to sleep with him.'

David's jaws clenched. 'If I thought he'd made you do it—'

'You're being silly, David. Why are you so upset?'

He sat up abruptly. 'Because if we ever get out of this, I want to marry you.' He hadn't realized what he was going to say before the words were out of his mouth.

'Oh,' she said. 'So does James.'

It was like a kick in the stomach. 'Have you accepted?'

'Yes.'

He slumped back, winded. 'Does he love you?'

'I don't think so. It'd be easier for him to marry me than anyone else. I already know all there is to know about him – he doesn't have to worry about me finding out he's different. And he's probably sized me up and reckoned I'd make a passable First Lady some day.'

'You make him sound so calculating.'

'He is. He has to be.'

David got up and walked over to the fire. He picked up the poker and toyed with the burning logs. Flames unfurled lazily up the chimney.

'What about me, Beth? Don't you feel anything for me?'

'Of course. But I think, being with me, you've suddenly

realized how lonely you've been without your family. It's been us against the world the last couple of weeks, and that's made us feel sort of close.'

'I get the message. Ours was a holiday romance.'

'Some vacation.'

He poked the logs savagely, making the flames leap.

She stood up and walked over to him, slipped an arm around his waist.

'You don't need me now, David. You've got Anna back.'

He dropped the poker, took her face in his hands and bent to kiss her.

'I want you,' he said. 'I really do.'

Two sounds, almost simultaneous. Anna screaming in her room upstairs, and, a split second later, footsteps along the path leading up to the house.

'I'll check on Anna,' David said, letting go of Beth. 'You see who's outside.'

As he headed out of the room he saw Beth reaching in her bag for her gun.

CHAPTER THIRTY-SEVEN

Anna was sitting up in bed, staring down at herself in horror. Blood was gushing onto the sheets from between her spread-eagled legs.

'Daddy!' she cried. 'It hurts!'

He ran to the cupboard in the corner of the room, dragged out a sheet. He balled it as he ran to the bed, jammed it between her legs. The sheet turned red in an instant. Panic gripped his chest. She was losing an enormous amount of blood.

The bedroom door burst open. James Lord stood framed in the doorway for an instant. He looked so old and gaunt he was barely recognizable. He approached the bed with awkward, lurching strides.

He told David to stand back, then placed a hand on Anna's head. She looked up at him, wonder mingling with fear.

'Yes, I'm like you,' he said. 'And I'm telling you you can stop it. You can stop the bleeding.'

David felt Beth grab his arm. The room was filled with a familiar buzz. James, feeding power into Anna.

'Can't!' Anna gasped.

'You can do it. Use my strength.'

She shook her head.

'Do it!' he shouted. 'I don't have much power left.'

Anna closed her eyes. The buzzing increased, became a deep thrum. The floorboards seemed to vibrate under David's feet. Beth tightened her grip on his arm.

There was a ripple across Anna's distended belly. She let out a yell.

'It's over,' James said.

The buzzing stopped. James shifted his hand round to the back of Anna's shaved head and lowered it gently onto the pillow. She began to pant exhaustedly.

'It's over,' James repeated. 'She'll be all right. She had an antepartum haemorrhage. That means the placenta becomes partially separated. Ann should be okay.'

Beth let go of David, went over to James. 'The baby?'

He blew air out from his cheeks. 'I think it's alive.' He gave a crooked smile. 'I'm not so sure *I* am. I need to lie down.' Beth placed his good arm over her shoulders, helped him out of the room. James's blond hair was hanging down over his forehead as he passed David. 'Hi, Dave!' he mumbled.

David followed them downstairs. He poured James a large brandy and handed it to him as he lay stretched out, white-faced, on the couch. James's hand was shaking as he took the glass.

'Beth, would you get my case? My car's at the gate.'

She nodded, left the room.

'You should have let the baby die,' David said as James sipped his drink.

'Anna might have died along with it.' He looked up at David. 'Anna's important to me as well, Dave.'

'I don't doubt that. After all, she's an emperor.'

'Empress,' James said. 'You're really pissed at me, aren't you?'

'Pissed off,' David said.

James grinned, but David didn't respond.

Beth reappeared at the door, carrying a suitcase.

'Food would be good,' James said to her. 'And some aspirin. My head's aching.'

Beth headed for the stairs, struggling with the heavy case.

'I thought they'd abolished slavery,' David said.

He followed Beth out to the hall, took the case from her.

'I'll fetch the pills. You'd better get on with the Master's food.'

He dumped the case in one of the bedrooms, looked in on Anna. She was asleep. He checked there was no fresh bleeding, gently rolled her over, and placed a thick towel over the pool of blood on the bed.

When he got back downstairs, he handed James a glass of water and a bottle of aspirin.

'You'll have to take the top off,' James said. 'One of my hands is fucked.'

David handed him three pills and James swallowed them.

He studied David for almost a minute. 'You and Beth, huh?'

'None of your business.'

James's eyes went hard. 'She's mine, Dave.' He turned over on the couch. 'Tell Beth to forget about the food. I'm finished.' His paralysed arm was hanging down awkwardly behind his back. As James began to breathe deeply, David shifted it to make him look less broken.

Spear sat behind his study desk dressed in a black silk robe with a yellow dragon design on the back. His hair was wet from standing for half an hour under a fiercely hot shower that had failed to dissipate his panic. He poured himself another glass of fifty-year old Burgundy from a dust-covered bottle. He gulped the wine. It tasted vinegary.

Spear clanged the glass down on the desk top.

He wondered how his colleagues would react to the news that the other side had gained possession of Anna. He would not remain their leader for long; they might not even let him live.

There was a twelve-inch globe of the world on the desk beside a personal computer. Spear grabbed the empty wine bottle by the neck and used it to smash the globe onto the floor.

Ruined. Everything *ruined*! Unless he could get Anna back. The phone on his desk rang. He snatched it up. Listened. Grinned.

'Did our gambling friend say which airfield the plane was due to land at? . . . He should have contacted us about it right away. Why didn't we get this information earlier? . . . Drunk? I suggest you have him disposed of, Señor Juarez.'

He put the phone down, pressed an intercom button.

'Hughes, come up here.'

Excitement, fierce and sweet, pierced the alcohol fog in his head. He got up and retrieved the battered globe from the carpet, set it back on the desk. It had acquired an odd tilt. He span the globe. The world screamed.

Hughes knocked, lumbered into the room. He was carrying what looked like a sliver of soft cheese in a cellophane wrapper.

'Semtex,' he said. 'There's enough of it in the conference room to destroy the whole house.'

'What is it?' Spear demanded.

'Plastic explosive. Czech-made. There was a remote-controlled detonator packed in the middle.'

Spear reached out, took hold of the explosive. 'They could have killed us all last Wednesday. I wonder why they didn't.'

'I don't know.'

'Of course you don't! The question was rhetorical.' Spear tossed the packet onto the desk. Hughes flinched. 'The girl was here. That must have stopped them.' He looked up at Hughes. 'You and your cyclopoid partner have allowed a washed-out hack and a silly little American girl to run rings around you. There'll be some personnel changes around here when this is all over.'

'Mr Spear, I—'

'Shut up! I'll give you one chance to redeem yourself. James Lord is here in England. According to our source in the States his jet was due to land here a couple of hours ago. I assume he's met up with Cauley and his daughter and this Palmer girl. Their next move will no doubt be to fly Anna out of the country. Your job is to prevent that happening. First, find out where the plane landed.'

Hughes nodded.

'If you fail, you'll lose more than an eye.'

The big man backed out of the room, as if afraid to turn his back on Spear.

CHAPTER THIRTY-EIGHT

Beth yawned as she stood at the kitchen window waiting for the kettle to boil. Her body was still aching, but twelve hours of sleep had taken the edge off her exhaustion.

Outside, the winter sun was making the frost on the lawn and trees sparkle like gems. David and James came into view, strolling around the garden. David was dressed in a denim jacket with a chunky fisherman's sweater underneath. James's cashmere coat was buttoned to the throat, where a white silk scarf formed a ruff. There was something about David's big man's shamble that reminded Beth of her father. She wondered what it would be like to be married to him. He would make her laugh, that was certain. Physically, he was capable of satisfying her; he had already proved that. But would he stimulate her mind the way James could?

She halted her speculations abruptly; she was going to marry James.

When she studied James, it made her feel sad. Before the assassination attempt he had been alive with such fierce energy it had hardly seemed possible for his body to contain it. Now, as he moved awkwardly beside David, head sunk between his shoulder blades, walking stiffly, slightly off-balance, he looked tired and vulnerable. She hated seeing him this way. She would nurse him back to health; she would prepare him for the White House.

She poured cereal into a bowl and checked the copper kettle on the Aga. It was taking an age to boil. She clanged it back down on the heat.

James had been cold with her when she had eventually helped him up to bed the previous night. At first, she imagined he had guessed that she and David had been sleeping together, but his coldness had seemed more the result of embarrassment than anger.

She had asked him if he would like her to stay with him.

'No, that's all right. I'll be fine.'

'Are you mad at me?'

'No, I'm not,' he had said, pulling the bedclothes over his naked body with his one good hand. 'You've done a good job. You got Anna back.'

She had bent down to kiss his cheek, but there had been no response. She had slept alone on the couch in the sitting room.

She spooned coffee into a mug, willing the kettle to boil.

Someone looking at her. She jerked her head up.

Anna Cauley was standing in the kitchen doorway in her kimono robe, one hand on the doorframe, the other on the swell of her belly.

'Who are you?' Anna asked. Her speech was blurred and her thin face looked numb, but her eyes were alert. And unfriendly.

'Beth Palmer. I help out James Lord, the man you saw last night.' She yanked her thumb over her shoulder at the kitchen window. 'And I'm a friend of your father's.'

'You're pretty,' Anna said. It didn't sound like a compliment. 'What do you mean when you say you're a friend of his?'

Beth felt clammy heat against her arm. The kettle was boiling at last, spewing out steam. She turned towards it, then found herself saying, 'I've slept with him.'

'Here?'

'Yes.'

250

Beth stood stockstill, staring at the kettle, wondering why she had admitted that. A sudden insight: *Anna's an emperor. She made me tell her.*

She heard Anna repeat the word 'Here!' There was disgust in her tone.

Beth rammed her own arm against the side of the boiling kettle. She opened her mouth to scream, found she couldn't. The pain was unbearable, but she couldn't move her arm away. *Couldn't!* She could see her flesh shrivel.

Then the spell was broken, and Beth was clutching her arm, whimpering.

She looked round to see Anna waddling slowly across the room towards her, back arched, one hand on her stomach, the other reaching out for support; table, chair, dresser.

Beth backed up against the sink, still cradling her burned arm. 'Keep away!' she moaned. 'Please!'

Anna halted by the table. 'I'm sorry, Beth. I was angry, because of my mother. You and Daddy, here, at *our* place. I . . . got mad. I'm sorry.'

She began heading towards Beth again. Beth froze, still frightened.

Anna placed a hand over the angry, oval-shaped burn on Beth's arm.

The pain disappeared. Just . . . went!

'Run cold water over it and put on a dressing,' Anna said. 'Tell me when it begins to hurt again. I'll stop it.'

Beth turned on the tap, felt the icy water bite her skin.

'Me and your father – there was nothing wrong in what we did, Anna.' Beth's voice was still shaking. She had been around James most of her life, and was used to emperors, but even she found this child's power awesome. She turned off the tap, looked round at Anna. 'Your mother sounds wonderful. I wasn't trying to take her place.'

Anna managed a weak smile. 'I know. Don't be scared of me. I'll never hurt you again, Beth.'

Beth realized it was the truth, and relaxed.

Anna's knees started to give way and Beth had to run over and help her to the nearest chair.

'Could Anna's baby really be an emperor?' David asked James as they headed towards a bench at the end of the garden. They could hear a horse clopping along the road behind a high hedge twenty yards to their right.

'Maybe,' James said.

'What if it's evil, like him? What do we do?'

'Whatever has to be done.'

David shivered. 'You're supposed to be one of the good guys, James.'

James halted. So did David. The expression on James's twisted face hardened.

'Dave, you still don't understand. You keep judging me by your own standards. That doesn't work. Deep down, we're more different than a Kalahari bushman and a Zurich banker.'

'You mean because you do mental fairground tricks, you're above morality? You ordered Beth to kill Anna if we couldn't get her away from Sorensen's Institute. What in God's name has happened to you, James?'

'I couldn't afford to leave Anna in Spear's hands. You know how dangerous that would have been.'

David turned away in disgust.

'You've got it all wrong, Dave,' James said. 'Emperors aren't morally superior. We've never claimed that. We're not *above* morality, either. We're like . . . we're like the Greek gods, capable of great good and great evil. Some of us are on the side of humanity, some of us aren't. But even when we're on your side, you have to accept us warts and all. We lose our tempers, we lash out, we're ruthless. We have to be, because we're not fighting *you*, we're fighting the other gods, and if we weaken, we go under. Hell, when we screw up, we don't miss out on promotion or lose an annual bonus – millions suffer.'

'So you think you're a god?' David said, turning to face James again.

'The Greek gods were *us*. Can't you understand? It makes perfect sense. They were constantly at war with each other, as we are. They helped or hindered human beings as they saw fit. Again, like us. Why do you think so many of the myths, so much of Homer's poetry, involve people hearing the gods speaking to them *inside their heads?* When you get down to basics, that's what we do to you.'

'James, this time I think you've really flipped.'

An odd, humourless laugh. 'Perhaps.'

They turned and walked in silence for a while around the perimeter of the garden, frost crackling under their shoes. David lit a cigarette as another horse passed by. He caught a glimpse of the rider above the hedge. A girl about Anna's age, wearing a brown velvet riding hat, cheeks glowing, eyes glittering with the cold. The contrast with Anna – pale and sick, her body swollen with the child of a beast – was poignant.

'We'll be leaving tomorrow morning,' James announced. 'Just after dawn. There's a jet waiting at an airfield a couple of hours' drive from here. There'll be a doctor on board to look after Anna.'

'Where will the plane take us?'

'The States. I have a secure base in Colorado, high in the mountains. Easy to defend and damned hard for enemies to find. We'll stay there awhile, till the baby's born. Then . . . well, I'm not too sure. Spear will be looking for us. If he doesn't get Anna back, my guess is his colleagues'll have him killed. They're not forgiving types. Without Spear to guide them there'll be more falling out between them, and that suits me fine. It'll give our side a chance to regroup.'

'About Beth,' David said. 'I've grown very fond of her. Do you think you're doing the right thing marrying her? Is she going to be happy with you?'

James shrugged. 'You're right, it wouldn't be fair. I'm not going to marry her.'

David's heart leapt. 'Does she know?'

'Not yet. I'll break the news to her soon.'

David couldn't help smiling. 'That's a good decision, James.'

'I thinks so, Dave. You see, I've decided to marry Anna instead.'

David halted, grabbed James's arms. 'Tell me you're joking!'

James stepped back, out of reach. 'I don't have to ask your permission, Dave. I could make you say "yes".'

'I want Anna to lead a normal life,' David said. His mouth was dry.

'Forget it. She's an empress. She's never going to be satisfied with some sort of "Honey, I'm home" suburban existence. Even if she wanted it, she couldn't have it. The other side won't rest till they've tracked her down. With me, she'll have protection. And she won't have to lie to her husband about her powers. She'll be proud of what she is. With me, she'll be fulfilled.'

'I don't suppose love and happiness matter.'

'She'll be as happy as I can make her. At least I'll understand her. Better than any ordinary husband.' He paused. 'Better than you.'

'What if she rejects you?'

'I'll persuade her not to.'

'You might not find that so easy. The one time she fought Spear on an equal footing, she crushed him. She may be weak right now, but she'd do the same to you.'

James smiled. 'Maybe, but I don't intend using my powers on her. She'll see things my way. No one turns down an invitation to Mount Olympus.'

'I would.'

'You're not an emperor, Dave.'

'Thank God for that!'

James's face spasmed with anger. He turned away and began walking crookedly towards the kitchen door.

As David watched him, a fully-formed plan entered his head. He'd wait till James was asleep, then he and Beth and Anna would escape, head for somewhere remote – the Hebrides, Cumbria, the middle of nowhere. He'd put the plan to Beth as soon as he could get her alone. She'd resist, of course. She'd been trained all her life to obey James, but David would convince her it was the best course. They'd find a small cottage somewhere, change their names, live off the land if they had to.

As David passed the kitchen window, he glanced inside. James was sitting at the kitchen table beside Anna. He had hold of one of her hands and he was talking rapidly. She was listening intently, nodding now and then, evidently fascinated.

Gods together, David thought.

James and Anna looked a team, somehow. Father and daughter? Husband and wife? It didn't really matter. They just looked *close* in a way that he and Anna never had.

His plan of escape crumbled.

Beth was moving carefully around the kitchen, giving Anna and James hurt, puzzled glances, excluded by their oneness.

David dropped his cigarette butt onto the grass, crushed it with his heel.

He had lost his daughter for the second time.

CHAPTER THIRTY-NINE

Something wrong!

Half-awake in the darkness, David could hear a car in the distance, faint, getting fainter.

He sat up in bed just as the bedroom door burst open. The overhead light came on. Beth entered, a sheet wrapped round her like a toga.

'They're gone!'

David jumped out of bed, rushed past her. He ran to Anna's room; her bed was empty.

He raced downstairs, Beth behind him. No one there.

He rounded on her in the sitting room. 'What the hell's going on?'

'I've no idea.'

'Tell me!'

'I *don't know*!'

'James snatched her. You helped him.'

'I heard a car taking off. That's what woke me up.'

He ran to the window, drew back the curtain. 'His car's gone.'

'What's this?' he heard Beth say.

He turned. She was walking towards the computer. The word 'message' was flashing in the top left-hand side of the monitor.

Beth pressed two of the buttons on the keyboard. Words filled the screen.

'It's for you,' she said.

He stepped closer to the VDU.

Sorry it had to be this way, Dave, but our little chat yesterday made me nervous. I got the feeling you were planning something crazy, like trying to get Anna away from me. Was I right? It's too late to matter now, but I felt I had to act on my instincts, and they told me to grab Anna and head for home before you could interfere. You know she'll be safe with me, safer than she would be with you. You've managed to sidestep the Dragon so far, but everyone's luck runs out eventually. I don't want Anna with you when yours does. I want you and Beth to wait for me at the cottage till I send for you. That'll probably be in a few days' time. Lie low, and don't do anything rash. And, please, try not to be too pissed (off) at me.

David felt Beth's hand on his shoulder, shrugged it off angrily.

'Are you sure you didn't know about this? Did he leave you behind to make certain I didn't try to follow them? Is that it?'

'David, that's cruel.'

'Maybe.'

'Were you planning to kidnap Anna?'

'Kidnap her? She's my daughter, for God's sake!' He saw her chin pucker. He knew she hadn't helped James steal Anna away. He had just lashed out at her in anger. He took a deep breath. 'It crossed my mind to get her away from James. I was going to ask you to come with us.'

'But why would you want to get her away from James?'

'He wants to marry her, breed more emperors.'

She frowned. 'You're wrong. I'm the one he wants to marry.'

'He changed his mind.'

'You're lying. You're trying to turn me against him.'

'Beth, he told me yesterday he was going to marry Anna.'

She covered her face with her hands, started to cry.

'You actually love him, don't you?' David said.

She nodded. David put his arms around her, held her.

'You said yourself he was ruthless, Beth. There really isn't that much difference between him and Spear. That's why I wanted to get Anna away. As for you, he's eaten up too much of your life already.'

Beth lowered her hands from her face. There was a terrible pain in her eyes.

'Maybe they belong together, David.'

'I can't accept that. She belongs with me. I'm her father.' He let go of her, shook his head. 'Maybe you're right. Otherwise, why would Anna walk out on me like that?'

'Maybe she didn't.'

'James couldn't carry her, not in his state.'

'He could have got to her when she was asleep. She'd have been unable to resist him. He might have got her to walk downstairs and into the car without her even waking up.'

'You really think that's possible?'

'Yes. I don't think she'd desert you.' She rubbed the burn on her arm. It was starting to hurt. 'She's crazy about you. That's obvious.'

'Perhaps.' He shrugged. 'You know what's so awful? She's sixteen-years-old and she's never going to have a boyfriend or go to college or have a normal family life. She'll just wind up as a breeding machine.'

The clock above the fireplace chimed five times.

Beth glanced at it. 'James's plane takes off at seven. We can just about make it.'

David nodded. 'Let's go!'

Anna awakened to find herself strapped into the passenger seat of a car travelling fast down a dark country road. She was dressed in her kimono, and a blanket had been thrown over her shoulders.

James Lord smiled at her, driving one-handed.

She twisted round, saw the backseat was empty.

'Where's Dad? Beth?'

'They'll be joining us in a few days.'

She didn't like the way he said it. Too glib.

'Are you taking me to the plane?'

'Yup.'

'How did I get to the car?'

A pause. 'Your father carried you.'

'Didn't he want to say goodbye to me?'

'He didn't want to upset you. He thought it was best to let you sleep.'

A memory floated up from her subconscious; walking down the stairs at the cottage like a zombie, feeling the buzz, James beckoning her down.

'You're lying,' she said.

He didn't respond.

'You've kidnapped me.' She was staring at him intently. 'Why?' The paralysed side of his face was towards her. Its waxy immobility made her flesh creep. She summoned her powers.

'Don't!' James barked. 'Save your strength for the birth. That's what matters. Besides, if we tussle now you're liable to get us both killed.' He tried his smile on her again. 'Driving one-handed isn't easy, kid.'

'I want my father,' she said.

He dropped the smile, scowled ahead through the windscreen. 'You'll see him soon enough.'

'When?'

'When our future's decided. After the baby's born. We'll have to find a safe place for you to live, somewhere where you can be protected. That'll take some time.'

'Dad should have a say in where we end up. After all, I'm going to be living with him.'

'You'll be living with me, Anna.'

'For how long?'

'Forever. You and me.' He laughed softly. The sound

258

chilled her. 'On Mount Olympus. Zeus and his wife, Hera. That'll be us.'

She'd heard enough of his crazy theories the day before.

She turned away from him, looked out the side window at the trees rushing past in the darkness. 'I don't want to be Hera. I want to be me.' She felt the tears welling up in her eyes. 'And I want to be with my father.'

'Anna,' he said quietly. 'You're an empress. You have duties, responsibilities. You know how important you could be to the world. I've explained all that to you. You can't just turn your back on it, pretend you're the same as everyone else. That's what your father wants you to do, but he's being totally unrealistic.' His voice turned sympathetic. 'I know it's frightening, and I know you've had a tough time, but everything's going to be okay.'

She laid the side of her head against the window, stared out miserably at the night, and let the tears flow.

CHAPTER FORTY

David Cauley drove the Mitsubishi through the entrance to the small airfield just after seven; one rickety control tower, two hangars like barns on a disused farm, and a single runway fringed by wind-bent trees on one side, with the East Anglian countryside rolling away forever, flat as a desk-top, on the other.

Dawn was just about to break, sullen and overcast, accompanied by a steady drizzle. The light streaming from the windows of the Lear jet parked at the start of the runway looked unnaturally bright, garish.

As the car sped past the control tower Beth shouted out, 'There they are!'

James Lord was helping Anna out of his Mercedes, parked twenty yards from the plane. Anna was struggling feebly. Two men were standing near James, watching his efforts to coax Anna out of the car. David assumed one was the pilot, the other a doctor.

James let go of Anna when he heard the Mitsubishi racing towards him. David brought it to a halt ten yards from the Mercedes. The pilot reached into his jacket for a gun as Beth and David stepped out. David put up his hands to show he wasn't armed. They approached James's car. Anna caught sight of him, squeezed out of the Mercedes past James and tottered barefoot towards her father through the drizzle. He hugged her. Beth came and stood beside them.

'Let her go, Dave!' James called out.

'She stays with me.'

'Don't try to stop me, Dave. You're way out of your depth.'

'I don't want to stop you. I'd be happy to see you get on that plane. Without Anna.'

Anna turned her face towards James. 'Remember,' she said. 'You've got me to contend with.'

James placed a hand on the roof of the Mercedes to support himself. He looked beaten. 'Beth, I'm disappointed in you, siding with them.'

Beth stepped in closer to David and Anna. 'How do you think I feel about what *you* did, James?'

Silence, apart from the patter of the rain.

David broke it. 'Well, do you want a fight?'

James looked down at the runway, exhausted. The doctor and the pilot were staring expectantly at him. Eventually, he shook his head.

David placed an arm around Anna's shoulders, began steering her towards the Mitsubishi. Beth remained where she was. David halted, turned to her. 'Aren't you coming with us?'

She was staring at James.

'No,' she said, her voice husky. 'I can't.'

David nodded. 'Go to him.'

She turned her head, looked at Anna, then David. 'I hope they never find you.'

'They won't.'

Beth began walking towards James. As David opened the passenger door of the Mitsubishi, he heard what sounded like a tree branch snapping somewhere in the woods to their left, beyond the plane.

When he looked round, he saw Beth staring down at her front, arms out by her sides, fingers splayed. She swivelled towards him, mouth open in horror.

There was a gaping crater where her stomach had been.

She toppled forward onto the runway, dead.

The doctor and the pilot were running towards the plane. Two more shots rang out. The doctor span round and ran, wierdly, backwards for a few steps before collapsing. The next shot gouged a chunk out of the pilot's arm, but he kept on running. The next got him in the throat.

James was crouching by his Mercedes, using the door as a shield. 'Get out of here!' he shouted at David. 'Now!'

David began to shove Anna roughly into the Mitsubishi. Bullets ripped holes in the bonnet. Steam, sparks. The car was useless.

'Get over here!' James shouted. 'Keep low!'

Crashing sounds. Three cars had blasted through the crumbling wooden walls of the aircraft hangars and were heading towards them, fast, lights on full beam. David bent low and, clutching Anna to him, staggered towards James.

Then, suddenly, it was as if a gigantic animal had bitten clean through one of his knees. He stumbled, overbalancing Anna. As she fell to the ground, her head hit the hard surface of the runway, stunning her. She lay, groaning, a few feet away from David. He was staring down at his leg. His knee was an oozing, bloody mess.

James was hobbling towards them, crouching low, as bullets bit hunks out of the tarmac around his feet.

James reached Anna, knelt down. He tried to lift her, couldn't.

'Drag her!' David yelled. 'Just get her away!'

James gripped one of Anna's wrists and pulled her on her back across the tarmac towards his Mercedes, bullets pinging around them. He bundled her into the front seat, turned and headed back towards David.

'Get away!' David screamed. 'GO!'

James halted. A bullet fragmented a corner of his

cashmere coat. He turned, scuttled back to his car, got in. The engine roared and the big Mercedes automatic shot forward, heading for the open fields.

Three Porsches screamed past David and fanned out behind the Mercedes. Hughes was driving one of them. Vercoe, one eye completely covered with a bandage, was at the wheel of another. David caught a glimpse of Spear sitting beside him as the car raced by.

James realized he'd made a mistake as soon as he drove the Mercedes off the runway. The bonnet reared up and for a moment he thought the car was going to somersault. As the front of the car smashed back down, the impact jerked his one good hand off the steering wheel. Anna was bouncing around on the seat beside him, screaming, trying to grab hold of something, anything. The front of the car reared up again as James tried to regain control of the steering wheel.

He couldn't do it one-handed. Impossible.

The car crashed down once more. He realized the suspension wouldn't be able to cope with the high ridges between the field's deep furrows.

James reached deep down inside himself, *commanded* his paralysed arm to shift. *Come on, you useless fucking lump of meat! Move, move, move!*

His arm jerked upwards. The dead hand found the steering wheel. His fingers curled round it. James let out a whoop, twisted the wheel so that the car was heading down a furrow, wheels spraying water out of it.

Anna had grabbed hold of the headrest and was clinging to it, moaning, clutching her belly with the other hand.

James checked the mirror. Two of the pursuing cars had followed his example, and were speeding down furrows to either side, keeping pace. As he watched, the third car hit the field way too fast. He caught a brief glimpse of Richard Spear's face as the car shot up into the air, twirled, and crashed down, landing on its side.

Suddenly he relaxed, grinned. At least he wouldn't have Spear to contend with. He doubted if any of their pursuers would dare open fire on the Mercedes with Anna inside.

Spear would have made it clear she was not to be harmed.

James's grin froze as the realization hit him that Beth was dead.

He heard David's voice inside his head. *You're supposed to be one of the good guys.*

Maybe he wasn't, after all.

Each raindrop falling on the gaping wound in David's knee was a blow from a hatchet.

The full pain had hit now, and it was like nothing he had ever experienced before. He had glanced down at the wound once or twice, but he really didn't want to look again – gristle, bone, and tendons mashed up into something that looked like it belonged on a butcher's slab.

He had glanced at Beth, too, but that wasn't a good sight either. He hadn't enjoyed seeing her lying there with her stomach torn away. He didn't want to think about Beth at all. Not yet.

He looked across at the field beyond the runway. James was managing to keep ahead of his pursuers. The Mercedes and the two Porsches following it were now almost out of sight. He had watched two people struggle out of the car that had crashed onto its side; they were now heading towards him.

He could sense Spear's dark murderous rage as he approached. Vercoe was behind him.

This time, David realized, as a fresh spasm of pain racked his body, there would be no escaping the Dragon. His luck had run out. At least Anna wasn't with him. The pain in his knee crescendoed and he gratefully gave in to unconsciousness.

As the wheels of the Mercedes moved from earth to tarmac, James offered up a silent prayer of thanks. It felt as if they'd spent a year driving over a cattle grid. Even with the smoothness of the two lane road under him he could still feel his body vibrating.

He took the car up to ninety miles an hour. His pursuers hit the road a quarter of a mile behind him. They were heading across flat, treeless country that reminded James of the Midwest. The rain had stopped, but vicious winds were buffeting the car. He needed both hands to keep the Mercedes on the road.

Anna was staring ahead through the windscreen.

'Where are we going?' she asked.

'Back to the cottage. I'll need to figure out how to get us out of the country. Spear'll have the airports covered.'

She was silent for a few moments. 'Is Daddy dead?'

'No. He got hit in the leg.' He paused. 'I went back for him after I'd got you to the car, but he told me to leave him, get you safe.'

'You're not going to try to save him.' Her voice was flat.

He'd been wondering about that. His first plan had been to take Anna to the cottage and arrange for another plane to come and pick them up. Even that wouldn't be simple. Spear was somehow getting hold of information about his flight plans.

'I honestly don't know if I can save your father, Anna,' he said.

'He's your friend.'

'I have bigger responsibilities. We both do.'

'He's your friend.'

He glanced at her. Her eyes made him feel as if his own conscience was staring at him.

'What happens if I die and Spear gets hold of you again because we tried to save your father?' he asked. 'Where does that leave the world?'

'I want my father back.'

He paused. 'Okay. I promise I'll try to rescue him later, after you've had the baby.'

'No, you won't. You're frightened of Spear. You think he'll beat you. It's been easy up till now, pushing ordinary people around. You haven't got the guts to face Spear. It would be a fair fight, and you might lose.'

In a way, it was true. He had been avoiding a direct confrontation with the Dragon Man for a long time.

'If you don't save my father, you'll be my enemy,' Anna said.

'Somehow, I can't see you siding with Spear.'

'I won't side with anyone. I'll just be your enemy.' She

placed a hand on her belly. 'And I'll kill the baby. I could do it right now. All I have to do is *think* it dead.'

'Please don't!' he said quickly.

'Then save my father.'

He checked the rear-view mirror. The pursuing cars were keeping pace, but at least they weren't gaining.

Suddenly, his paralysed hand slid off the steering wheel. The Mercedes veered across the road as he fought to control it. He slammed on the brakes. The car juddered to a halt, skidding on the wet road. He opened the door, and stepped out, gathering his mental strength.

The lead car was a hundred yards away. James flung a bolt of energy at the driver. The car kept on coming. James took a deep breath, tried again. Still too far away. A hand holding a gun emerged from the window. Fifty yards, forty. A bullet shattered the back window of the Mercedes. Anna screamed. James could see the driver's face now, *blasted* him.

The driver's mouth opened in a scream. The car whiplashed, went into a complete spin, then it was hurtling towards James, tumbling end over end, shedding chunks of metal. It cartwheeled past him, missed the Mercedes by a couple of feet.

James turned his concentration on the next car. He caught a glimpse of the driver – a hideous white face above enormous shoulders – and recognized him as Hughes.

The Porsche was heading towards James at a fantastic speed, too fast for him to react . . .

The car fishtailed as the driver slammed on his brakes. The windscreen shattered as the man in the front passenger seat shot through it. The passenger tried to grab hold of the bonnet, but slid off. He shrieked as the wheels went over his body. The driver was still trying to brake. The Porsche was twenty yards from James, fifteen, ten . . .

It shuddered to a halt inches away from him.

Hughes and another man stared out. James looked round, following the direction of their gaze. Anna was standing on the other side of the Mercedes. It was she who had made Hughes bring the Porsche to a halt.

Hughes jumped out of the car, a gun in his hand. He aimed it at James.

James gave the monster a crooked smile. He was about to make him drop the gun when he felt a stream of energy emanating from Anna.

Hughes turned the gun on himself, pointed it at his own face.

James was awed by the power coming from Anna. He could see how she had managed to defeat Spear the one time they'd met on equal terms. She was in a class of her own.

Hughes started screaming.

'This is for Beth,' said Anna.

Hughes's face disappeared. He crashed down onto the road like a felled tree.

The man still inside the car leapt out, tossed his gun aside, and began running down the road away from them.

Anna gasped and clutched her stomach. 'I think . . . it's coming.' She let her breath out slowly, looked at James. 'I'll let it live if you save my father.'

James stared back at her. So far his tactics had proved disastrous. Running and hiding hadn't worked. Beth was dead. David Cauley was in the hands of the enemy. And the girl with whom he had dreamed of ruling the earth was on the verge of turning into a foe; a foe even more powerful than himself. He suddenly saw that he had been greedy and cowardly. He had wanted Anna and the baby without having to fight for them. The battle could no longer be avoided. In a way, the realisation came as a relief.

'Okay, Anna. It's a deal. Let the baby live and I'll get your father back.'

She nodded. Clutching her stomach, wincing, she got back into the Mercedes.

James stared up at the lowering dawn sky as wind whipped hair across his face.

What if David was already dead?

CHAPTER FORTY-ONE

He had no idea how long he had lain on the chaise longue. The green velvet covering under his smashed knee had turned black with blood; he could hear it dripping onto the carpet. He knew if he lost much more, he'd die, but the prospect wasn't that unappealing. Anything would be preferable to the pain he was suffering – that, and the anguish of knowing that Beth was dead.

He tried to move, but leather straps around his chest and ankles held him in place.

The door opened. Spear stepped into the room, followed by Sorensen. The doctor was carrying a small felt bundle.

Spear walked over to the chaise longue and gazed down at David for a while before speaking.

'You've been extremely troublesome to me, Cauley.'

'Likewise.' The word emerged as a croak.

'You're going to tell me where James Lord has taken Anna, and you're going to tell me quickly.' David watched Sorensen untie the ribbons holding the felt bundle together. 'I could force the information out of you myself,' Spear continued, 'but I'm saving my strength for worthier opponents. I've wasted enough energy on you.'

As Spear retired to a chair in the corner of the room, out of David's range of vision, Sorensen unfurled his felt bundle on a small side-table to reveal a row of orthodontic instruments.

'Too dark,' he said. He moved to the nearest window, opened the curtains. Grey, watery light trickled into the room.

Sorensen pulled the side-table close to the chaise longue and selected one of the instruments from the bundle. He examined the curled tip of the steel probe.

'First, a demonstration,' Spear said.

Sorensen jabbed the probe into David's wounded knee. David howled.

'It's quite simple, Cauley. The doctor is going to keep doing that until you tell me where James Lord has taken Anna. Understood?'

'So, your goons let her slip away, Spear. Ever thought of hiring professionals?'

'Once more, doctor,' Spear said.

Sorensen inserted the probe back into David's knee. Its tip found a nerve and lingered there. Pain flared through his body. He shouted, felt himself beginning to black out.

'Careful doctor,' Spear said. 'You almost lost him.'

Sorensen mumbled an apology, removed the probe. His enormously magnified eyes studied David's face without emotion.

'Sorensen assures me he can keep you awake for hours,' Spear said. 'But we haven't got that long, so just tell me where Anna is.'

'I have no idea,' David said. The probe approached his knee again. 'I expect James has got her out of the country,' he added quickly.

'Impossible. We have the main airports covered, and he hasn't had enough time to organize another private flight. Besides, I'm sure he wouldn't leave without you.'

'You're wrong. James kidnapped Anna this morning. He was going to leave me behind. He wants her to himself.'

A pause. 'You had a falling out?'

'His plans for Anna weren't that much different from yours.'

He could almost hear Spear's gut twist at the thought.

The door opened and Vercoe entered the room. His one eye glared at David.

'Are the men in place outside?' Spear asked.

'Yes.'

'Go and join them.'

'Let me stay,' Vercoe said. 'I want to see this bastard suffer.'

'Stick around,' David said. 'Judging by past performance, that'll probably guarantee my escape.'

Vercoe moved fast. His balled fist crashed against David's cheekbone.

'Leave!' Spear shouted.

Vercoe stalked across the room and slammed the door on the way out.

'He seems a trifle upset,' David said. He could feel his cheek already swelling, but the pain was nothing special; he was getting used to pain. 'By the way, Spear, do your overseas pals know you've lost Anna? James reckons they'll have you killed when they find out. What do you think?'

'Doctor!' Spear said.

As his knee exploded with pain, David heard Spear shout, 'Where *are* they?'

'Don't . . . know!' David forced out. He'd been wrong about getting used to pain.

The probe was removed. A fragment of gristle was hanging from the spike at the end. Sorensen wiped the instrument with a tissue.

'Afraid I'll get an infection, doctor?' David asked through gritted teeth. His body was covered with sweat.

Sorensen ignored him, selected another probe.

'My guess is they've returned to wherever you've been hiding out for the past few weeks,' Spear said. 'Where might that be, Cauley?'

'Over the rainbow. The back of beyond. The middle of no—'

The last word turned into a scream as Sorensen located an interesting new nerve.

'FUCK YOU FUCK YOU FUCK YOU!' David bellowed as agony roared through him.

Spear was leaning over him. 'Where were you hiding? Tell me that and we'll fix your knee and give you painkillers.'

There was a mad hunger in his eyes.

'James thinks you people were the old Greek gods up there on Olympus.' His voice was juddering. 'Well fuck you, and all the other tin gods, Spear!'

'James Lord is right. We *were* the old gods. *And* we're the new ones. But we're not made of tin, Cauley. We're made of steel.'

'Steel gods,' David said. 'May you melt in hell.'

Spear waved Sorensen away.

'You're going to tell me where your daughter is, Cauley. And quite soon afterwards, you're going to die.'

David felt a white-hot needle point inside his brain, digging and gouging, questing for information.

'Where are they?' Spear said.

The mental probe stabbed harder into his mind. David bit his tongue to stop himself telling, tasted blood. Then the probe found the spot, rested for an instant, *dug*.

And he heard his own strangled, tearful voice coming from a thousand miles away, giving the address of the cottage.

David thought, *You've betrayed her. You've betrayed Anna!*

Suddenly, Spear was no longer inside his head. He was standing above him, smiling down. 'Thank you.' His smile broadened. 'By the way, Anna was an excellent lay.'

David lunged against his straps, breaking the one round his chest, making the couch shift. He was growling as he tried to grab hold of Spear. Spear jerked the probe out of Sorensen's grip, buried it three inches inside David's knee. He let go of it, stood back.

It was a few seconds before David experienced the full force of the pain. His whole body writhed. He opened his mouth wide to scream, but agony had stolen his voice. The probe was slimy with blood. It took him several goes to grasp it. As he pulled it out, something twanged deep inside his knee. He realized that everything he had experienced before couldn't really be described as pain. What now burned through his body was of a different order. He found his voice; his high-pitched scream went on and on until there was no more air in his lungs. The bloody probe slithered from his fingers, and he fell back on the couch, panting.

'Now, you die,' Spear said.

David felt Spear gather his power. *Please let it be swift!*

Cracking sounds from outside the house; two in quick succession.

Spear flinched like a startled fox.

'Shots,' Sorensen said.

Spear glared at David. 'Later!' he growled.

He headed for the door, Sorensen following in his wake.

CHAPTER FORTY-TWO

'Spear, come on out here!'

As David heard James Lord calling from the front of the mansion, he struggled to sit up. What was James doing here? He had what he really wanted – Anna. Why would he risk a confrontation with Spear?

His knee was bleeding freely again. He untied the strap around his ankles. He grabbed hold of Sorensen's instrument bundle and tied the felt strip around his knee. Gritting his teeth, he stood up. He took one step, fell down. He crawled over to the wooden chair Spear had been sitting on, levered himself up. Using it like a walking frame, he made his way slowly to the door and out into the main hall.

Spear was standing behind the front door, eyes wide, taking quick, shallow breaths. Sorensen had disappeared. Spear's hands were shaking.

'Come on, Spear!' David heard James shout. 'Let's settle this thing now.' There was no hint of fear in his strong, confident voice.

Spear squeezed his eyes shut, muttered something to himself. He heard David's chair scrape on the hall flooring, looked round.

Spear's face was grey.

'Scared?' David asked.

All at once, Spear's hands stopped shaking. His back straightened. 'As I said, I'll deal with you later, Cauley.'

'Not after James is through with you. This is Judgment Day, Spear.'

Spear pulled the door open, stepped outside.

In his eagerness to follow, David pushed the chair he was using to support himself too violently, and it collapsed under him. He found himself lying on top of the inlaid figure of the monstrous dragon-man, Typhon. He looked down at Spear's face. A flame flicked out at him from the demon's mouth. David felt the heat of it against his cheek. He began crawling as fast as he could across the floor to the open front door.

James was standing half-way between the gate and the house. Behind him, near the gate, two guards lay sprawled on the ground, their guns still in their hands. It looked as if James had made them shoot each other.

Spear was standing a few feet from David, in front of the door. He rubbed the palms of his hands against the sides of his trousers, as if to remove sweat from them.

James started moving towards the house. He was walking normally; no hint of paralysis. As Spear took a small backward step, David could sense his pungent terror.

'You and me,' James said. He smiled his crooked smile.

A Doberman came bulleting round the side of the house and headed straight for James. Vercoe was behind it, gun out. He glanced at Spear. Spear nodded.

Vercoe halted, aimed the gun at James.

The Doberman slid to a halt a few yards from James, who was staring at it. The dog turned swiftly, and sped, sleek and deadly, back towards Vercoe. Vercoe was squeezing the trigger of his gun as the dog launched itself at him. The impact sent him crashing to the ground. He shrieked, tried to club the animal with the .38 he had retrieved from David. The dog ripped the bandage away from his face, revealing an empty eye socket.

Vercoe's shriek turned into a gurgle as the dog sank its fangs into his neck. His blood spurted up over its face. It held on grimly as Vercoe clubbed its head again and again with his pistol.

The gun eventually slid from his grasp. The animal jerked its head up, tearing out his throat. Vercoe's body spasmed, then he lay still.

The dog gazed at Spear, tendrils of flesh hanging from its mouth. It growled, baring its fangs. It was preparing to attack.

Spear stared at the dog. As he sent a mental bolt at it,

David saw a brief flash of *something* through the air, like electricity.

Like a machine that had been switched off, the dog slumped down dead.

David saw doubt in James's eyes; just a flicker. But it was enough to make his stomach sink. Spear began walking towards James. There was something in his confident stride that suggested he'd also detected James's sudden uncertainty. James began walking forward as well, but now he was limping.

The two men approached each other like gunslingers.

David realized that this was his chance. Spear's entire attention was focused on James. Now would be the perfect time to strike.

Pain shrieked from his knee as he crawled past the dead dog towards Vercoe's body. He gripped Vercoe's gun. The butt was slimy with the blood still gushing from the dead man's throat. David forced himself to stand up. He swung round and aimed the gun at Spear, fired twice. The first shot missed altogether. The second made Spear stumble. At first, David couldn't tell where he'd hit him, then saw a shallow rut along the Dragon Man's temple. Spear blinked. David prepared to fire again.

He saw the light coming off Spear, saw it darting through the air towards him. It blinded him, set fire to his brain. He was dimly aware of the gun dropping from his hand. He sank down onto the ground.

'No!' he heard someone shout.

The fire in his brain was extinguished. He could see again. He realized it was James who had called out.

'You and me, Spear!' James shouted. 'No more pawns.'

Spear turned away from David. 'We could join forces, Lord. We could rule the Earth together – if you weren't so sentimental about these creatures.' He waved a dismissive hand in David's direction. 'You actually *care* about them, don't you?'

'Ever thought these people might not want us, Spear? Ever thought they might be happier without us?'

'Evolution, Lord. We're superior. We deserve to take over. We *have* to. That's nature.'

'We're not natural, Spear. We're freaks.'

'The first example of the species *homo sapiens* was a freak.' He paused. 'Come on, let's form an alliance. There's no one to oppose us. We have the girl. In a few generations it'll be us, just us.'

James shook his head. 'And there'd be someone like you facing someone like me all over again. Let's fight that battle now. Let's save a lot of people a lot of misery.'

'You're a fool.'

'Probably. But I'm not a monster.'

As they began moving towards each other again, the sky darkened. David looked up to see an impossibility; ugly, roiling stormclouds racing towards Spear's mansion from every corner of the sky, gathering into one enormous teeming black ball directly overhead. It seemed the heavens had come to witness the fight.

David had experienced the power of the emperors in many forms. He had felt it as a gentle nudge from Anna when she was a child, as a black oppressive cloud when Spear had tried to make him take his own life, as a blinding fire just a few moments back. On the night the emperors had gathered here, at the mansion, he'd felt it as a dark, wicked pulse. Now, as Richard Spear and James Lord approached each other, it was as if the very nature of reality had been warped, as if they had entered another dimension. Their power made the air around them ripple. David could almost *see* the energy flowing from the protagonists, melting the air like the exhaust fumes from a jet plane, turning everything liquid.

Then there was thunder inside his head; great crashing, rolling echoes, followed by the sound of breakers roaring over rocks, impossibly amplified, so that he thought his head would break with the cacophony; and a screaming, raging wind so *real* he wondered why it didn't simply blow him away, carry him beyond the trees like a leaf. Then came a blast that rocked the ground beneath him, as if two massive cymbals, many miles wide, had been brought crashing together by the hands of God Himself.

He saw James halt, shudder. For a moment only the whites of his eyes were visible, and it seemed he would fall. When his pupils reappeared, his eyes looked hollow, exhausted. James's shoulders narrowed. His head appeared to be retracting between them, like a turtle's. Spear seemed to be increasing in stature, growing huge. As he continued to move forwards, it was with a giant's swagger.

James straightened suddenly. He raised his paralysed arm, pointed at Spear, and roared, eyes blazing. He looked terrifyingly inhuman, an elemental force made flesh.

The roar blasted against David like a hurricane. He felt himself driven backwards by it. His body was moving, slithering back across the drive. His fingers scrambled at the gravel as he tried to keep himself in place.

Spear halted. His whole body trembled violently. He staggered back, and then he was on his knees, clutching his temples.

All the while, James was roaring, roaring and pointing, and it was as if white fire was spurting from his fingers towards Spear, and Spear was yelling, 'No! No! No!' It was as if his voice had been slowed down; it sounded like that of a gigantic animal, horribly wounded . . .

David heard the thunder again, inside his head, but now it was as if he was there at the very heart of the storm, at the very point from which the thunder was emanating.

A blood vessel burst in one of James Lord's eyes, turning the white a vivid, burning red. He was moving again, walking towards Spear, who was still on his knees, eyes squeezed shut, hands over his ears. A sliver of blood shot out of one nostril.

James was standing over him, pointing down, still roaring, like some vengeful Old Testament prophet, like a figure from mythology – like a god.

Spear rolled over onto his side and furled his body into a foetal ball, drawing his knees up to his chest.

And David knew James would show no mercy. Spear was going to die. Here. Now. Finally. And David was crying, with terror and relief and awe . . .

The shot sounded insignificant. David only realized a

gun had been fired when the back half of James's head exploded.

His roar was still echoing in the air as he toppled forward, across Spear. One red eye glared sightlessly at David.

It took him fully ten seconds to realize what had taken place. Slowly, he turned his head and saw Sorensen standing by the front door of the mansion, holding the biggest handgun David had ever seen.

CHAPTER FORTY-THREE

For several moments there was no sound at all. Then, as David looked up at the sky, the vast stormcloud that had gathered overhead burst ferociously, forcing him to shield his eyes against the downpour.

Sorensen was heading towards Spear, who was lying motionless underneath James Lord's body.

Was Spear dead? Had James destroyed him before meeting his own end? Had they perished within seconds of each other, like Thor and the dragon, Midgard? David would make sure Spear was dead. He reached for Vercoe's gun, lying on the ground a few feet away from him. Sorensen caught the movement, pointed his Smith & Wesson .44 Magnum at him.

'Don't!'

'Sorensen, you know what Spear is. Why are you helping him?' The rain was so loud David had to shout to make himself heard.

'I *must* help him. He's a superior being.'

'Superior to who?'

'Us.'

'Shoot him, Sorensen. He may be dead anyway. If he isn't, you could do the world a favour!'

Sorensen smiled, showing yellow teeth. 'I'm not sure I particularly like the world.'

The doctor reached down and rolled James Lord's body

off Spear. Spear did not move. David offered up a silent prayer; *Please let him be dead! Let the monster be slain!*

Spear's body gave a twitch. David heard him sob. Sorensen got down on his knees, and helped Spear sit up.

Spear was trembling, crying. He had his hands over his face. 'He doesn't look like a superior being to me!' David shouted. 'James Lord beat him, Sorensen. You killed the wrong emperor!'

Sorensen's saucer eyes goggled at David for a few seconds.

Spear lowered his hands. He sat, weeping, the rain mingling with his tears. David found himself staring at an old man. The battle with James Lord had aged Spear twenty years in a couple of minutes.

David let his head sink down onto the cold, wet gravel. The fierce rain was blasting against the ground, big drops of it bouncing up like hailstones. He felt blank, empty. He had witnessed a cosmic battle; he had seen the triumph of evil. The world now belonged to *them*, the steel gods.

He thought of Lauris, and Beth, and James, and of Sammy Moss. What had befallen them would now become the fate of millions. How David felt now, that sense of bleak desolation, millions would soon feel.

He did not want to live. He did not wish to see the earth become a charnel house.

The baby was moving inside her, thrusting against the frail shell of her body, eager to emerge into the light. The first contractions had started before she and James had even reached the cottage. Now they were coming every two or three minutes, each one lasting up to a minute. James Lord had told her what to expect. She knew the birth could not be that far off.

She reached for the phone on the bedside table. She had been trying to hold on until James returned with her father, but she wasn't sure she could stand the pain any longer. She got hold of the receiver, lifted it from its cradle . . .

The earth shifted on its axis – or so it seemed to her. *(Something wrong something horribly wrong.)*

And then a foul, fetid dead wind raced across its surface. It shook the cottage. It felt as if the evil wind was blowing right through her body. She shuddered. The telephone receiver dropped from her hand.

She thought she understood. James was dead. The earth shifting was her experiencing James's death. The wind was a premonition of doom that made her soul shrivel. It meant Spear was alive.

Was her father dead too? A numbing loneliness enveloped her at the thought.

She bit her lip, determined not to cry. She had to be strong now. It would only be a matter of time before Spear came to claim his baby.

The thought of the beast slouching towards her almost made her forget her pain.

As Spear's Rolls-Royce headed for the cottage through the thickening twilight, David found himself praying that James hadn't taken Anna there. But where else would they have gone?

Sorensen was driving, whistling to himself. *Whistling*. David, lying on the back seat with his wounded leg out straight, switched his attention to Spear, in the passenger seat beside Sorensen. He was holding the Magnum that had killed James. The gun was aimed at David, but it was a pointless precaution. He was too weak to fight. The length of felt wound around his knee was soaked through with blood. He looked at Spear. The Dragon Man's eyes were on him, but they weren't seeing anything. David could *feel* Spear's squirming, turbulent emotions – fear, excitement, *hunger*. Some colour had returned to his face, but he still looked dreadfully old and tired, evidently too exhausted to maintain the barrier between his thoughts and the outside world.

If Anna was at the cottage, and if she was sufficiently alert, she'd be able to blow Spear away. James had taken Spear to the edge; Anna would be able to push him over. But what if the events of the previous twenty-four hours had precipitated the birth? If she was in the middle of giving birth when they arrived, she'd be powerless against

Spear. David guessed that he had been brought along as a hostage to guarantee Anna's co-operation. Spear didn't look like he had much fight left in him.

David closed his eyes. He had seen enough of the Dragon Man. If it hadn't been for the pain in his knee he would have sunk into an exhausted sleep . . .

The Rolls came to a halt. David opened his eyes. He had managed to doze, but felt no better for it. They were parked in front of the cottage. The sky was dark, and there were no lights on inside the house. Spear got out of the car and stood, holding the gun. He cocked his head to one side, and seemed to sniff the air.

He opened the back door of the Rolls. 'She's here.'

David knew it was true; he could feel Anna's dark, lonely pain.

Sorensen got out, dragged David roughly from the car, and let him drop onto the ground.

'Follow us,' Spear commanded.

David had to crawl after them on all fours. As he did so, he saw that Spear was walking like an old man, on frail legs.

Spear pushed the front door open.

'Where's the light switch?' he demanded.

'To your left.'

Spear reached inside and the hall light came on. David crawled through the door after them, made it to the bottom of the staircase. Spear and Sorensen made a hasty search of the ground floor rooms, but David knew where Anna was. He could sense her pain piercing the house from above. He heard a rapid series of shrieks.

Sorensen and Spear came to the foot of the stairs and stood to either side of David, listening.

'She's in the final stages,' Sorensen said.

'But it's not due for weeks,' Spear said.

'Not my responsibility. I told you, her pre-natal routine's been severely disturbed.'

'No more mistakes,' Spear said, quietly, and there was a mad quality to his voice. He looked down at David. 'You go up first.'

'I need help.'

Spear motioned at Sorensen. The doctor leaned down and slung one of David's arms over his shoulder. They made their way slowly, painfully, up the stairs. Spear followed, still holding the Magnum.

Anna's panic and agony were blaring inside David by the time they reached the door to her bedroom. Sorensen grasped for the knob, pushed the door open, and switched on the overhead light.

Anna was lying naked on the bed, head writhing from side to side, hands clutching her belly, legs drawn up, knees wide apart. Her face was covered in sweat and her jaws were clenched. Each time her head moved, she emitted a desperate shriek.

Shocked, David shrugged away Sorensen's arm and stumbled towards the bed, calling her name. Sorensen caught up with him, grabbed his arm, shoved him to the floor.

'Over in the corner,' Spear said.

'Let me stay by her side!' David pleaded.

'Move!' Spear shouted.

David crawled over to the far corner of the room and sat with his back to the wall. Anna's helplessness made his stomach churn.

'I'll fetch my bag,' Sorensen said, and left the room.

Spear went to the foot of the bed, gazed down at Anna. There were tears in his eyes. 'Cauley, you're about to witness the birth of a god.'

'I pray it's stillborn.'

Spear wasn't listening. 'The birth of this child will make me the most powerful emperor who ever lived. This is as significant as the birth of Christ. You're in the presence of history.'

'The end of it, more like.'

Spear pointed the Magnum at David. It was like staring down the barrel of a small canon.

'I wouldn't,' David said. 'The bullet could go anywhere.'

'Daddy!' Anna moaned.

'I'm here, darling.'

As Sorensen re-entered the room carrying his black bag, Spear reluctantly lowered the gun.

CHAPTER FORTY-FOUR

It took well over an hour. All the time, Spear stood at the foot of the bed, watching intently, his neck craning forwards. David had found his excitement somehow obscene. Sorensen had been calm and efficient, whistling abstractedly to himself between his teeth.

At one point, after Anna had been shrieking constantly for half an hour, Sorensen administered an injection. David cried out in anger.

'It's only pethidine,' Sorensen said. 'It'll help speed the birth. The longer it takes, the more danger there is that the baby will be starved of oxygen. Besides, your daughter will feel less pain.'

The drug seemed to do the trick. Anna's cries gradually became less urgent.

Several times, David found himself drifting into unconsciousness, only to be awakened by the pain in his knee. He had tried to think of a means of escape, but had failed. As soon as the baby was born, Spear would kill him, that was certain, and Anna would be too befuddled to prevent that happening. Spear would let Anna live, naturally, but what sort of a life could she expect? Years lying drugged in a prison cell?

And, then, suddenly, it was over. Anna screamed as Spear's child slipped from her. Sorensen held the baby up by its feet. He smacked it once, twice . . .

'No!' Spear whispered, horrified.

Sorensen placed the baby on the bed, hurriedly prepared a fresh syringe.

'What are you doing?' Spear demanded.

'Giving it an injection of naxolone. It'll counteract the pethidine, start it breathing.'

He emptied the syringe into the baby's bottom, lifted the child up off the bed. David noticed a constellation of sweat-drops on the doctor's brow.

'It's still not breathing!' Spear hissed.

Sorensen smacked the baby, holding its ankles with one hand.

'*Do* something!' Spear shouted.

Sorensen smacked it again. Still no response.

'Damn you!' Spear yelled. 'I told you to *do* something!'

'I've done everything I can.'

The baby opened its tiny mouth and wailed. Sorensen snipped the umbilical cord.

Anna raised her head from the pillow for a moment, gazed at her baby daughter. She closed her eyes, let her head drop back.

A smile spread across Spear's face. He stepped around the side of the bed and took the child from Sorensen. He held its bloody body against his chest.

'History!' he said, his voice cracking.

The infant's tiny fingers spasmed uncertainly. Spear took hold of one minute wrist and studied the baby's hand, still smiling.

His smile froze.

'It's normal,' he whispered.

'Impossible,' Sorensen said.

Spear thrust the infant's hand close to Sorensen's goggling eyes.

'The fingerprints, Sorensen. See them? They're not straight.'

Sorensen opened his mouth, but wasn't able to get any words out.

'IT'S NORMAL!' Spear yelled. He tossed the baby onto the bed beside Anna.

Sorensen found his voice. 'I'm sorry. I don't know what went wrong. There was every indication that it would be an emperor. But we can try again. Yes, that's what we'll do. We'll try again—'

'No,' Spear said. 'You had your chance. You botched it.'

David could feel Spear gathering his power. It was as if

he was sucking energy from the room into himself. David found it difficult to breathe. Sorensen seemed to be experiencing the same problem, but that might just have been fear. The doctor stepped backwards until he reached the wall, his eyes now so wide they seemed to cover most of his face.

'You can't,' Sorensen said. 'You *wouldn't*. I'll get it right. I *promise* you. This is a setback, just a set—'

He clutched his head, displacing his glasses as he did so. David was disconcerted to see how small his eyes really were.

'You failed me,' Spear said.

Torrents of blood spurted from Sorensen's eyes and from his mouth, spraying across the room. David jerked his head away as blood spattered his face. He felt it hot against his lips. He wiped it away with the back of his hand as the doctor fell forward onto the floor.

Spear turned towards the bed, lifted the gun and aimed it at the screaming infant.

'ANNA!' David bellowed, crawling towards Spear. 'STOP HIM!'

Her eyelids flickered open. She lifted her head, saw Spear.

David had seen what looked like an electrical flash in the air during Spear's battle with James Lord. Now, the flash that leapt from Anna to Spear was a hundred times as bright, a fireball. David threw an arm across his eyes to stop it blinding him. When he lowered his arm, he had to blink several times to make sure that what he was seeing was real.

Spear was standing by the bed with the nozzle of the Magnum inside his own mouth.

Anna was sitting up, staring at him. The room was pulsing with the energy flowing from her as she tried to force Spear to pull the trigger.

A gurgling noise sounded from the back of Spear's throat. His whole body was shaking as he tried to resist the power flooding from Anna.

The buzz in the room suddenly grew weaker. Anna's shoulders sagged. She looked spent, finished.

Spear began to remove the gun from his mouth.

David got onto his good knee. He launched himself up off the floor, both hands out in front of him, caught Spear in the small of the back.

The shot echoed in the small room for a long time.

CHAPTER FORTY-FIVE

The Dragon Man turned almost casually towards David. As he stared down at him, fire was flickering in his eyes.

'Die!' David whispered. 'Oh God, please die!'

For an instant, Spear's eyes blazed with rage. Tongues of flame leapt from their depths towards David . . . but never reached him.

Spear toppled over sideways onto the floor. Blood trickled from a gaping hole in the back of his head.

He was dead. The Dragon was slain. The coppery stench of blood made David gag. Then, suddenly, it was as if a fresh, sweet-scented breeze was blowing through the room. It was warm and healing and carried with it the fragrance of hope.

David sucked the air deep into his lungs; it gave him strength. He crawled past Spear's corpse to the bed.

Anna's eyelids were closing as he reached it.

'Over?' she asked.

'Yes. It's over.'

She let her eyes shut. Her head sagged back onto the pillow, and she was unconscious. David levered himself up and sat hunched on the edge of the bed for a few minutes, holding Anna's baby in his lap as it cried itself into its first sleep. He thought he could feel its unfocused panic blare inside himself, just as he had felt Anna's soon after her birth, but he knew he was imagining it.

The child was as normal as he was. The fingerprints proved that.

When it was asleep he laid the baby carefully beside

Anna and propped a chair against the bed so that it would not fall onto the floor. He made his way to the bathroom and removed the felt strip from above his knee. The resulting throb of pain almost caused him to pass out. He got an elasticated bandage out of the cabinet above the washbasin and wound it above his knee to form a rough tourniquet. He waited until the pain had eased, then hobbled down to the sitting room. He slouched down on the chair next to the phone.

The world had to be warned against the emperors. It was time for humanity to decide its own destiny.

He rang the Capital Television switchboard and asked to be put through to Whitley Chamberlain.

'David? I can't believe it. Where are you? Where've you been?'

'Battling the forces of darkness, Whitley.'

'Hiding from the tax inspector, huh?'

'Even worse than that.' Despite everything, Whitley's big, warm voice made him smile.

'The last I heard, you were on the run from the police. We've been talking about nothing else around here. Calvin Scott said something about paranoid delusions. What the hell is going on?'

'Whitley, I'm at a cottage in Wiltshire. My cottage. I want you to get down here with a camera crew as soon as you can, and bring a doctor with you. That's important. And whatever you do, don't tell Calvin Scott what you're up to.'

'David, I'm on air in six minutes.'

'Leave as soon as you've finished. The traffic'll be light this time of night. It shouldn't take you more than an hour to get here.'

'I have a dinner engagement, David, and she's amazingly cute.'

'Whitley, do as I say and you'll have the biggest scoop of your life. You're famous now. After this, you'll be a megastar.'

'I *am* a megastar, but I get your drift. At least give me *some* idea what it's about. Surely you can do that much.'

'Richard Spear's upstairs. He's dead. Sorensen too.'

A pause. 'Give me the address.'

'You won't tell Calvin Scott or the police?'

'Is the bear a catholic? Does a Pope—'

'You'll get your reward in heaven, Whitley.'

'I don't accept post-dated cheques. The address?'

Whitley could sling a piece together and have it ready by morning. He could tell whoever was editing the Breakfast Show that the item was about something entirely different. Editors rarely saw pieces before they went out. Besides, Whitley now had enough clout to get anything he wanted on the air. By the time the editor realized what the item was about, it would be too late for him to do anything about it. By then the world would know all about the emperors. For the first time, David found himself wondering how the world would react.

'For fuck's sake, David, hurry up with the address! The editor's having a coronary here. I'm on in two minutes. I—'

David slammed the phone down.

He blinked, wondering what had made him hang up.

He looked round. Anna was slumped against the sitting-room doorway, cradling the baby in her scrawny arms. Her naked body was smeared with blood. David realized that *she* had stopped him giving Whitley the address.

'You mustn't tell,' she said. 'Daddy, we must keep it a secret.'

'Spear's friends will come after us, Anna. It's better if it's all out in the open. We'll have some protection. The more people that know, the better.'

'*I'm* the only one who can protect us. We must make everyone believe we're dead.'

To David, she looked impossibly wan and frail. He stood up, hobbled over to her. She half-turned away, as if to hide the baby from him.

'Anna, you need a doctor. So do I.'

'We'll find a doctor. After he's taken care of us, I'll make him forget we ever existed. Then we'll go somewhere far away, where nobody will know who we are.'

'What'll we do for money?'

'I can walk into any bank and make them hand over as much as we want.'

'But what about Hung Xiang and Marenkev and the others? You can't let them take over.'

'No, I can't. I thought I could, but when I realized James was dead, I knew it was my duty to carry on the fight. That's how it has to be, Daddy. It's down to us now. You and me.'

His heart plunged as he looked into her eyes. There was a steeliness there he hadn't seen before. Like James, she was turning ruthless.

'What about the baby? Doesn't she deserve a normal life?'

Anna looked down at the child. Her expression was grave.

'She wouldn't have a normal life if everyone knew I was an emperor.' She sighed. 'She couldn't lead a normal life anyway.'

'Why not?' David asked. But he thought he already knew.

'Look at her fingers,' Anna said.

David peered closely. The skin on the child's tiny palms and fingertips had begun to flake. He rubbed some of it away with his thumb.

Underneath, the prints ran in straight, parallel lines.

THE END

A SELECTED LIST OF HORROR TITLES
AVAILABLE FROM CORGI BOOKS

THE PRICES SHOWN BELOW WERE CORRECT AT THE TIME OF GOING TO PRESS.
HOWEVER TRANSWORLD PUBLISHERS RESERVE THE RIGHT TO SHOW NEW
RETAIL PRICES ON COVERS WHICH MAY DIFFER FROM THOSE PREVIOUSLY
ADVERTISED IN THE TEXT OR ELSEWHERE.

☐ 09156 1	THE EXORCIST	*William Peter Blatty*	£2.99
☐ 13034 6	COME DOWN INTO DARKNESS	*Clare McNally*	£2.99
☐ 12691 8	WHAT ABOUT THE BABY?	*Clare McNally*	£2.99
☐ 12400 1	GHOSTLIGHT	*Clare McNally*	£2.99
☐ 11652 1	GHOST HOUSE	*Clare McNally*	£2.50
☐ 11825 7	GHOST HOUSE REVENGE	*Clare McNally*	£2.99
☐ 13033 8	SOMEBODY COME AND PLAY	*Clare McNally*	£2.50
☐ 13277 2	NIGHTSHADE	*Gloria Murphy*	£2.99
☐ 12705 1	THE DEVIL ROCKED HER CRADLE	*David St. Clair*	£2.99
☐ 12587 3	MINE TO KILL	*David St. Clair*	£2.99
☐ 11132 5	CHILD POSSESSED	*David St. Clair*	£2.99
☐ 10471 X	FULL CIRCLE	*Peter Straub*	£2.99
☐ 13466 X	STILL LIFE	*Sheri S. Tepper*	£2.99

All Corgi/Bantam Books are available at your bookshop or newsagent, or can be ordered from the following address:

Corgi/Bantam Books,
Cash Sales Department
P.O. Box 11, Falmouth, Cornwall TR10 9EN

Please send a cheque or postal order (no currency) and allow 60p for postage and packing for the first book plus 25p for the second book and 15p for each additional book ordered up to a maximum charge of £1.90 in UK.

B.F.P.O. customers please allow 60p for the first book, 25p for the second book plus 15p per copy for the next 7 books, thereafter 9p per book.

Overseas customers, including Eire, please allow £1.25 for postage and packing for the first book, 75p for the second book, and 28p for each subsequent title ordered.